D0385521

Also by Jay Bonansinga

The Killer's Game
The Black Mariah
Sick

HEAD CASE

Jay Bonansinga

Simon & Schuster

Simon & Schuster
Rockefeller Center
1230 Avenue of the Americas
New York, NY 10020

This book is a work of fiction. Names, characters,
places, and incidents either are products of the
author's imagination or are used fictitiously. Any
resemblance to actual events or locales or persons,
living or dead, is entirely coincidental.

Simon & Schuster and colophon are registered trademarks
of Simon & Schuster Inc.

Designed by Deirdre C. Amthor

Manufactured in the United States of America

10   9   8   7   6   5   4   3   2   1

Library of Congress Cataloging-in-Publication Data
Bonansinga, Jay R.
Head case / Jay Bonansinga
p.   cm.
I. Title.
PS3552.05927H43   1998
813'.54—dc21   97-36464   CIP
ISBN 0-684-82514-7
ISBN 0-684-84931-3 (signed edition)

Acknowledgments

TWO PEOPLE WERE particularly indispensable to me in the creation of this story: Norm Kelly, PI par excellence, for sharing his tricks of the trade and his many years of experience as a working investigator; and Bob Mecoy for brilliant input during the gestation stages, not to mention the delicate business of editing.

Special thanks to Jeanne Bonansinga for love, patience, and incredible instincts; Peter Miller for managing my life; Jennifer Robinson for continued advice and friendship; Elizabeth Hayes and Louise Braverman for amazing support above and beyond the call; Don VanderSluis for educating me in blue steel; Jodee Blanco for her Teflon enthusiasm; Bill and Mary Bonansinga for their love and hospitality; and Andy Cohen for being a true mensch *and* the smartest guy in Hollywood.

Additional *gracias* to Yvonne Navarro, Chris Vogler, Pete Fornatale, Tom Cassidy, Shasti O'Leary, the folks at PMA Literary and Film Management, Bruce Clorfene and the folks at Something Wicked, Dennis Armstrong, Ben Adams, David A. Johnson, Aaron Vanek, Tina Jens and Twilight Tales, David Quinn, Norm Pokorny, Richard Chizmar, Harry Jaffe, MD, John Buckley, Di & Sully, Alice Bentley and The Stars Our Destination.

To the Memory of Jim Andrews (1923–97)

(Everything is all right, Jimmy, 'cause we're all still sitting at that kitchen table covered with oilcloth, laughing like hell under that one bulb overhead.)

Part One

John Doe in Purgatory

The most merciful thing in the world, I think, is the inability of the human mind to correlate all its contents.

—Howard Phillips Lovecraft

1

White Noise

BEFORE THE PAIN, before the blind terror—even before the man on the bed realized anything was wrong—there was the beeping that seemed to come from everywhere and nowhere simultaneously.

The man on the bed tried to open his eyes, tried to move, but he found his body as heavy as granite. Breathing was a chore, and even his eyelids felt inordinately heavy.

The delicate *blip* continued to chime in his ears, a rhythmic tattoo in the dark, becoming more and more prominent with each passing second—*blip-BLIP!—blip-BLIP!—blip-BLIP!* But was it real? Or was it a fading vestige of a dream?

Again the man on the bed tried to move, tried to focus on some familiar object in the room, and that's when he discovered the pain.

It started in his chest, a sharp jab beneath his heart that then sliced down his rib cage. The man sucked in a breath, and the sudden inhalation made a whistling sound across his clenched teeth. And all at once, the pain was everywhere. This pain had a texture to it, like razor wire tightening around his joints, very sticky, like ground glass in his marrow. Another twinge in his chest, and he winced.

He managed to moan.

The beeping continued impassively—*blip-BLIP!—blip-BLIP!—blip-BLIP!—*

Now his eyes were adjusting to the darkness, and certain shapes were coming into focus around him. Rectangular panels overhead, little pocked squares in the ceiling, the gleam of metal, some kind of monolithic shape looming to the left of his bed—blinking lights and numbers?—and metal railings all around him. He licked dry, chapped lips, and tried to assimilate all these unfamiliar elements. *Wait a minute, wait, wait just one minute, this isn't my bedroom, this isn't even my house.*

—*blip-BLIP!*—*blip-BLIP!*—*blip-BLIP!*—

That's when the man on the bed started to get very, very frightened.

Across the room, the door burst open.

"Call Dr. Cousins—"

A large figure in white was coming into the room now, followed by more figures in white. It was like a white tidal wave pouring into the room, and the man in the bed tried to take it all in, tried to understand it, but his eyes were still caked with mucus, and his body was still racked with spasms of pain, and the best he could do was moan again—his mouth was so dry he could barely make a sound—and now he was making feeble attempts to focus on all that stunning whiteness gathering around him. He felt a wasp sting above his wrist, and almost instantly he sensed something cold entering him.

Another figure was entering the room now, a woman in a physician's coat. "Okay, kids, what do we got?" Her voice was pleasant, almost maternal, as she approached the bed.

"BP's one-fifteen over seventy—"

"Okay, could we get that CBC and CT scan up here right away, please—"

The realization flowed through the man on the bed, galvanizing his terror. He was in a hospital room, tethered to IV tubes and EEG cables, and there were three nurses and a doctor gathered over him now, peering down at him. The doctor was using an ophthalmoscope on him, and the light was violently bright. He felt as though his body were pitching back and forth on a faulty gyro. The pain was easing slightly, most likely due to the narcotics being pumped into his veins. But his mouth was so dry it tasted of bitter almonds, and his eyes were still teary, obscuring his vision. He tried to focus on the woman doctor dominating the group, her voice clear and pleasant.

"The scans look just wonderful, Sandy, that's just great, thank you." She leaned over the bed, and her face coalesced over the man, only inches away now. "Looks like somebody's coming around," the doctor said genially, and then she winked. She seemed to be an attractive middle-aged woman with dishwater-blond hair pulled back in a tight bun.

He looked up at her dumbly, trying to say something, but his mouth wouldn't work.

"Easy does it, *amigo*." The doctor touched his cheek and her fingertips felt like cold kisses. "You don't have to talk just yet."

The urge to speak was so strong now, he could feel the tears tracking down his temples on both sides of his head, and he could hear them hitting the mattress. Little muffled raindrops. The room was coming into better focus, and he realized he was in some kind of modified surgical suite paneled in some kind of high-tech black cork, with high windows, vertical blinds, acoustic tile on the ceiling, and racks of equipment on the left wall. Syrupy Mantovani-like Muzak played softly out in the hallway, syncopated beneath the beeping of the nearby cardiac monitor.

The doctor must have noticed the man's frantic need to communicate, because she leaned over and nodded. "You're going to be fine. Can you understand me? How about blinking one for yes, and twice for no? Does that sound okay?"

He managed to blink once.

"Good, great, you can understand me." She gazed around the room and shared a series of glances with the others. Then she looked back down at her patient. "Sure gave us quite a scare there for a while."

He tried desperately to speak, but found his mouth filled with glue.

"Do you remember what happened?"

He managed a couple of labored blinks.

"My name is Marie Cousins, and I'm a neurologist. You're at the Reinhardt Rehabilitation Center in Joliet, Illinois. Do you understand?"

He blinked once.

"Looks like you had a nasty little tiff with a semitruck out on Highway Eighty yesterday," she continued in her surreal-sweet voice. "Tore up a big old chunk of cartilage in your legs, busted your noggin pretty good. They brought you out here last night. Folks at ER thought you might be headed for a long-term coma. Looks like we all got pretty lucky, huh?"

She might as well have been speaking Swahili. He blinked twice, then he blinked twice again, then he blinked twice again and again and again, as though sending a Morse code for *Help!* The pain was being replaced by a swirling dizziness, a pitching, yawing disorientation, like he had been out to sea in a nasty storm and had just landed. He couldn't remember the first thing about any accident with a semitruck, or being in Joliet, Illinois, or being on the road.

"Okay, easy, easy does it," she said, stroking the side of his bandaged shoulder. She turned and whispered something to a nurse, and the nurse dug in the pocket of her light blue pinafore, rooting out a small tablet of paper.

The doctor took the tablet and positioned it under the man's right hand, which lay flaccid and heavy at his side. He could just barely see over the folds of his hospital gown, around the tubing that twined along his arm; the doctor was urging a ballpoint pen into his hand. He tried to grasp it. It was like moving a dead fish. Finally he managed to curl his index finger around the ballpoint.

"Let's just start with a few simple questions," the doctor said then. "Since we couldn't find any identification on you, why don't we start with any family members you might want notified."

He couldn't think of anything to write.

"That's okay, take your time."

He took his time, and he thought and he thought, and it dawned on him that he had no idea whether he had any family members, or whether he had any family at all, come to think of it. This desolate sort of realization sent a shiver up his spine. This was not good. This was perhaps even a bit terrible. He concentrated on remembering, and found it somewhat similar to tuning a shortwave radio in a storm. Nothing but static. Like a television station at the end of a programming day.

White noise.

"Listen, don't worry about it," the lady doctor was saying. She was being monumentally patient. Cheerful, calm, maternal—like a den mother. He wanted so badly to connect with her, to please her, to communicate something of substance to her. "Why don't we just start with the simple facts," she said finally. "Your name, for instance."

He closed his eyes and began to weep. Finally, he managed to write something on the tablet.

A question mark.

2

Someone Else's Laundry

"THEY'VE GOT A lot of fancy names for it, but in most of the literature it's referred to as episodic amnesia." Dr. Cousins was standing next to his new bed, holding a vinyl binder to her chest, a strand of ashy-blond hair dangling in her face. Dressed in her white jacket, with half-glasses perched on the bridge of her nose, she looked like a Junior Leaguer about to award a blue ribbon for the best key lime pie. "The thing of it is," she continued, "it's really not that godawful rare, believe it or not. We see it in stroke victims, overdoses, and—"

"Head tr-traumas?" he interjected awkwardly. It had been only forty-eight hours since he had awakened—and only twenty-four since he had regained the ability to speak—but already he had countless questions.

"Yeah, John, that's exactly right!" She nodded enthusiastically, referring to the man as "John," as in John Doe, as in Patient 436. Evidently it was Dr. Marie Cousins's idea to assign him a name rather than a number. Better for promotion of memory recovery.

That was the theory, at least.

"But what I'm w-wondering is, how I—you know—got to this point," John Doe said, speaking in a sort of halting stammer. It was driving him crazy, this weird nervous flurry with which he communicated. Was this the way he always talked? Or was this a result of his injuries?

At the present moment, in fact, he didn't know much of anything. All he knew was that he was a patient in a small clinic south of Chicago, reclining on a motorized bed in a private room, talking with a neurological specialist who sounded as though she were hosting *Romper Room*, and he was scared to death. Early this morning, they had moved him to this two-hundred-square-foot cell of sterile tile, cork walls, and institutional furniture. He was still fairly woozy with painkillers, not to mention bound up in splints and braces and bandages, but now he was starting to make several observations about himself.

First, he could plainly see that he was an extremely hyper man with a host of nervous tics and mannerisms. Sitting with his back against the head-board, his torso wrapped in gauze, his arms wound with IV drip tubes, his wiry frame felt like a spring coiled way too tight. He was not a large man, not particularly fit by any means, but thin. Maybe five feet ten, a hundred fifty pounds, short-limbed, with small feet and delicate, double-jointed fingers. His fingernails were bitten down to the quick, and his fingertips were chain-smoker yellow. In fact, at this very moment he felt an odd, inchoate urge for a cigarette, and the weirdest part of all—he knew what brand he smoked: Marlboro Menthols.

Second, he wanted a drink very badly. Simple as that. He wanted either a Tanqueray and tonic with a twist of lemon or a couple of cold glasses of Pilsner Urquell. Wasn't that strange? How did he know what brand of beer he liked? Especially when he couldn't even remember his name. As a matter of fact, there were all sorts of personal minutiae and preferences boiling under the surface of his thoughts, but whenever he tried to figure out who he was, it was like scanning that dead radio dial—nothing but sizzling hiss.

The worst part, though, was the "face thing." In the past twenty-four hours, he had had numerous opportunities to look in a mirror at his own face, but had avoided it at all costs. The prospect of looking at himself ter-rified him. Why? Why did he not want to take a look at his own face? Wasn't that the quickest way to jar his memory?

What the hell was wrong with him?

"Okay, why don't we start with the incident on the highway first, shall we?" the doctor said.

"Yeah, yeah, that would be good."

"Here's what we know," the doctor began, pulling a chair beside the bed, then taking a seat. "According to eyewitness reports, you appeared out of nowhere, darting out of the woods along I-Eighty." She paused for a moment, looking at him. "Does that mean anything to you?"

He thought about it, turning that dial in his head, and there was nothing but static. "No, actually, it doesn't—I mean—it doesn't really ring any bells."

"Do you remember ever having been on Highway Eighty?"

Again, he thought about it for a moment. "I've heard of Interstate

Eighty—I mean, I know where it is—but beyond that, you know, there's not much—I mean, there's not really much of anything."

"Well, it turns out you darted directly into the path of an oncoming truck."

"Jesus."

The doctor looked at her notebook. "Yeah, I understand it was a Kenworth refrigerated tractor-trailer, and I understand one of the witnesses claimed they saw dark wet spots across the front of your shirt prior to impact."

John swallowed air. *"Prior to impact?"*

"That's right, John. So maybe that means you had some injuries before you ran out onto the highway. Do you have any memory of that?"

John shook his head.

The doctor looked down at her notes. "Well, luckily, the truck was already slowing down at that point. It was downshifting onto an exit ramp when it hit you. I understand you were thrown over fifty feet and landed in those nasty old weeds out there along the shoulder."

"Jesus Christ."

"Yeah, well, the good news is, John, even though you got banged up pretty darn good, it looks as though you're gonna make a full recovery. You got a minor contusion on your forehead, your right femur has a tiny little incomplete fracture—not enough to warrant a cast—and both your knees have transverse cartilage tears—"

"Wonderful."

"Oh, yeah, and three of your ribs have minor compound fractures. And I'm also thinking a couple of disks in your spine were compressed a teeny-weeny bit."

John shook his head, taking a deep breath, feeling a delicate, stringy pain knitting in his left side again. The pain was dull yet constant, swimming beneath the surface of the Dilaudid like a shark. His spine felt like a fuse, burning hotly, sparking and sputtering. His knees were throbbing with a dull, distant ache. He couldn't decide whether it was better to know all the medical terminology at this point or just be blissfully ignorant.

"What about the amnesia?" he asked finally. "You say it's called—what?—episodic amnesia?"

"That's exactly right, John. They used to call it old-fashioned amnesia, because Freud was the first one to catalog it and study it. Sometimes you hear it referred to as anterograde organic amnesia, sometimes transient global amnesia, but a rose by any other name is still a rose, am I right?"

The doctor smiled, her dimples deepening. John managed a tepid grin, wringing his hands now, fidgeting against the headboard. He was trying to tune in some station in his head, any station would do, but the static continued to sizzle.

"See, John, a person with AOA usually loses all episodic memories. In other words, they lose track of real-life events, real-life people, and circumstances that got them where they are . . . and yet they retain most of their knowledge and most of their skills."

"Yeah, but the thing is—how do I put this?—I can remember all these little details about myself—"

"And that's totally normal, John."

"But I can't remember any of the major stuff, like who the hell I am, for instance."

"Again, that's exactly how it works. The patients remember their general knowledge, their likes and dislikes, even their favorite flavor of ice cream. Do you remember your favorite ice cream, by any chance?"

The doctor was smiling again, and John felt like vomiting in her face. Instead, he just muttered, "Actually, uh, I was never really . . . what you would call, fond of ice cream."

"That's right, that's right!" she enthused. "See what I mean? The fact that you know that about yourself—that's part of the profile."

"But how the hell could—you know—how could that be?"

The doctor shrugged. "We're learning more and more about the human brain every day. With the new MRI technologies, we can map the brain, we can test it, but the truth is, we still have a long way to go. The latest thinking is the brain is just chock-full of compartments, and the injury to your brain probably jostled the compartment that processes the *chronological* aspect of memory."

John thought hard about it for another moment, then said, "What about the clothes I was wearing?"

The doctor nodded. "That's a good point. I was wondering myself about that—whether or not your personal effects might jog your memory a little. Hold on."

The doctor rose and stepped into the hall. She returned, carrying a square of folded clothing with a large Ziploc bag on top. She handed them to John.

It was like holding someone else's laundry.

"Take a good look and see if it sparks any connections," Dr. Cousins urged.

John lay the clothing on his lap. His hands were trembling now, and he felt another strong urge to suck down a few dozen ounces of gin. The shirt was a faded-blue chambray, a big black Rorschach of a stain along the front, with tattered gouges here and there—presumably from tangling with the Kenworth's grill. The trousers were worn khakis, the shoes beat-up sneakers. John could smell the faint odors of stale smoke and stick deodorant—were these his scents?—and he was feeling sick to his stomach all of a sudden. But the nausea was not the foremost thing in his mind at the moment. The thing that had caught his eye was in the Ziploc bag. They had already told him that his wallet had been missing—if there had ever been one in the first place—but they had neglected to mention the object in the bag.

"What the hell is this?"

Peeling open the bag with his shaky hands, he pulled out the key chain—a tiny plastic grand piano with half a dozen keys of various sizes attached to it—and held it in his palm for a moment, and the weight of it, the contours of the tiny piano, the *rightness* of it in his palm, all washed over him at once. In his head there was a crackling sound. Static electricity, static sizzling. He was remembering something in half-formed images. Flashframes flickering in his head. He was beginning to make something out.

And, quite frankly, he didn't like it very much.

3

Man with Meat

THERE WERE ROWS of blurry, indistinct ribs, blotchy spots of red, a black arrow, and an icy-white face with muscles constricting—forming a rictus . . . all of them etched in dark, fervid pencil sketchings on eggshell paper that he had been pilfering from the art-therapy room down the hall. Over the last twelve hours, he had been drawing compulsively, drawing on a rolling tray that they positioned across the center of his bed, sketching images in tiny squares, like those of an obsessive little comic book. Every now and then another one would flicker out of the darkness in his mind, bubbling up through the static and white noise like a distant satellite transmission. Most of the feelings and images and sensations revolved around two things: a man and a slab of meat.

He had no idea what they meant.

John stopped sketching for a moment and sat back against the headboard, chewing his fingernail, thinking about the images in his head. He looked at the clock. It was almost three A.M., and he was still wide awake. This damn insomnia was making him crazy. For a man who could remember nothing, his head was sure noisy. He took a deep breath and tried to clear his mind. His foot would not stop tapping against the bed's railing, and the motion was making the metal brace on his knee click and squeak. The sound of it was driving him nuts.

He badly needed a change of scenery. He had been a guest of the Reinhardt Rehabilitation Center for three days now, and he had yet to take one step beyond the hundred-foot corridor of green tile that defined his world.

And he still had not looked in a mirror.

He found his pack of Marlboros sitting next to a Styrofoam pitcher, rooted out a smoke, and sparked it with a Bic. Then he reached over to the portable cassette player sitting on the windowsill next to the bed, flipped the tape over, and pressed PLAY.

Dizzy Gillespie moaned out of the three-inch speaker—"Cool Blues," with Ray Brown on bass, John Lewis on keyboards, Kenny Clarke on drums, the great Charlie Parker on alto sax—and the haunting heartbeat of the music, the tom-tom tattoo, and the plaintive call and response, all made John feel slightly less alone, less rattled.

The tapes and cigarettes and art therapy had been Dr. Cousins's idea. The theory was, anything that John remembered—no matter how banal or trivial—might trigger other, more significant memories. The doctor had convinced John to write a list of personal preferences—favorite musical selections, favorite movies, brands of cigarettes and coffee and snack foods, and anything else that he could think of. He'd been given everything he requested except a half-gallon bottle of Tanqueray gin; Dr. Cousins had nixed that on the grounds that it would not only interact with the painkillers but retard John's progress as well. Now John was finding it difficult to think about anything else but that bottle of Tanqueray.

He closed his eyes and tried to concentrate on the music, foot tapping compulsively.

Somehow he had known that jazz was his passion. The knowledge seemed to simply *be there* in his forebrain, like the distinct odor that a house always has but that its occupants rarely notice. He especially liked Kansas City blues and hard-core bop from the fifties and sixties. Count Basie, Dizzy, Bird, Monk, Jay McShann.

How the hell did John Doe know these things about himself? How could he access these things and not even know his own name? God, he needed a drink.

When he closed his eyes, it was worse. Then the white noise became something he could see, like a movie traveling far too quickly through the projector, the images strobing up through static and noise. He saw quick flashes of stiletto heels, sides of beef, fishnets stretched over pale flesh, teeth, and heavy purple velvet fabric billowing in some otherworldly breeze—

"Dammit!" he heard himself utter, pushing the tray aside and painfully climbing out of bed.

He grabbed the crutches that were canted across the side of the bed and then scuttled painfully across the room, puffing his cigarette, trying to clear his mind. His body was still very tender, his ribs throbbing as he moved, his knees complaining with each shuffling step. But the more he moved, according to Dr. Cousins, the quicker he would mend.

He leaned against the window and looked out at the night. He could see the dark, deserted grounds, the empty parking lot bathing in sodium-vapor light, and the man-made pond in the distance, the black water dappled with moonlight. The building itself was desolation personified—an I. M. Pei monstrosity of jutting wings and monolithic steel and glass. Inside, the sterile carpeted corridors and starkly appointed rooms were as silent and gray as the deserted valleys of the moon. The atmosphere made John feel like a laboratory rat.

The worst part was the imagery in his head. John didn't have to be the Marquis de Sade to know that much of what he was remembering—albeit fleetingly—was bizarrely fetishistic. The meat and the stiletto heels and the teeth and the blotchy spots of red.

"Excuse me, sir?"

The voice came from the doorway across the room, and it nearly made John jump out of his skin.

He pivoted toward the sound and saw a figure standing in the gap between the jamb and the half-ajar door, backlit by the fluorescent lights of the corridor. At first it was hard to make out the face, but it was clear that the figure was a large, barrel-chested man wearing maintenance dungarees and holding a mop. There was a newspaper rolled up under one of his arms. "Mr. Doe, is it?" he said.

"H-hello—yeah—that's me," John said, nodding, trying to control his fear, his nerves.

"I saw the light on," the man said. "Heard somebody moving around."

"Yeah, I'm sorry—been having trouble sleeping, you know—bad case of insomnia."

"That's a pisser."

There was an awkward pause, and John managed a wan smile. "Is there something—you know—something I can help you with?"

The big man grinned. "Thought you might be interested in seeing this." He unfolded the newspaper, then took a couple of steps toward John. "One of the boys in Maintenance showed it to me."

"What is it?" John was trying to mask the alarm in his voice.

"Here, lemme show ya," the big man said, and started thumbing to the middle of Section Two. It looked like a small-town newspaper. Probably less than a hundred pages. "Orderlies must have snapped the picture during your walk yesterday. Sold it for a pretty penny, I bet."

John took the newspaper in his shaky grasp and looked at the bottom of the page. There, under the bold headline LOCAL CLINIC HOUSES MAN WITH NO NAME, was an article three columns wide. A photo was nestled in the center of the story. It was a close-up of a pale, wiry man being helped along the corridor in a metal walker.

The patient's face was clearly visible.

"You're a regular celebrity, Mr. Doe," the big man gushed. "Whattya think about that?"

4

Billy Marsten's Thing

HE WAS COMING out of Durkin's Pancake House on 159th Street, making his way through a narrow foyer, when he noticed the tabloids at the bottom of a wooden rack near the door. He rarely paid any attention to these trivial little rags, but this time, something reached out to him from that cover page.

Perhaps it was the caption in the lower right-hand corner, which said: "Amnesia Victim on the Mend—Inside Section Two."

Billy Marsten knelt down by the bottom rack, his black duster blossoming on the tile floor like a great hoop skirt. He grabbed the last issue of the *Times-Weekly,* which was sandwiched between a couple of *Chicago Readers* and a stack of *Illinois Entertainers*. Billy rose back up to his full height—which was a daunting six feet five—and leaned against the edge of the news rack. The wooden frame creaked under his weight as he scanned the first section.

To say Billy Marsten was a rather large young man was somewhat akin to saying the Hindenburg disaster was a minor glitch. Nearly three hundred pounds in his underwear, he was shaped like a gigantic pear, with a delicate little head that was too small for the rest of him, an eyeliner-thin goatee, and a pair of piercing, dark eyes that seemed to catch the daylight like obsidian stones. He was currently dressed in his customary funereal black—black Uomo T-shirt, black leather pants, black motorcycle boots. He had a small tattoo on his neck in the shape of a black hand, a symbol whose impenetrable meaning was way beyond most of his bumpkin classmates at Lewis University.

He continued scanning the tabloid until he came to the article buried in Section Two.

Billy's gaze landed on the headline first—LOCAL CLINIC HOUSES MAN WITH NO NAME—and then he saw the photograph at the bottom of the page. He stared at it for a good long moment, until he realized what the gist of the article was about, and all at once Billy's entire posture changed. He straightened slightly, and his lungs filled with an exalted breath of air, making his entire frame expand—which was truly something to see.

It seemed impossible to stumble across the man in such a random fashion. Could it be a mistake? Could it be some kind of a cruel cosmic joke? Billy's hands were tingling now as he closed the tabloid and gazed around the foyer. There were a couple of other patrons coming through the door now—an elderly couple in their threadbare Sunday best, hunched over like polyester-clad supplicants, murmuring banalities; they would never understand Billy's Thing. It took a very special person to hook into Billy's Thing.

Like the man in the photograph.

Billy put the folded *Times-Weekly* under his arm and strode through the exit, his heart beating a little faster.

5

Torture Chamber

AT THE END of the main corridor, there was a large, airy room known as the physical therapy center. Two thousand square feet of parquet floor worn down to a velvet burnish over the years, walls of ancient white plaster, and ceilings ornamented with crumbling Victorian fixtures, the room was a pure anachronism in the stark Bauhaus world of the Reinhardt Rehab Center. Sunlight streamed in through the high arched windows along the west wall, igniting dust motes and heating up the musty air. The room looked like a ballet school rehearsal space, retro-fitted with rows of elaborate stationary weight machines. Each machine was planted on a spongy rubber mat, and along the windows ran a line of parallel bars to aid patients in the baby steps of early walking.

For John the room had become a torture chamber, the bane of his existence.

They started him on the leg machine this morning, and it was excruciating. Every repetition felt like rusty railroad spikes being driven up through his knees, every stroke accompanied by corresponding bolts of agony in his ribs. But John kept at it. Sixty reps on the leg machine, sixty reps on the hip flexor, thirty minutes on the walk bars. It was draining, but John had myriad incentives to keep him going, not the least of which was a little dynamo named Jenny Withers.

Jenny Withers was the physical therapist whom Dr. Cousins had assigned to John's case. A dark-skinned African-American woman with a Medusa tangle of dreadlocks and glistening, sinewy muscles, Jenny Withers had the same sort of kinetic energy that all physical trainers seem to radiate. Dressed in her spandex and terry cloth, constantly clapping her cable-taut hands, shouting out encouraging bromides—*"You got it now!"* and *"That's the way!"* and *"Make it burn!"*—she was a whirling dervish of adrenaline, a funnel cloud of motivational psychology.

The moment John laid eyes on her, he liked her.

"I supposed you've heard about me," he had said to her this morning, a few moments after they met.

"The man with no name," she had replied with a grin.

"Yeah, right, that's me—the mystery man, enjoying my fifteen minutes of fame."

"Enjoy it while it lasts," she said, then pointed to a nearby mat on the floor. "Why don't you lie down and we'll start out with some stretching exercises while we talk."

John obliged. "I've been trying to get to know myself again," he grunted, lying back, allowing Jenny to raise his knees, then lower them. "I mean—you know—rediscover myself, or something like that."

"Must be pretty terrible."

"Oh, I don't know—you don't have to worry about filling out your taxes."

"You don't remember nothing at all?"

"Nope, nothing—not even my face."

"You don't remember your own face?"

John shook his head. "I look in the mirror and, you know, all I see is this forty-something guy with an average-looking face, starting to bald a little bit, and that's about it. He's somebody I've never met. Isn't that crazy?" There was an awkward silence, and then John told her about the trivial stuff that he couldn't get out of his head—Miles Davis, oysters on the half-shell, great saxophone solos. Of course he neglected to tell her about the slabs of meat, and the icy-white face, and the stiletto heels, and the toothy rictus of a smile.

"That ain't so trivial," Jenny said.

"What do you mean?"

She shrugged. "What else is there to life than music and food?"

John smiled. "Yeah, I suppose you're right."

"Why don't you roll onto your side now, and just bend your right knee back as far as you can without hurtin' too much, then bend it on back."

John obeyed. He could feel Jenny's strong hands lightly brushing his calf and his hamstring as he flexed his injured knee as much as possible without peeling off the top of his skull from all the pain. "That smarts—*ouch!*—that burns quite a bit," he said with a grimace.

"Okay, no problem, we'll back off a little bit," she said, slowing him down with her steel-cable fingers. "What you got there is a partial tear to one of the four ligaments in your knee, which is messed up by the hairline fracture in your femur. Why don't you tell me, on a scale of one to ten, when the pain rises above . . . let's say, about a seven or an eight."

"Okay, fine, no problem."

After another moment, she said, "I bet music and food weren't the only things you remembered."

"What do you mean?"

"Y'all gotta taste for the drink, don't ya?"

"What?"

"You know what I'm talking about. Alcohol—beer, wine, liquor?"

John peered up at her. "How did you—yeah—that's right. How did you know?"

"Woman's intuition," she said. "Now turn over slowly, and then do the other knee."

John did as he was told, and he lay there for a moment, wondering if this woman was secretly some kind of shaman, some kind of good witch who could lay her hands on a body and discern the maladies in an instant. He glanced at her fingers, her lovely ebony fingers lightly guiding his knee brace, and something crackled through the static in his mind for just an instant . . . a trace of a woman's voice, pleading inarticulately, mewling like a cat . . . and then there was nothing but a whisper of chills along John's spine. He closed his eyes and murmured, "That hurts a little bit—yeah—that's about a seven."

"Sorry about that," she said.

"How did you know—really—about the booze?" John asked.

Jenny shrugged. "Don't have to be no doctor to see the signs, the shaking, the sweating."

"Is it really—ouch, that's about an eight!—is it really that obvious?"

After a long pause, Jenny said, "Guess it helps when you have an alcoholic for an ex-husband."

There was a long stretch of anguished silence, and then the workout continued.

John tried to fill the remainder of the session with nervous small talk.

The rest of the day was spent in a sort of furious denial, limping along the hallways with his metal crutches, keeping his head filled with great saxophone solos from the past that he found himself remembering note-for-note. There was the velvet buzz saw of Sonny Rollins on "Dancing in the Dark," and the leaping quarter-notes of Coleman Hawkins on "Beyond the Blue Horizon." But the greatest of all was Charlie Parker's runaway riffing on "Lester Leaps In." How the hell did John know all these tunes? He found the music bubbling out of his subconscious like a wellspring. Later on, while working on his flexibility in the Reinhardt Center's pool, he found himself humming the rhythm section to "Opus One" over and over, an endless mental mantra that kept the dark images at bay.

Late in the afternoon, he suffered through a series of standardized psychological tests with Dr. Cousins, such as the Thematic Apperception Test, which involved impromptu verbal reactions to an array of cartoon scenarios. Unfortunately, nearly two hours of staring at flash cards of domestic scenes, lost children, angry daddies, and lascivious mailmen did very little to rattle anything loose in the jammed clockwork of John Doe's mind.

That night, for the first time since he had been a patient at the center, John took dinner in the cafeteria. He sat alone near the window, ate his chicken teriyaki and rice, and tried not to stare at the other patients. Most of them kept to themselves as well, sensing a certain tension in the air.

John felt as though everyone else in the world knew something that he didn't.

He wasn't too far off the mark.

By nine P.M., the Orland Park Public Library was closing down for the night. Several announcements had been made over the loudspeakers at ten-minute intervals, and most of the patrons had wandered downstairs to the loan-out desk. And now Sylvia Sunnheimer sat at her cluttered station under the REFERENCE sign, waiting to power-down her computer, waiting to punch out and go home. But Sylvia Sunnheimer could not leave yet, oh, no, Sylvia couldn't budge. There was still a straggler lingering across the room near the periodical stacks.

There was always one in every crowd, every doggone night, making life difficult for the late shift.

Sylvia had been the reference clerk at the library for almost ten years now, ever since her husband, Bernie, had passed away. Sylvia had seen every type of yay-hoo you could ever imagine come into the library. Derelicts looking for a corner to flop in, prostitutes, drug addicts, hyped-up high school kids looking to cause a ruckus. But somehow, the worst types were the stragglers. Lost in their own little worlds, thumbing through old issues of *The New York Times,* whizzing through endless spools of microfiche.

Sylvia knew some of them were lawyers, some were reporters, some were insurance investigators, some were small-town private detectives, some were merely bored housewives looking for a new recipe for clam dip. But they all shared a profound disregard for the feelings of others, and that just burned Sylvia up.

She stood up and came around the rear of the desk, smoothing the wrinkles in her new Ann Taylor skirt. Fast approaching her sixtieth year on the planet, Sylvia was a petite woman with a thin, leathery face, impeccable grooming, and the posture of a Marine Corps drill sergeant. She suffered very few fools lightly, and she was getting too old to let a straggler keep her from seeing the Barbara Walters special. That's why she decided to go say something to the man.

He was sitting at a round table near the window, his back turned to Sylvia as she approached, a microfiche screen glowing next to him, a spray of recent local papers spread across the table in front of him. From behind, it was difficult to see his face, but it was clear that he was in a professional trade of some sort. Teacher, cop, professor. Medium height, broad shoulders, he wore a tan sport coat with patches on the elbows. Probably in his mid-forties. Sylvia could see his hands sorting through the newsprint, and they were strong hands, dexterous, powerful. He paused on a copy of *The Joliet Times-Weekly,* and Sylvia could see him studying a photograph at the bottom of one of the pages. The man's temples were pulsing busily.

Sylvia was about to go tap on his shoulder and give him a brusque message, requesting that he finish his business at once, but she froze for some reason, standing next to a magazine rack ten feet away, the overhead fluorescents buzzing in the stark silence of the deserted library. She couldn't help staring at the man. Something about the way the back of his finely groomed head was cocked, the way his jaw was set in that odd tableau, the way his powerful shoulders filled out the padded seams of his sport coat. Sylvia felt an odd sort of reticence washing over her all of a sudden.

This man meant business.

Sylvia stood there for a moment, too rattled to return to her desk, too flustered to say anything. And a moment passed, and then the man at the table did something that Sylvia had never seen a visitor do before—and, God knew, Sylvia had seen it all—and it all happened in a snap. The man at the table reached down and tore the article right out of the *Times-Weekly*— just like that—and he did it with such nonchalance that Sylvia felt the strangest sensation of being violated.

Then the man rose, folding the article and putting it into his pocket as though he had every right. He turned away from the table and started toward the stairs, and his face came into full view as he passed Sylvia, his severe features, his lantern jaw and perfectly hooked aquiline nose. His hair was the color of morning sunlight on a wheat field, and his eyes glinted with a kind of worldly knowing. The truth was, he looked like a movie star. But mostly what Sylvia saw was the way he glanced at her—*a haunted look* was how Sylvia would describe it—and that look lingered, lingered on his face as he crossed the room and paused at the staircase, nodding one last farewell and then vanishing down the steps.

Making Sylvia forget all about Barbara Walters.

6

News

AMONG THE NEARLY three dozen men, women, and teenagers at the Reinhardt Rehabilitation Center, there were numerous automobile-accident victims. One of the worst cases was a baby-faced young man named David Eisenberg who had lost control of his Nissan Sentra while driving home from his senior prom ten months earlier. The young man had sustained severe damage to the lower and central sulci of the frontal lobe, which devastated his motor and speech capabilities, and he was just now learning to communicate through an electronic touch pad. John felt an odd empathy for David Eisenberg, and was already showing his fondness for the boy through a series of spastic waves and sidelong glances as they passed each other in the hall, John with his crutches, the Eisenberg boy in his wheelchair. There was something about the desperate glimmer of hope in the boy's eye that simply broke John's heart.

Perhaps this was why, late in the afternoon the next day, in the physical therapy room, John broached the subject with Jenny.

"Have you worked with the Eisenberg kid yet?" John asked, grunting, urging the iron footrail of the leg machine forward with the flats of his feet. In his imagination, he could hear the boogie-woogie pulse of Jay McShann doing "C-Jam Blues," and it was driving him on. It was his sixth day in purgatory, and already he was feeling strong enough to walk without the crutches. Notwithstanding his amnesia, he was starting to contemplate leaving the facility, striking out into the world and searching for his lost self. It was a terrifying proposition, but he knew it was something he would have to face soon.

"Sweet boy," Jenny said. "Been doing some basic stuff with him—five more, John, come on, make it hurt!—been doing some eye-hand coordination stuff, nothing too strenuous."

"Will he eventually—you know—will he bounce back?"

Jenny shrugged. "That's somethin' we take one day at a time around here."

"It seems like—I don't know—there's a lot going on inside him."

"I know what you mean."

"But you don't have any idea whether he'll be able to speak again?"

"I really don't."

John started to say something else, then gulped the words back as he realized the very same prognosis probably applied to him. The reality was, nobody could say whether John would ever recover his memory. The odds were probably about even. And that's probably why John felt such an affinity for the Eisenberg boy. "It's none of my business, you know, and I'm not a doctor," John muttered as he finished the last painful push. "I just think the kid's mind is okay, you know? Like it's trapped inside his—"

"John!"

The voice sliced through the musty air, coming from the doorway across the room.

John looked up and saw Dr. Cousins entering the therapy room, striding toward him, clutching a clipboard to her white jacketed breast, her eyes aglow with excitement. Her heels clicked on the hardwood as she approached. "You're not going to believe this!" She came over to the leg machine and hovered over John. "You're just not going to believe it."

John let his legs relax, and he sat back in the padded chair. "At this point, Dr. Cousins, quite honestly, I'll believe just about anything."

"You've got a visitor," she answered, grinning.

"I've got a what?" He wasn't sure that he had heard her properly. It sounded as though she had said "visitor," but she might have said "whistler" or "blister." He swallowed dryly and gripped the sides of the machine.

"A visitor, John, a real flesh-and-blood visitor!"

The room seemed to change suddenly, the passage of time screaming to a halt, as though the entire world were a grandiose video program and someone had just pressed the PAUSE button. John's ears were hot all of a sudden, his scalp too tight for his skull.

"A visitor?" He was still semistupefied by the news, as though he hadn't yet processed it fully.

"Isn't that just the greatest news? He's waiting for you in the lounge—as we speak!"

"That's pretty cool," Jenny said, taking a step back, her hands on her bony hips.

"Oh. My. God," John uttered finally.

It felt as though his heart had just jammed. Chills swept up the back of his legs, up his spine, tightening the tiny hairs on his neck. His stomach tightened. This was too abrupt. He hadn't expected the moment of truth to come from the outside world. He had expected it to come from within, to result from some quiet internal epiphany. But now it felt as though he had been sitting in a comfortable chair and suddenly realized it was a seat on a roller coaster, and it was moving, climbing up a steep incline, about to plunge into oblivion. He looked up at the neurologist and said, "Who—who is it?"

"It's your brother, John . . . it's Robert."

John kept staring at her, unable to speak.

7

The Man in the Lounge

JOHN DECIDED TO go back to his room first and make himself presentable.

The housekeeping staff had been there that morning, and his bed was made with crisp white sheets, the pillow fluffed, the blanket turned down with military precision. There was a small glass vase on the bedside table. Somebody had replaced its shriveling contents with a fresh flower: a yellow daisy. Behind the bed's headboard was a small bulletin board. A couple of newspaper articles about the man with no name were thumbtacked there. There was a pile of cassettes on the window ledge, his tape player, a box of pastels and charcoals, reams of paper, and a carton of Marlboro greens. He stared at the room for a moment, thinking, marveling at the fact that these items were currently the sum total of his identity.

Now all this was about to change.

He went over to the closet and, hands trembling, put on a fresh T-shirt, jeans, and loafers. The nursing staff had been nice enough to purchase him some new street clothes. The tiny piano key chain was sitting on the top shelf of the closet, and John grabbed it. He stared at the keys for a moment—an odd habit he had developed over the last couple of days, thinking that maybe if he studied the shapes of the various keys, they might somehow unlock something in his memory—and then he put them in his pocket. The keys had become a talisman, the only tangible link to his former life.

Finally, he crossed the room and stood in front of a floor-length mirror that was mounted on the back of the door, and he looked himself over one last time. His heart was thumping steadily in his chest, his mouth as dry as paste. He wanted a gin and tonic so badly now, he could feel the low, buzzing vibration of need cramping his gut.

Why was it so hard to look at his own face? It wasn't that it looked particularly odd to him. The truth was, it was a very average-looking face. A little ruddy-complected, a little jagged maybe, but it was certainly not about to scare any children. No distinguishing marks other than the fading smudge of a bruise over his temple, as well as the centipede of stitches where his head had connected with the truck's grill. His hair was beginning to thin, and it also seemed to cowlick naturally, as though he had spent his days and nights compulsively running his hand through it, thinking, ruminating.

He must have been a heavy thinker.

As well as a heavy drinker.

John McNally.

He knew his name now and—irony of ironies—it really *was* John. John Winston McNally. Dr. Cousins had gotten a huge kick out of *that* little coincidence. The man waiting in the lounge was named Robert McNally, and he was John's only brother, and he had stumbled across John's photo in the *Times-Weekly.* Then he had tracked down the clinic, and oh, boy, was he excited to see John. Dr. Cousins was understandably excited herself—this was the breakthrough she had been hoping for. She had already gleaned several salient points of interest from the man in the lounge—such as the fact that John was divorced and that both his parents were deceased—but she didn't want to learn too much too fast. She felt that it would be better for John to absorb his background gradually, person-to-person.

Or brother-to-brother, as it were.

John found a hard-bristle brush on the closet shelf, grabbed it, and brushed his hair. It felt strange to have a real name now: John W. McNally. Sounded like a real "regular" guy. Like a good neighbor, a life insurance agent maybe, a high school football coach. Irish-American—Catholic, perhaps? But how in God's name was it connected to those flash-frame visions of black leather and scalpels?

The name was making a weird noise in John's mind, like a high-tension wire vibrating at dissonant frequencies. There were echoes in it, after-echoes. A name whispered in a dream, reverberating faintly in the light of day. A distant broadcast wavering in and out of reach.

It was finally time to tune in a station.

He turned away from his reflection and limped out the door.

The lounge was situated halfway down an adjacent corridor, beyond a row of meshed windows radiant with overcast daylight, and it took John a couple of minutes just to make the trip. He could walk only so fast, and the last Percodan he had taken for the pain was beginning to wear off. Unfortunately, he wasn't due to take another one for at least an hour, so he had to tough it out. The fact was, his entire waking life had become a game of staving off pain, and satisfying his urge to drink with painkillers. The Percodans lasted just long enough to allow him enough mobility to exercise, but the last hour of each cycle was murder.

He reached the door to the lounge, and paused. He realized that he wanted so badly for this to go well. He wanted to burst into the room, rush over to this man—whoever he was—give him a great, big, brotherly bear hug. He wanted to be John McNally again: whoever that was.

He opened the door.

A great, big empty room glared back at him.

John stood there for a moment, scanning the room, wondering if he had come to the wrong lounge. There were no long-lost brothers, no other patients, nobody—only a few oversized sofa groupings placed along the edges of brightly colored Mojave area rugs. There was a large-screen TV in one corner, and the far wall offered an expansive view of the outer grounds and the forest beyond. The room smelled of day-old popcorn and lemon wax. On the wall to John's immediate left was a Rembrandt knockoff of a Spanish conquistador.

John stepped into the lounge and let the door swing shut behind him.

There was a sound behind him.

John tried to turn, but something wrapped around his neck, freezing him where he stood, cutting off his air. John's hands instinctively shot up and clutched at the object, and he realized at once that it was a thickly muscled male arm, and that it was strangling him. John tied to say something, but he couldn't get the words out—either the shock or the pressure on his Adam's apple was stifling his voice. Then John felt something pointed and sharp pressing into the small of his back.

"Don't move," the voice said in his ear, and it made his neck rash with chills.

"Let go," John hissed.

"I got you where I want you now."

"P-please," John stammered, and tried to wriggle away, but the arm was pig-iron stubborn.

"Don't you recognize my voice?"

"N-nn-no, I don't—"

"Liar," the voice growled, and John could feel the hot breath on his ear-

lobe, he could smell the cologne, a faint hint of spice and cigarette smoke.

Suddenly, the arm dropped away as abruptly as it had appeared, and John staggered for a moment, stunned silly, and laughter pealed through the room—great, booming belly laughter in John's ears—and John managed to spin around and get his first glimpse of the assailant.

"I'm sorry, Johnny, I couldn't resist!" the man chortled. He was laughing so hard now, his eyes were welling with tears. A handsome, square-jawed man in his early forties, he was pointing his finger at John like a gun—presumably this was what had poked John in the back—and the guy was in stitches, absolute stitches, laughing at the sheer absurdity of it all.

John was rubbing his neck. "W-what's the idea?"

"I'm sorry, Johnny, I'm being a shit again."

"Who—who are you?" John was trying to get his bearings back.

The laughter gradually sputtered and died, and then the man looked sad, eyebrows furrowing. "Poor Johnny," he said. "You really are messed up in the head."

"Yeah, I guess that's one way of saying it."

"I'm sorry, Johnny."

"They told me—I mean—I understand you're my brother? Robert?"

The man smiled. "Big brother, Johnny, and don't you ever forget it."

There was an awkward moment of silence, and John found himself gawking at the man. Dressed in a tan sport coat with patches on the sleeves, a black Ban-Lon shirt, khaki slacks, and expensive loafers, Robert McNally carried himself with a weird kind of authority. His features were finely chiseled, his hair meticulously coiffed. He looked like a soap opera star. And yet, there was a faint undercurrent of nervous tension in his gaze, a subtle wired quality, as though his mind were occupied by more troubling urgencies. And the more John looked at his face, the more John heard that crackling, indistinct static in his own mind. Unfortunately, this was the extent of the reaction that this unexpected visitation had conjured. "I apologize, but, you know, the thing is—this is very difficult," John finally stammered.

"You don't remember shit, do you?" the man said.

John shook his head.

"Okay, no problem, we'll just take it nice and slow," the man said, making his way over to a nearby sofa, taking a seat. He patted the seat next to him. "C'mon, Johnny, take a load off and let's talk."

Another moment of stark silence, and John remained standing. "You're my only brother?"

"No, actually we do have two Siamese twin sisters—Chang and Eng—who run a worm ranch outside of Kankakee."

John gave him a sidelong glance.

"I'm completely serious, Johnny." Robert's face was grim and set. "Mom and Dad used to travel with the carnival down around the Smokey Mountains." And now he started smirking a bit, his eyes beginning to water. "They used to book themselves as the Marauding McNallys—" Then Robert started giggling, his eyes tearing up again—he was having a grand old time.

"Yeah, right, that's very funny," John said, swallowing back the bile. His legs were killing him, and his neck still stung from the stranglehold that Robert had had on him.

"I apologize, Johnny, but this is just too much fun."

"How's that?"

Robert wiped his eyes and said, "Having someone who's a blank slate, it's just too much fun."

John sniffed back his anger. "Yeah, it's a real barrel of monkeys."

"Sorry, sorry." The man straightened up suddenly like a child being punished. "Go ahead, Johnny, ask me anything."

"Okay, let's start with marital status—am I single?"

The man grinned. "I'm sorry to tell you this, Johnny, but you're a Mormon—and I believe—I think at last count you had seventeen—sssseven—sss—" He burst out laughing again, slapping his palm against the cheap woven fabric of the sofa seat, and he laughed and laughed like it was just the best old time he had ever had.

"Stop it—*just stop it!*"

John's anguished cry seemed to have an immediate impact, as though he had just slapped Robert in the face. Robert's laughter wilted, and then something changed behind his eyes. A dark glint of pain, like a cinder smoldering faintly. His expression hardened. He glanced around the room for a moment, nodding obscurely, as though the circumstances he found himself in were simply par for the course. "You're right," he murmured, almost to himself rather than to John. "This is serious business, very serious, not the kind of thing to be taken lightly."

"Look, Robert, the thing is . . . I just need some time, you know, time to reorient myself."

"No-no, no, you're right," he said, and raised his hand deferentially.

"I didn't mean to—"

"You're right, brother. When you're right, you're right."

"Look, Robert—"

"Nope!" He stood up, clapping his hands. "I've been a shit, and I'll tell you what we're going to do. We're going to take this thing one step at a time, just like the good doctor said. We'll go on a walk."

"A walk?"

Robert gestured toward the leafy vista outside the windows. "There's at least an hour of daylight left, whattya say? We'll catch you up nice and easy."

John felt nauseous. "I don't know—"

"Come on, Johnny, take a walk with your big brother and I'll reintroduce you to yourself. What harm could it do?"

John looked at the man and thought about it for a long moment, and he was hard-pressed to put into words all the myriad kinds of harm it might do.

8

Freak

"THERE'S A BENCH up ahead, behind those trees." The man named Robert motioned with his manicured finger, urging John toward a stand of poplars.

They were strolling along the periphery of a man-made reservoir that snaked through the grounds of the clinic. It was nearly dusk, and the air was turning cold, even for mid-April in northern Illinois. The massive terraces of the clinic rose around them like some ancient Mayan village, the terra-cotta turning gunmetal purple in the dying light. A handful of other patients were wandering hesitantly around the courtyard behind them, and a flock of sparrows flew overhead in formation.

The birds looked like stitches.

"Sorry if I seem—you know—kind of anxious," John said earnestly, trying to keep up with the other man's big, robust strides. John had been walking without crutches only for a little more than twenty-four hours now, and he was still a tad rusty. His heart was hammering in his chest, not only from the strain of keeping up but also from the sensory overload of being outdoors for the first time since he had awakened at the clinic six days earlier. None of it looked familiar; and the wind on his face, the odors, all the sensations, were overwhelming. For some reason, he kept hearing *Bird with Strings,* one of his favorite records, endlessly churning in his head, conjuring vague images of sunlight on his bare feet, running along the mud-smooth banks of a river as a child. He felt a strange sort of shame and embarrassment for his outburst back in the lounge—after all, his brother was probably just as unnerved by this whole thing as he was. "I'm trying to take it all in," John added. "It's just that I'm, you know, kind of starving for information."

"Don't blame you one bit, Johnny."

"You say I'm divorced?"

"Hideous woman," Robert muttered, glancing over his shoulder at the other patients shuffling silently along in the near distance, the sun glimmering off the frames of their metal walkers. Robert McNally seemed exceedingly nervous, hyperaware of the gazes of other patients, and he seemed determined to get behind those trees. Was this whole process embarrassing him? Was it too painful to undergo in front of other people?

"What did you say her name was?" John asked.

"It's . . . uh . . . Myra."

"Myra?"

"Complete bitch," he said, rolling his eyes. He was leading John around a hedgerow that bordered the clinic's property line, across a scabrous carpet of crab grass. They were far enough away from the other patients now that they could drop their pants and nobody would be the wiser. Still, Robert charged toward the lengthening shadows of the poplars like a man possessed, and John started wondering what kind of brother this man had been. For that matter, what kind of brother had John been? All the angst notwithstanding, it was oddly liberating to be amnesic. All the personal baggage was lifted from one's shoulders, all the issues between one's relatives positively evaporated. John had no reason to love or hate this man. Robert was simply a designated relative: Older Sibling.

John looked at him then. "No children?"

"What?" Robert's mind had been wandering for a moment. "Oh, uh, yeah, that's right. You don't have any kids."

"What about our parents? You say they're both deceased?"

"Yeah, that's right."

"How did they—?"

"Cancer, both of them." Robert shuddered as he walked. "Horrible thing, really. You took it pretty hard. Dad got sick first. Started in his spinal cord, then spread, and by the time they diagnosed it, it was too late. It was burning up his brain. His last few weeks were pretty tough. He had the mind of a one-year-old, wearing diapers, shitting all over himself, playing with the shit. It was too much for Mom. She found the lump in her breast exactly one month after they put Dad in the ground."

There was a pause then, and John noticed how his older brother seemed fairly nonchalant about such terrible memories. John started to say: "How long ago did all this—?"

"Come on," Robert said suddenly, motioning toward the cool shadows.

"I think it'll all make more sense if I start at the beginning. There should be a bench around here somewhere. Come on."

John followed the man through a patch of weeds and into a dimly illuminated grove of hardwoods. It smelled of mossy decay and something richer, more alkaline, like the spoor of a possum or a skunk. The flesh along the back of John's neck crawled suddenly—he wasn't sure why—and he looked over at Robert. Robert was standing a few feet away in the shadows, peering back through the foliage at the clinic grounds, as though he were making certain that positively no one could see them.

John shrugged, getting fidgety. "Listen, um, Robert . . . if this whole thing makes you feel uncomf—"

Robert spun around suddenly, grabbing John by the T-shirt. "Look at me!"

"What?"

"I said, look at me!"

"What are you talking about?" John was dumbstruck, his back pressed against the bark of an elm tree.

"You're telling me you have no fucking idea who I am?" Robert's hands were tightening on the T-shirt.

"What do you mean? You're my brother."

"I'm your brother, sure."

"Aren't you?"

"Look at me, you idiot!" Robert roared, his eyes blazing now, his teeth clenched. His breath smelled bad, a mixture of hot tar deodorized with stale mint. A tiny pinhead of saliva clung to his sculpted chin. "You still have no idea who I am, do you? *Do you?*"

"No—dammit! I don't!—I—I can't—"

"Shut up!" Robert shoved John hard across the clearing.

John tripped on an exposed root and stumbled to the ground, his shoulder smacking hard-pack. The pain trumpeted in his ribs, in his knees, in his groin, and he lost his breath. He lay there on his side for a moment, gasping, trembling like a fish on the dry hull of a boat. He tried to rise to a kneeling position, but a shadow was looming over him.

"Look at me, you sick freak!"

The iron fingers closed around John's shirt again, and John managed to look up and utter, "Please—"

"No! You have no fucking idea what you've done, do you?" the man said then, almost playfully, as though he were talking to a recalcitrant hunting dog.

"I don't, I really don't—I don't know what you're talking about."

"Shut your mouth!"

John swallowed dryly and rose to a kneeling position, favoring the less sore of his two knees. His brain was buzzing now like a hive of bees, his chest thumping painfully. He tried to swallow again, but his throat was filled with sawdust.

Robert grabbed John's T-shirt again with one of his powerful hands. "They told me to leave it alone," he growled. "They told me to stay away from it."

"I really have no idea—"

"I told you to shut up!"

There was a taut moment of silence then, and it looked as though the man named Robert were turning something over in his mind, his rage-glazed eyes sparking with an idea, a thought. And then, just for an instant, the corners of his mouth twitched, a smirk playing across his lips. Could he possibly be enjoying this? Or was he so intoxicated with rage that he was literally giddy?

"You see this?" he said suddenly, reaching into his breast pocket. He pulled out a small leather billfold, then flipped it open with a flick of his wrist, revealing a tarnished silver star embossed on a metal shield. The words INGHAM COUNTY SHERIFF'S DEPARTMENT were stamped across the top, and SPECIAL DIVISION along the bottom scroll.

John's mind screamed, *Cop!*—a torrent of harsh, squealing feedback—the realization hitting him all at once that this man who called himself Robert was a detective.

"You see this shield?" Robert said evenly.

John managed to nod.

"It doesn't mean anything to me anymore," he said, and tossed the shield into the shadows and weeds. It made a *foof*ing noise as it landed.

Then John felt the vise grip around his left wrist again, yanking him to his feet.

"Turn around, freak!"

John was spun around and slammed against the shank of an elm tree. His teeth cracked loudly in his skull as his face was mashed up against the rough bark, vision blurring, head spinning. He could smell the moist decay. His stomach was turning inside out, threatening vomit. A familiar jangling noise rose up behind him, the sound of heavy metal jewelry.

The handcuffs closed around one wrist, then another, the steel cold against his skin.

"C'mon," Robert said flatly, then yanked John violently back around so that he was facing west. "You want to see what you've done? Huh? Take a little trip down memory lane?"

"Wait, wait, please—"

"C'mon, let's go."

"But—"

"Now!" The cop grabbed John under the elbow and urged him toward the far end of the tree line.

John couldn't think of anything else to say or do, so he simply followed orders.

9

Snake Eye

THEY EMERGED ON the other side of the grove, stepping over thick cords of ancient roots. There was a parking lot in the distance, filled with scattered cars. From the window of his room he had been able to see only up to the tree line, and this had seemed a placid, peaceful place. But now, as dusk closed around the grounds, he felt a surge of dread. This wasn't a friendly place, no, sir, it was turning downright forbidding.

"Last car on the right," the cop muttered, and ushered John down a gentle slope and then across the football-sized pea-gravel lot. The rhythmic crunching of their footsteps was the only sound John could hear over the timpani of his heart. His mouth had gone completely dry, and his fingers were tingling from the handcuffs cutting into his circulation. They approached a milk-chocolate-colored sedan. "Hold it, please," the cop said flatly, and then managed to open the passenger door with one hand while holding John with the other.

John climbed into the car.

It was a Toyota Camry with a lot of miles on it, and the interior smelled of stale cigarettes and pine-scented deodorizer. John watched as the cop strode around the front of the car, opened the driver's side door, then climbed behind the wheel. The seat springs groaned under the man's weight. He started the car, put it in gear, and pulled out of the lot.

A moment later, they were heading down a winding access road toward the main artery.

"Can you at least tell me, you know, what it is I did?" John said.

"Be quiet, you," the cop murmured.

John sat there silently, flesh crawling with nervous tension, the handcuffs cutting into his wrists. The car was picking up speed, and John was starting to come to painfully obvious conclusions. *One, this man is definitely not my brother. Two, this guy is either going to kill me or arrest me, and right now the bastard isn't exactly paying attention to my Miranda rights.* John realized he had better do something about it soon.

Unfortunately, the handcuffs were limiting his options.

Outside the car, darkness was falling, and with it came the glacial air of a spring evening. The sedan was making its way down the access road, tooling around the hairpins in a mist of carbon monoxide, the vapor lights playing across its hood like droplets of liquid mercury. John glanced into his side mirror, watching the blue glow of the clinic grounds shrinking into blackness behind them. Soon they were on the two-lane macadam that routed traffic toward the highway, red reflectors glowing back like angry eyes.

"They said I should walk away from it," the cop blurted suddenly.

"Pardon me?" John's shoulders were cramping, the cuffs digging into his wrists.

"They said I should walk away, said there wasn't enough evidence."

"Evidence of what? Jesus—I think I have a right to know what I'm being accused of."

"Shut up, freak, you don't have any rights in this car!"

"All I'm asking is that you—"

John fell abruptly silent, his words clogging in his throat as the cop's hand came out of his coat with a weapon in it. The gun was carbon-steel black, glimmering in the low light, and it seemed to swing toward John with an almost dreamlike motion. "I told you to shut up," the cop said softly, his gun in John's face.

John was silent then, clenching and unclenching his fists, trying to keep his hands from falling asleep.

"I'm gonna show you what you've done," the cop purred softly, after turning his gaze back to the road. His arm lay across the back of the seat. He tapped John's head with the pistol almost absentmindedly, like a man soothing a nervous pet. The cop's smile was gleaming in the dashboard light, and in the dimness it was hard to tell whether it was full of mirth or a toothy rictus of rage. "I'm gonna rub your nose in it, Johnny-boy. How do you like that?" John offered no reply.

They reached the mouth of a narrow entrance ramp and accelerated down the grade. Then they lurched into the northbound lanes of Highway 53, racing past the gray monolith office plazas on one side and the dense wooded darkness of a river on the other. The two-lane was dark and silent this evening, the sedan's headlights washing the gravel shoulder, reflectors and broken glass strobing in the magnesium beams. John stared at the desolate landscape rushing by as though he were being hypnotized by the blur. His eyes ached, and he had that coppery taste of panic in his mouth. He closed his eyes and tried to breathe deeply.

Something flashed in his mind.

—a shard of broken glass embedded in a slab of raw meat—

His eyes popped open.

It was as though something had suddenly bubbled out of the mire of his amnesia, unannounced, just for an instant. A flashbulb on the inside of his eyelids. A glimpse of something, like a jagged piece of colored glass impaled on a piece of rotting beef—that goddamned meat imagery again—and the accompanying after-echo of a sound. A voice, perhaps, maybe a scream. It was as though it had just suddenly *existed* in his mind, like a snippet of a film soundtrack running backward through a sputtering projector.

And then there was nothing.

He heard himself say, "Okay, listen—all I'm asking is that you tell me, you know, tell me what it is I did."

"I'm gonna do more than tell you," the cop murmured, more to himself than to John. "I'm going to rub your nose in it."

"Rub my nose in what—what the hell are you talking about?" John was raising his voice now.

Robert snapped the Glock's hammer back into its firing position.

"Okay, all right, I'm sorry, sorry," John stammered. He was petrified now, and all he could think about was getting out of this car, getting away from this angry vigilante, this avenging angel. Perhaps if John stalled long enough, he could figure out a way to get the door open and bail out without getting shot or dying, broken on the highway. Maybe if the cop slowed down enough while rounding a corner. "All I'm saying is," John continued stalling, "if I did something before I got injured, I'll be happy to take responsibility for it, but you can't just start condemning me, and, and, and, and—and not even tell me what I did, see, because I'm completely in the dark here."

There was a pause as the cop shook his head slowly, as though he were deeply amused by it all.

John started concentrating on three things: the motion of the cop's gun hand, the cop's eyes as they shifted from John back to the road, and the cop's right foot on the accelerator pedal. If he could just find the right instant in the triangulated relationship among those three actions, perhaps there was a way out of here. He almost laughed. How in the world did he expect to escape with a gun in his face and his hands cuffed behind him?

A moment later, the man named Robert made John's passive observations academic.

"I should kill you right now," he said, brushing the gun barrel across John's earlobe.

What happened next occurred with a sort of time-lapse swiftness—the kind of swiftness that was exclusive only to things like traffic accidents, muggings, and random acts of violence—and at first John was not even aware that he had initiated the process until he saw his left foot shoot out across the center hump, arcing over the shift lever and slamming down on the cop's right leather loafer. At that moment, John was also unaware that his action had been perfectly timed with a lucky break—an act of God, actually—in the form of a six-ton truck barreling toward them in the opposing lane.

Several equal and opposite reactions happened almost instantly.

The Camry's engine growled, the car lurched, the cop's arm flew backward, and the gun went off. There was a sledgehammer pop that burst in John's ears and a blinding flash of light as the side window blossomed outward. Then the car was sliding into the supernova of the truck's headlamps. An air horn bellowed loudly, and Robert frantically yanked the wheel with both hands—the gun lost and forgotten. But he overcompensated, and the Camry swerved violently back across its own lane, skidding across the shoulder, the wheels gobbling the guardrail, keening like a freight car, throwing sparks, the entire chassis shivering furiously.

Now we're both going to die, John thought wildly.

It was the last thing to occur to him before the sedan broke through the guardrail and went over the edge of the embankment.

10

Alligators in the Sewer

AN ENORMOUS OAK leaped out of the shadows.

The impact was bone-rattling, the car smashing head-on into the tree, slamming both men into the dash. The driver-side air bag erupted, engulfing the cop, and the rubber edge of the glove box punched John in the face, jarring his teeth, igniting stars in his vision and whiplashing him back into his seat. And then there was silence, *silence,* falling as abruptly as the car had crashed, and John managed to gaze through the soupy air over at his adversary, who was semiconscious, wedged between the air bag and the door. Fine strings of blood were spattered across the cop's face, across the upholstery, across the rosette of cracks in the side window behind him, looking like black thirty-weight in the darkness: The cop's skull had connected with the side window.

"Jesus," John uttered dumbly, trying to make his body move, but his ribs were wailing, and his knees were like broken china, all brittle and hot. His hands were ice cold behind his back, the cuffs biting into his skin. Something was hissing outside the broken window.

The cop moaned, his face slack with shock, the whites of his eyes showing.

John started moving on instinct, twisting his body around so that his hands were pressed against the cop's torso. A spike of pain drove through John's side, but he worked through it, breathing hard, thick, pained breaths, his head throbbing. He could feel the folds in the cop's jacket, the scaly leather belt around his waist—was it lizard skin?—and the seam above the cop's right trouser pocket. John swallowed all his pain and quickly thrust his cuffed hands into the pocket, fishing around for keys, any keys, anything. The pocket was empty. The cop moaned again, and John shivered with agony, groping for the key, but knew it was futile and he was trapped.

Then John felt something cold and hard on the seat next to the cop.

Loose change and a key ring.

John started frantically fiddling with the keys—they must have slipped out during the collision—and felt a couple of larger, rubber-coated keys attached to a plastic tag—probably the car keys, either from a rental firm or some police fleet—and also a smaller key with a tubular head. John's heart started racing, drumrolling in his chest, drumming like Krupa's tom-tom riff on "Cherokee," because this tiny tubular key was the key to John's freedom. The cop mumbled something suddenly, the words garbled, his throat clogged with blood and phlegm. John was already working the tiny key into one of the wristlets, worrying it back and forth, and finally hearing the heavenly *click!*

The rest of the liberation happened fairly quickly: John twisting around, unclasping the other wristlet, then dropping the cuffs and key to the floor.

Then John was turning toward his door, clawing for the handle. The car had those maddening Euro contours with the recessed handles, and John couldn't find the damn door lever at first, and he heard the cop moaning louder behind him, leather upholstery creaking, and John tried to focus his groggy, gummy brain on the task at hand—getting the hell out—but things were starting to get all syrupy for him, the sounds becoming muffled, his vision getting silvery and diffuse as the pain started washing over him. Finally he got his hand on the lever, but he couldn't make it work, the blood making his fingers slippery. His blood? The cop's blood? A moment later he got the door partially open, but found it blocked by a deadfall, and he was having trouble mustering the strength to push it open.

That's when John felt fingers clutching at the back of his T-shirt.

"*No!*" John yelped, tearing out of the cop's grasp, trying to squeeze through the narrow channel, gouging his T-shirt and his belly on the crumpled interior trim. Something gleamed dully on the floor to his left, and he looked down. *The pistol.* It had fallen to the floor mat on the passenger side, and now the cop was reaching for it. John acted without thinking. He slammed his foot down on the cop's hand, hard enough to snap cartilage.

The cop bellowed a garbled cry, and it was just enough time, thank God, for John to squeeze out through the breach and sprawl to the cool earth.

John hit the ground, and felt the chilled dampness on his hands and knees, and now things were happening around him all at once, happening fast, and all he could manage was a labored crawl toward the shadows of the woods. There was another vehicle approaching behind them, a pickup truck, its headlights sweeping out across the shoulder and down the embankment, and there was a grinding sound, as though the cop were racing the sedan's engine and getting nowhere, and there was the sound of the cop's voice, yelling something—John couldn't make it out but it sounded threatening just the same—and, finally, the click of the pistol's slide.

The first shot rang out just as John reached the edge of the forest.

The leaves sizzled above him as he dove for cover behind a huge deadfall log. His sore shoulder slammed against the timber, and a blast of pain jolted up between his shoulder blades. He bit down hard on his lower lip, swallowing the scream, trying to stay as silent as possible. The deeper woods were only twenty to thirty feet away, and somehow he knew that if he could just make it into the womb of darkness, he might have a slim chance of slipping away.

The cop was coming; John could hear him, huffing and puffing, footsteps crossing dead leaves.

John rose to a crouch position and made a decision in the space of a heartbeat: *Go.*

He lurched into the darkness, weaving around a tangle of birch trees, their bark like pale muslin in the darkness, and then he was stumbling down a gentle grade of roots and stones, clamoring into the darker woods.

It wasn't easy. Never mind that he was in severe pain, his lungs burning, his injured knees and spine twinging with every stride, the pain-stars bursting flares behind his eyes; and never mind that he had no earthly idea where he was heading, the woods closing in around him, his attempt at following a meager little dirt path thwarted by the riot of foliage in his face. The worst part was the madman on his tail, the sound of the cop's footsteps snapping twigs, the threat of a bullet shattering the back of his skull at any moment like a cold kiss on his neck. The only thing John had going for him was the darkness.

A moment later, another blast popped a hole in the dark behind John.

This time, the bullet chewed a piece of bark off a tree ten yards to John's left, and he could tell the cop was getting desperate, firing at shadows, losing John in the pitch-black. If his luck and his knees and his lungs held out, perhaps he did indeed have a chance.

He ran.

A moment later, a narrow stream loomed in the darkness ahead of John, the trickle of water shimmering in the intermittent moonlight. John was hyperventilating now, his heartbeat hammering in his ears, his legs aching, and he suddenly decided to follow the stream. It seemed as good a strategy as any, so he hopped up on the mud-packed edge and started tightroping alongside it, keeping as quiet as possible, hyperaware of the cop's faint footsteps falling farther and farther behind him. The stream began to widen, the edges hardening into concrete as it snaked through the woods. Soon the thing started to resemble a runoff ditch or culvert of some sort, and John realized that he had inadvertently chosen a direct route back into civilization.

At the moment, however, it wasn't clear how this would affect his flight.

When he finally emerged from the woods, he got his answer.

The water-treatment facility was immense, dark and brooding under the clear night sky. It lay on the far horizon, across a vast vacant lot, its gray stone buildings vaulting up over the surrounding trees. At first glance John figured it might be some kind of deserted college or university, but then he saw the grimy windows, the hydroelectric towers in the rear, and the black glassy surface of the reservoir to the east, and he smelled the burned-metal, alkaline odors on the breeze. And that's when he started panicking. The wind was rustling through the trees behind him, and he heard something like a twig snapping. The cop was still back there, pursuing John, and John had better do something quick, or he was a sitting duck out here in the open.

Across an access road to his right was a grouping of box-shaped trailers, each facing a common cul-de-sac, each of their gates in the open position for public loading. John crept across the middle distance, staying low, hyperaware of the swaying shadows behind him. As he approached the deserted boxcars, he saw huge signs rising up near each trailer's gate, labeling each recycling bin—this one for glass bottles, that one for plastics, the far one for newspapers and magazines.

John climbed into the trailer labeled PLASTICS HERE and looked for a place to hide.

The semitrailer was a cornucopia of filthy plastic, with jugs and bottles and tubs of myriad sizes piled in the rear of the thirty-foot-long box of filthy corrugated iron. The air was fetid and thick, and John had to breathe through his mouth as he swam through the detritus, looking for a place to sit. The floor was sticky. Luckily there was a spot in back—which was actually the *front* of the trailer—where an empty pallet sat near a latched side door. John squeezed past a stack of smashed milk cartons and collapsed onto the pallet.

It seemed like a safe enough spot to hide; it was obscured by all the plastic, and it lay near a possible alternate escape route. John took deep breaths and tried to settle and think. It took several moments just for his heart to ease back and his ears to stop ringing. The gun blasts had rattled his brain, and daggers of pain were stabbing his ribs, slicing up his spine, and he sat there huddling in that pungent dark stench for several moments, breathing deeply.

The sound of footsteps outside the trailer were icy fingers on his neck, making his flesh crawl.

He turned to the side hatch to see whether he could indeed slip out unnoticed. But when he grasped the handle and gently pushed, the door held firm. Probably padlocked from the outside. The footsteps were approaching—John could hear them crunching over the gravel of the cul-de-sac— and he ducked behind the pile of plastic, heart pulsing in his veins. There wasn't anything he could do but stay silent, stay still, and pray.

The footsteps were outside the mouth of the PLASTICS HERE trailer.

John heard the footsteps pause, shuffling in the gravel for a moment, then falling silent. What the hell was this guy doing? Was he waiting John out? Then a realization struck John like a lightning bolt: *The cop was out there listening, listening for any sign of a human being in here.* John was sweating profusely now. His shirt was plastered to his back, and sweat was beading on his brow. He closed his eyes and held his breath—as though, in some elemental, childlike part of his brain, he figured he would be harder to detect with his eyes closed. The silence stretched for what seemed like an eternity, and John became faintly aware of a change in the stench around him. Amid the rancid-sweet odors of moldy soda and old laundry soap, there was a soupier smell rising around him. Musky. Like spoiled beef.

Something moved next to him.

Out of the corner of his eye he caught a glimpse of a gray ropy object snaking between an empty two-liter Diet Pepsi bottle and a spent carton of 2 percent on the floor, a ridged gray centipede like an enormous cable, contracting into the shadows, and his brain screamed: *A tail!* It was a rat's tail, and the thing must have been enormous, just like one of those urban folk myths—the alligators in the sewer, the maniac on the loose with the hook for a hand—and now it was real and it was slithering through the shadows only inches away from John.

Outside, in the dark, the footsteps shuffled, then paused again.

John tried to shift his weight without making a sound, because his spine was throbbing unmercifully, and his injured knees were cramping. When he inched to his left, the subtle change in posture must have jarred the vermin next to him, spooking it into fight-or-flight, because all at once a ball of gray fur pounced on John's right ankle.

The possum glowered up at him with tiny black cinder eyes, hissing like a cat.

Razor teeth bit into John's flesh just above his ankle.

John's entire body convulsed suddenly, an involuntary spasm, as the pain surged up the tendons of his right leg, and his hand flew up to his mouth, clamping down on the scream. He saw nothing but bright fuchsia pink for a moment, the pain like a jolt of electricity, but somehow he managed to stay mute. Through his tears he gazed down at the monstrosity on his leg. It was *enormous,* the size of a dachshund, with a hunched back and a long scabrous tail. Its tiny snout remained vise-gripped around John's ankle, its delicate little eyes rolling back in its head, turning white as maggots, as the blood started soaking into John's socks, spraying out of the edges of the animal's jaws in delicate, tiny filaments in rhythm with its hyperventilated breathing.

Outside the trailer, the footsteps shuffled closer, then paused.

There was a dry, metallic snapping noise, like a match being struck.

Cold panic spurted through John's belly, overriding the pain, overriding the shock, and he reared back suddenly—almost involuntarily—then kicked the possum off his leg. The creature spun against a heap of greasy plastic containers, digging its claws into the floor, whining like a mutant baby. It was hissing now, spitting, trying to burrow back into the garbage, when all at once the air seemed to pop open like a champagne cork, and John saw bright yellow flames in his mind's eye.

The bullet struck the possum dead center in its back, tossing it three feet across the narrow aisle.

The animal slammed against a moldy cardboard box, shuddering convulsively, a delicate stream of entrails glistening on the floor behind it. More gunfire rang out in the darkness—three quick pops, like a ball-peen hammer striking an anvil—and three tufts of fur suddenly blossomed in sequence along the creature's back, the bullets shattering its spine. Hind legs jittering, eyes washing blood red, the animal was all nerves and muscle reflex now, shivering against the box only inches away from John.

Then silence fell.

John closed his eyes, held his breath, and waited for the next volley of gunfire to turn him into possum-burger. His heart was beating so loudly now, he could have sworn it was echoing across the length of the trailer like a tiny skin drum, bouncing off the walls, reverberating noisily. John's ears were ringing from the gunshots, and he could not get Gene Krupa out of his head—that *bap-bap-BAP-bap-bap-BAP-bap-bap-BAP!*—and it took every last ounce of strength just to keep himself from shivering out of his skin. But then he heard the blessed sound of footsteps pivoting on the gravel, then starting to walk away. The cop was finally giving up, the sounds of his footsteps receding back into the symphony of night breezes and crickets.

Leaving John alone with the possum guts and the silence and the hideous ringing in his ears.

John tore a hank of cloth off the end of his shirttail and wrapped the ragged strip around his ankle. For all the pain and shock and struggle, the wound wasn't that godawful deep—an oval of tiny punctures filled with blood as black as tar. The bandage seemed to stem the bleeding. It was infection that John was worried about now. Somewhere in the back of his mind, he knew that possums carried rabies. But on the positive side, a case of rabies was still better than a bullet, and the psychotic cop was gone, and now John had time to think.

At length, he managed to rise to his feet and limp back to the mouth of the trailer.

Taking deep breaths, shivering in the chilled breeze, he gazed out at the shadows, and he saw the faint burnish of light on the treetops from the distant highway, and the lacy shadows of the wooded path down which the cop had retreated. The eastern edge of the treatment facility was smoldering with the muddy glow of a small town on the horizon beyond it. John wondered if he should try to get back to the clinic. The cop was probably heading back there at this very moment, anticipating his return. The breeze picked up suddenly, and it rustled the trees. John saw the willow branches swaying in the distance, and just for a moment, amid all the turmoil and tension, he thought of an old Art Tatum classic, "Willow Weep for Me," an incredibly beautiful, mournful jazz ballad, and the sound of it—that delicate cascade of sixteenth notes like the sigh of an angel—was swirling through John's brain now, penetrating his fear, seeping down into his soul, finding the pain there.

Unarticulated pain and grief.

Why?

Finally John looked up and saw the vast spattering of stars in the black void of the night sky, and at that precise moment he felt just about as alone as a human being can feel.

11

Too Late

BLUE AND RED fire swirled around the clinic's front entrance, painting the walks and the gravel and the shrubs with garish Day-Glo colors, deepening the shadows behind the east woods and distant grounds. Three police squad cars were canted at awkward angles near the front walk, and for a while bodies swarmed around the glass doors, patrolmen busily coming in and going out, radio voices crackling, and the faces of curious patients gaping behind the lobby windows. Then the flurry seemed to subside, and two out of the three cop cars pulled away, their lights extinguishing as they vanished over the hill.

That was when the enormous figure finally emerged from the shadows and drifted toward the entrance.

He entered the clinic cautiously, heart thumping in his chest, dark eyes scanning the lobby like a lost child. A stark, cold, high-ceilinged affair, the lobby had a strangely hushed quality to it now, like a waiting room in a morgue. The air smelled of astringent and disinfectant-swabbed tiles. Off to the right, a pair of plastic ficus trees flanked a forlorn little couch. Off to the left, a reception desk was planted near a bank of elevators. A uniformed policeman was sitting on the edge of the desk, spiral-bound in hand, quietly scribbling notes. A middle-aged nurse sat behind the desk, softly murmuring into a phone.

Billy Marsten stood there for a moment, holding his briefcase, indecision seizing his massive limbs. His barrel chest burned with cold dread, and his fingers tingled, and just for an instant, standing there in his black jackboots and gothic regalia, frozen with angst, he looked like some sort of hellish trophy, like some mutant breed of Siberian bear posed in Madame Tussaud's dungeon of wax horrors.

He glanced around the lobby, and he tried to breathe and he tried to think.

The problem was, all this police activity more than likely meant one thing: Billy was too late. His hero had already been discovered, ferreted out, captured, taken into custody, or maybe even—God forbid—killed. If only Billy had come directly from Durkin's Pancake House to the clinic, he might have made it in time. But *no,* not Billy, not fucking-shit-for-brains Billy. He had to go home first, get cleaned up, and then get all his stuff, his camera and his tape recorder and his photo album and all his bullshit souvenirs. All because he was naïve enough to think that *he* was the only one who would recognize the man in the newspaper photo. As if Billy were the only one who had a thing for this guy.

"Sir—?"

Billy nearly jumped out of his boots at the sound of the nurse's voice behind him. He dropped his briefcase, and he heard something crack inside— maybe a cassette breaking or one of the film canisters snapping open. He leaned down, gathered up the case, turned to the receptionist, and uttered, "Yeah—hello—how ya doing?"

Both the cop and the nurse were staring at him now. "Can I help you?" the nurse asked.

Billy ambled over to the desk, trying to appear as nonchalant as possible. His mind was going a mile a minute now, grasping for some acceptable approach. What the hell was he supposed to tell them? The truth? Finally, after nodding warmly at the cop, Billy turned to the nurse and said, "I'm with *The Joliet Times-Weekly,* and I was just wondering if I might get an interview with the—uh—uh—the guy with amnesia."

The nurse looked at the cop, and the cop looked at the nurse, and then both looked at Billy. "Thought you folks already ran something," the cop said icily. He was a ruddy-complected young man with steely blue eyes, and the way his chin jutted made Billy want to rip the man's tongue out.

"Yeah, we did," Billy said, "but the thing is, we wanted to do a follow-up."

"Follow-up?"

"Yeah, you know, maybe show how he's getting on . . . you know."

The cop exchanged a glance with the nurse, then turned his ice-blue gaze back toward Billy. "The way he's getting on," the cop said softly, "is not for public consumption."

They got to him, Billy thought. *Goddamn motherfuckers got to him.* Swallowing back his anger, Billy put on his most innocent face and said, "Is anything wrong?"

"You interviewing *me* now?" the cop asked tersely.

"No, sir, no, I just wondered, you know, if he's okay."

"He's fine," the cop said, and then shot another glance at the nurse. The nurse was looking down at her desk blotter, rearranging her paperwork, trying awfully hard not to get involved. In fact, it was becoming painfully obvious to Billy that the nurse was downright spooked. For that matter, the cop seemed a little jittery himself. And the more Billy thought about it, the more he liked it.

There was a pall hanging over this place, as thick and as palpable as a rotting smell. The sweet bouquet of buried secrets being dug up and exposed to the night air. A surprise party. The man with no name had surprised everyone—the clinic staff, the cops, the doctors—*everyone.* It was obvious what had happened.

The man with no name had escaped.

"Sorry, sorry to have bothered you," Billy was saying now, backing toward the door.

"Wait a minute, hold it—" the cop was saying, starting after Billy.

But it was too late.

Billy was already slipping into the glorious darkness outside.

12

The Killing Floor

. . . the man with meat . . .

. . . his face rising like a cold stone planet, eye sockets deep and dark, lips peeled back over lifeless teeth . . .

. . . then something terrible is happening, and John is helpless, power-less, adrift in its relentless current, because the face is contorting, the mouth gaping wide, wider, eyes shocking open, and the great side of beef is tipping toward John, and John finds himself scooting backward, frantically trying to escape across a platform of some kind, in some kind of a ware-house or slaughterhouse—the killing floor?—scooting away from the falling meat like a frightened child.

Then the beef lands hard across John's legs, a great, fleshy weight against his thighs, and John looks down and sees the pale, doughy texture of the meat protruding across his lap, and he sees something that screams like a banshee in his brain, the realization pouring over him as he focuses on the blunt end of the beef, the bulbous tip hanging over his lap.

It has human fingers.

The image erupts into a kaleidoscope of broken glass, spinning, swirling, jagged shards of color, forming a mosaic of a single hideous scene: John cradling an unconscious man in his arms. The man's head in John's hands. The unconscious man is smallish, wiry, with a delicate little mustache and goatee. His hair is long and unruly, silvery gray. Something is happening to the man, something fascinating and horrible.

The light is going out of his eyes like a candle flame flickering out, a pair of tiny sparks in the centers of the man's irises, dwindling, contracting, shrinking down until there is nothing but a needle prick of life. Then the fire finally goes out and it's incredible. Moving. John looks down at the man's hands, and they are closing, curling inward like the petals of a lovely flower at sunset.

Then the final transformation, a time-lapse ballet of shifting color as the man's flesh goes from pink to white to a dull putty gray.

It is so sublime, watching this tranquil atrophy.

John sat forward with a violent start, his brain flaming with heat and dizziness.

He scanned the shadows in a momentary frenzy, his heart racing, his mouth dry and pasty. Where was he? What the hell had happened to him? He could feel a hard, clammy surface on his back, and he smelled the suffocating odors of ink and damp cardboard. He was running a temperature. The sick-chills were creeping up the backs of his arms and legs. Eyes adjusting to the gloom, he looked down and saw a soggy morning edition glued to the floor. All at once he realized where he was.

He wrenched around and saw that he had fallen asleep in the NEWSPAPER HERE trailer, on a bed of soggy late editions.

It was morning.

The newspaper trailer had been a bit drier and cleaner than the plastics trailer, and he had planned to sit here only for a few minutes—just to get a handle on things—but then another spell had washed over him.

It had started like all the others, a wave of dizziness coursing through him, then nausea turning his gut over, and then flashing images. It must have been the worst yet, because John could vaguely remember collapsing to the damp floorboards, then passing out in a whirlwind of odors and noises and bright flashing shapes. He wasn't sure if he had immediately plunged into some kind of latent fugue state, or had merely passed out into exhausted sleep, but now he couldn't stop thinking about the dream—and the accompanying images—that had ushered him through the night.

John wondered whether this horrific dream was some kind of terrible breakthrough, the first fully formed episodic memory he had had since he'd managed to get himself shattered into a million pieces out on the highway last week. The specificity of it. The detail in the dying man's face. The textures, the tactile qualities. It seemed like a dream that had to be shaped from experience. Which, needless to say, was the most terrifying aspect of it. Was *this* the atrocity the cop had accused John of? Who the hell was this diminutive, goateed man? And what was his relationship to John?

A sudden sound clanged outside the trailer.

It came from the front, and was accompanied by a hard thud that rocked the entire structure. John braced himself on a nearby wooden rail, and he tried to stand, but he was light-headed and the trailer was pitching slightly now. Then the realization suddenly flooded his brain: *We're moving.* For God's sake, the entire semitrailer was moving. He could see the cul-de-sac through the rear opening, the landscape slowly shifting, the rays of sunlight sweeping lazily across the threshold of the trailer as it pulled away.

In the space of an instant, a series of presumptions flashed through his mind. He presumed that this exodus was probably part of the morning recycling routine, and that they were likely bound for some industrial plant or weigh station. He also concluded that maybe he shouldn't panic right away, that perhaps this was a stroke of luck. He could safely ride the trailer out of the hot zone, discreetly fleeing the area in which the cop and God-only-knew-who-else were most certainly searching for him.

Meanwhile, the trailer was rattling and vibrating on its merry way.

He managed to stand, and he instantly became aware of his injuries, both old and new, as the dizziness washed over him, threatening to take his breath away, the pain gripping his knees and spine and bandaged ankle, his stomach churning emptily. He realized that he probably needed prompt medical attention, but he was damned if he was going back to the Reinhardt Clinic. The best bet was an anonymous hospital somewhere, if for nothing else than to get a tetanus shot. But for that he needed money, or at least an identity, and at the moment the only personal effects he had in his possession were the following: a plastic laminated patient card from the clinic, used to charge meals and incidentals to his account; a small plastic comb missing a few of its teeth; a half-empty pack of Wrigley's spearmint; and the piano key chain.

The semitrailer shuddered and shivered. It was pulling onto a main thoroughfare—John could tell by the steadier hum against the oversized wheels beneath him—so he squeezed through the stacks of newspapers and limped his way back to the rear opening. Gazing out at the passing landscape, he saw that they were rolling along a two-lane blacktop access road, wending through a nondescript industrial park. Miles of low-rise foundries lay on the gray-cement horizon, stitched together by Hurricane fences and high-tension wires. He didn't want to get too far away from his geographic reference point of the clinic, so he waited for the next opportunity to make his exit.

When the trailer stopped at a railroad crossing, he slipped out the back.

The moment his feet hit the ground, a series of sensations engulfed him, nearly tossing him off balance—a warm gust of diesel-scented air, the odors of garbage and asphalt and chemical pollution, and the harsh rays of the sun in his face. He hobbled as quickly as possible across the intersection, skull throbbing, the *clang-clang* of the rail warning shattering his feverish eardrums. He didn't even bother looking back over his shoulder to see if the anonymous driver of the semi had spotted him.

There was a small convenience store straight ahead called Pick Kwick. He found a pay phone outside the store's entrance, under a metal awning. He dialed the operator and asked to place a collect call to the Reinhardt Clinic in Joliet. Moments later, the clinic receptionist was on the line, stammering something about Dr. Cousins being on call, and that unfortunately it would take a few moments to track her down through her pager.

John waited.

And waited.

It seemed to take forever, and while he stood there, dazed out of his wits, heart chugging, the wind was playing with the metal awning above him. It made a vibrating, tattletale sound, like a child shaking a noisemaker, driving John buggy, making his flesh crawl and his sphincter muscles contract. Then the doctor's voice was on the line.

"Hello, this is Marie Cousins."

"Dr. Cousins—it's John—it's me." His voice was clogged with phlegm, mushy.

"John, good God! Hold on."

There was an awkward pause then, followed by a muffled rustling sound, as though the doctor were holding her hand over the mouthpiece.

"Dr. Cousins?"

"You gave us all a real scare, John. When you both disappeared, we didn't know what to think."

"I don't really—I don't really know what happened myself—if you want to know the truth."

"Are you all right?"

"A little banged up, you know, a little rattled—but nothing too serious."

"That's good, John, that's really good to hear."

"The thing is, I have no idea—you know—what's going on. The guy who came for me, the guy claiming to be my brother . . . um, he wasn't my brother."

"What do you mean?"

"Actually, he tried to kill me."

Another pause, shuffling sounds. Above John, the awning buzzed furiously. He was getting very frustrated, tense. "Hello? Dr. Cousins?"

"He tried to kill you?"

"Yeah, right, that's correct," John said, and then he told her all about the man who had called himself Robert, and how he had gotten John alone, and how he had sprung the surprise. John told her all about escaping into the woods, and spending the night in the recycling trailer, and even about the possum attack. Finally, John said, "He accused me of a lot of things, Dr. Cousins—nothing specific, mind you—but I'm thinking the best thing for me right now would be to stay out of sight, lay low for a while, sort things out. If you could meet me, help me stay out of sight . . . that would be best, I think."

Shuffling sounds, whispers, then: "You've got to come back to the clinic, John."

"No, actually, I'm thinking it would be best if . . . you know . . . I stayed out of sight."

"You've got to come back, John. That would be the best thing."

"Why?"

After an awkward pause, "Okay, look . . . I'll come get you, and, um, I'll bring you back . . . and then we'll sort things out."

What the hell was wrong with her? Marie Cousins had always impressed John as the perfect den mother—decisive, helpful, nurturing. She hadn't seemed tentative once since John had checked into her little universe of schedules and therapies and immaculate fluorescent corridors. But now she was sounding as skittish as a laboratory rat.

"Okay, fine," John said, cringing at a twinge in his spine. "I'm at a phone booth near—"

He froze suddenly. He was about to give her the number printed on the pay phone, and the approximate location relative to the train tracks and the neighboring street signs, when he heard two distinct sounds in the background, coming over the line in rapid succession. One was that sudden clicking noise heard occasionally with faulty connections—which, as John somehow knew, was also the telltale sound of somebody messing with the line—and the other was the sizzle of a voice from a two-way radio.

"John—hello? John?"

John could tell she was getting nervous. His hand was gripping the phone so tightly now, it felt welded to the plastic. He couldn't think of anything to say, and yet he couldn't motivate his arm to hang up.

"John, are you there? John, don't hang up. Please—John—say something."

He slammed the phone down, disconnecting the line and sucking in a breath. His heart was in his throat now, the chills crawling up the small of his back. He realized at once that Dr. Cousins had been stalling him, keeping him on the line long enough for the cops to trace the call and locate him. Anger stirring in his gut, venom tightening his stomach muscles, he started hearing the whip-crack drumming of Max Roach in his imagination—*baddap-baddap-BAP!-BAP!-BAP!-BAP!-BAP!*—syncopating with his mounting rage, making him fidget restlessly in the blustery air, involuntarily tapping his foot against the rusted metal standard. He was a fugitive now and still had no clue as to what he might have done. That wasn't all of it, though. Something else was happening. Something deep down in his marrow—inchoate and instinctive—welling up in him like poison. The cocktail of rage and fear and desperation yielding a new feeling, a new emotion, impossible to articulate but bizarrely seductive, like a tuning fork in his groin. A reptile brain buzz that made him feel filthy and powerful at the same time. Was he a bad man? Was he evil?

BADDAP-BADDAP-BAP!!

A noise pierced his reverie.

John spun toward the sound of tires crunching in the gravel behind him, and he saw the sun glinting off the hood of a minivan as it pulled up to the door of the Pick Kwick. The driver's door sprang open, and a teenage girl in a tie-dyed top and torn jeans scurried inside the store.

Leaving her car idling.

Idling, for God's sake, *unattended,* with the keys in the ignition.

At first, it didn't even compute in John's overloaded brain: this bizarre little window of opportunity that had just opened up before his eyes. But in the space of an instant he realized that he might never get another chance like this, and he would have to act quickly, without hesitation or deliberation, without even considering the morality of the act.

He rushed over to the car, opened the door, and climbed behind the wheel.

The interior reeked of stale beer and marijuana smoke, and there was a little plastic ZZ Top logo hanging from the mirror, and the radio was buzzing with hideous heavy-metal music, and John started thanking Christ that these minivans were easy to drive, with automatic transmissions and power steering; he wasn't certain that he could have managed a stick. He put the thing in reverse and lurched across the lot, then slammed it down to drive. The girl was coming out of the store just as the minivan was blasting off in a thundercloud of dust and carbon monoxide.

John was surprised at how easy it was *not* to look back.

Part Two

Descent

Man is a rope stretched between the animal and the Superman—a rope over an abyss.

—Friedrich Nietzsche

13

A Suitable Candidate

RANDALL, ILLINOIS, WAS a godsend.

The little hamlet came looming out of the distant morning heat waves as John pushed the minivan southward. The town was calm, and discreet, and was far enough off the interstate to blend in with the patchwork of surrounding farm fields. A population of just over ten thousand. John figured it to be mostly farm trade and the families of blue-collar workers from the nearby Armour Star plant. He found the main drag and made his way eastward through the World War I storefronts, the weathered brick buildings, and the feed-and-seed stores. He noticed that most of the residents were nestled to the north in old wooded neighborhoods lined with herringbone brick roads, in great Victorians shaded by ancient elms. And there was even a real, honest-to-goodness town square, complete with a white-wood gazebo planted in the heart of a little antebellum park. It was small-town permanence and stability personified, and it was as good a place as any for John to try to get his bearings back.

His first stop was a filling station catercorner from the town square, a Sinclair job with the two pump islands and the single-lift garage. The manager was a gentle behemoth in greasy overalls and ham-hock arms, and as he came out to greet John, his eyes twinkled with the kind of earnest goodwill and trust you find only in little towns. John gave him a hard-luck story about losing his job at the plant, and losing his family in the divorce settlement, and all that John had left was this little old minivan. John laid it on thick, and he probably looked convincing because of the bloodless pallor of his face. He was gripped in severe pain—his ankle was throbbing, his lower back was throbbing—everything was throbbing; he was one great throb.

The station manager had mercy on him and bought the minivan for thirty-five hundred dollars in cash, most of which was stashed in the station's safe. The man didn't even ask questions when John handed him the registration—which John had found in the glove box—and explained that there was no other paperwork.

The station owner probably got the better part of the bargain; John couldn't have cared less.

John's next stop was a doctor's office over on Losey Street, the one with the white picket fence out front and the quaint little wrought-iron sign hanging from the gaslight: MILLARD PENNY, M.D., S.C., FAMILY PRACTICE. John limped in and gave the blue-haired old woman behind the reception window the same song and dance about getting laid off, losing his insurance benefits—et cetera, et cetera—and then asked if there was any possible way the doctor might agree to see him without an appointment. The old crone had hesitated a moment, but when John started wobbling on weak knees, bracing himself against the counter, she finally had pity on him.

The doctor turned out to be Millard Penny, *Junior,* a skinny young man fresh out of his second-year residency. He saw John in a tiny examination room with yellowed Norman Rockwell prints on the wall. John told him the animal bite on his ankle was from his ex-wife's poodle, and they had a good laugh together—Dr. Penny and John—commiserating over the vagaries of divorce and the torments of life in general. It turned out that John's temperature was only 100.5 degrees, not as bad as he had thought. The doctor cleaned his wounds, gave him a tetanus shot, prescribed some painkillers and antibiotics, and told him to take better care of himself. John thanked him and then walked out into the overcast afternoon, marveling at the degree of anonymity a little cash can buy a person.

At this point, as John wandered west along the railroad tracks, he had his first lucid moment since he had awakened at the Reinhardt Clinic more than a week ago: he realized he needed somebody else on his side. Somebody he could trust. Somebody who would be able to trace the twisted path that had led him here. Somebody experienced in matters such as these. Somebody smart, professional, and, above all, discreet.

That's when he saw the pay phone across the adjacent street, mounted on the side of an Ace Hardware building, complete with a tattered Yellow Pages stuffed into a battered metal case underneath it.

It didn't take John long to find a suitable candidate.

14

Nervous Bird

THE SOUND OF the front doorbell lilted across the backyard, alerting the Huntress that an intruder was attempting to breach the castle door. She immediately darted behind a tree, then stood there for a moment, her heart thumping wildly in her tiny chest, her head spinning as she planned her next move. The element of surprise was important. Surprise was the best way to ward off vampire intruders.

Surprise and garlic-soaked silver bullets.

Gripping her magic plastic sword, crouching down low, the Huntress silently crept across the lawn to the corner of the house where the early tomatoes were just beginning to take root and climb their respective paint stirrers. She hunkered down there in the dirt for a moment, the morning sun warm on her freckled forearms and flaxen hair, the air filled with the musky odors of fertilizer and tilled earth and dandelion milk. Summer was on its way, and the Huntress could barely wait for the sound of the Mr. Frostee truck to come down the lane with its broken-bell chorus. The Huntress was especially fond of the blueberry snow cones and the chocolate-dipped bananas. Unfortunately, these treats were still a couple of weeks off, and besides, the Huntress couldn't afford to think about snow cones right now because there was somebody ringing her doorbell.

From her vantage point, peering around the edge of aluminum siding, the Huntress saw the strange man standing on the porch, ringing the doorbell a second time.

All of a sudden, Kit Bales forgot all about pretending that she was the Huntress—her favorite comic-book character—and was abruptly yanked back to reality. Now she was a skinny little second-grader again, enjoying the last day of Easter vacation, dressed in faded OshKoshes, Jack Purcell tennis shoes, and a makeshift superhero cape fashioned out of her mother's old afghan that had long ago gone to the moths. Dropping her plastic sword smack dab on the tomato plants, Kit gawked at the man on the front porch.

If Kit had possessed the proper vocabulary to describe her first impression of the man on the porch adequately, she might have said that he was tightly coiled, wound as tight as Mom's alarm clock. Ringing the doorbell a third time, glancing over his shoulder, fidgeting restlessly, the guy had a haunted kind of face, his deep-set eyes filled with a kind of knowledge he was better off without. He was not an ugly man, either. He had close-cropped dirty blond hair that Kit and her school pals might call "pretty cool," and he seemed to be in fairly decent shape in his tapered Levi's and pocket T-shirt. But it was the subtler stuff that really captured Kit's imagination. The dark stains on the man's shirt and pants, the way he jerked at noises like a nervous bird. Kit had found an injured bird once, a sparrow with a torn wing, on the roof of the tool shed. Kit had tried to nurse the bird back to health in a shoe box with Bactine and cotton balls. The bird had managed to survive for a day and a half before keeling over. Kit would never forget the way that bird's eyes had shimmered with pain and fear. This man's eyes looked just like that.

When Kit's mom finally came to the door, the man looked as though he were about to drop. A few words were exchanged—Kit couldn't really hear what they were saying, but it was clear that the man needed help—and Kit's mom finally nodded and invited him inside.

The man nodded a silent thank-you and went in.

Now Kit's heart was racing again as she turned back toward the rear of the house. She crept across the tomato garden, then around the rose trellis toward the back door. She was as quiet as possible; she didn't want to alarm anyone. There was a strange and handsome creature inside her house now—a wounded bird—and Kit was dying to know just what this man wanted from her mom. Carefully climbing the deck steps, Kit tiptoed across weathered gray wood toward the door.

She paused just outside the screen and listened to the murmur of voices coming from inside.

The man was saying something about being in an awkward position.

Kit listened closely to the exchange, hanging on every word, understanding very little of it. Deep down, Kit knew that what she was doing was naughty—Mom had always told Kit that nobody likes a snoop—but the fact was, Kit's own mother was a snoop, a professional snoop. A private eye. And Kit was going to be a private eye herself when she grew up. So technically, it was okay that Kit was snooping right now. Besides, it wasn't every day that a weird guy with such cool hair showed up on Kit's doorstep. Kit put her ear to the screen and concentrated on the conversation.

The man was doing most of the talking now, telling a story about how he had come to call on her mom's services. Something about waking up at a medical *clink* up north, and having *am-lesia*, and *convollesking*, and something about a man claiming to be his brother but turning out to be a *vigiyante* cop. And then Kit's mom asked him a couple of questions, and the man's voice got really low. Kit strained to hear.

The man was saying something about a *gun*.

This was just too cool to miss out on, so Kit carefully pushed the screen door open and sneaked inside the house to get a better angle.

15

Tied in Knots

"THAT'S QUITE A story."

Jessica Bales pushed herself away from the imitation-veneer desk and rose to her full height. She wasn't a bit self-conscious about her six feet and one-half inches; as a matter of fact, she'd made her height work in her favor more than once over the years, just as she had made her other statuesque attributes work for her. Jessie was not the kind of woman to be shamed by some bullshit social norm. As a road-tested, seasoned private investigator, Jessie knew one particular axiom: You take advantage of everything.

"I'm getting the feeling—I mean, it seems like—you don't quite believe me," John said.

He was sitting in the wicker divan across from her desk, his brow furrowed, his hands still nervously clasped the same way they had been ever since he had walked through her door half an hour ago and started his story. The man was clearly tied in knots; it was easy for Jessie to see that much. The rest of it was still open for interpretation.

"Can I get you a refill?" Jessie asked him, turning toward the Mr. Coffee machine behind her desk. Jessie's office was in the front of the house, adjacent to Kit's room, so that Jessie could keep tabs on the girl during late-night paperwork sessions. The office was a three-hundred-square-foot cubicle of carpeted hardwood, cheap drywall, and Sears paneling slapped onto the east corner of the ranch home as part of a whole-house renovation done back in the eighties. It had a separate entrance, Levolor blinds, a Tiffany ceiling fan, and a stereo currently tuned to Jessie's favorite country-western station.

"No, thank you," John said, shaking his head.

"I'm going to have another one if you don't mind." She poured the last of the crappy coffee into her commemorative Yellowstone Park cup. Then she turned back to her desk and sat down, leaning back, paying special attention to the man's gaze as she crossed her legs. It was something Jessie often did at the outset of a client meeting—especially with a male client—in order to take the guy's temperature. A flash of a long, shapely leg peeking through the seam of her skirt. If the guy copped a look, he was probably shoveling her some shit, shucking and jiving some angle on her. If he didn't notice, he was either telling the truth or he wasn't breathing.

This guy didn't notice.

Jessie looked at him and said, "To be honest, I don't quite believe anybody until I get to know them a little better."

"I promise you, you can believe *this*."

"All right, let's pretend I do. What makes you think I can help you?"

"You're a private investigator, right?"

"I have my moments."

"There must be some way you can—you know—discreetly track down my true identity."

Jessie didn't respond right away. Instead, she merely sipped her coffee and continued sizing up this wiry little guy in the wrinkled T-shirt and stained jeans. At the moment, Jessie was less concerned with the validity of his story than with the man himself. There was something interesting about this guy. Something about the way he moved. He was jumpy enough, sure, but he also had that desperate, stranded quality of someone lost in the wilderness. It was in his eyes, in the way he listened. What a wonderful world it would have been if all of Jessie's male acquaintances could have had this same neediness.

"I have been known to locate a somebody or two from time to time," Jessie finally remarked, reaching into her top drawer for a Carlton, smiling at her shameless Philip Marlowe-ism. She'd been a regular smoker since seventh grade, and had been trying to stop since her kid was born. At this rate, by the time she hit fifty, her voice was going to be a couple of octaves south of Louis Armstrong. "But I've never had the body and needed to find everything else. Still, it all depends on who, when, where, why, and how much," she said, and blew a wreath of smoke out across the desk blotter as though punctuating her understatement.

Jessie Bales's face was a collection of angles, all cheekbones and tulip lips, like a Hurrell photograph from the fifties, like she should be walking around with a gauzy nimbus of light behind her. She was wearing a cranberry sweater today, with her black lace Chantelle underneath, accentuating her figure. Jessie knew how to parlay her looks into results. She knew how to sleaze down to get into the back room at the county lockup; and she knew how to class up to get past a receptionist at a corporate headquarters. She knew how to provoke a testosterone overdose better than a runway dancer at a men's club. Simply put: Jessie knew how to take advantage.

Which made a lot of people wonder why she was wasting her talents in such a pissant little burg like Randall.

The answer was currently dressed in a cape, playing somewhere out in the backyard.

Jessie's daughter was born at Chicago's Northwestern Hospital a mere three months after Jessie had received her private investigator's license. Rather than subject her baby to the daily flotsam and jetsam of big-city PI work, Jessie decided to move south to Mayberry, U.S.A. Raise her daughter in a calmer atmosphere and learn the ropes on safe little cases like lost dogs and cheating husbands. But the irony was, Randall turned out to be as rotten to the core as any other place in this wild and woolly country. Kidnappings, drug deals, highway prostitution rings, local courthouse embezzlement scandals, family farms burning up for no reason, Mob hideaways erupting in storms of automatic gunfire, bodies being dumped into the Vermilion. The big city had nothing on this little hellhole. Jessie Bales ended up establishing a permanent investigation business here—with Kit settling into the school system—and for more than seven years now, business had been brisk.

"Well, then . . . what do you think?" John was staring at her, looking as though he were about to pop. "Would you be willing to take my case?"

Jessie thought about it for a moment, taking a lush drag off the cigarette. "Tell you the truth, honey, I'm still trying to decide whether I swallow the whole thing." Jessie smiled sympathetically. "Nothing personal, you understand."

"You can easily check it out," he said tersely. "Find a back issue of *The Joliet Times-Weekly*."

"How about I just call the clinic?"

"No, no, no." He raised his hands on that one, waving them in alarm. "They'll send somebody for me—you've got to trust me on this—that's a very bad idea, that's not a good way to go, believe me. I just need some time, you know, I need to get my life back on my own." He paused then, and rubbed his face. He looked bone-weary, exhausted down to the marrow, like a man who had tried to climb a mountain and had failed. After another moment, he looked up at Jessie and said, "I don't want to sound, you know, melodramatic, but *you* are my last option here. I'm not exactly looking forward to turning myself in—getting beaten to death in some holding cell for some untold crime against nature—I just want to find out who I am, and what I did, and then maybe—maybe I can—I don't know—apologize for it." He paused again, exhaled sharply, half a dry laugh, half a pained grimace. *"Apologize—Jesus—that's a good one."*

Then he collapsed like a rag doll, burying his face in his hands, his shoulders starting to spasm. At first, Jessie thought he was giggling—his breath puffing rhythmically into his hands, giggling at some cosmic irony—but then she realized with an odd sort of dismay that the man was actually weeping right there in her imitation knotty-pine office. And it wasn't a mere sprinkle either. No sirree. This was an all-stops-pulled-out, body-convulsing, mucus-running-out-of-his-nose downpour that went on for endless moments.

Jessie felt her face flush hot for a moment, and she started to get very self-conscious, watching this total stranger's crying jag. Was it a command performance? Could this guy possibly be on the level? For some reason, Jessie hadn't gotten a handle on this thing yet, and all the waterworks now were just making this guy even tougher to decipher. She had seen every kind of flimflammer imaginable in her day, but this guy seemed different. This guy seemed desperate with a capital *D,* and Jessie was inclined to proceed with caution. "It's okay," she said softly, snubbing out her cigarette in a plastic ashtray. "Take your time."

John still had his face in his hands, trying to rein in his emotions, trying to breathe normally. He took a few pained breaths and wiped his face on his sleeve, a string of mucus and saliva roping across his arm. His cheeks were hectic with color, his eyes swimming in tears. Jessie looked away, feeling a weird jolt of shame running through her. She heard him sniff, then take a few more uneasy breaths.

When Jessie looked back at the man, he was sitting back in his chair, eyes closed, taking deep breaths. "I'm sorry," he uttered breathlessly.

"Don't sweat it, honey," Jessie said, and waved at him.

"No, really, I'm sorry—I'm all right—it's just—"

He stopped abruptly, and for a moment Jessie thought he was remembering something, maybe getting a flash, seeing a ghost of a memory off in the middle distance. Then Jessie heard a creaking sound behind her, and she realized that John was staring off toward the arched doorway into the kitchen. Jessie spun around and saw the face of a little gnome peering around the jamb.

"What are you doing, Boodle?" Jessie asked somewhat rhetorically, knowing full well that the little girl had probably been eavesdropping on their conversation from the beginning. "Boodle" was a nickname that Jessie had started using years ago, and to this day she couldn't remember if it was derived from the phrase *kit and caboodle* or from the movie *Carnal Knowledge,* where Jack Nicholson calls Ann-Margret "The Boodle."

"Nothing, Mommy," the child replied in a sheepish tone, her gaze still riveted to the stranger.

"You know it's not nice to spy on people, right?"

The little girl shrugged.

"Kit . . ." Jessie said in a warning tone.

"Yes, Mommy, I know it's not nice to spy on people, but you said sometimes you gotta spy because it's all part of the job."

Jessie tried her damnedest not to grin. "All right, smarty-pants . . ." Jessie pushed herself away from the desk, stood up, turned to John, and said, "I'm sorry, just gimme a second." Then she went over to the doorway, knelt down by her daughter, and said softly, "Mommy's working now, Boodle, and you know the rules when Mommy's working."

"Yeah, but—"

"No *but*s about it, Boodle. I want you to go into the kitchen and wait for me, and I'll be there in ten minutes to make your lunch."

"Okay, Mommy, but can I tell you something?"

"What is it, Boodle?"

The little girl leaned over and whispered into her mother's ear: "That man needs a Kleenex."

Jessie smiled, then whispered, "You're right."

The little girl said, "Can I give him one?"

After a moment's thought, Jessie just shrugged. "Sure, why not?"

The little girl went over to the desk, pulled open the top right drawer, and yanked a couple of tissues from the slot. Meanwhile, John was still trying to get his bearings, swallowing back all the bile, watching the child. Kit walked around the front of the desk and then calmly offered the Kleenex to John. There was an awkward pause as John stared down at the little girl for a moment, blinking away his tears. Then he smiled for the first time since he had entered the house—his eyes crinkling warmly at the corners—and he took the Kleenex from her. "Thank you very much, young lady," he said.

"My name's Kit," she told him.

"That's a nice name, very nice, I like that."

"What's your name?"

John took a deep breath, wiping his eyes and his nose. Then he said, "McNally. My name's John McNally. Call me John."

Jessie watched from across the room, an undercurrent of contrary emotions swirling around inside her. It was like watching her daughter pet a stray dog—it wasn't clear whether the animal was harmless or rabid. And yet, there was something completely mystifying going on between the man and the little girl right now, something unspoken passing between them. Kit was not the most extroverted child in the world, but once in a while she instinctively latched on to somebody. "Come here, Boodle," Jessie said finally, crossing the room to her desk, sitting back down.

The little girl came back over and hopped up on her mom's lap.

Jessie looked at John. "So, you believe the cop was using your real name yesterday? John McNally?"

The man looked out the window for a moment, noodling on it, licking his dry lips. Then he looked back at Jessie, and his expression had cleared. "Yeah," he said. "Yeah, actually, I do think he was using my real name."

"Why?"

"I don't know, maybe he was using it to see if he could break through the amnesia."

"How do you think he knew your name?"

John shrugged. "I guess that's why I'm here."

After a long pause, Jessie lifted her daughter off her lap and shoved her toward the doorway. "Go wait for me in the kitchen, honey."

"But Mommy—"

"No *buts*, I'll be there in five minutes."

The little girl ambled out.

Jessie turned to John. "Okay, let's say I take on your case. I gotta tell ya, Mr. McNally, I'm not sure you've got enough of that thirty-five hundred dollars left, after young Doc Penny got through with you. Besides, that dough is hot enough to fry eggs on. The minute the cops catch you—and they will, by the way—that cash is outta here."

"How much do you charge?" John asked.

"I usually charge by the hour, and it's usually a hundred bucks an hour for a missing-person case, with a minimum of five hundred a day. Plus expenses and mileage."

"I've got plenty left," John said. "And if we go through the rest of it, I'll refund all your expenses and fees once we recover my identity."

"Assuming it's possible."

"Pardon me?"

"You're assuming we'd be able to recover your identity, and frankly, John, I'm not convinced that's possible."

She was lying through her teeth, of course. Jessie Bales could find almost anybody simply by picking up the phone and making a couple of calls. Even the most difficult cases—people who didn't *want* to be found, or people in the witness protection program, or people on the lam, or any garden-variety bad buy. They required a little bit of shoe leather, but Jessie could usually find them in just a few days. Finding people was pretty simple; you just had to know were to look. It was what you did with them *after* you found them—or what they did with *you*—that got complicated.

"Listen, Mrs. Bales—"

"Ah, Christ, I hate the sound of that *Mrs. Bales* business. Besides, it's not Mrs. It's *Miss.* I've been flying solo since the day Kit was born. Why don't you just call me Jessie?"

"Fair enough, then—Jessie—listen. I can't offer you much more than what I have in my pocket, and maybe what I've got blocked in my brain, but I'm asking you—pleading with you—to please help me."

Jessie regarded the man for a moment, watching that shimmer return to his eyes. So many unanswered questions, so many red flags. Was the story on the level? Or was it all a scam? And even if the story was true, Jessie couldn't help wondering about the most ominous question of them all— *what the hell did this guy do?* Jessie kept thinking about what this alleged cop had allegedly said: *"I'm gonna show you what you've done. I'm gonna rub your nose in it!"* Was the cop lying? Or was there an ongoing investigation? It was a Chinese puzzle box that was beckoning to Jessie, and even if it all turned out to be a fiasco, it sure would be an *interesting* fiasco.

Truth be told, this was actually Jessie's favorite part of the gig. The beginning. The first moments of every job, when things are new and fresh and interesting. When the challenge is laid out like a long clear road on a beautiful day. It was better than foreplay; it was what she lived for.

Jessie suddenly spun on her swivel chair toward the beat-up credenza behind her. She pulled out the standard job invoice form—the one with all the waivers and caveats—and turned back to John. She laid the form on the desk in front of him. He looked at it, momentarily stunned, like a man gazing across a prison cell at an open window.

"That's a standard form," Jessie said, plucking a ballpoint from her top drawer and laying it neatly beside the form. "I'll need a deposit of two hundred and fifty bucks in cash up front, the rest at the end of the job, regardless of whether we get results or not."

John just stared at the paper.

Jessie lit up another cigarette and looked at him. "Well? You gonna sign the damn thing or not?"

16

Long Night

JESSIE BALES WAS born and raised in the heart of the heartland: East Peoria, Illinois. She spent her summers detassling corn stalks, autumns working nights at the A&W, and winters playing first-string guard for the East Peoria High School Panthers girls' basketball team. Mama Harriet was a registered nurse—now retired—with more than four decades of service down at Saint Vincent de Paul Parish Hospital in Creve Coeur. Daddy Jerome had been a stern, demanding Welshman who had taught physical education at a local middle school and ruled his home with an iron fist. Probably an undiagnosed manic-depressive, Jerry Bales had forced his only daughter to grow up fast, hard, and with a restless spirit.

After graduating high school, Jessie enrolled at Lewis University up in Joliet, studying criminology, psychology, and pre-law. But all she really learned was how much she hated college. The day after her twenty-third birthday—much to the chagrin of her father—she quit school and enrolled in the police academy. It was grueling, and it chewed up the best years of her young-adult life, but Jessie had made up her mind: She wanted to wear a detective shield.

She completed the 650 academy hours with honors.

Her first job was working dispatch at a small police department in a western suburb of Chicago. Seemed like total shit-work at first: twenty-eight months of working the mike for union minimum, dispatching units throughout the suburbs, chattering with the boys on the streets, calling in 10-200s and 10-33s galore. But the more Jessie worked that mike, the more she worked her fellow cops, the more she learned. From her vantage point she could see the big picture, and she learned about the bad guys and the good guys and every other kind of guy imaginable. She learned just exactly what makes the street tick.

The day she quit, she had already decided she was going into the investigation business for herself.

The only problem was one idiotic, drunken evening that Jessie had spent with a desk sergeant named Rick Stallworthy. Stallworthy had been Jessie's supervisor, and the two had developed a grudging friendship based on verbal sparring, off-color jokes, and mutual respect. On one particular occasion—only a month before Jessie submitted her resignation—they found themselves working a double shift together in an empty squad house. It was the night before New Year's Eve, and it was fairly dead, and around eleven o'clock Stallworthy broke out an illicit stash of Maker's Mark. The twosome proceeded to drink themselves into oblivion. By three o'clock that morning, they were making sloppy love on the cot behind the interview box.

It was the only time that Jessie had been with a man without protection; and a month and a half later, she became a statistic.

For his part, Stallworthy had offered the obligatory support of an average man cornered by his own unexpected circumstances. He managed to keep the whole situation confidential; he offered either to marry Jessie or to pay for an abortion; and he offered to give Jessie her old job back, or at least extend her benefits through the childbirth. But something had changed deep inside Jessie Bales. She didn't want a husband, she didn't want her old job back, and she didn't want an abortion. She wanted the child, and she proceeded accordingly, with no strings attached to Mr. Stallworthy.

Oddly enough, the pregnancy seemed to focus Jessie's energies on starting her own investigation business. She got a part-time job doing telephone work—skip traces, mostly—for a big Chicago detective agency called Truth Finders while she worked on the rigorous requirements for earning a PI license in the state of Illinois. It took her four months, but she eventually got a sponsor, passed the written test, and borrowed the rest of the money required by the state for liability insurance. By the time little Kit Bales was born, Jessie had found a place in Randall and was already doing phone cases.

Over the seven years since then, Jessie had lived several lifetimes, working through a succession of day care, baby-sitters, and juggled schedules. Although she had pulled her gun only a handful of times and shot it only once—and that was to scare some son of a bitch off her tail more than anything else—she'd threatened a few people, she'd been threatened herself, she'd been chased, she'd chased others, and she'd even chased her own tail a few times. She'd been hurt a couple of times, and she'd hurt others. She'd put more miles on her Caddy than a damn Fuller brush salesman. But at the end of the day, she and that brush salesman had one thing in common: They were both getting the job done with plain, old-fashioned hard-goddamn-work.

Which was precisely what she was doing tonight, speeding eastward along Interstate 80 in her powder blue Sedan DeVille convertible.

Jessie was squinting against the wind and the glow of the setting sun, a Reba McEntire song blasting on the radio. A couple of car lengths away, a rowdy bunch of teenagers in a Range Rover were all lit up like Times Square on New Year's Eve, swerving around a semi, throwing bottles out their windows. Jessie eased off the foot-feed and turned on her lights.

The evening had turned mean, the Hawk swooping down from the lakeshore, the gusts like razors slicing across the Caddy's bonnet, tossing Jessie's mane of Clairol desert sunrise. The dusk had come early, and it was almost completely dark now, the air sharpening with the odors of diesel and leaf-smoke from surrounding farms. Jessie flipped on the heater, and the rush of warm air blanketed her legs. She realized she should have worn long pants tonight, but there was still no telling whom she might run into, or who might be persuaded a little further by a pair of gorgeous gams. She reached into her pocket, pulled out another Carlton, and lit it with the car's electric lighter.

She felt good, sober as a judge, focused.

Her first stop this afternoon had been the Fitzgeralds over on Cherry Street, where she had dropped Kit off for the rest of the day. Kit went to school with the youngest Fitzgerald girl, and Martha and Dick Fitzgerald didn't mind looking after Kit when the need arose. Jessie had done a few favors for the Fitzgeralds over the years, and they'd come to be like family. Unfortunately, Kit was becoming increasingly surly about these impromptu visits. When Jessie had told the child that it might be a late one again tonight, Kit had fallen into one of her silent slow burns, especially since tonight was a school night. Not even Martha Fitzgerald's lemon bars could change the child's demeanor.

Jessie's next stop had been the Highway Star Motel on the east side of Randall. Jessie had convinced John to lay low at the motel for a while. The Highway Star was run by an old friend of Jessie's, a black old-timer named Walter Sass. Walter never asked questions, usually slept with one eye open, and was the perfect baby-sitter for Mr. Amnesia. Thankfully, John had agreed to stay put—at least for the next twenty-four. He welcomed the refuge, the time to think, the chance to try to remember something, anything, while Jessie went off on her wild-goose chase.

The Randall Public Library was next.

In most missing-person cases—especially the ones with a name attached—Jessie would invariably make major progress at the local library. Most libraries, even the smallest, had databases known as city directories. These directories dated back decades, and included names, addresses, nationalities, occupations, birth data, and more. But Randall's database came up empty. There was only one John McNally—and he was deceased for more than thirty years. Then she tried old phone books, and although *McNally* was a common listing, there was only a handful of *J. McNallys* in the immediate region, and none of them turned out to be a possibility. Each was either dead, the wrong gender, or so far removed from the subject who was back at the Highway Star, pacing feverishly, nursing his wounds, that Jessie didn't even bother digging any deeper. It was possible that one of the J. McNallys had been John's father, but Jessie had a gut feeling that she was off the track.

At this point, she decided to take a trip up north.

In Jessie's experience, the hottest information was often found right smack dab at the scene of the crime. Whether it was a kidnapping, a theft, a disappearance—whatever—the clues were often sitting around at ground zero: the last place anybody saw the person alive. In John McNally's case, the theory was inverted. It would be the *first* place anybody saw him alive, and that would be Joliet. Specifically, the woods along I-80. More specifically, Higinbotham Woods, a grungy little forest preserve just west of Mokena, the place from which John had emerged on the night of the accident.

Jessie had learned from local newspaper accounts that the trucker involved in the incident had given a statement to both the police and the clinic staff, and he had pretty much said it was a freak accident. John had simply *appeared* in the glare of the semi's high beams like a ghost, and may or may not have been covered with blood already. But when Jessie arrived at the spot, she found nothing but a nondescript stretch of cracked pavement littered with shredded tire rubber like great blackened strips of bacon. The forest was an endless wall of misshapen hardwoods and riotous foliage, and was equally unyielding. Jessie must have sat there on the shoulder for nearly half an hour, just staring, turning things over in her mind, putting herself there on the night of the hubbub, putting herself in John's shoes.

All to no avail.

Next she tried all the standard sources around the Joliet area. She went to the library, and she went to the post office, and she looked through all the change-of-address directories and phone books and old census guides. She went to the Will County courthouse and got on their computer, looking through birth-certificate records, tax and mortgage records, probate histories, wills and divorce decrees, and she came up with jackshit. She was starting to wonder about fingerprinting, but even *that* was a long shot. John would have to have either been arrested or served time in the service to have one on file. And to complicate matters further, Jessie had a lousy relationship with local law-enforcement folks. It was the bane of the PI's existence: the police playing the adversary role. Jessie had tangled with more than her share of vindictive cops, and lately she had made it a policy to stay as far away from the police as possible.

The only other avenue down which Jessie had yet to travel was the little plastic piano key chain that John had showed her. Normally, an original key would bear some kind of manufacturer's serial number, maybe even a job number. An enterprising PI could trace the key back to the maker, then figure out where the hell it belonged. Unfortunately, most of John McNally's keys were copies, either unadorned with any numbers whatsoever or embossed with the Ace Hardware logo. The only original was a car key, unmarked, of course, probably matching some foreign job—a Toyota or a Nissan, something like that—which told Jessie absolutely nothing.

An air horn suddenly blared ahead of Jessie, snapping her back into the here and now.

A sign loomed, glowing in the wash of her headlights, a green rectangle emblazoned with the words HIGINBOTHAM WOODS—NEW LENOX—NEXT RIGHT.

Jessie took the exit going more than sixty miles per, a funnel cloud of carbon monoxide swirling after her, the Caddy's brakes complaining loudly. She squealed to a stop at the foot of the ramp, then turned left. She rumbled north in a haze of black smoke, roaring back through the preserve, back through the region from which John McNally had first appeared. A few minutes later, she crossed the north border of the woods, emerging into civilization. Now Jessie found herself tooling past endless ribbons of strip malls, and miles and miles of innocuous trailer parks and industrial warehouses. It was the land of suburban sprawl, the land of low-slung prefab buildings and abandoned gravel lots washed in dirty fluorescent light. It stretched all the way back to Chicago, and it was a perfect place to start looking for a needle in a haystack.

Moments later, Jessie came upon a Dairy Queen and pulled into its gravel lot.

The place was a blocky little whitewashed building with two service windows out front and vapor lights overhead swarming with insects. Jessie walked up to the first window, taking her place in line behind a teenage boy in a leather jacket. The leather boy paid for his Dilly Bar, turned, and slunk off toward his beat-up Trans Am. Jessie stepped up to the window, leaned down to take a good look at the girl behind the screen, and said, "How ya doing, sweetheart?"

"I'm not bad," the girl replied softly. She was an acne-scarred waif in a stained jumper, her fingernails chewed down to the nubs. "What can I get ya, ma'am?"

"Jeez, I hope you can help me with something." Jessie spoke as genially as possible, reaching into her purse. "Been looking for a particular gentleman all day, and I wondered if you might remember seeing him, you know, buying an ice cream cone, or walking by the shop, or whatever." Jessie pulled out three Polaroid snapshots that she had taken of John McNally at the Highway Star earlier that day, and she showed them to the girl.

The girl stared at the photos.

They were mug shots really, nothing more than John standing in front of the yellowed drapes that stretched across the front window of his motel room—one of them in profile, the other two straight-on shots. But somehow they had an odd personality to them. Jessie had noticed it even while she was looking through the viewfinder of her 600, taking the shots. The way John had gazed directly into the lens, his eyes wide and bright, his head tilted at a subtly confident angle. Later, studying the Polaroids, Jessie had come to the conclusion that the man must have been strangely comforted by the process, like a person with a terrible disease who is finally getting some medical attention.

"Nah, I ain't never seen that guy." The girl was shaking her head, chewing her fingernail.

"Now, you're real sure about that, sweetheart?"

"Yeah, I'm sure." The girl looked up at Jessie then and smiled, and Jessie saw how lovely the girl was, pimples and all. "I remember most people I see," the girl said. "My dad says I got a photograph memory."

"Is that right?" Jessie put the snapshots back in her purse.

"Yeah, like the last math test I took, I got a ninety-seven, which was the best grade in the whole class."

"That's incredible, honey."

"Can I get you anything, ma'am."

"Sure, why not? Why don't you give me one of those chocolate-dipped babies, and make it a large."

Jessie paid for the cone and then went back to the Caddy. She climbed behind the wheel, pulled out of the lot, and headed north toward the endless miles of strip malls.

Moments later, she tossed the cone out the window.

17

Silver Bullets

IT HAD STARTED with the nausea—just like last time—and the hot poker of dread burrowing up his gorge, and the dizziness, and soon he was pressing his throbbing brow against the cheap laminate desktop, feeling as though the shards of fractured memories were about to burst through his skull. The desk was adjacent to the room's queen-sized bed, the taffeta spread covered with leaves of motel stationery, each one scrawled with a different pencil sketch of some indistinct object—a grimacing face obscured by smudges, a stiletto heel, rows of medical sutures, slabs of beef, and partial faces distorted with gaping holes.

John turned away from the desk—away from his compulsive sketching—and surveyed the tawdry little motel room. It was typical roadside Americana, a sparse rectangle of aging textured wallpaper and imitation Bauhaus furniture. Above the bed's chipped particle-wood headboard was a framed flea-market seascape. The air was heavy with Lysol and stale bodily functions, and the walls were warping inward on John, the white noise from the malfunctioning television set layering over the static in John's brain, the hideous crackling shortwave of half-formed memories and traumatic images, all of it syncopated against the sizzling cymbals and gurgling Hammond organ runs of a Jimmy McGriff tune like incessant waves crashing against the sand—

John had to do something to buffer the noise in his head.

Another silver bullet, right between the eyes.

He grabbed his glass—sanitized for his protection—rose to his feet, and staggered on wobbly knees over to the Formica counter next to the closet. There was a meager little refrigerator there, wedged under the counter, rattling its death throes. John had been keeping his silver bullets in its freezer, along with a couple of Snickers bars that he had bought at the liquor store a block west of the motel. Throwing open the fridge door, John yanked out the bottle of Tanqueray.

It was already half gone.

He poured another couple of fingers into the tumbler, the gelid liquid so cold and silver it looked almost like mercury. He knocked back a great gulp, and the quick-frozen fire swirled down his throat, the crisp tang of juniper berries igniting his nasal passages, and it was so good, so bracing, it was positively erotic. He inhaled the rest of it and poured himself another.

Then he went over to the bed, sat down, and waited for the storm in his brain to subside.

18

Pinhole in a Box

THE DARKNESS HAD brought a chill to the air, and it seemed as though the old man in the booth had been staring at the photos of John McNally for an eternity. The geezer looked like a shriveled apple core, the park service uniform buttoned up tight around his grizzled turkey neck, his hound-dog eyes nestled in loose folds of skin. Finally he glanced up at Jessie and said, "Yup."

"What was that?" Jessie's mind had been wandering. She was standing in the raw wind outside the desolate little gatekeeper's shack, trying to light a cigarette. The gusts were buffeting her, toying with her Bic lighter. Behind her, the shadows of the Shawnee Forest Preserve swayed and pitched on the night breezes. The preserve was a modest little seventy-acre patchwork of dense hardwoods and dirt campsites. A few minutes ago, Jessie had turned into its entrance on a gut hunch. She had pegged the little ranger at the mouth of the woods as a busybody, the type of fellow who would remember a face, especially that of a loner wandering the night, running from some unidentified threat.

"Yup," the old man said again. "And by the way, ma'am, there's no smoking in the park."

"Sorry." Jessie nodded and put the stubborn cigarette back in her pocket. "You said *yup*. Yup—what? Yup—you remember seeing this guy?"

"Yes, ma'am, I saw him."

Jessie could feel the tingling sensation at the base of her spine, the skin along the back of her neck crawling. It was better than drugs, better than sex: the first real break in a case. It was like a pinhole in the side of a box, letting in the first ray of sunlight, painting the beginnings of an image on the blank canvas of a job. She licked her lips. "You remember when exactly?"

"Yes, ma'am—it was two weeks ago."

"Two weeks exactly?"

"Yes, ma'am. Believe so."

"He was here? Visiting the preserve?"

"No, ma'am, I saw him up to Gordon's place."

"Gordon's?"

"Yes, ma'am. Local fella, friend of mine, runs a liquor store out at Waverly Road. Most nights I stop by on the way home, pick up a six-pack, maybe some pork rinds, you know. Saw this fella buying some booze."

Jessie lifted the collar of her Ultrasuede jacket, thinking. "Did he say anything special?"

The old man looked away, sucked his teeth for a moment. "Not that I recall, no."

"You remember what he was wearing?"

"Yes, ma'am, I remember 'cause I got the feeling he was from out of town. He was wearing one of them tweed sport coats with the patches on the pockets, and jeans, faded jeans. Can't tell ya why exactly, but he sure didn't look like a local. Not to me, anyway."

"But you don't remember if he said anything out of the ordinary?"

"No, ma'am. Don't recall much of anything he said."

"Do you remember what he bought?"

"Yup. I remember what he bought 'cause it seemed like he was stocking up. Got a gallon jug of Black Label, a gallon jug of gin—can't remember what brand—and a case of beer—some Kraut import, I seem to recall. And mixers too. Tonic. The whole shot. I remember thinkin', This fella's either on one hell of a bender, or he's stockin up for some big shindig."

"Do you remember if he paid with cash or a check or a credit card?"

The old man thought about it for a moment, and then said he couldn't remember.

Jessie nodded and started gathering up the pictures. "You say this liquor store's on Waverly Road?"

"Just north of here, about five miles. You take the Southwest Highway to Waverly, then shoot north."

"Sir, I truly do appreciate the information."

"Ain't no skin off my nose," the old man grunted. And the sad fact was, there wasn't much skin *left* on the old coot's nose. Judging from his big, pockmarked, ulcerated schnozola, it was pretty clear the old geezer had bought *himself* a few gallon jugs in his day.

"You take care of yourself now," Jessie said, then turned and headed back toward the Caddy.

"What did he do?" the old man called after her.

Jessie shot the geezer a look over her shoulder. "God only knows."

Then she climbed back into the Cadillac and roared off.

Don Gordon's Trading Post sat at a busy intersection on the north side of town, flanked on either side by fluorescent-drenched gas stations. It was a modest little prefab building, with a brick façade and a grimy display window filled with huge paper signs emblazoned with the current specials. Jessie parked in the gravel lot near the entrance. There were only two other vehicles parked in front, a rust-bucket pickup and a Chevy SS.

Jessie went inside.

The place had that pungent, fermented smell of all great liquor stores. Stained, sticky floor tiles impregnated with years of rancid overflow, and beer-sodden mats at the threshold of each cooler. The ceiling was festooned with foil-lined displays of dancing bears, Joe Camel, the Budweiser frogs, Elvira—an F.A.O. Schwarz for boozehounds. Jessie went over to the front counter, which sat beneath an enormous hooded dispenser of cigarettes. The clerk sat on a stool behind the cash register.

"Help you, sweetheart?" The man was a beefy, middle-aged jock gone to seed. He wore a Ban-Lon golf shirt and had a toothpick stuck in his mouth.

"You Don Gordon?"

"Guilty as charged."

"Got a question for you," Jessie said, pulling one of the photographs out and showing it to the man. "Was talking to the ranger over at Shawnee, and he said this gentleman was in your store a couple of weeks ago. You don't happen to remember serving this guy, do you?"

The man behind the counter grinned. "You a detective?"

"You could say that, yeah."

"This guy do something?"

Jessie sighed. "Don't know for sure. I'm just supposed to find him."

There was an awkward pause then as the owner gave Jessie the once-over, his gaze lingering here and there. By this point, the other customers—a lanky white farm kid and an older black man—were converging on the counter, either to make their purchases or simply to eavesdrop or both. Jessie cleared her throat. She could feel every gaze in the place on her body like leeches, and that always pissed her off.

"Well, now, I'll tell ya," Gordon finally said, chewing lustily on his toothpick. "Tonight's your lucky night."

"How's that?" Jessie's heart started pumping again, that tingle back in her spine.

"Because that brainy son of a bitch was in here probably a half a dozen times over the last couple of months. I talked to him a lot."

"Is that right?"

"Yeah, and I can tell you why he kept coming back, too."

"Tell me."

"Because he was staying at the Wagon Inn just down the road, and that fleabag would drive anybody to drink."

There was another pause then, and it took all of Jessie's self-control and willpower not to lean over and kiss that ugly bastard right on the lips.

19

The Worm Turning

JESSIE WAITED UNTIL the following morning to return to the Highway Star, so full of anticipation she was about to pop.

Walter was gone, probably out back watering the tomatoes. A little cardstock sign that hung in the front-office window said WE'LL BE BACK AT (and then a little plastic clock read ten o'clock). Jessie glanced at her watch; it was just after nine o'clock. Something was wrong; she could feel it like a bad mood swing. She had wanted to return late last night—immediately after striking paydirt at Gordon's—but her maternal duty had compelled her to pick up Kit, take her home, and get her safely to school this morning. Now Jessie was certain she had left McNally sitting alone too long.

She strode past the office and down the cracked sidewalk toward the guest rooms. The sun flared magnesium hot off the flagstones as she approached the door to room 21, the sound of a heater motor rattling arrhythmically. Her reflection in the shaded windows revealed the tension in her stride, the way her spine had gotten erect all of a sudden. She had worn her brightly colored cable-knit sweater today, and white jeans, and now she was wishing she had dressed in commando black. It was a gift Jessie had enjoyed since her teens: this ability to sniff out trouble in the air before it even happened. Some might call it extrasensory. Some might even say she was psychic. But Jessie had never put much stock in that hoodoo crap. She had simply developed a keen nose for a kettle of fish.

And on this particular morning, approaching the door to John McNally's room, the whole goddamn motel stank to high heaven.

"John?" She rapped on the door as she called out.

No answer.

Jessie looked over and saw that the drapes had been hastily drawn across the window, but had parted slightly in the middle where something had fallen against the inside of the glass. It looked like the back of a chair or the edge of a desk. Looked as though there might have been a struggle.

"John!"

Jessie knocked harder, now wishing she had brought her gun along this morning. She owned several firearms, and had a legal owner's ID that qualified her to keep the iron for sport, limited to the shooting range. In the state of Illinois, it was illegal for a civilian to carry concealed, although Jessie had done it time and time again. The largest of her arsenal was a big old Beretta nine-millimeter with a fifteen-round magazine that she really used only to impress the good old boys down at the Gun World range. The Beretta had a selective fire capability that allowed a shooter to fire off three-shot full-auto bursts. It was so illegal, she was surprised the gun didn't glow in the dark. She also owned a couple of Smith & Wessons, a .357 magnum and a .38 snubbie. The .357 was strictly for show, since it had a kick like a goddamn bucking bronco, and the snubbie she kept back in her kitchen for home-defense purposes. Her favorite carry piece—the one she wished she had stuffed in the back of her belt at the moment—was the Raven Arms MP semiautomatic. The little .25-caliber job fit under just about anything, and it fired five hollowpoints—four in the clip and one in the breech—just as pretty as you please.

Unfortunately, all she had with her was the .22 Short tucked underneath the Caddy's driver-side seat, and that little novelty carried about as much persuasive power as a harsh word from a substitute teacher.

"John! Open up!"

She tried the door and found it locked. She went over and peered through the curtains, but all she could make out were a few shadowy shapes on the carpet inside the room. Maybe a fallen water glass, a chair, some scattered pieces of paper. She turned and called out for Walter, which was futile since the old man's hearing had gone kaput sometime back before the Nixon administration. She turned back to the door and rammed it hard with the meat of her shoulder. The door held firm. She tried again, and again, and again.

Goddamn thing was the only piece of wood in this whole rundown place that was solid.

Jessie was about to go find a telephone when she heard the steel-wool wheeze of Walter Sass coming around the corner of the last room. "What in high-jumping Jesus is going on?" Dressed in filthy denim overalls, his face

the color of rich dark loam, he was hobbling toward her with a bamboo
fishing pole in his hand, grimacing, showing his yellow teeth. "What the
hell you doing, woman?"

"Walter, thank God." Jessie motioned at the door. "Gimme a hand with
this, will ya?"

The old man approached and leaned the pole against the building. "You
don't have to rimrock my entire place."

"You got a skeleton key?"

"What's the problem?"

"Walter—for Chrissake—the place is a disaster area in there! My guy's
in trouble—come on!"

"Hold your horses," the old man grumbled, and fished through a ring of
ancient keys. He found the right key, stepped forward, and worried it into
the lock, his crooked old brown hands trembling with excitement.

The door flew open, and Jessie darted into the room.

McNally was unconscious on the floor.

A wave of details flooded Jessie's mind as she knelt down by McNally.
The man lay at the foot of the bed, one hand still clutching the blankets, his
face bloodless, his chin glistening with saliva, his eyelids slightly parted, revealing the whites. The television was tuned to snow in the corner, and
countless sheets of paper from the motel's scratch pad were strewn about
the floor, odd scribblings and diagrams, some of these pages stuck to the
wall, some wedged behind the mirror or impaled on a lamp.

The man had been busy doing *something*.

"Walter—get Mel Penny over here," Jessie said urgently as she cradled
John's head in her hands. She pressed her fingertips to his neck and found
his pulse, and it felt pretty normal. A little fast maybe, but strong and
steady. He seemed to be breathing normally as well. She didn't like the
look of his eyes, though, or the drool on his chin. Was this guy an epileptic?
Was he having some kind of a seizure? Or was the injury still short-
circuiting his brain? Or perhaps he was simply nuts. It was something that
had been bothering Jessie from the start: the possibility that this guy was
nothing more than some head case from the local loony bin.

"What's going on?" Walter was lingering in the doorway, pursing his lips
indignantly.

"Walter, goddamnit, go call Doc Penny, and tell him it's a goddamn
emergency!"

The old man whirled and then vanished into the morning sun.

"John? Can you hear me?" Jessie gently disengaged John's fingers from the spread, and then laid him on the hideous orange carpet.

Toward the back of the room, the bathroom door was ajar, a nimbus of fluorescent light spilling out, vibrating nervously. It seemed that every fabric in the room, from the fly-specked drapes to the yellowed lamp shades to the ancient shower curtain, was impregnated with a sour, rubbery urine smell. But the worst part was the incongruity of all those notes strewn about the floor, the table, and the bedspread.

At a glance, they looked like diagrams, doodles, haphazard formulas of words and phrases strung together compulsively. The notes of a man trying to piece together the slippery components of his past. For a brief instant, Jessie found herself wondering if John had broken through to something important, and that's why he had fainted.

"John!"

She lifted him gently by the shoulders and shook him; she didn't want to move him for fear of damaging something. She had no idea how hard he'd fallen, or if he had injured his spine or his neck. She shook him again, gently. His head lolled. "John? Can you hear me?"

His lips moved.

"John—it's Jessie Bales." She shook him again, lightly slapping his cheek. "Can you hear me?"

His jaw trembled, his lips moving again, twitching, something clicking in the base of his throat. He was trying to say something. His eyelids were fluttering now, the pupils dilating back into focus.

"It's okay," Jessie assured him softly. "You're safe, you're in a motel room. Can you understand me?"

He whispered something.

Jessie leaned in close and said, "What was that?"

Then he whispered it again, and it sounded like, "It's the method . . ."

"What was that?" Jessie wiped a bead of perspiration from his brow. She felt the fresh scar above his temple, a row of recent sutures, the place where the truck grill had connected with his head. She lifted him up into a sitting position and leaned him against the bed. "Take your time, John, it's all right."

He was swallowing hard now, blinking, focusing on his surroundings. His face was still as pale as alabaster, his bloodless lips moving. He looked up at Jessie. "Oh . . . Jesus," he uttered, his choked voice barely a whisper.

"What's 'the method'?"

He blinked again. "Pardon me?"

"You said, 'It's the method.'" Jessie looked at him, studied his drawn face. "Do you know who I am?"

"Yes . . . yes . . . I do."

"Who am I?"

"You're . . . you're Jessica Bales . . . Jessie for short . . . the best private investigator in Randall, Illinois."

Jessie smiled. "That's not funny. I'm the *only* PI in Randall, Illinois."

Another awkward pause as John tried to focus and get his bearings.

Jessie motioned around the room. "Looks like you've been a busy boy. Doing your homework?"

John tried to stand, but the moment he tensed his legs, his whole body seemed to collapse, and he sagged back to the floor, grimacing at the pain. "Ouch!"

"Easy there, pardner." Jessie braced him against the bed. "Let's take things one step at a time; I've got Mel Penny on the way."

"I'm all right, really. I'm okay." John grimaced. He wiped the moisture from his chin and brushed back his hair. He looked like a man who had just been in a burning building. But even amid all the drool and the trembling and the writhing, Jessie couldn't help noticing that the guy was a handsome son of a bitch. "My legs, they're still—you know—pretty messed up," he said finally. "But I think I'm making progress in other areas—in the memory department, at least—a little bit."

"What happened?"

"I believe it's called a blackout." John rubbed his eyes.

"You think it's the injury?"

"No, not exactly, no."

"What do you mean?"

He glanced around the room for a second. "What I mean is, I'm pretty sure about what caused the blackout."

Jessie waited. "And that would be . . . ?"

John glanced over his shoulder and saw something on the floor behind the bed. He leaned over and scooped it up, and then he showed it to Jessie. "That would be *this*," he said somewhat sheepishly.

The empty bottle of Tanqueray gin had a fuzz of carpet fibers around its rim.

Jessie nodded. "I get it."

"It's funny, you know, most small towns—wherever you go—you always find a liquor store within blocks." John set the empty bottle upright on the floor. "I suppose I should look on the bright side. At least now I have another piece of the puzzle."

Jessie looked at him. "What—that you're a juicer?"

John smiled wearily. "Yeah, well, I've always preferred the term chronic recovering substance abuser."

"Welcome to the club." Jessie grinned, extending her hand.

John stared at her for a moment, then grasped her hand and managed another feeble smile. "You too?"

"Guess you could say I'm fully recovered." Jessie shrugged. "Been clean and sober for almost five years."

"That's great."

"What's 'the method,' John?"

He grimaced again and took a couple of shallow breaths to stave off the pain. "It's something that bubbled out of my drunken stupor—the words themselves—I'm not sure what they mean. I was doing my little art therapy, trying to make connections between the images in my nightmare and the names and places on the tip of my tongue—and there it was: *the method.*" He closed his eyes then, pausing as though waiting for the latest twinge to subside. "The bad news is, that's all there was to it—the words—and I have no idea what they mean."

Jessie sighed and glanced around the room. The sheets of notepaper were everywhere. Some of them had odd little sketches of objects that looked like cuts of meat, others that looked like human limbs, faces, arms with outspread hands, more faces, fingers pointing with biblical purpose. And the words and phrases—much of them variations of the words *the* and *method*—scrawled in tortured symmetries. The mystery seemed as stubborn and opaque as a rock.

But the rock was about to be turned over.

"I've got some good news," Jessie said finally.

"I could use it."

"I found the hotel room you were staying in."

John looked up at her, licking his lips thoughtfully, yet saying nothing.

"According to the desk clerk, you had been there for several weeks," Jessie added. "Prepaid through the rest of this month. Which means everything is just as you had left it."

After a long pause, John said, "Did they let you go in?"

"I sort of figured it might be better if we go in together."

After another agonizing pause, John took a deep breath and said, "What are we waiting for?"

20

Room 213

IT WAS A few minutes before eleven o'clock, and the sun was already heating up the morning, when Jessie pulled the Caddy into a vacant lot behind the Wagon Inn's property. She didn't want to leave the vehicle sitting in plain sight—after all, the Caddy *was* a breeze to identify—so she pulled behind a neighboring power transformer and parked. She turned the car off and sat there for a moment, glancing over at her passenger.

John sat in the shotgun seat, chewing his fingernail, scanning the distant complex, his eyes darting back and forth from one dirty brick building to another. He looked as though he were trying to take it all in at once. It had been less than two hours since he had awakened from his blackout, but he seemed to be bouncing back heroically. Doc Penny had given him a complete going-over, and Walter had cooked up some eggs and home fries for breakfast. Afterward, Jessie had recommended that John rest for a while before they jaunted off to see his room, but John had been too anxious to wait.

Now they sat poised on the threshold of John's recent past.

The Wagon Inn was a strange, decaying carnival of highway hospitality. Crouched beneath an enormous neon wagon wheel, the central building was a three-story edifice of peeling cinder block that housed the main lobby and cavernous restaurant—*Friday night fish fries, kids under seven eat for free, try our new chicken-fried pork patty.* The guest rooms and conference areas were in back, lined up along two adjoining split-level buildings, offering lovely views of both the local landfill to the east and the scarred, graffiti-stained ramparts of the Ninety-sixth Avenue overpass to the west. The place looked as though it hadn't been painted since the Korean War, and the pollution, lake winds, and jet fumes had darkened the walls with a patina of age and grit. Along the north edge of the parking lot, a muddy pasture was sparsely populated with emaciated farm animals—*visit our petting zoo, bring the whole family*—while a nearby billboard garishly lured passersby to visit the Bare Assets Gentleman's Club.

The inn was relatively slow this morning, only a few cars parked in the lot, the surrounding wings pretty quiet. But Jessie could tell by John's face that the joint wasn't ringing any bells; he seemed lost. "Tell you what," Jessie said, punching the cigarette lighter deeper into its socket. "We'll take this one step at a time, nice and slow."

"It's not that," John muttered. "I'm all right, really, I'm just trying to remember."

"Nothing looks familiar?"

"Not yet." He glanced over at the petting zoo. "I mean, maybe—"

He stopped abruptly.

"You see something?" She lit a Carlton and took a quick drag.

"I don't know." He rubbed his mouth, staring at the sickly little ponies and goats, and Jessie could tell that his wheels were working overtime. "Maybe, maybe not," he said. "It's hard to explain—it's like—like being in a perpetual state of déjà vu or something."

There was a pause then, and Jessie tossed her cigarette away and opened her door. "Whattya say we go inside and see if the front-desk clerk recognizes you."

Jessie grabbed her purse and got out of the car.

Before ushering John over to the building, Jessie asked him to wait for a second, and she went around back to the Caddy's trunk. She had stopped by her office that morning and picked up her Raven MP .25—for reasons she would be hard-pressed to explain. The gun was still in its leather pouch, wedged between the spare tire and the box of road flares. She rooted it out and checked the magazine. The bullets were nestled there like little brass jelly beans. She snapped the magazine back into the pistol, and then stuffed it into her purse for safekeeping.

"Here goes nothing," she said, coming back around the front of the car.

They crossed the lot, circled around front, and went inside the main entrance.

The lobby looked like somebody's rec room from the 1950s, a narrow, low-ceilinged affair with imitation-hardwood paneling, orange fabric chairs, and a console TV in one corner tuned to a rerun of *The Jeffersons*. A greasy-haired kid with a peach-fuzz mustache sat behind the front desk. He was dressed in a pathetic little maroon blazer, a tiny wagon wheel sewn on the pocket. As Jessie and John approached, the kid gazed up, eyes twinkling, gum snapping. "Welcome to the Wagon Inn. How can I help you folks this morning?"

John stepped forward. "Hello there."

There was a beat of awkward silence—just a blip—as the kid made eye contact, and all at once the kid's expression got a little glitchy, as though he were searching some menu for the proper response. Jessie watched him grope for the right words. "Hello, Mr. Mc—Mc—"

"John," said John evenly, his smile plastered to his face.

"We haven't, like, seen you for a while, you know," the kid stammered, typing madly. "You know, since you gave us orders not to clean your room on a daily basis—we just wondered, you know, if everything was, like, okay."

John and Jessie exchanged a look.

The kid kept typing away. "Just checking to see, you know, if you have any messages." Another pause. "Nope, don't see anything, no sir, no messages, nope."

The kid was really babbling now.

"That's fine," John said softly, tapping his fingertips absently on the counter. "But I gotta ask you another favor. Seems I've misplaced the key to my room."

The kid looked at Jessie, then looked back at John, then reached into a drawer.

He gave John a key with a tiny tag attached that said ROOM 213.

John nodded and then turned toward the hallway just off the east side of the lobby. Jessie followed. But before they got halfway across the room, the kid called after them, "Hey, Mr. McNally!"

John paused, turning back to the desk. "Yes?"

"Your room is this way," the kid said, pointing at the opposite side of the lobby.

"Of course, yes, of course." John was nodding sheepishly, heading back the way he had come.

Jessie followed him through a glass door and into a narrow corridor lined with cheap outdoorsy portraits on paneled walls—pheasants, fox hunts, geese flying in formation—the air thick with a pasty, fibrous odor like old, spent carpet. Jessie had a tightness in her stomach, but it was a wonderful tightness, invigorating, a feeling of imminent riches. They reached the end of the corridor and climbed the steps. The second-floor corridor was even more airless, and smelled as though a grease fire had recently broken out in one of the rooms.

When they finally reached the door to room 213, Jessie's heart was beating harder than ever.

John put the key in the lock and opened the door, then let himself inside. Jessie followed.

There was an awkward silence at first, as Jessie watched John.

And John watched the room.

21

Technicolor Banshees

IT WASN'T THE spaciousness of the room, or the two queen-sized beds pushed against the north wall, one of them still unmade, its blankets bunched at the foot. It wasn't the grouping of overstuffed chairs and work desk in one corner, the little veneer minibar in the other, or the large bathroom area in back sectioned off by the cheap Oriental repro divider. It wasn't the typical chintzy decor, the mail-order Leroy Neiman prints over the bed, the Colonial lamps with their tacky little wagon-wheel bases. It wasn't even the air, which had a terrible pungent closeness to it, a musty stench like wet fur, petrified food, and old newspapers. No, the truth of it was, it wasn't any of these things that first set off the inexplicable silent alarm in Jessie's brain.

It was the array of unidentified photos—both glossy black-and-white stills and images clipped out of magazines—taped and hung and squeezed into every available inch of wall, lamp shade, desktop, and counter space.

They looked like photos of women.

"Good God," John was uttering breathlessly as he entered the room.

Jessie stood in the doorway for a moment, trying to get a handle on things. There were other incongruous items among the photos, scattered throughout the room, strewn amid the empty fast-food containers and liquor bottles. Old dog-eared folders and portfolios, notebooks worn down by relentless scribbling and fiddling, stacks of magazines and newspapers. Scanning the room, swallowing back the bile that was rising in her throat, Jessie Bales realized beyond a shadow of a doubt that this was no traveling salesman. This was no account executive with a few product samples or spec sheets lying around. This guy was pathological. Obsessive-compulsive to the extreme. Maybe worse, maybe . . .

"Oh, Jesus, Jesus, Jesus . . ." John's voice was strangled, tortured.

"Take it easy, John," Jessie managed to mutter. "Just take it one step at a time."

She moved slowly into the room, carefully shutting the door behind her. Then she paused for a moment, noticing the drapes next to the door, completely drawn across the front window, their fabric so old and worn it was nearly transparent. The corridor outside was faintly visible through it, as well as the balcony and the strip-club billboard beyond it. Jessie turned back to the room and started to say something.

That's when she saw the photo by the bed. It was pinned to a lampshade, a glossy photo of a model from some show-business agency roster, a gal who looked vaguely like Jessie. This lady was a strawberry blond, baby-doll lips, come-hither pose, gazing demurely over her shoulder at the camera, backlit by diffuse silver light.

Somebody had cut her eyes out.

Jessie reached into her purse and put her fingers on the beaver-tail grip of the Raven, gently wrapping her hand around it. Not exactly because she wanted to use it; it was more of an involuntary reaction. She merely wanted to know that the weapon was there. In her purse. Available. She kept her hand wrapped around it and she said, "Talk to me, John. What's the deal? What's it all mean?"

"I don't—I don't really know," he muttered, and it was the mutter of a child, a child who believed in bogeymen and space aliens and magic. He was moving deeper into the room, shuffling slowly like a zombie in one of those drive-in movies, his knee brushing the corner of the bed, the photos and documents all around him, his gaze flitting from pictures of surgical instruments to S&M paraphernalia to countless beautiful women, some famous, some anonymous, each with a different part of their anatomy excised from their picture.

"John?"

"I don't really know," he was murmuring softly now, almost whimpering. His expression had gone sour; he looked ill, sounded like a wounded animal.

Jessie walked over to the unmade bed, looked down, and saw a manila folder lying open on the rumpled sheets. The contents of the folder had spilled out across the bedding. More photos. These were different somehow, mounted on stiffer cardstock, maybe cut out of books. Industrial maybe, scientific, agricultural. Jessie picked one of them up and took a closer look. The image trumpeted at her. A grotesque black-and-white photo of a rendering vat at a slaughterhouse, a severed calf's head floating on a pool of offal. Jessie picked up another photo. This one showed a woman lying on a gurney, nude, one of her breasts flayed open with a metal speculum, a crudely drawn harlequin's mask overlaying her features.

Jessie dropped the photo, and it skittered across an array of similarly macabre photos.

"This—isn't me—"

The voice came from the bathroom, and Jessie whirled toward it. John was in there. The shuffling noises, and the strangled mewling sound of his voice, all of it barely audible above the rattle of the ceiling fan. Jessie lifted the Raven out of her purse. She thumbed the safety off and started toward the bathroom, walking with the gun at her side, her senses hyperaware now, her fingertips tingling, the backs of her arms and legs rashing with goose bumps. What had she gotten herself into? What kind of monster had she taken in? There were other noises now, behind her, coming from the outside, the crunch of tires on gravel, the squeal of brakes, radio voices, but they seemed a million miles away.

She peered inside the bathroom.

He was sitting on the edge of the tub, crying, cradling a worn leatherette notebook on his lap. The bathroom was a pigsty, clogged with trash and empty bottles, roiling with stench, the walls strafed with deep-red graffiti, cryptic singsong that made no sense other than adding to the overall shocking din, and the photos, many of them in color, autopsy shots, graphic images of flesh curled like paper, organs splayed like fruit, musculatures pink and glistening and screaming at Jessie like Technicolor banshees.

Jessie pointed the gun at John.

Gazing up at her, eyes liquid, terrified, he uttered, "This is *not* me."

Jessie started to say something when she heard the unmistakable *shuck* of a weapon chambering a round. Jessie knew that sound as an animal knows the sound of its trainer's voice—it was one that automatically put the squeeze on her heart. She looked up. The wall of the shower stall had a louvered window—about the size of a manhole—that opened out over the rear parking lot, bordered by a narrow balcony. There was a figure out there on the balcony, fifteen feet away, coming toward the window. Middle-aged, pot belly, sport jacket, laminate-steel shield hanging around his neck, the sun glinting off the metal. He was carrying a cut-down pistol-grip twelve-gauge.

Had to be a cop.

John rose to his feet and then shot a glance out the rear window. "No, no, this isn't—it's not *me!*"

"Okay, fine, I believe you," Jessie was murmuring now, glancing back across the bathroom. She could see out into the main room. Outside the front window, there was movement. Jessie could see them through the drapes, the pale outlines of more middle-aged men in sport coats coming toward the room. They were shuffling sideways, their backs against the walls, their handguns drawn and raised and ready to rock: This was not good.

All at once, things were starting to happen.

Jessie turned back to the bathroom and started to say something when John shoved her out of the way, vaulting across the shower stall. Jessie slammed backward into the tile, and then things were happening so quickly it was hard to keep up, because Jessie was slipping to the floor, momentarily dazed, and John was clawing at the screen, tearing it out of the window frame, shoving the louvers open with the edge of that worn black notebook. "Wait a minute!" Jessie cried, but it was futile now, because she had dropped her gun, and the window was collapsing outward, and John was squirming through the breach into daylight, his desperate loafer-clad feet cobbling up the mildewed tile.

Outside, the cop's startled voice: *"Hold it right there, friend!"*

Then John was out, and Jessie heard the sound of the shotgun going off—a dry blast ripping open a hole in the sky outside and ringing in Jessie's ears—and all at once it became clear that John had surprised the cop, sending the shotgun blast wild into the sky. The cop had tumbled backward then, careening over the balcony railing and landing in a Dumpster down below. John fled across the remaining stretch of balcony, heading toward the far stairwell, one hand still clutching the notebook.

But Jessie was too busy to worry about John right now. Scooping up the Raven, sucking a breath, lurching toward the window, Jessie heard the angry voice behind her. *"Chicago police! Open up now or we break it down!"*

Jessie was moving on instinct now, all the contradictory impulses jamming the switchboard in her head: She knew that if she took off, she would be considered an accessory, but that if she stayed, she would be busted for sure, might even lose her license. She had no choice.

"Last chance!" The bark of the cop's voice shattered the stillness.

Jessie climbed over the edge of the tub, grabbed the ledge of the breached window, and boosted herself up. The jagged edges of broken screen tore at her sweater, gouging a tuft here and there, but she managed to squeeze through quickly and quietly, grabbing an electrical conduit pipe outside for leverage. She landed on the narrow rear balcony. Peering down through the railing, she saw the dummy in the Dumpster.

The cop was still trying to find his shotgun, which had sunk into an oblivion of cabbage leaves and wet cardboard.

Jessie started toward the far stairwell.

In the distance, she could see John. He was stumbling toward a strip of trees on the horizon, climbing a Cyclone fence that bordered the Wagon Inn lot, then running with that weird half-limp. His weakened legs suddenly buckled under him, and he went down hard. Ate a mouthful of dust. Then he scooped up that goddamn notebook and continued hobbling off into the trees, vanishing in the cool shadows.

Jessie rushed down the steps and crept silently across the rear lot.

She found the Cadillac where she had left it, obscured behind the fifteen-foot-high tangle of rusty power lines and transformer boxes. She threw her purse on the backseat, slipped behind the wheel, fired it up, and quickly pulled away, careful not to make too much noise.

A moment later, she was hurling down the narrow dirt road behind the Wagon Inn's lot.

It felt as though she were going a thousand miles an hour.

22

The Fan

THE DOOR BLEW open, a big black hurricane pouring into the cluttered studio apartment, its wake sending posters and Post-It notes flapping, yellowed window shades billowing, lamp shades shivering. The hurricane slammed the door, then stormed over to the kitchen sink. Angrily tossing his leather knapsack on the counter, the hurricane ran some water. Then he leaned over the sink, splashed cold water on his face, and shook off the rage like a huge canine tossing moisture off its back. All the money and effort he had invested over the last two days had just gone up in smoke.

Billy Marsten grabbed a moldering dish towel off a nearby rack and wiped his face, smelling the congealed mustard impregnated in the terry cloth. His stomach was churning with frustration and disappointment. The plan had been so simple, so fucking simple, it was a bloody miracle that he had blown it, especially when everything had been moving along so well.

The plan had started with Dr. Harkonian, a little bald-headed criminal psych professor with ties to the local police department. Billy had called the teacher up two nights ago—after losing McNally at the Reinhardt Clinic—and bribed Harkonian to dig into whatever cop files he could access for information. It had taken three hundred dollars in cash and a promise to fix up Harkonian with one of the friskier coeds, but ultimately the little fart had delivered the goods. One of Harkonian's pals was a shift commander at Area Thirteen, and word among CPD insiders was that the force was spending a lot of resources surveilling a place called the Wagon Inn in Blue Island. Billy had immediately started his own little surveillance, spending eight to ten hours a day hanging out in the weeds across the street. Unfortunately, just as he was arriving this morning, the big safari was already coming to a crashing climax. Billy never even saw McNally. All he could manage were a few hastily snapped photographs of plainclothes guys swarming down the steps in back and a few peripheral onlookers.

In other words, a total washout.

"Fuck!" Billy spat the word, hurling the towel in the sink, then grabbing the camera case.

He stomped across the apartment, sidestepping jumbles of memorabilia and collectibles. The seedy little cold-water flat was a virtual museum of serial-killer lore. Peach crates filled with laminated news clippings and magazine articles were stacked along the east wall, meticulously indexed and well thumbed. Bookshelves groaned with the weight of countless volumes and monographs, annual reports from VICAP—the Violent Criminal Apprehension Program—as well as dog-eared documents from the National Center for the Analysis of Violent Crime and the FBI's Behavioral Science Unit. The west wall was a gallery of original mass-murderer artwork. Among the bizarre collection were "Skull Clown" paintings by John Wayne Gacy, ballpoint doodles by Richard "the Night Stalker" Ramirez, and even cute little koala bears sculpted out of dirty socks by Charles Manson. Much of the paraphernalia was extremely rare and valuable, many items having cost Billy several months' worth of his meager salary as a bookstore clerk.

Billy belonged to several organized fan clubs, including the Official International Ed Gein Fan Club. Gein was one of the most celebrated and notorious serial killers of this century. A shy little Wisconsin farmer raised by a cruel, domineering mother, Gein achieved notoriety after police broke down his door and found a true house of horrors—headless corpses hanging upside down in his kitchen, chairs upholstered with human skin, and shoe boxes full of female genitalia. Gein immediately achieved superstar status—his autograph is now more valuable than Winston Churchill's and Mickey Mantle's combined—and went on to inspire such horror classics as *Psycho, The Texas Chainsaw Massacre,* and *Silence of the Lambs.* Billy owned a rare facsimile of Gein's official death certificate, copies of obituaries, and a handsome membership certificate currently framed and hanging in his bathroom next to a wilted spider plant.

There were other collectibles too, touching on every conceivable corner of serial-killer culture. There were neatly boxed sets of serial-killer trading cards sitting on the radiator near the window, and comics and fanzines and calendars and videos by the bed. There were figurines of Henry Lee Lucas, Ted Bundy, Berkowitz, and Speck lining the bookshelves. In other words,

every possible artifact available that celebrated the underside of human behavior filled the room—and yet the collection was still flawed, imperfect,
incomplete.

All because Billy Marsten had lost the trail of the most fascinating
celebrity of them all.

"Fuck-fuck-fuck—*FUCK!*" Billy growled as he clamored into the bathroom.

He slammed the door, shrugged off his coat, and flipped on the safelight.
A sickly red glow filled the tiny chamber, making both the cracked porcelain and Billy's pale skin appear almost luminous. Billy was a fairly decent
amateur shutterbug, and he had built a fairly well-equipped makeshift dark-
room inside his tiny bathroom. He yanked the shower curtain aside and revealed a bulky old enlarger and a series of plastic trays lined up in sequence
inside the bathtub. Chemical bottles sat on the soap-dish shelf, and a large
timer clock was mounted above the shower nozzle.

Billy knelt down by the tub and began developing his photographs.

The first step was processing the negative, then enlarging the image into
five-by-seven black-and-white proofs. Billy had managed to snap off
twenty-odd shots during the chaos at the Wagon Inn, and then had managed
to flee the scene without getting stopped by the cops. It was doubtful that he
had captured any shots of McNally—or the mystery woman with whom he
had come—but it was still worth checking. He started the first blowup,
holding the paper with rubber tongs, dipping it into the developer mix, then
the stop bath, then the fixer, then the rinse. The image was a blurred mess,
an out-of-focus shot of the Bare Assets billboard behind the Wagon Inn.
The next frame was the same story, another blurry image snapped while
Billy was scrambling to get out of sight. The next one was the same, and
the next, and the next. Finally, Billy started dipping shot number six—into
the developer, the stop bath, the fixer, the rinse—the final image emerging
under harsh red light.

Billy sucked in a breath.

Although the shot was poorly framed—tilted into the sun and light-
struck—it clearly showed an overgrown stretch of dirt access road behind
the Wagon Inn, snaking through a grove of spindly trees, leading up a gradual incline toward the neighboring highway ramp. In the middle distance,
slightly out of focus and blurry with motion, was a car. Most of it was
cropped by the right side of the frame, but enough was visible to make out
the make and model.

A late-model Cadillac with a statuesque woman behind the wheel.

Billy lifted the photograph from the rinse bath, the liquid dribbling off its corner, tiny droplets falling like tears into the bath, a wave of emotion pouring over Billy. His chest was swelling with hope. All was not lost. Thank God, all was not lost. There was still a way to find his hero.

Reaching across the tub, Billy grabbed the hair dryer, which hung on a nail. He flipped on the dryer and started drying the wet photograph, careful not to warp the paper. He worked with the utmost caution. Finishing a photograph is delicate work, especially one with such an important clue buried in its grain. Billy knew he would probably have to enlarge the shot even further in order to be sure, and resolution goes all to hell when you keep pushing something bigger and bigger, but that didn't matter. The important thing was that Billy had found a way to track down McNally, and it was going to be his little secret.

When the photo was dry, Billy took it over to the sink and turned on the overhead light. There was a magnifying glass sitting in a cup next to the soap dish, and Billy grabbed it and took a closer look at the clue in the photo. Sure enough, down in the extreme right-hand corner, just clear enough to make out the series of embossed letters, was a license plate.

The statuesque lady's license plate.

This was how Bill was going to find McNally.

Tossing the magnifying glass back into its cup, Billy tore the right-hand corner off the photo.

There was a load of work to do now, and not a lot of time in which to do it.

Part Three

The Method

I have felt the wind of the wing of madness pass over me.
—Charles Baudelaire

23

Disintegration

THERE WAS A grimy, fly-specked mirror above the sink in the transient hotel bathroom. At approximately ten o'clock that evening, the man slipped into the darkened bathroom, flipped on the bare lightbulb hanging overhead, and saw his reflection glowering back at him. The lightbulb swayed on its own cord, the shadows lazily contracting and expanding around the man like a hellish bellows stoking a flame. Then the man moved closer and stood there for quite a long while, staring at himself. His ears were ringing, his heart like a trip-hammer in his chest.

At first, it was as though he were simply confirming his own existence. Double-checking to make sure he hadn't metamorphosed into some demonic beast, some oily little gargoyle. But oddly enough, he found himself staring at a perfectly ordinary face, ordinary in every way. And the face stared back in a perfectly ordinary fashion. A little frightened, perhaps, a little unhinged from reading the terrible words that were written in his own handwriting, but other than the fear, there wasn't anything extraordinary about this face.

The minutes passed.

And John McNally started to calm slightly, a Charlie Parker tune in his head.

He lifted the pint bottle of Tanqueray to his lips and took another bracing swig, wincing at the metallic burn, sniffing back the blast of junipers. The bottle was getting low, and John was not nearly drunk enough, not nearly enough to deaden the fear. He looked back up at his reflection and tried to make the connection between himself and the guy writing the journal. "No fucking way," he murmured at his reflection. "No fucking way are you this guy."

Outside the bathroom, the noise of buzzing neon filled the room like bees.

John had been locked up in the transient hotel for nearly two hours now, pacing, reading passages out of the worn leatherette notebook that he had pilfered from the Wagon Inn. He had gone through nearly half the journal entries, and with each successive page of feverish, tightly kerned ballpoint-ink handwriting, he had been getting sicker and sicker. An hour ago he had opened a window in an attempt to flush away his terror with some fresh air, but the noxious sweet wind from the distant steel mills and factories down in Gary and Hammond had only punctuated his malaise.

"No fucking way," he muttered again, as though repeating a mantra.

Glancing away from the mirror, he peered out the bathroom door at the seedy little hotel room, his gaze taking in the spartan furnishings, the ratty little single bed, the hideous Greco-Roman wallpaper, and the ghostly water stains on the ceiling. He was on the fifth floor of a ten-story building, and the weight of all the other rooms seemed to be pressing down on him. Outside, through the open window, the dusk was infecting the sky with black lung disease, and the dirty green buzz of a neighboring neon sign leaked through the blinds, radiating the room with a sickly pallor. It was almost humorous, how his lodging had deteriorated in a geometric spiral downward since he had fled the clinic grounds three days ago. Now he was in the seventh circle: the Blue Island Hotel—Transients Welcome!—festering on the south side of the great and weary city of Chicago.

Truth be told, it was a miracle that he had made it here without being apprehended.

After escaping the ambush at the Wagon Inn, John had crept through what seemed like miles of overgrown thickets and trees, lugging the ancient vinyl-bound journal the entire way. Every now and then he would hear the squeal of tires or loud voices, at which point he would drop to the ground for several minutes, heart chugging, waiting for the footsteps to surround him, with the dogs and the shotguns and the radio voices. But each time, nothing would happen. Finally, he emerged from the trees and hailed a yellow cab. He told the cabbie to put some miles behind him, and the cabbie took him clear across the southern metro sprawl to Lake Michigan, where John finally located a suitably innocuous transient hotel.

He ended up in Blue Island, in this godforsaken room, suffering through the hellish diary.

Looking back out at the room, he saw the journal lying on the bed, a tattered husk of simulated leather wrapped around a three-ring binder of college rule paper. It looked as though it had once been maroon, but the years or moisture or God-only-knew-what-else had seasoned it to a dull blueblack, like the color of a scab. It was hard to tell how old it was—the paper had not yet yellowed—but it certainly radiated a malignant kind of weight. Like mummified skin wrapped around some hideous manifesto.

It's in my own handwriting.

John looked back at his reflection and felt a pang of something new, something almost beyond description radiating out of his own reflection, seeping out of his pores. It was as though he had pushed too hard on some internal envelope, and the elastic had finally snapped, and suddenly he found himself thinking the unthinkable. *What if I really am this guy?* At first, the thought positively strangled him, making him dizzy, drying his throat. But then something quite unexpected happened. John found himself looking at a new face in the mirror.

There was something imperceptibly different about his own features, a glint in his eye, a certain jaggedness. The feeling lasted only a moment, but the worst part, the most puzzling part, was the ambiguity. There was a trace of fascination mingling with the repulsion, a certain narcissism with the horror. He was staring at his own eyes, wondering what it felt like to look into the eyes of pure evil, pure madness, and he felt a wave of sick warmth rushing over him: looking into the eyes of the beast. *What if I am this guy?* The feeling curled around his gut like a blast of heroin, making his groin tingle.

"Okay, stop it!" He looked away, realizing his heart was pumping madly again.

He lifted the pint to his lips, polished off the rest of the gin, grimaced, tossed the empty in the trash. His mind was reeling now, floating on the juniper fumes and echoes of the journal. There had to be an answer in the pages of this hideous diary. There had to be some sign that it was *not* him, that it was a mistake, a frame job, a nasty coincidence, a joke.

There had to be.

He reached down and ran some cold water in the sink, splashing some on his face. He was ready to go back and read some more obscenities, clinging desperately to the hope that he would find a clue, a sign. He dried his face on a towel, then turned and walked out of the bathroom.

Into the buzzing dimness of the hotel room.

Where the journal awaited like a tumor.

24

Warping

7 August, 1991 *A day filled with ideas, projects GALORE. The life of the mind is truly a blessing and a curse. Is it my medical training? Maybe it's something else. PRIMAL STUFF???? I feel compelled to lay down the essence of my method, all the tributary projects leading toward the one great experiment. But that's in the future.*

Nowadays, I spend much of my time seeking the perfect specimen. It takes forever sometimes—often an entire lunch hour—sometimes longer—but they always appear. Always. Like clockwork. Every time.

She'll be emerging from some middling fashion boutique like The Limited or Ann Taylor or—HEAVEN FORBID!—The Gap, and I'll see the posture first. It's not difficult to detect. A slight slump in the shoulders, a certain ennui, a sort of laziness in the stride, and I know immediately I've got a candidate.

I'll quickly leave a few bills on the table and follow this sad little specimen.

Invariably she leads me from one boring, pathetic diversion to another. Cleaners, supermarket, manicurist, health food store, therapist, chiropractor, tanning salon, tae kwon do, fortune-teller, sensory deprivation tank and whatever-ad-nauseam. Anything to occupy her desperately AVERAGE life, her numbingly empty hours. And then—and only then—do I know for sure:

She's perfect.
Perfect.
PERFECT.
P-E-R-F-E-C-T!

11 August, 1991 What was I writing about last time before I was so rudely interrupted?

Oh yes: The acquisition of the PERFECT specimen.

The acquisition usually happens at night. If she lives alone, I do it in her upper-middle-class home on her upper-middle-class street. If she has family around her, I do it in a dark parking lot or neighborhood square. Whenever the most expedient window of opportunity opens—and it isn't difficult to encounter one, especially with such a lonely, empty, unhappy human being—I catch them alone somewhere, absently walking along, their thoughts blank. Their thoughts as WORTHLESS as their life, and then I move in for Phase One.

PHASE ONE:

I've found the best technique is the atomizer. An inexpensive little cologne bottle, sold at any beauty supply shop—the eight-ounce size works best; it's small enough to conceal in the palm, yet voluminous enough to get the proper amount of the chemical into the nasal passages. I fill the atomizer with a solution of laboratory grade atropine and water. I've tried formaldehyde—which is certainly fast-acting, instantly incapacitating the woman the moment she encounters it—but formaldehyde is noisy and messy. It irritates the respiratory tract and causes vomiting and abdominal cramps. Atropine is cleaner and instantaneous. All I have to do is stroll past the woman—usually in the opposite direction, gazing around as though I'm a lost tourist—and the moment I come within a couple of feet, give her a nice SPRITZ in the face.

They often drop without knowing what hit them.

PHASE TWO:

The relocation; and this is more difficult than it sounds. A hundred and twenty pound woman knocked completed unconscious—dead, sometimes, if I happen to use too much atropine—is quite a LOAD, believe me, like hauling around a burlap sack full of bowling balls. The poor miserable soul is completely limp. I usually take advantage of my little Japanese hatchback station wagon for this task; I wrap the girl in a blanket, stow her in back, and take her to the lab.

The lab is where I make her whole, where I transform her. Not a pleasant place, I'm afraid, but private, and quiet, and well equipped. In reality, it's nothing more than a cellar. Originally a root cellar, I believe.

Now, of course, it's a place of transcendence.

PHASE THREE:

The transformation: There are many decisions to be made at this stage.

The appropriate incision site, the implant type, placement of the implant in relation to the surrounding tissue, the type of medium to be introduced. Let's say I choose a submammary site, or lower, perhaps something along the triangular fascia. I'll infiltrate the torso with a local—usually Marcaine with a tad of epinephrine to keep the girl from moving—and I'll use an Irons curved scalpel to make the incision. I retract the dorsal flap, and gaze into the void.

In most of the chosen ones, the subglandular tissue looks like wet bark, spongy to the touch, but the closer you look, the more you realize it's an endless patchwork of dark, fetid NOTHINGNESS. Like a black night sky. A galaxy of infinitesimally meaningless cells. The void. The manifestation of the girl's useless, empty, vacuous life. I fill this empty space with me. Sometimes I use my hair, or my fingernails, or my saliva, or even a tincture of my own blood. It depends on my mood. I usually bow to the muse and let inspiration rule.

I fill the void with meaning. I imbue the empty cells with my own purposeful ones.

John closed the journal.

The room seemed smaller all of a sudden, the seams of the wallpaper warping inward. It was stuffy, despite the open window, miserably stuffy, and ripe like a hothouse. John swallowed hard and took some deep breaths. He was drunk-dizzy, and nauseous, and sick with confusion. Was this him? Could this kind of insanity ever be eradicated by a simple case of episodic amnesia? It was as though he were on a roller-coaster ride now, a ride through his own past, and the ride was becoming quite bumpy.

He managed several moments of deep breathing before he gathered enough nerve to open the journal again.

I always implant a good portion of my cells—MYSELF!—into the woman—which usually involves stuffing a wad of hair under a muscle flap, or sticking a few nail clippings inside the dissected pocket, or injecting a couple of cc's of my own blood into the tissue. Then I hastily close the incision site, stitching it subcutaneously. Mostly I use dissolving sutures to avoid an obvious SCAR in the event that the girl survives. And then I close all incisions with surgical tape. I administer some antibiotics, just to give her a fighting chance—not that I give a democrat's damn one way or the other—and I wrap her back up in the blanket. I take her out the back way, put her in the wagon and drive her a good fifty miles or so out of town.

Then I lay her gently under the stars in some remote pasture, her LIFE-LESS EYES—I's?????—gazing up at all the celestial bodies, unaware that her own body has just been transformed.

This is the part where I drive off into the night, full of peace and satisfaction again; I've done my part; I've filled an empty vessel with MEANING AND VALUE.

Sometimes the girl survives.

Sometimes not.

The wave of nausea washed through John like a hot poison current.

He pushed himself away from the table, stumbled across the room to the bathroom, and roared vomit into the toilet.

When he had emptied his gut, he managed to stagger back across the room to the window. He leaned against the window frame and let the polluted breezes cool his sweaty brow. The night was bright with neon and silver sodium light, and long shadows were gouging jagged troughs in the sides of buildings. John stared at the cityscape for a moment, his brain vapor-locked with wooze and confusion and terror.

These journal entries.

These were not his thoughts.

This was the world's most brilliant frame-up.

Yet somehow, there was something familiar about the words, something personal. It was subtle, and if asked to explain it, John would have been at a loss. Except: There was something behind the words, underneath the narrative, as though the story were an iceberg, the words merely superficial, masking something even more vast and hideous underneath. John was certain of it, and now, in the wake of this discovery, he was growing more and more obsessed with not just finding his true identity but getting underneath these rambling words.

The method was the key. He had flashed on that phrase the previous night, just before blacking out. He had murmured it in his zombielike state the following morning, murmured it to Jessica Bales. And he had seen it referenced in the journal. Was it the method described by the narrator? Or was it something else? For that matter, to whom could this pathetic diary belong, if not to John?

He was going to find out.

Just as soon as he replenished his gin supply and had another drink.

Maybe several more drinks.

25

Nighttime

"WAIT—DON'T—NOT yet!"

The child had the covers pulled up to her chin, her little cherubic face buried in the pillow.

"Say when," Jessie said, her fingers poised on the light switch, her statuesque form filling the doorway. It was a ritual dance they went through each night regarding the number of hall lights left on, the amount of inches the door was cracked, and a host of other safety precautions designed to soothe the little girl's feverish imagination. Kit Bales was a big fan of spooky stories, horror comics, and scary TV shows—*during the daylight hours*—but come sunset, she reverted to childish wimphood and required as much hand-holding as any ordinary seven-year-old. Jessie was always happy to oblige.

"There!" the little girl blurted. "Right there, that's good."

"You sure?"

"Yeah, that's just right."

"Thank heavens," Jessie said with a cackle.

"Mom?"

"Yeah?"

"What happened to that man?"

Jessie took a breath before answering. She had been expecting this, but she was still much too unnerved by the day's events to plan out a response. The truth was, she had no idea how to discuss the situation with her child. Kit was whip-smart, and Jessie knew there was no way to tap-dance around the truth with the kid. "He got himself into some trouble," Jessie said at last.

"What kind of trouble?"

"I'm not sure, honey, but the thing is, we won't see that man ever, ever again."

"Why?"

"Because he ran away from the police, and if he comes back, the police will get him."

After a long pause, the child said: "Did he do something wrong?"

Jessie sighed, thinking to herself, *Why in God's name couldn't I have had a stupid child? Stupid children are so much easier.* "I think," Jessie replied finally, "he might have hurt some people."

"Hurt them how?"

Jessie chewed the inside of her cheek, thinking, then walked back into the room, pulling a lacquered chair beside Kit's bed. The room was pure Kit, an amalgam of early Grimm's fairy tales and *Star Wars* plastique, the shag-carpeted corners clogged with toys, the unicorn-print walls slathered with posters of Chewbacca and Joey Lawrence. Jessie took a seat next to the bed and said softly, "Honey, you remember when I told you there were some things about Mommy's job that were not really good for a little girl to hear about?"

Kit nodded grudgingly.

"Well . . ." Jessie gestured vaguely at the window. "This is . . . one of those things."

The little girl crossed her arms defensively, looking somewhat comical for a moment, like a pint-sized Egyptian pharaoh lying in state. "I'm gonna be eight years old, Mommy, I think I can handle it now."

Jessie smiled. "Maybe you're right, Boodle, but the fact is, I don't really know what he did. It's a job I never should have taken in the first place."

"But he needs your help."

"That may be true, Boodle, but I think he's done some bad things and I really don't want to help somebody who's done bad things."

"How do you know?"

"How do I know what?"

"How do you know he's done bad things?"

Jessie's smile faded. Once in a great while she would experience moments like these, when she would abruptly realize her daughter was on a completely different wavelength than she. Something was wrong here, and Jessie could tell it was important to the child. "What's the matter, honey?"

The little girl shrugged, looking away.

"Are you okay, Boodle?" Jessie asked, realizing that something was eat-ing at the child. The little girl was shrugging again. Jessie said, "Kit . . . are you all right?"

"Mommy, you always said you liked to help people, and that's why you're a private eye."

"That's true, Boodle, but the thing is—"

"That man named John McNally needs your help, and you said you would help him."

There was an awkward pause then, as Jessie tried to figure out what was going on. She stroked her daughter's baby-fine hair and said, "You like John McNally, don't you Boodle . . . ?"

The little girl shrugged again.

Jessie grinned. "It's okay to like somebody from the moment you meet them, Boodle—God knows, I liked you the moment I met you." Jessie leaned over and rubbed her nose across the little girl's nose, making the child giggle.

"That's silly, Mommy."

"Why is that silly?"

"Because you're my mommy and I came out of your vagina, and you *had* to like me."

Jessie laughed out loud despite her nerves. "Right again." She reached down and gently tucked the blankets around Kit's shoulders, then touched her cheek. "Now, that's enough sex education for one night. It's time to shuffle off to dreamland, honey."

Jessie kissed the child's forehead and went over to the door, pausing once to glance back in at the world's smartest kid, then turning out the lights.

Miles away, huddling in absolute darkness, another individual was being tucked in for the night.

Standing near the mouth of a putrid alley, the stench of rotting garbage engulfing him, Death ignored all external stimuli now and concentrated on the task at hand. His mind was focused like a pinpoint of sunlight refracted through a magnifying glass, focused on shapes moving behind stained venetian blinds fifty meters away. It was as though Death were being tested by this endless pursuit. His entire being—every fiber, every last molecule—hungered for relief, hungered for peace. It was a furnace inside him, speeding up his metabolism, sharpening his senses.

A sound skittered through the refuse behind him. Probably vermin. The opposite end of the evolutionary spectrum. It barely fazed him.

Death moved closer to the mouth of the alley, paying no attention to the scuttling noises behind him, paying no attention to the stench, paying no attention to the sounds of footsteps coming from the north or the distant sirens coming up a parallel street to the south. He was a machine, calibrated for results, as fit as any man his age had ever been. There was not an ounce of fat on his tapered, sinewy body. Shaped by obsessive weight training, yoga, and meditation, his powers of concentration were honed to those of a snake.

It was a good thing too, because he needed all his powers to find relief.

His grand experiment.

All the years of planning, strategizing, and dreaming—they were all coming to fruition now. It was so thrilling, it was positively intoxicating. He felt a buzzing at the base of his spine, and his ears were ringing. His fingers tingled. It was a feeling he knew all too well. The need was returning like a tide rolling in.

Soon he would find another sacrificial lamb.

26

Sinking the Hook

"WHAT ARE YOU doing?"

"Whattya mean, what am I doing?"

"I mean, what the hell are you *do*ing—calling me at home on this thing?" The voice on the other end of the line was stretched as taut as a banjo string. "Word gets out I'm talking to you on this deal, I'm out of a job."

"Who the hell am I gonna tell, Dolores? It's not like I chew the fat with the shift commander at the precinct house every morning." Jessie was gripping the receiver a little tighter than necessary. Standing in the middle of her kitchen, clad in a terry-cloth robe and fuzzy slippers, she had been pacing the rooms of the ranch house for the last half an hour, thinking about her conversation with Kit, thinking about how the child had instantly bonded with the amnesic stranger. Even Jessie herself—in spite of all the abominations at the Wagon Inn—still felt a certain ambivalence toward the man.

By the time the credits for *Nightline* had started rolling on the kitchen TV, Jessie had broken down and called an old comrade from her dispatcher days.

Dolores Loeb was a tough old broad from Area Thirteen who had started out as a second-shift dispatcher right behind Jessie, working under Stallworthy. A couple of years ago, Dolores had been promoted to desk sergeant in Violent Crimes, and she and Jessie had stayed in touch. They still played canasta every few months with a couple of gals from Homicide. But since Jessie had gone private, the two women rarely talked shop.

Until now.

"All right, look," Dolores's voice returned suddenly, sounding a tad weary. "You didn't hear this from me; you didn't here this from anybody, and if you say you did, I'll have you busted . . ."

"Fair enough."

"They got a gag on this thing like you wouldn't believe. Press is totally locked out. Everything's still so speculative, it's not worth talking about."

"I understand."

"The thing is, this guy—this amnesia guy—they like him in a serial-murder investigation."

"They like him?"

"They like him a lot."

"Any other suspects?"

"Nope. This guy is *The Guy.*"

Jessie felt a faint little tremor travel up her spine, and she glanced over at the back door. Beneath the darling little ruffled curtains, the dead bolt was secure. She said into the phone: "Can you tell me anything about the case?"

"Goddamnit, Jess, why the hell are you so interested in this thing?"

"No reason."

"Then, how come you want—" Dolores's voice halted suddenly, and there was a slightly breathy inhalation over the line, as though the woman had suddenly touched something hot. "Oh, Jesus, Bales, if you're working this thing—"

"I'm not working this thing, Dolores."

"—and it comes that I talked to you."

"Would you calm down, Dolores, I'm not working this thing."

But Jessie *was* working it, she was working it like crazy, she was working it overtime in her mind.

It was obvious to Jessie that McNally had been truthful about the amnesia—why else would he lead a private investigator to the smoking gun?—but the rest of it was shrouded in gray. On a superficial level, McNally certainly came off as innocent, and Jessie knew it wasn't beyond the realm of possibility that he had been framed. But it was a long shot at best, and long shots were better suited for federal authorities to sort out. Still, there was a nagging compulsion deep down inside Jessie to pursue this thing. Had McNally gotten to her? Had the white-hot desperation in his eyes sunk a hook into Jessie? *So what* if she was desperate herself?—desperately lonely—and *so what* if most of the men she encountered wore bib overalls and thought that the last great television show was *Green Acres?* That was no reason to become an anatomy experiment on some psycho's wall.

"Look, Jessie." Dolores's voice came back over the line sounding drained, washed out. "I gotta get back to my cats. Snoozer's got a bladder infection, and if I don't let her out before I go to bed, the kitchen'll smell like a urinal."

"Just a couple more questions, Dee, please. You haven't heard of a cop named Robert, or R, McNally, have you? Works County somewhere—Ingham or Ingram? Tall guy, broad shoulders, sandy-blond hair, wears expensive sport coats, Versace maybe."

After a long pause: "McNally? Did you say *McNally?* As in . . . John McNally?"

"Calm down, Dolores."

"You *are* working this thing, aren't you! Goddamnit, Jessie, you're gonna get me canned as sure as I'm standing here. This is a goddamn serial-murder case—total red-line case—and I'm singing karaoke to a goddamn PI, Jesus Christ Almighty, I'm finished—"

"Dolores, simmer down, Chrissake, you'd think I was asking you the combination to your kid's college fund."

"There won't *be* a college fund, I tell you anything else."

"Just tell me one thing. You haven't by any chance heard of some kind of screwy secret vigilante force working underneath the CPD, have you?"

"Vigilante—*what?* What the hell are you talking about?"

"I dunno. Maybe nothing. But let's say some Homicide dick gets a little frustrated, can't close a file. You know. Guy decides to play a little Charlie Bronson, Judge Dredd, whatever. I'm just wondering."

There was a long, awkward pause.

"Dee? You still there?" Jessie could tell she had struck a chord.

"Yeah, I'm still here," the voice returned, beaten. "I'm just trying to figure out whether or not I'm ruining my career by talking to you."

"Calm down, Dolores. Who's gonna know? Besides, last time we played cards, I told you all about Sy Weisman having the affair with the receptionist down at Keeler Brass, and Sy's my attorney, for Chrissake. Gimme a break."

After another moment: "All right. There are a few detectives who've been getting a little—I don't know—*carried away*. On this serial case, I mean. But I wouldn't call 'em vigilantes, Jess. For God's sake."

"What would you call them, Dee?"

"Jessie, if you saw some of these victims, these poor girls, I'm telling you—"

"If they're not vigilantes, Dolores, what would you call them?"

A pause, and then: "I would call them detectives who've been getting a little carried away."

Jessie pondered the possibilities for a moment, staring out the kitchen window. The backyard was buried in darkness, a thin glaze of moonlight on the grass, a latticework of shadows from the tool shed and the grapevine arbor. It was edging toward midnight, and the neighborhood was already fast asleep. "Lemme ask you one last thing, Dolores," Jessie said finally.

"Jessie, for God's sake . . ."

"Would you be willing to meet me down at the precinct house sometime? I'll buy you lunch, and I could take a quick gander at any group photos you might have of the various divisions, softball teams, ID photos, whatever."

"Absolutely *not*."

"C'mon, Dolores, you do me this one favor and—" There was a muffled noise outside the back window, cutting off Jessie's words, making her jump slightly. Sounded like someone nosing around the back of the garage, maybe bumping into the barbecue grill. "I gotta go, Dolores," Jessie muttered softly into the receiver, slowly moving over toward the wall phone. "I'll call you back."

"Don't call me anymore, Jessie, not about this McNally thing."

"I'll talk to you tomorrow," Jessie said, and gently hung up the receiver.

On the counter by the stove was a metal sugar canister with no sugar in it. Instead, it had a Smith & Wesson Model 442 snub-nosed revolver tucked inside. Jessie quickly turned off the overhead light and carefully dug the handgun out of the canister. She checked the cylinder and snapped it closed. Gripping the gun with both hands, defensive posture set, she backed over to the rear door and peered through the curtains.

There was another rattling noise out on the patio that made Jessie jerk slightly.

She glanced over toward the chain-link fence on the east edge of the yard and saw a little dark bundle of fur waddling along the fence line. It paused for a moment, turning toward the house, its tiny black-bead eyes shining orange, its ashy-white snout twitching.

Goddamn raccoon.

Jessie lowered the gun, turning back to her darkened kitchen, her heart still racing, her mouth dry with panic. She cursed herself for being so jumpy, and she took deep breaths until her pulse slowed back to normal. Goddamn raccoons had been a major nuisance from the day she had moved into the place. She was going to have to do something about it, get some traps or repellent or something.

She put the gun back in the canister and walked out of the kitchen.

Before going to bed, she went into the bathroom and searched through the medicine cabinet for a sleeping pill.

It was going to be extra difficult getting to sleep tonight.

27

Desolation

LOOK UP *desolation* in the dictionary, you'd be apt to find a picture of the Blue Island Hotel's front lobby at three A.M.: long shadows on the scarred parquet floor from the cracked front window, silhouettes of sickly yellow streetlights outside on the deserted corner. The front desk was a cage. The mesh window sat on the painted particle-board counter. Handwritten signs all around in blunt Magic Marker, phrases like NO PERSONAL CHECKS and NOT RESPONSIBLE FOR ARTICLES LEFT IN ROOMS. A wire-encased fan sat in one corner, rattling, circulating the stale air.

Polly Koslowski was sitting behind the counter, doing a crossword, trying to ignore the gloomy ambience. A stocky little forty-something woman with a bulldog face and spit curls so peroxided they looked almost silver-plated, she had been working the graveyard shift for so long now, she hardly noticed the desolation anymore. She was a second-generation Pole from the south side, married and divorced three times over, a couple of miscarriages and a current boyfriend doing three-to-five at Marion for two counts of theft by deception. Polly Koslowski was not the type to get spooked.

But tonight, for some reason, Polly had a nasty case of the willies.

It sure as hell wasn't because the place was full up. At the moment, there were only about a baker's dozen checked into the eighty-room flophouse. A handful of regulars on two—Fellson, Carmine, Biggs, and Jimmy Pete—all of them weathered, wasted old men trying to stay out of the drunk tank and hold down menial jobs down at the Catholic mission. On three, a couple of hookers and their respective johns. On four, some mealy-mouthed little salesman, his plump wife, and his two snot-faced ragamuffins. On five, that flaky bastard with the haunted eyes. Polly wondered if the reason for her edginess was *that* guy—with that bogus name he had he given—what was it? Johnson? Ralph Johnson?

The guy definitely seemed a couple of credits short of a degree. He had arrived earlier that day, sweating like a pig, his eyes bugging like he had electricity flowing through him, and clutching a moldy old notebook like it was the crown jewels. No baggage, no belongings, just the shirt on his back and that frigging notebook. He checked in, paid cash, and asked where he could buy some hooch. Then he holed himself up there all night, didn't eat, didn't show his face except to go out and buy more booze. In fact, he had just gone out for another pint less than fifteen minutes ago. Came back minutes later, expression knitted with pain, staggering across the lobby like the captain of the Titanic. He gave Polly the big, fat creeps.

A sudden noise drew Polly's attention away from the crossword puzzle.

It came from behind the scarred metal door to her left, the one that led into the corridor. A creaking sound, like a crack rippling through the ancient joists. Polly pursed her lips skeptically. In the seventeen years that she'd been working the front desk, she'd grown accustomed to every sound the old fleabag had to offer, from the groan of the radiators to the *foosh* of the window units, from the grinding sounds of the ice machine to the drone of faulty fluorescent tubes, from the muffled moans of frenzied fucking behind paper-thin walls to the sounds of arguments, yelling, drunken blubbering, even murmured prayers. The hotel was a menagerie of noises, and Polly Koslowski knew every one. Except the one she had just heard. It seemed incongruous, so incongruous that it made the stubbly hairs on the back of her neck stiffen.

She scooted off the edge of her stool and climbed out of the cage.

Padding across the lobby toward the metal door marked GUEST ROOMS, Polly had a premonition. In her mind's eye she saw the flaky character with the notebook, all sweaty and worked up with those weird eyes, huddling in the shadows, waiting for her with a big, fat butcher knife in his hand. It was a vivid image, and it lasted only a split second, but it was enough to make Polly's scalp crawl, and the back of her throat dry. Polly had a second cousin, Leanu from Romania, who was supposedly psychic. Operated a little fortune-telling parlor back in Bucharest. Polly had never believed in any of that crap.

But, then again, when it's three A.M. and you're alone in this dive . . .

"Bullshit," Polly mumbled to herself, stepping up to the door and gazing through the porthole of grimy glass.

She could see the empty hallway, the ratty maroon carpet stretching back into the shadows. Dim pools of sepia light from wall sconces shone down at irregular intervals, only deepening the shadows. But there was no movement, no sound. Polly chewed on her cheek, thinking, wondering about that goddamn vision she just had. She chewed and she thought and she finally got up enough nerve to push the door open.

The first thing that struck her as she entered the corridor was the odor.

It took her only a few seconds to place it, but during that span of time, a number of things suddenly happened so swiftly that Polly didn't have time to react or scream or even move: a glint of glass arcing out from the shadow behind the door, something sweeping around her from the opposite side, a strong male arm wrapping around her collarbone, a hand clamping over her mouth, and then something beginning to fizz—fizz like an Alka-Seltzer. The black ink had already started to cloud her vision, the invisible weight pulling her down into unconsciousness by the time she finally recognized the smell, and it was a smell that harkened all the way back to high school biology class, when a young Polly Koslowski had gotten squeamish dissecting a frog.

Formaldehyde?

28

Dark Ribbons

THE IMAGES coming furiously—warping, short-circuited kinetoscopic memories bursting through the static—*FLASH! Feather-thin blades ripping fabric—FLASH!—magenta stage lights flaming on—a small town in Michigan buried in the snow, faces vacu-forming, young women torn from yearbooks and student catalogs—SHOOP!-SHOOP!-SHOOP!—the countless little blurbs and notes and scribbled journal entries crackling like heat lightning through the static. Now the memories were flashing, sparking, arcing—a curtain parting in a darkened theater, a lone man silhouetted in the spotlight—leaves covered with blood, red paint spattered across rotting hardwood—CLICK-CLICK-CLICK!!—people, places, blood, faces, teeth, screaming, paper tearing, BLOOD!*

"No!"

John jerked awake on a carpeted floor, his heart doing a tribal-drum number, his head throbbing.

He lay there, prostrate, for a moment, blinking fitfully, his legs streaked with white-hot pain, his body partially wedged inside his half-ajar door. At first he didn't know where he was. He was fully dressed, and he could smell a musty, fibrous odor, like a dirty rug. He blinked some more, and swallowed the dry, pasty panic in the back of his throat, and turned his sore neck to gaze across the faded pastels of the ancient carpet, realizing suddenly that he was lying in the hallway outside the door to his hotel room. Had he fallen there in the night?

Had he been sleepwalking?

The flashbulb images from his dreams still clung to his consciousness like retina burns on the backs of his eyes. More information crackling through the white noise in his mind. More lightning bursts. He could still remember some of them—the yearbook photos, the blood, the scenes from the snowy little town in Michigan. How had he known it was Michigan? He tried to get up, but the moment he motivated his legs and his torso, the pain bolted up his carriage, flaring in his hips. He collapsed back to the floor, gasping, holding his ribs as though they might burst under the pressure.

Good Lord, he was a mess. Between the injuries that were still mending and his insatiable thirst for alcohol, he was destroying himself. He hadn't had a moment's peace or a decent meal in more than three days. Worst of all, he kept rationalizing the need for booze: He needed it so he could think straight, and he needed it to squelch the pain in his joints, and he needed it to dull the horror that had come with each page of that hideous journal. At this rate, he was going to drink himself right back into the hands of the law, and probably an institution, for the rest of his life. He shivered suddenly, feeling bone-cold.

A street noise swirled outside a nearby window, drifting up on the morning breezes. Sounded like the squeal of a police patrol car, maybe the sharp bleat of a PA speaker.

John managed to rise to his feet and hobble over to the barred window. Pressing against the grimy glass, he strained to see over the ledge. He could just barely make out the street corner five stories below, the row of stone bus-stop benches, and the entrance into the subway. There was a flurry of activity down there. A pair of Chicago police cruisers and an EMT ambulance were parked in front of the hotel at various haphazard angles, several scores of neighborhood people crowding around the yellow cordon tape just beyond the vehicles. A fourth cruiser had just pulled up, nearly knocking a dozen or so gawkers over like bowling pins. The cops were yammering at the onlookers through bullhorns, trying to keep the throngs backed up toward the opposite sidewalk. It was pandemonium.

Just then, the sound of rickety elevator doors came rattling down the corridor from the opposite end.

John whirled and rushed back into his room, supercharged with animal-instinct panic. He slammed the door shut, threw the dead bolt, and hooked the chain lock. His heart was racing again, tumbling in his chest like a loose bearing. He had no hard evidence to think the cops were here for him, other than his raging paranoia and his suspicions that he might have given himself away during his little fugue-state sleepwalk last night. He hurried over to the desk, grabbed the journal, scooped up some stray notes, and stuffed it all into a cheap nylon rucksack that he had purchased at the liquor store next door.

There was a fire escape outside the rear window; John had noticed it the previous night and had made a mental note that it was there in case he needed to make a hasty exit. The question was, could he get the congealed window open? He went over, unlatched it, and tried to muscle it up. No good. The thing was welded shut with age and countless coats of paint.

Outside his door, something moved, and then loud, abrupt knocking. "Mr. Johnson?" a voice asked. "Chicago police."

Then another voice: "Anyone home? Hello? Mr. Johnson? Just need to ask you a couple questions."

John grabbed the desk chair and slammed it against the window.

It took several tries, but the fourth blow broke the glass. A fifth wallop collapsed the pane, but then there were other concussive sounds behind him, across the room, outside the door in the hallway. Big, beefy bodies slamming into wood, the ancient hardware creaking, the chain jangling. John squeezed through the window, hauling the rucksack over his shoulder, his mind racing, wondering wildly if he was doomed to make these desperate exits through windows for the rest of his natural life.

And then he was out.

He found himself on the waffle-iron grating of the fire-escape platform, the noxious wind buffeting him, the city smells of malt, mold, and monoxide surrounding him. He crept over to the rusted iron ladder that was mounted off the end of the platform. The ladder was eighteen inches wide, and bracketed to the ancient iron foot rail, and the moment John started down it, the whole assembly seemed to pitch to one side and then the other like a faulty lifeboat. John held on for dear life, the pain surging in his joints, the rusty metal shrieking. It took him several frenzied moments to reach the last iron rung. Then he jumped.

He landed on the scarred pavement, the impact like a shotgun blast up each leg.

Radio voices echoed off a nearby wall, and John saw that he was standing in a narrow alley cut between the two tall buildings, dark as the deepest forest, ripe with garbage, lined with wet cardboard boxes on either side. The pain was making him woozy, and his knees were weak, but he managed to stay standing. His adrenal glands were revving now, sending spurts of energy-rush to his organs and limbs. To the east, about fifty yards away, the alley opened out onto the same street that ran past the front façade of the Blue Island Hotel. About twenty yards in the other direction was an intersection of three buildings, bordered by a tight passageway, closed off with chain-link fencing. The fencing looked old, ragged enough to break through.

John started padding toward it, but just as he approached the chain-link, something caught his eye in the darkness off his right. Something in the passageway that led toward the street, a sudden flash. Then another. And another. Dry silver light, like an artificial sun, pulsing rhythmically. John moved behind a Dumpster, crouching down and peering around its corner, and he saw the filthy ground-level window embedded in the side of the hotel. There were shadows of people moving behind it, and the flash of a camera strobe, and John had to really squint and concentrate to see what was going on. Then he realized he was looking into the tawdry little lobby of the Blue Island Hotel.

Then he saw the blood.

It was tossed all around the lobby like party streamers, ribbons of it, arterial spray painting the broken-down counter, the mesh cage and the walls, so dark it looked like chocolate syrup in the sudden bursts of strobe light. Forensic technicians were huddling over something slumped in a chair behind the counter, their white-gloved hands working at it, brushing it, taking photographs of it.

It was the night clerk, the woman with POLLY on her name tag, facedown, her hair matted with blood. The back of her blouse was flayed open. John inhaled a shocked breath, convulsing against the Dumpster as though he had been punched in the stomach. The poor woman had been stabbed repeatedly from behind, her flesh blooming deep scarlet flowers. Whoever did the deed had wanted to make a point, and the obscene banality of it, the pathetic little lobby striped in blood, and the bored night clerk doomed to slump in eternal tableau, made John look away.

Tears burned his eyes, and his stomach seized up all tight and hot.

He realized that this brutal murder was meant for him, the next phase of his damnation, and he was powerless to stop it, powerless to fight it. It was as though the underside of the city and Fate itself were conspiring against him, swallowing him, digesting him in their rancid, evil juices. He tried to motivate his legs and convince his body to get the hell out of there, but he was paralyzed, riveted to that cold, scabrous cement, gazing off at the dark ribbons crisscrossing the lobby. Why? Why this poor, morose woman with her peroxide curls and sad eyes? Was she one of the "empty ones" mentioned in the journal? If only John could remember his past life—and the etchings of lost memories that were tormenting his dreams—perhaps he could learn *who,* and *what,* and *how.*

And *why.*

Another spurt of radio voices came from the nearby street, closer this time, and John stiffened. He could see the long silhouettes of patrolmen slicing through the dust motes seventy yards away, entering the mouth of the alley, their shadows pouring across the pavement like cancer, guns drawn, hands cupped in the tripod posture, ready to fire.

John found his legs.

He sprang from the stench of the Dumpster and crept across the passage to the fencing, crouching down as low as possible, keeping as quiet as possible, finding a rip in the chain-link, pulling it up like a doggie-door flap and then squeezing under it.

Then he vanished into the shadows between the buildings.

29

Agony in the Heart

BEFORE THE PHONE started to ring, Jessie was treating herself to her morning ritual—soaking in a hot tub of bath salts, nursing a cup of French roast, smoking a Carlton, and trying to imagine that she and Kit were anywhere but in Randall, Illinois. It was nearly nine A.M., and the Fitzgeralds had just picked up Kit for school, and now the house had that pristine, sunny silence that houses get after their morning rush has passed. It was the time of day that Jessie usually spent in delicious limbo, spoiling herself with a quiet hour of woolgathering.

Today, however, her thoughts were churning furiously, making her crazy.

She was thinking about John McNally, and wondering why she was so ambivalent about him. She was thinking about trust, and fate, and her rotten track record with men. From the moment she had set up shop in Randall, she had suffered through a succession of disastrous relationships. There was the junior college professor whom Jessie had frightened off with her rabid libertarian politics. There was the insurance agent whom Jessie had scared shitless on the dance floor. There was the bartender who couldn't get it up, the college student with the mommy complex, and the cook with the chip on his shoulder. All disasters. But now Jessie had topped even herself in the catastrophic relationships department.

The handsome client who turned out to be a homicidal maniac.

Maybe it was simply a family curse that went all the way back to Jessie's relationship with her father, Jerome "Jerry" Bales—gym teacher extraordinaire, friendly neighborhood fascist. To say that the old man was uncomfortable around the female of the species would have won the Understatement of the Century. The truth was, Jerry Bales was excruciatingly inept with women, especially those in his immediate family. But his strained relationship with his daughter reached its nadir one humid August night in the seventies.

It began like any other night during Jessie's halycon teenage years. She had been out cruising the main drag with three of her girlfriends, looking for trouble, passing around a bottle of Annie Green Springs apple wine. For some reason they had ended up on Northmoor Road, a local lover's leap, and had stopped to take a potty break. Creeping through the woods, looking for a private place to tinkle, Jessie had heard noises coming through the foliage. A pair of young lovers huddling in the weeds. Jessie cautiously approached, expecting to see one of her high school pals, but when she got close enough to make out the faces, Jessie got the shock of her life. Her father was nuzzling Miss Lochman, the girls' P.E. teacher, in the moonlight.

Jessie had rushed out of the woods that night as though she had seen a ghost, never looking back, never even acknowledging it to anybody, including her mother and father. But the experience had changed Jessie forever, curdling something deep down inside her, sealing her destiny. She would never completely trust another human being again, and it probably was the first step toward her becoming a professional snoop. But now the old man was long gone—succumbing to a protracted case of liver cancer six years ago—and Jessie was a thirty-something single parent struggling to keep her investigation firm afloat in a leaky ranch house.

And the damn phone was ringing out in the living room.

"Shit," Jessie muttered, emerging from the tepid suds of the bubble bath.

She snubbed out her cigarette in a little clam-shell ashtray and quickly toweled off, dripping all over the bathroom floor, smelling of herbal soak and liniment. She threw on her terry-cloth robe, wrapped a towel—turban-style—around her hair, and rushed out the door, padding wetly across the hardwood.

She answered the phone on the fifth ring.

"Jessie Bales."

"Jessie, it's John, John McNally."

There was a taut, awkward pause then, an odd ambience in the background, a rushing noise. John's voice sounded weak, squeezed dry.

The pause stretched on, and Jessie found herself wondering where she had stashed her guns, whether she had locked all the doors, and who she might call first—the sheriff, who was a complete idiot, or the state police, who would be less likely to question her inexplicable delay in turning this psychopath over to the authorities.

"Jessie? You there?"

"I'm here," she said finally, gazing out through the front curtains. Morning sunlight was filtering down through the leaves of her maple trees, dappling her lawn. The neighborhood was bustling with morning activity, school buses coming and going, men in pickups with lunch boxes heading off to work at Armour Star. It was all a little too cozy for a showdown between a private investigator and a suspected serial killer. "Where are you, John?" she asked softly.

"I'm at a pay phone. It's not—not too far from your place."

Cold panic spurted through Jessie's stomach. "What in God's name are you doing?"

"I wanted to make sure I wouldn't be ambushed again—you know—if I came to your office. I was hoping and praying you hadn't contacted the police yet."

"Turn yourself in, John."

"Listen to me, Jessie—I'm not a psychopath—I'm telling you right now—I'm innocent."

"What do you want from me, John?"

"I want you to finish the job—the job I hired you for."

Jessie could hear the emotion strangling the man's voice, the way he nearly ran out of breath at the end of each sentence. It was obvious that he either believed he was innocent or was the greatest living actor in the world. The jury was still out on that one. But regardless of how believable he was to Jessie—or how tantalizing his case was becoming—she preferred to stay as far away from this lunatic as possible. "With all due respect," Jessie said evenly, "I believe I found your identity." She wiped a bead of moisture off her nose with her sleeve. "Now, if that particular identity doesn't suit your needs, well, then I'm real sorry, I don't know what to tell you."

"That isn't me, Jessie, I promise you."

"How do you know?"

"I'm certain of it . . . you're just gonna have to trust me on that."

"Trust *you?* Jesus Christ, John, how can *you* even trust you? How do you know the amnesia didn't split your personality into two halves?"

"What do you mean?"

"This other guy—he might be exactly that—another guy who's really *you.*"

There was a long, noisy pause, and Jessie heard the sound of a truck in the background, rumbling by the pay phone. She guessed that McNally was probably calling from the corner of Losey and Chatham, near the old fairgrounds. It was a ten-minute walk from Jessie's house.

When John's reply finally came back over the line, his voice had gotten weaker, yet somehow more resolved. "I would never be capable of doing those things, Jessie."

"How do you know that for sure when you don't even remember your own name?"

After another anguished pause: "Because of my heart."

"Your heart?"

"The pain in my heart—that's the only way I can explain it to you—it's like agony. This journal that I found in the Wagon Inn room—Jessie, you wouldn't believe some of the things in there, horrible things."

Jessie thought about it for a moment, and she thought about who would frame a guy like this, and why. Certainly, stranger things had happened in this crazy, imperfect world. Overzealous police had been known to fudge a little bit to put a serial case to bed. But, then again, what were the odds that a guy who was being framed would get amnesia? It seemed too damn bizarre, not to mention too damn convenient. Could John have been framed *after* the amnesia-causing injuries? It just seemed too weird, even for Jessie Bales to swallow. "You can't come here, John," she said finally. "I'm sorry."

"Give me one chance, Jessie," his voice urged desperately. "That's all I'm asking."

"John . . ."

"Five minutes—five minutes face-to-face, and I think I can convince you."

"John, come on . . ."

"You can throw me out on the street if you're not convinced—please, Jessie—I'm asking you to take a chance. If I was this monster, and I wanted to hurt you, don't you think I would have done it by now?"

"I don't know what to think anymore," she told him.

"Five minutes, Jessie, please. I need your help."

Jessie gazed across the living room at the linen curtains, open slightly in the middle, bulging inward on subtle breezes coming through the screens. Thank God, Kit was safe at school—for the time being, at least—but she would be coming home in a few hours, and the last thing Jessie wanted to do was put her in harm's way. Jessie took a deep breath and thought about it. She could smell the odors of freshly cut grass and motor oil wafting through the window. Frank Peets must have mowed his lawn this morning, the first cut of the season. Peets was a long-haul trucker in his late fifties who lived next door, a real redneck who tended to stare at Jessie's ass every chance he got. The good thing was, if there was a problem, and Jessie got in trouble, Peets would be over here in a flash with that hog-leg twelve-gauge he kept in a strongbox out in his garage.

"All right," Jessie said after another long moment of deliberation. "Five minutes, and not a second more. You understand?"

"I'll be right there."

There was a click, and the line was disconnected.

30

Death Wish

JESSIE SLAMMED THE phone down, cursing herself for being so stupid. She stormed back into the bathroom, finished drying off, then went into her bedroom to get dressed. Hurriedly pulling on her clothes—nothing too provocative; baggy cotton blouse, khaki slacks, hair pulled back in a pony-tail—she found herself wondering if she had a death wish. Up to now, her anonymity had been fairly protected; if McNally had been busted and he had mentioned her name, she could have pleaded ignorance. But the moment he walked back through her door and into her life, she was an accessory, pure and simple. So, why was she doing this? Why was she doing this to Kit? Was Jessie's ego *that* weak? Was her curiosity *that* uncontrollable?

The last thing Jessie did before going back into the front room was dig out her Raven .25. She checked the magazine, snapped the clip into the butt, and yanked the slide—that reassuring *snick-clang* noise in her ears as a round slid into the chamber.

Then she went into the living room and waited.

A few minutes later, the doorbell chimed.

"Hold on a second," Jessie called out, getting out of her chair, going over to the door. She stood behind the hinges, feet shoulder-width apart, knees slightly bent. The Raven was gripped tightly in her right hand, her finger on the trigger guard. She firmly grasped the doorknob and said, "I'm going to open the door, and I want you to take one step inside and turn to your left with your hands in plain view."

"I understand," the muffled voice said from outside the front door.

Jessie opened the door.

John took a careful step into the house, then turned toward the east wall, his arms raised in surrender. Jessie slammed the door shut. John was wearing the same jeans and T-shirt—which were surely getting pretty ripe by now—and a beige windbreaker that appeared to be recently purchased. He had a nylon rucksack over his shoulder—also newly purchased. Jessie kept the gun aimed at the back of his head. "You can turn around now," Jessie told him.

John turned.

Their gazes locked.

Something deep down inside Jessie turned suddenly like a tumbler in a combination lock. Maybe it was the watery glaze in John's eyes, the desperation welling in him, or the way his lower jaw shivered slightly as he waited for Jessie to call the next play. Or maybe it was something else entirely. For a while now, Jessie had been entertaining errant thoughts about getting close to a man with amnesia. How strange it must be to reteach a man everything about himself, about his past. But in another way, there was also something liberating about it—to be able to reshape a man from scratch—it seemed almost seductive. No baggage, no expectations, no built-in hostilities. Just a blank slate.

The perfect man.

"After what you saw the other day," John said finally, "I don't expect you to ever trust me completely, all right?"

Jessie kept the gun aimed at his left eye. "What's in the backpack, John?"

"The journal," he said softly. "The one I took from the Wagon Inn."

"Keep talking," she said.

"If you think about it, there are only two possible explanations for my situation."

"And those are . . . ?"

"Either I'm guilty and—you know—I don't remember it, or I've been set up and I don't remember it."

Jessie thought about it for a moment, the gun still poised. "Okay. Sure. So what?"

"Therefore," John continued, "you've got an unbelievable opportunity here."

"What are you talking about?"

"What I'm talking about is the missing-person case of the century, Jessie—think about it—I'm talking about accomplishing something important, something a lot more significant than catching the local druggist cheating on his wife . . . or, or, or, or finding lost dogs."

"That's good, John," Jessie said, the gun staying right where it was. "Appeal to my ego, that's a good approach."

The only problem was, the son of a bitch was right. This whole thing had taken root in Jessie's brain, and now there wasn't anything she could do about it. Her resistance was weakening like flowers wilting in time-lapse.

"What would be the point?" John said. "I mean, if I was playing games, wouldn't I just vanish?"

Jessie shrugged, the gun wavering now. It was as though she had discovered that her dance partner was Charlie Manson, and then had discovered that he was a damn good dancer. The worst part was that Jessie actually liked this guy. She actually *liked* him. She wondered if it had anything to do with the fact that her daughter had taken to John right off the bat. Kids have a weird sixth sense about adults. Kids can see through a lot of things that adults don't necessarily see. "How the hell do I know why you haven't vanished?" Jessie finally said with a weary smile. "I'm just a lowly dog chaser."

John looked deeply into Jessie's eyes then, so deeply that Jessie felt a tightness in her stomach. "I promise you this, Jessie," he said evenly. "If I'm the one, if I've done these things—" He stopped suddenly, swallowing hard, very hard, as though he were swallowing ground glass, as though the very possibility of such a thing were almost too much for him to bear. "If it's me, then I'll shoot *myself* and leave a note giving you the credit for catching me, and I'm serious about that, totally serious."

Jessie let the gun drop, her entire body relaxing. "Jesus Christ, McNally, you don't have to shoot yourself—I'll do it for you."

John let out a sigh of relief, smiling. "Fair enough, Inspector."

Jessie shook her head, reaching around and shoving the Raven into the back of her slacks. "For now, I think I'll just try and kill you with my coffee."

For the better part of two hours, they sat in the kitchen and talked and drank coffee, and John drew diagrams on napkins, describing images from his blackouts and fractured pieces of his memories. He showed her passages from the diary, and he spoke of darkened theaters, and sides of beef, and snowy towns in Michigan, and yearbooks, and broken colored glass, and a whole host of odd, esoteric little images that made no sense whatsoever. Throughout most of the morning, Jessie kept that little semiautomatic tucked into the back of her khakis. Sure, it was uncomfortable while she was sitting at the kitchen table, the gun digging into her back, but it was more uncomfortable being around John without it.

Around noon, Jessie put a call in to an old friend, Tom Beavers.

A big, overgrown farm kid partial to greasy Caterpillar hats and baggy dungarees, Beavers was a night security guard at a local Wal-Mart, an amateur artist who had done sketch work off and on for the Will County Sheriff's Department. Jessie wanted to get a working sketch of the cop who had tried to erase John from the earth, and Tom Beavers seemed the logical choice to draw it.

Beavers and Jessie went way back. They'd even gone out a few times, but Beavers had one helluva drinking problem, which had put the kibosh on further dates. But Jessie had stayed close with the man, and she trusted him enough to do a sketch or two and stay quiet about it.

Sure enough, the moment Jessie got Beavers on the phone, Beavers told her he would be happy to oblige.

Fifteen minutes later, Tom Beavers was standing on Jessie's doorstep with his leather-bound sketch pad and a toolbox full of art supplies.

They did the sketch on the back porch. Jessie made a pitcher of iced tea and some chicken salad sandwiches, and they sat at the round metal table on metal chairs and ate and tried to make a picture of the detective who had come to kill John at the clinic. The back porch was screened in to keep the insects away, the floor covered with all-weather AstroTurf, the ceiling festooned with hanging plants, brimming with flowers and ivy and ferns. John sat on the edge of his chair for most of the time, describing the cop in great detail, every once in a while pondering Beavers's sketch, making suggestions and midcourse adjustments. Jessie kept quiet mostly, just watching, thinking about the man who was materializing on Tom Beaver's pad of onionskin.

Asked to describe the face, Jessie would have said it was perfectly average. Maybe a little angular, sure, a little gaunt, certainly, but nothing outstanding. Good cheekbones, stylish haircut, vaguely foreign-looking, almost Scandinavian. If Jessie were forced to come up with a celebrity he most closely resembled, she probably would have said the man was a cross between Max Von Sydow and that actor who played Jesus in *The Last Temptation of Christ*, what's-his-name—William? Willem? That's it. *Willem Dafoe.*

Jessie really had to hand it to big old Tom Beavers, though; the boy sure could draw.

After the three-by-five-inch sketch was done, Jessie offered Beavers a beer. Beavers happily accepted, and ended up inhaling three Budweiser longnecks, proceeding to tell John some tall tales about Jessie's checkered past. An hour later, Jessie looked at her watch and told Beavers thank you so much for the great work, but it was getting late, and Kit would be coming home soon, and they all had a lot of work to do. Beavers eventually got up and made his way to the front door, getting all drunk-sentimental all of a sudden. Jessie ushered him down the front walk to his car, slipping him five twenty-dollar bills and telling him to take care of himself.

Beavers roared away, his car stereo blasting an old Lynyrd Skynyrd tune.

When Jessie returned to the patio, she found John staring at the sketch.

"You okay?" she asked.

John just nodded and kept staring at that drawing. "Goddamn psychopath—tried to kill me in cold blood."

"I know, John," Jessie said. "And that's why we're going to track him down and find out why."

Then, just for an instant, before she started to clear the table, preparing for the afternoon ahead, Jessie found herself wondering whether there was something that the goddamn psychopath had known that she didn't.

31

No-Man's-Land

THE WIND CLAWED at John's face as he sat in the passenger seat, watching the landscape stream by either side of the Cadillac. The ridiculous disguise was driving him batty, the blond wig itching unmercifully under his Cubs cap as they sped northward on Highway 57, the ashen overcast sun beating down on them. The sunglasses kept sliding down the bridge of his nose, and the ponytail that dangled out of the back of the cap kept whipping back and forth in the wind. But Jessie had insisted on the ludicrous disguise, explaining that it was the safest way for John to be in public.

"I want you to do something else for me," Jessie was hollering now over the din of metal-thunder and wind. "Before we get to the precinct house."

"Name it," John said, his heart galloping in his chest, faster and faster as they closed in on the city. He was watching Jessie drive, a cigarette poised between her pink lacquered fingernails, the wind playing havoc with her hairdo. She was a real character, this woman, a complete original, and for some reason John had the feeling he had gotten extremely lucky when he had stumbled upon her little display ad in the Randall Yellow Pages.

"I want you to promise me," Jessie said, "you'll do whatever I tell you to do when we're out in public."

"Of course," John said.

"I'm talking *to the letter,* John. Down to the tiniest detail. Whatever I say, you do."

"Yeah, absolutely, you bet."

"I want to hear you say it."

"Say what?"

"*Promise* me," she barked at him.

John felt a twinge of dread in his gut. Back at Jessie's house, they had argued over whether it was a good idea for John to come along on this little reconnoitering mission. John had thought it better for Jessie to venture out on her own, keeping in contact via telephone while John waited either at Jessie's or at the motel. He'd been spooked by the events at Blue Island, and wasn't exactly ready to plunge back out into no-man's-land yet. But Jessie had been adamant about bringing John along. She claimed she wanted them to become leaves on the wind, following any clue, no matter how trivial, *together*, in order to get closer to John's past. Jessie wanted to keep him moving, to keep him stimulated. She wanted to play free-association games, utilizing key images and phrases from John's spells and blackouts. She also wanted to try to precipitate another blackout by getting John drunk, then record his murmurings, making notes, then feed them back to him. She also was thinking about hypnosis. She told John that they might be able to find a psychologist or therapist somewhere who would put John under deep hypnosis.

All this made a great deal of sense to John. He felt as though his brain were one of those little plastic puzzle games, the ones with the little tiles that slide from one configuration to another, successively making room for one another, and the more you worked the puzzle, the more it gelled into a single, recognizable shape.

But John also knew that the real reason Jessie wanted him by her side was to keep him away from Kit.

John and Kit had hit it off from the very first moment they had laid eyes on each other—a fact that made John wonder if he had any kids of his own. But John could also tell that this attraction had stymied Jessie. It was obvious that Jessie still didn't trust John around Kit, and the truth was, John didn't fault Jessie one little bit. The child was a gem—a seven-year-old going on forty—and John would be hard-pressed himself to trust a stranger around her. And even though a simple solution would have been to ensconce Kit at the neighbors' house while John waited at the motel, John could certainly understand Jessie's overprotectiveness.

"I promise," John said softly, "I'll do whatever you want me to do."

"Raise your hand, and repeat after me—I, John McNally—come on, say it!"

John smiled in spite of his nerves, then raised his right hand and said, "I, John McNally—"

"—do hereby swear that I will follow to the letter every single command of the great detective goddess."

John dutifully recited the oath.

Jessie looked at him. "That's good, John, because what we're about to do is really go out on a limb. You understand what I'm saying?"

"I understand."

There was a stretch of windy silence.

"The Area Thirteen precinct house is in a scroungy little section of Pullman," Jessie told him, lighting another cigarette. The smoke swirled around her head and diffused wildly. "About six blocks from the Calumet. I saw it a couple times back when I was working for the CPD."

"You're thinking our cop might be working out of this precinct house?"

Jessie shrugged. "It's not the closest squad room to Higinbotham Woods, but it's the closest one with a bunch of Chicago Homicide dicks."

John nodded.

Jessie's plan was to begin at the police precinct house closest to the Reinhardt Clinic north of Joliet. (John was amazed to learn that Jessie was once a cop herself, and that she still had quite a few friends on the force, and that she could probably bribe one of her cronies to take a look at the composite sketch of the killer cop.) The idea was to track down the cop and then have Jessie pose as an eyewitness. She would claim that she had seen this dastardly villain, John McNally, not three days ago running across her tomato patch—or some such nonsense—and that she thought she should report it right away. She would engage this man in a conversation and get as much information as possible. Jessie also wanted to get John's fingerprints and run a check on them, but this was going to take some time and maneuvering. Such a check might also give them away and get them apprehended.

He turned and gazed out through his tinted glasses at the passing terrain.

The strip malls and scattered woodlands had deteriorated into a vast sea of rooftops and wasted cement as the highway climbed its trestled path into the south side. The overcast light accentuated the hazy afternoon pollution from Midway, Gary, and the steelworks to the south. The air had a thick, medicinal smell to it, like sticky syrups that had spilled and commingled.

John was just starting to think that maybe he could use another stiff drink when the sound of Jessie's voice cut through the wind.

"John? You with me on this?"

John looked over at her. "Sorry, I was just . . . thinking."

"Yeah, well, think about this: There's an alley across the street from the precinct house. While I go inside, I want you to wait there for me. The alley's our best bet because it's got several escape routes—in case things get dicey. There's one at the opposite end, one that leads into a neighboring building, and one that goes up the fire-escape ladder. You following this? John?"

John told her he was following her perfectly.

They got off the highway at 111th Street and drove eastward toward the lake.

Ten minutes later, Jessie pulled into a Self-Park lot a block and a half south of the precinct house. She parked, opened up the Caddy's trunk, and pulled out a few items: a large leather satchel in which she had stashed the composite sketch of the cop, the dog-eared journal, and her Beretta nine-millimeter pistol with two extra clips. She gave John the satchel, and then ushered him across the street. They made their way down an alley behind two dingy gray-brick warehouses, then headed north. Jessie had been wrong about the alley. Turned out it wasn't directly across the street from the precinct house—not even close.

It was half a block south.

"I shouldn't be more than fifteen minutes—tops," Jessie said as she ushered John behind a metal Dumpster near the mouth of the alley. From this vantage point, John could just barely see the front steps of the precinct house. "You stay there until I come and get you. Understand?"

John told her he understood.

Then Jessie dug into the satchel—which was still hanging off John's shoulder—and rooted out the composite sketch. "I'm gonna take the sketch with me," she said. "The gun I'm gonna leave with you; the metal detectors at the doors would pick it up. Do *not* touch it. It is strictly a throw-down weapon, meaning you get caught, you throw it down. You understand what I'm saying?"

John nodded, then watched Jessie turn and stride toward the street.

It took her only a few moments to cross the half-block and vanish inside the precinct house.

John shivered in the cool, dank shadows. In the distance, he could see that it was just another day for the Chicago police, their squad cars canted along the curb in front of the precinct building, a few beat cops leaning against the hoods of their vehicles, drinking coffee from paper cups, kibitzing idly. John scanned both ends of the street. It was a gray, depressing area, industrial warehouses mostly, with a few brownstones, studios, and lofts mixed in. The results of creeping gentrification—a spindly tree here, a new bus-stop bench there, everything sandblasted, prefabricated.

But mostly it was the old, slumped, road-weary universe of the beat cops and the homeless.

If there was ever a time John needed a drink, it was now. He wanted one so badly, it felt as though his throat were constricting, his gut turning inside out, his scalp itching under the absurd wig and baseball cap, his lips burned and cracked, his nostrils seared from the heat of his need. Just a simple drink. Nothing fancy, just a jigger or two of Tanqueray. Yes, that would be just fine.

John closed his eyes and prayed to God that he would be able to get a drink soon.

All at once, a jolt of nausea gripped his insides, and he wavered dizzily, grabbing the greasy corner of the Dumpster to brace himself, a succession of firecracker-bright images assaulting his brain—images of mutilated faces, a theater stage, rotting rib meat, the sound of a madman's words: *"I imbue the empty cells with my own purposeful ones, then I drive off into the night, full of peace and satisfaction again; I've done my part; I've filled an empty vessel with meaning and value"*—and, finally, a powerful wave washing over him, just for a moment, a feeling of primal, animalistic lust. It was a sensation an animal must get in the wild while stalking its prey—a feral blood-lust, all white teeth and saliva hot—erupting like pure adrenaline from John's innards.

The thrill of the hunt.

Then it flickered out as abruptly as it had first materialized.

And then there was nothing but a blank screen in John's head, and the sound of his own whisper.

"Just one little drink, God, just one . . ."

A block north, a very large young man dressed all in black was hunched over the steering wheel of his rust-pocked import, breathing hard, squinting against the glare of the overcast sun on the car's hood.

He was sweating profusely, trying to gather his wits about him, trying to make his heart stop chugging.

Billy Marsten had never attempted to follow anybody without being noticed—at least not on Chicago's crowded thoroughfares—and the strain of it had taken its toll. Billy's eyes were stinging, and his arms and legs ached, and his throat was as dry as a salt mine. But it looked as though he had been successful. Neither McNally nor the lady detective seemed aware of Billy's presence, and that was good. It meant that all the money that Billy had shelled out to Professor Harkonian to get the ID run on the Caddy's license had not been in vain. More important, it meant that he could go on observing his hero from a distance, and maybe even capture the ultimate collectible for a fan such as Billy.

A photo of a famous maniac in the commission of a crime.

Reaching over to his camera case, Billy pulled out the baby Nikon, checked its frame indicator, then checked its batteries. Then he stuffed it into the side pocket of his black leather jacket.

He was ready now.

Twisting around toward the backseat, Billy peered through the cracked rear window at the mouth of the alley in the distance. He could just barely make out a thin shadow slicing up the side of an adjacent brick wall, the silhouette of John McNally. Beautiful, delicate. As soon as McNally continued on, Billy would be ready. Billy would be right behind him. Everything was perfect.

Almost.

The only problem was the slight prickling sensation along the back of Billy's neck that had started all the way back when he had picked up the Cadillac's trail down in Randall. It wasn't anything concrete, just a tightness in Billy's gut, a vague uneasiness that could certainly turn out to be nothing but Billy's imagination. Still, the sensation was real, and Billy figured he might as well face the fact.

It felt like somebody was following *him.*

32

Red Line

IN THE DISTANT haze, the precinct house was shimmering in waves of heat and pollution, and John kept his gaze riveted to the shadows of the entrance. Minutes later—a stretch of time that seemed an eternity—a shapely figure emerged from the ancient double doors, shuffling quickly down the steps. It was Jessie, and she looked nervous.

John met her at the mouth of the alley.

"Something pretty goddamn weird is going on," Jessie was murmuring softly as she ducked into the shadows of the alley and led John over to the wall. Her face was flushed slightly, moist from the effort of trotting across the street as well as from the excitement of her discovery. She loosened the top of her blouse and reached down into her brassiere—a gesture that took John by surprise; it was something he thought only characters in pulp novels and movies did—and pulled out a small black-and-white photograph mounted on cardstock. The man in the photo bore quite a resemblance to the man in Beavers's composite sketch.

"What is it?" John asked, taking the photograph from her and inspec-`ting it.

"Either I'm crazy or that looks like our boy," Jessie said, buttoning her blouse back up.

John took off his sunglasses and looked at the photo in the dim light, a sharp metal scalpel of chills slicing up the backs of his legs.

It was the man who had come to the Reinhardt Clinic to kill him. Posed against an airbrushed backdrop, dressed in a smartly tailored suit, he sat at an angle to the camera, his face turned toward the lens. His smile was pure public relations. All stiff and Bachrach-wooden. The picture was dated, maybe circa early eighties, judging by the style of the three-piece suit and the amount of sandy-blond hair on the man's head. But the eyes were the same. Cold, chiseled gemstones the color of deepest cobalt blue.

"Where did you find this?" John couldn't take his eyes off the photo.

"Okay, here's the thing." Jessie was still breathing hard as she spoke. "I weasel my way in to see a friend of a friend, girl named Marylou Champion, works in Property Crimes. She doesn't know much of anything about anything. Doesn't recognize the sketch—blah-blah-blah. Shows me a couple group photos, one shot of the Area Thirteen bowling league. Nothing. Then she gets called away from her desk. Lucky me. Her office is right next to Homicide, across the hall from their file room. I slip in there and start snooping around."

John looked up at her. "And you found this in the file room?"

"I didn't find much of anything at first, but then I see this basket over by the window, wedged between a couple of old boxes of files. It's got a little label on the side with a big red slash in Magic Marker, and I'm thinking *red line,* which in cop lingo means a big, hot, important case. Looks like old, forgotten case files, something like that. I hear the gal coming back down the hall, so I hurry over and start rifling through the stuff. Bunch of documents, depositions, notes, and a manila file filled with photos—"

"This guy's photo was in there?" John asked.

"Sitting on top of the other shots, just as big as life. Problem is, I was about to grab the rest of the file—some really juicy stuff in there, pictures of weird, distorted faces, stuff that didn't make any sense—but then the gal was coming back to her desk, so I just grabbed the photo and slipped out, went to the ladies' room, and that was that."

John frowned. "Weird, distorted faces?"

Jessie nodded. "I know it sounds bizarre, but that's the only way I can describe it—paintings and sketches of contorted faces, people missing huge chunks of their faces—either they'd just undergone cancer surgery or the artist was doing acid at the time he painted them. And there was something else . . . the word *bacon.*"

"Bacon?" John shook his head at the non sequitur, the complete absurdity of it.

"Yeah, bacon, I'm sure I saw the word *bacon* scrawled across one of the notes."

John wondered if this was the "meat" he'd been seeing in his visions. He looked back down at the photo of the smiling man. "I'm not sure about bacon or distorted faces, but this is definitely our guy."

"Look on the back," Jessie said then.

John turned the photo over and saw a small Avery label with a name typed across it.

In the millisecond it took John to comprehend the word, it seemed as though a pinball had leaped up from the paper and hit him in the center of his forehead—striking a trigger hot-wired to his nervous system—and all at once lights starting blinking, bells started ringing, and jolts of sense memories started bolting through his brain, filling his mind with something bright and glittery and terrible. Something beyond words, beyond light or sound or feeling.

"Arthur Glass?" John had recovered enough to say the words with hushed awe.

Jessie nodded. "Yeah, Arthur Glass. That mean anything to you?"

"Glass?" John was looking away from the photo now, trying to recover from the shock, trying to think, his heartbeat in his ears, a rushing sound, and something faintly shrill, like a distant tea kettle. The name had triggered something in him the same way his *own* name had done it the very first time he had heard it.

"Ring any bells?" Jessie asked.

"You could say that," John said, gazing across the alley at a pile of garbage festering on the pavement, fizzing with flies.

"What's the matter?" Jessie was getting nervous.

"It's hard to explain—" John looked back down at the photograph, the man's radioactive eyes boring holes in his brain. Who *was* this bastard, and how in God's name had he found John at the clinic? John started to say, "You gotta give me a little more time to—"

A swirl of noises came from the street outside the alley—voices, radio voices—and both their gazes simultaneously snapped toward the street, toward the distant stone steps leading up to the precinct house. "Jesus, don't tell me," John said, slipping the photo into his windbreaker.

"Shit!" Jessie hissed.

The street was a flurry of action, several uniformed officers trotting down the stone steps of the precinct house, their nightsticks drawn, a group of office workers behind them, huddling in the doorway, watching.

"It's Dolores," Jessie said breathlessly. "She must have showed up right after I walked out."

"Who's Dolores?"

"Dolores Loeb," Jessie replied, pointing at the group huddling in the doorway. "The one with the bouffant hairdo, the one yapping at Marylou."

In the distance, a pair of women had emerged from the swarm and were now standing at the bottom of the steps. The dominant one—the one whom Jessie had referred to as Dolores—was a heavyset lady with a graying bouffant hairdo and loud print dress. She was gesturing wildly at the other woman—the one named Marylou—and their voices were nearly audible above the wind and the traffic. Dolores kept poking Marylou in the collarbone, pointing at the precinct house, ranting angrily, poking Marylou some more. Other cops were coming out of the building, their gazes shifting from the two women to the surrounding area to the street to the storefronts across the street. They were looking for someone. John's heart started racing, because the uniformed officers were making their way across the street, turning south toward the alley.

And now the woman named Marylou was pointing at the shadows in which Jessie and John were standing.

"Oh, shit, she just made us," Jessie uttered. She grabbed John's arm and quickly turned him around toward the rear of the alley. "Walk quickly, John," she said, "but do not—repeat—*do not* run."

They headed toward the rear junction of the alley, walking briskly, hyperalert, John's heart pumping now, his eyes watery with panic. The rear of the alley intersected another, narrower alley running perpendicular to the main passage, its stone walls stained with years of lampblack and pollution, and spattered with gang graffiti. John could smell the odors of garbage and urine as they approached the intersection. His ears—finely attuned with adrenaline—were picking up a new layer of noises now, footsteps, more radio voices.

"Wait!" Jessie whispered suddenly, urgently, clutching John by the arm.

She yanked him back against the filthy wall and peered around the corner of the smaller passageway, and John peered around Jessie's shoulder toward the north end. Fifty feet away, coming toward them through the shadows, was a beefy middle-aged man in a cheap sport coat and cheaper tie, his hair cut marine-style, his weathered face like a basset hound with a five-day shadow of a beard. This guy screamed *cop*, probably plainclothes, probably stationed out of the very same precinct house that Jessie had just raided. His hurried footsteps echoed and bounced off the stone walls.

"Come on," Jessie was whispering, dragging John back into the main alley.

John whispered, "Cop?"

Jessie nodded tersely. "Yeah, and I'll give you three-to-one odds he's been getting a little carried away lately."

"What? What are you talking about?" John was getting confused.

"Tell you later—come on," Jessie said, urging John toward the mouth of the alley.

They barely got ten feet before another burly figure filled the opening of the alley—definitely another plainclothes cop—his corduroy sport coat flapping in the breeze. This fellow was younger, prematurely bald, with the telltale shield clipped to his blazer pocket. He had his gun drawn, and his grim expression was all business. *"Hold it, Bales!"* he yelled, and raised his gun in a tripod posture.

Things started happening rather quickly.

John felt a vise grip on his arm again as Jessie jerked him across the alley—hard enough to make the hat and sunglasses slip off his head and tumble to the ground—and then into a shallow alcove no more than two or three feet deep, shrouded in shadows, stinking of cool stone and urine, its metal service door locked tight—no doorknob in sight—and then Jessie was doing something that John couldn't quite believe—*she was digging in John's pocket for the gun*—and John started to say something when—*BOOM!* A small thunderclap erupted in the alley behind them, making John flinch, probably a warning shot from the bald detective.

"Bales!"

"Cover your eyes!" Jessie said, then raised the Beretta, aiming it directly at the dead bolt on the service door and pulling the trigger—*BANG!*—a sharp crack like a lightbulb bursting in John's head, and then a hot spit of dust on John's cheek as he was looking away, ears ringing, vision going blurry. Everything started moving quickly again, Jessie slamming her foot down on the service door, the door collapsing inward with a shrapnel squeal and rush of noxious air.

Jessie pushed the door open, then yanked John inside the gaping darkness.

The door slammed shut behind them, a broken latch bolting it home.

33

Deep Cover

THE DARK CORRIDORS and labyrinthine rooms of the abandoned Dayton-Hudson warehouse were like the bloodstream of a corpse, the hardened arteries and hollowed-out veins leading into dead chambers like so many dissected and forgotten body parts. The sound of footsteps were echoing now, like whispers of the dead, crackling over broken glass and ancient candy wrappers. But deep within the dead leviathan, huddling just out of sight—just beyond the edges of the shadows—was a foreign substance. A virus. *A smart-virus.*

It had a will of its own, and a tortured sort of purpose, and it thought of itself as Death.

Death moved stealthily through the dark passageways, his senses keen and sharp, his focus laser-locked on the two targets ahead of him. They were feeling their way along charred walls, moving toward the dim light emanating from one of the arched doorways. Death knew where they were headed before *they* did. The doorways led into the tenants' corridor, where the merchants who rented space in the complex kept their back rooms. Staying just out of sight, just out of earshot, controlling his breathing, controlling his vitals, Death was able to silently track the twosome toward the light.

Toward the next leg of the journey.

Toward the next discovery.

The room was a flickering green fluorescent den of iniquity, the walls covered with butterflies, dragons, death skulls, flames, naked ladies, and burning roses, and Jessie entered it like a force of nature, and John tried to take it all in as Jessie dragged him toward the front, her Beretta hidden behind her back, murmuring banalities—"Honey, I told you we took a wrong turn at the tourist center, but would you listen? Nooooooo"—and it was several moments before John realized that they were rushing through an airless little tattoo parlor, and that the buzzing sound was the needle. A Credence Clearwater tune was sizzling through busted loudspeakers and the air was so thick you could spread it on toast, and all the inhabitants were pasty-skinned, heavyset men with shaved heads and leather vests and baleful gazes, dumbstruck, their bloodshot eyes tracking John and his alien partner, with the long nails and shapely legs and Clairol desert sunrise hair tossing with each powerful stride—"Honey, I'm telling you, from now on we use the triple-A map"—and soon Jessie was sidestepping a ratty old dentist's chair and squeezing between a pair of rusty autoclaves and apologizing to everyone concerned as she neared the front door.

A leather-clad behemoth stepped out of the shadows and blocked her path. "The fuck's going on?" It sounded more like a broken boiler pipe than a voice, the words more like an imperative than a question. He had an enormous head and long, stringy, thinning hair that hung down his back like delicate rat tails. There was a tattooed tear on his face.

"Excuse me, Ace." Jessie spoke genially, albeit quickly, her gaze darting toward the door behind him. Outside: the sounds of sirens, voices.

"What the fuck you doing in my stockroom? You trying to rip me off?" The behemoth was standing his ground and was either grimacing or smirking; it was hard to tell by the crescent of rotting teeth unveiled behind his lips.

"I'm sorry, Ace, the hubby and I are a little turned around, you know how it is." Jessie was craning her neck to see over the behemoth's hamhock shoulder.

"No, I don't know how it is." He shoved Jessie back, then crossed his big arms across his chest—two great, scabrous tree trunks that had grown together. "What the fuck kinda scam is this?"

John was about to step in and say something when Jessie raised her hand, waving him off. "It's okay, darling, the nice man has an excellent point." Jessie's gaze was glued to the behemoth. "He simply wants to know how we could get so turned around."

"That's right, lady," the behemoth grunted. "I wanna know how you got so fucking turned around you ended up in my fuckin' back room."

"Fair enough," Jessie said, and took a tentative step closer to the behemoth.

All at once, John realized exactly what Jessie was doing, and there was nothing tentative about it. She was moving with a purpose, quickly getting into position in front of the behemoth. It was obvious by the way she was squaring her shoulders, spreading her feet to shoulder width, and balling her fists. She had plans for this man beyond mere conversation. Yes, indeed, she had big plans for this muscle-bound lummox.

"Sir," Jessie said softly, "it was an honest mistake. We passed your service door out back, and we thought it was a way back to the street. We apologize for any inconvenience it may have caused."

"Fuck you," said the giant, his noxious breath engulfing her.

Jessie grinned. "Don't tell me I'm gonna have to drag out the old Persuader."

The big man's expression changed ever so slightly. "What the fuck is the Persuader?"

What happened next transpired so abruptly, so swiftly, that for a moment John wasn't even sure he had seen it. Jessie's entire body seemed to surge forward like a ballet dancer dipping into an arabesque, and then her knee came up like a piston into the behemoth's groin. It happened with the speed and suddenness of a cobra strike—and the force of a drill press—and the effect was instantaneous. The behemoth gasped, then staggered backward for a moment, his lips curling away from his teeth, his entire body closing down like a clenched fist.

He slammed into the back wall, rattling portraits of butterflies and dragons.

Jessie grabbed John and yanked him across the threshold and out the door.

The street was boiling with activity, sirens swirling in the distance, window shades winking open, people leaning out, coming out of their doors, coming down the steps of their two-flats and brownstones to get a better look; it was nearly rush hour, and the neighborhood traffic was coming alive. The wind smelled of exhaust and garbage. Jessie ushered John across the sidewalk, then started southward, marching along at a crisp pace—not suspiciously crisp, yet fast enough to put some distance between them and the cops. Occasionally looking over his shoulder, John kept glancing around like all the other rubberneckers, trying to find the action, searching for the scene of the crime, looking for carnage. Finally, John motioned back at the tattoo parlor and started to ask, "How the hell did you—?"

"It's nothing, really," Jessie murmured, cutting him off, scanning the street ahead of them. "Something I learned back in the Girl Scouts. But we're not out of the woods yet. Keep moving, and don't look back, but don't look like you're in too much of a hurry either."

"What's going on, Jessie? What did you mean back there when you said the cop was getting a little carried away?"

Jessie was glancing over her shoulder at the commotion behind her, the gawkers, and the cops in the distance, coming down the street. "It was something I've been wondering about ever since you told me your story," she said. "The killer cop who came to the clinic."

"Arthur Glass—what about him?"

"Once in a while, you hear tell of underground groups in the department, vigilantes, cops taking matters into their own hands." Jessie paused for a moment, and John could tell she was getting nervous again. She kept glancing over her shoulder—just as she had told John *not* to do—and her face was covered with a sheen of sweat, her eyes glassy from the nerves and the pain. "My friend Dolores confirmed it the other night," Jessie finally said.

Then she launched into a brief dissertation on vigilantism in the police force.

John listened closely as they strode quickly toward the corner. The back of John's neck felt hot, the tiny hairs standing at attention. The rest of him ached, his muscles cramping with every stride. He felt like a target. And that name flitting about the dark recesses of his mind—Arthur Glass— sounding like fingernails on slate.

Up ahead, the street dead-ended in a three-way intersection. Beyond it rose an enormous, monolithic factory of gray mortar and brick, stretching several city blocks. The perpendicular street that ran in front of it was a narrow one-way ribbon of blacktop, more of an access way than a road. The onlookers had thinned; now there were only a couple of teenage boys perched on the hood of a muscle car at the end of the street, watching.

"But you don't think Glass was one of these rogue cops?" John asked.

"I have no idea," Jessie said, walking exceedingly fast, eyes shifting back and forth, scanning the cross street. "There was a reason his photo was clipped to that red-line file. Maybe he left the force, got suspended. Maybe he was part of some deep-cover thing, some kind of task force—who the hell knows?"

They reached the corner and quickly turned east, John murmuring, "All I know is, somebody murdered that poor desk clerk at the Blue Island Hotel. And the others. The victims from the diaries."

"Yeah, well, you can be sure—"

Jessie fell silent.

"What's the matter?" John was glancing up and down the narrow asphalt street, looking up at the vast brick monolith with its countless grimy windows, many of them blinded by coats of black Rust-Oleum. There were huge garage-style doors sliding open, scattered movement in doorways. It was getting close to the shift change, and workers were clocking out.

"How are your legs?" Jessie asked suddenly; she had started moving sideways now, tense as a cat with its back arched.

"What do you mean?"

"I mean, we're probably gonna have to do a little bit of running."

She gestured over her shoulder, toward the west end of the street, where a black-and-white with a whip antenna and blue bubble lights had just turned onto the asphalt road. There were two uniformed officers inside it, and it was prowling slowly, a hundred yards away and closing. "Oh, Christ," John muttered, making eye contact with the cop behind the wheel.

The engine roared suddenly.

And the cruiser started after them.

34

The Monster's Throat

"THIS WAY!" JESSIE started sprinting toward the far corner of the factory.

John chased after her.

It took less than a minute to reach the east end of the factory, John running full bore, the satchel flopping behind him, his legs flaring hot and sharp, Jessie racing a few paces ahead of him, her sweater buffeting in the wind. She was a damn good runner, probably played sports in high school, and John had some trouble keeping up with her as she zoomed around the edge of the building. But just as John made the turn, the air seemed to erupt in his face, an explosion of noise and metal.

A semitruck was coming at them, its air horn blaring, engine bellowing.

"Look out!"

Jessie darted out of its way, and John followed suit, and they both slammed against the side of the building as the eighteen-wheeler thundered past them in a whirlwind of dust and diesel fumes, and John realized instantly that they had turned the wrong way down a narrow one-way street, probably a loading dock or truck lane, and just then the *skreee* of tires on cement behind them squealed above the truck noise, and the thump of car doors slamming and the chorus of warning voices signaled that the cops were on foot now, that the cops were pursuing them *on foot,* and more trucks were coming now, box trailers, flat beds, cement mixers, and the dust was as thick as a desert sirocco.

John felt another tug on his arm.

"This way!" Jessie pointed east, and led John out the opposite end of the street, then up a scabrous sidewalk toward the intersection of Sallee and Wayne Streets. John glanced over his shoulder and saw no sign of the cops.

Had they gotten hemmed in by one of the trucks? Had they called for backup? Had they taken a short cut?

"We gotta get off the street!" John hollered, turning back to Jessie.

"Shut up and follow me!" Jessie was yanking him toward the intersection. There was a bus stop at the crossroads, a crumbling little stone bench with a peeling picture of a local TV news team on the slatted backing, and next to that, the graffiti-stained windows of a subway entrance. "Down here!" Jessie motioned at the dark entryway.

John followed her down the steps into the cool, pungent shadows.

The subway had a strange, ethereal atmosphere that most urban dwellers took for granted. It was the land beneath the city, a vast skeleton of granite and steel, and it was a different world, its air as close and ripe as a root cellar. It was cold and clammy in the summer, warm and noxious in the winter, and always musky with human by-products—urine, old saliva, body odor, melted bubble gum, and a hundred years of grit. Footsteps seemed to echo endlessly in the subway, and graffiti stained everything. But there was also something mystical about the place—chimeric—as though anything could happen at any time. Maybe it was the constant motion of the trains, the speed, or the perpetual transience. Whatever the source, John was feeling as though they were inside the monster's throat.

John and Jessie paused for a moment at the bottom of the stairs, where three metal turnstiles were flanked by ticket cages on either side. Jessie hurried over to the cage on the right, digging in her pocket, slamming down a five on the counter. She didn't even wait for change.

John followed her through the turnstiles, then across the concrete platform.

The Wayne Street station was fairly crowded today with commuters waiting for the northbound B train: matrons with grocery carts and cloth bags standing under fluorescent tubes near the tracks; teenagers loitering by the pop machines near the back; scattered businessmen in trench coats and distracted expressions leaning against dirty tiles, reading newspapers, glancing impatiently at their watches. Halfway across the platform, a lone street musician in ragged denim and fingerless gloves played "Sweet Home Chicago" on a saxophone, paying little attention as Jessie ushered John across the lighted area and into a shadowy alcove beyond the platform. The alcove was formed by two huge cement ramparts that bordered the far edge of the platform. The floor was littered with cigarette butts and empty bottles, and the air smelled of urine and alkaline rot, and something was happening to John all of a sudden. He was getting dizzy. His skin was crawling, and he felt that telltale throbbing in his temples, throbbing that signaled the onslaught of a fainting spell.

"Jessie—" he started to complain, but she cut him off with the flick of her wrist.

"Wait, hold on—" She was craning her neck to see around the edge of the alcove, to see if the cops had followed them into the subway. "There's a train coming; if the cops don't show, we'll get on it."

"I'm not feeling too well all of a sudden," John muttered.

"Just hold on, John, hang in there."

John swallowed a mouthful of wooziness, his head spinning, his stomach roiling. The stench of the subway was mingling with the dizziness, threatening to topple him, threatening to tug him down into blackness. He tried to focus on the darkness of the tunnel across the station, the pinpoint of light coming at them. There were two trains coming, almost simultaneously from opposing directions, moving on parallel tracks. Their dissonant wails rising, squealing in pain. The commuters were moving toward the edge of the platform, preparing to board the northbound train. Luckily, no cops were in sight.

"Jessie, umm, I'm having a little, uh . . . *problem*," John said, clutching at her arm. His chest was seizing up, making it difficult do draw a breath. Sounds and colors were blurring together, flares bursting behind his eyes like fireworks. His ears were ringing now, drowned by the keen of the trains as they approached. The tunnel was filling with light and noise, the platform quaking.

Jessie took John's arm. "Hang on, John, we're almost home free. Soon as the train stops."

"Jessie—"

John staggered backward, striking the filthy concrete, a sharp pain stabbing his temple. He brushed his fingertips along the line of stitches above his right eye. It felt like a zipper in his skull. His vision was popping and flaring now, the noise of the train engulfing him. He felt Jessie clutching his arm, preparing to pull him toward the northbound train as it rumbled into the station, slowing noisily to a stop.

Just then, across parallel tracks, the southbound express roared through the station in a thunderhead of dust and debris, and John gazed up at the strobe of passing windows, and he saw the somber faces looking out.

Something clicked in his head.

A single instant that seemed to stretch for an eternity, bringing his past flooding back to him.

He is twelve, and he's in his parents' room in their long, narrow trailer home, and he's an only child—his parents call him John-John. He's rummaging through his father's tiny closet, full of naïve curiosity and raging hormones. He finds a shoe box, and inside he discovers a cache of illicit magazines, Argosy *and* Gent *and* Police Gazette *and* Dude *and* Real Detective, *sweaty little digest-sized pamphlets with scantily clad women, gagged and bound, breasts heaving, and tough guys with fedora hats and glowering eyes. He is transformed. To think his father would keep these nasties, his devout Catholic insurance salesman of a father. He steals one, takes it out to his tree house, and masturbates furiously. Later, he dreams of becoming one of the tough guys.*

A bloom of light.

The scene flickered away as quickly as it had appeared, leaving traces of brilliant veins across the orbits of John's eyeballs.

The windows of the passing train were flashing rhythmically now, like an old-fashioned nickelodeon, the stoic faces of commuters winking from light to dark, blinking semaphore signals in the magnesium darkness, magically metamorphosing, sparking into symbols, images, patterns that seemed to freeze time and spot-weld John to the filthy wall, gasping for breath, trying to move, but he couldn't move, he couldn't tear his gaze from the snake charmer's flip-card movie show:

—A snowman melting, its lopsided head and its cinder eyes falling out of its face (Mom and me), a German shepherd galloping down a winding autumn road in a whirlwind of dead leaves (me and Laddie Boy), a canvas sail flapping in the lake wind, a young woman glowering out at the horizon (Gail), a dim, narrow aisle in a library (me), tiny droplets of blood on the floor, these tiny droplets fading into black-and-white photographs—

Again John flinched against the wall, gasping for breath as though he were being dunked underwater.

Then another tommy gun eruption of light and sound forming an epileptic fit of images, a series of tiny vignettes in the moving windows, a spike of neurological energy making another connection, another palpable-real scene:

He's alone, barely eighteen, dressed in his high school graduation gown;

he's the valedictorian, first in his class—all the guys call him "Egghead" and none of the girls want to have anything to do with him—and he's walking along the edge of an ancient rock quarry filled with rainwater, the moonlight shimmering off the brackish ripples. He comes upon a couple lying seminude in the cool shadows near the bank—John-John knows them from English class; it's the captain of the football team and the head cheerleader—and there are empty bottles of Mad Dog in the grass next to them, and their gowns are wadded in the weeds, and John-John hides in the foliage nearby, and he watches them make love, and he watches them share a joint, and he watches them sleep, and he wonders what it would be like to be the class jock, or what it would be like to be the cheerleader. He feels as though his soul is floating out of his body and entering them, becoming them, feeling as they feel—

Mortar blasts of light, his gaze riveted to the train windows as they flashed and crackled with lightning-cured images from his past:

Alone, always alone, he sits in the narrow aisle of the graduate stacks, hunched at the narrow table, his back sore against the rigid-back chairs. The green-glass library light glows in his face, the solitary soul alone in the wee hours, eyes sore, driven, obsessed, reciting the litany in his mind: "Death is not anything . . . it's the absence of presence, nothing more . . . the endless time of never coming back . . . a gap you can't see, and when the wind blows through it, it makes no sound."

A *fffooosh*ing sound, as the train roared, the filaments igniting like tungsten arc lamps behind the windows, and then there were many colored lights within the frames:

He stands on a platform in a drafty, cavernous room that smells of musty fabric, old paste, and paint thinner; the floor is hardwood slats, elevated by oak risers that creak with each footstep; and there are silhouettes of figures out in the darkness, watching, and he crouches in a pool of broken light (the method), gazing up with tears on his cheeks as if he's about to curse God, his hands wet with something sticky (blood?), and his clothes are torn, his flesh mottled and scarred, and he's crying, the loss of innocence, the loss of childhood, the sorrow so deep it feels like bone cancer—

(The method!)

Now the light blossomed into a sun, and the sun was a supernova, the train windows shrinking into its brilliance.

Writing, feverishly writing, tiny-tight scrawl in tiny-tight notebooks, he is absorbed by The Method, consumed by sketches of women, mathematical equations, mythical creatures, demons, his life consumed with hunting targets over long stretches of lonely highway, no family anymore, mother dead, father dead, job gone, no identity anymore.

The light exploded, obliterating everything, leaving only a single image:

A road sign, lettered in green reflective paint, YOU ARE NOW LEAVING EAST LANSING, *shrinking away into the void of absolute blackness.*

Then . . . a sharp snap on his cheek.

Shattering the images.

35

Ghosts

"JOHN, DAMMIT, SNAP out of it!" Jessie slapped his cheek a second time, shaking him silly against the subway tile, frantically trying to get him moving. She could hear the train doors sliding shut behind her. She spun toward the train and saw the conductor three cars ahead of them, craning his head out an open window. He was a skinny black man in his early thirties with thick Coke-bottle glasses.

"Last chance, ma'am," he called back to her, sliding the doors back open.

"Wait a minute, for Chrissake!" Jessie yelled indignantly at him. "We're coming!" Jessie turned back to John and saw his eyes blinking, his lips moving groggily. He was coming out of his spell or seizure or whatever it was. Jessie shook him again, and urged him forcefully, "C'mon, John, goddamnit, we gotta get you out of here!"

"I'm okay now," he uttered breathlessly, then managed to push himself away from the tile.

Jessie ushered him on to the crowded train. They took a seat in back, where they could keep tabs on the comings and goings of the commuters, the fidgety teenagers and weary businessmen. Within moments, the train was rattling back on its way, and after a few moments of settling in, catching their breath, and trying to gather their bearings, Jessie said, "You sure you're okay?"

John nodded, but Jessie wasn't convinced.

The poor man had just suffered some kind of a fit. It reminded Jessie of those tent revival meetings they used to hold outside the Heart of Illinois Fair when she was a kid. She used to sneak into them and watch the worshipers dance with snakes and speak in tongues. Once in a while some poor old gal in the audience would get to praying so hard she would go into a trance, her head lolling backward like a felt puppy, her eyes rolling back in her skull like hard-boiled egg whites. John had gotten like that, standing there against the cement rampart, gawking at the passing southbound. What the hell had he seen in that passing train?

"I know who I am," he said suddenly.

"What did you say?" She turned and stared at him. His face was flush with emotion, eyes glimmering, the window behind him flickering with sparks from the wheel friction. The halo of light around his head made him look otherworldly.

"I said, I know who I am, or at least I know where I came from."

"What are you talking about? You remembered something back there?"

He nodded, then began describing the miniblackout he had experienced while staring at the passing train. He told Jessie about the things he had seen in the windows of the train, images from his childhood, faces of his parents and friends and teachers. He spoke in low, measured tones, so softly that Jessie had to strain to hear him over the rumble of the train and the voices of the other passengers, and as he spoke, his eyes welled with tears and his chin trembled. "I didn't realize it," he said finally, "but I was starting to wonder if—you know—whether I ever even *had* a childhood."

Jessie reached over, patted his shoulder. "I never doubted it."

John looked at her. "Certainly glad *one* of us was confident."

Then Jessie reached down and opened the satchel, which was still looped around John's shoulder. She pulled out a small notebook that had a ballpoint pen clipped to its spiral binding. She opened the notebook and began making notes: *midwestern town, only child, bookworm. Dad's an insurance salesman. Mom a homemaker?* Jessie paused and looked up at John for a moment. "Anything else?"

John gazed out at the tunnel walls rushing past them, the occasional bursts of bright blue sparks like capillaries across the darkness. "I was a nervous kid," he murmured softly.

Jessie turned back to the notebook and wrote: *Lonely, raging hormones, outsider, frustrated, always observing, outside looking in.*

"My parents are dead," John blurted suddenly.

"You know this for a fact?"

"Don't ask me how, but I'm sure of it."

Jessie wrote another note, then asked, "You remember going to college?"

John nodded. "Yeah, certain images, probably of graduate school—I'm not sure—I remember disappearing into my studies, hiding behind the walls of books—oh, and also—these lines keep running through my head: 'Death is not anything . . . it's the absence of presence.'"

Jessie looked at him. "What is that? A poem?"

John shook his head. "I think it's from *Rosencrantz & Guildenstern Are Dead.* It's a play from the sixties."

"You think it's something you were in as a kid, maybe in college?"

John shrugged.

Jessie thought about it for a moment. "Any chance you remember where you went to college?"

After a moment, John said, "Yeah, as a matter of fact, I do. I saw a sign."

"A sign?"

"A green highway sign—YOU ARE NOW LEAVING EAST LANSING."

"East Lansing? The one in Illinois?"

John shook his head. "Michigan. It's near the little town I grew up in. East Lansing, Michigan. State capital is there, and Michigan State University."

Before Jessie could say another word, the train lurched, then pitched to the right as it rounded a forty-five-degree curve. Jessie looked up. Some of the passengers had risen and were moving toward the exits in front and in back. The trains was heading into the next station—probably either Seventy-ninth Street or Comiskey Park, Jessie wasn't sure which—and the tunnel was widening, filling with the strobe of fluorescent lights and the echo of humanity.

Jessie glanced over her shoulder at the rear hatch. Only two other cars were strung behind them, filled with commuters, and for some reason Jessie started wondering if she and John might be able to make a quick exit out the back, if push came to shove. Only two cars to traverse, then it was an easy hop out onto the tracks—watch out for that third rail!—and then into the darkness of the tunnel.

"What's wrong?" John asked.

"Nothing," Jessie said, and glanced back toward the front of the car.

The train rattled into the station and came to a stop.

The doors slid open, and passengers started disembarking, shuffling out, new ones shuffling in. Jessie stood up, her skin prickling on the back of her arms. Something was wrong again, she could feel it. John rose next to her and scanned the car from front to back. He seemed to sense the trouble as well. Then Jessie saw the problem: the two plainclothes cops from the Calumet precinct house—Baldy and Mr. Whistler—getting on the car behind them.

"Oh, shit," she uttered.

"What?"

"Deputy Dogs just got on the caboose," Jessie said, and took John's arm and gently ushered him out into the aisle, smiling at the other commuters—no big deal, no fugitives here, just us chickens—and then she was quickly leading John toward the next car. "Just act casual, no sudden moves," Jessie instructed under her breath. "Just gonna check out the next car."

The train was pulling out of the station, pitching and yawing and rattling on its merry way, and Jessie quickly led John to the next pass-through door. Jessie muscled it open, and they stepped out onto the coupling platform. The noise and odor assaulted them——a loud mélange of moist stone, heavy stench, and cacophonous noise, the iron wheels doing a drum solo on the ancient rails beneath them—and then Jessie was hurriedly yanking John through the outer door and into the next car. Before sliding the door closed behind her, she glanced over her shoulder and got some bad news.

The two cops had noticed them.

Rushing down the aisle, flashing their shields at people, hollering for everybody to get down, the cops were coming fast and furious now, halfway across the car behind Jessie. From the looks on their faces, it was clear that these guys were more than a little upset. They were all jacked up now over Jessie and John evading them in the alley. Now it was a new ball game. Now it was personal.

"Change of plans," Jessie muttered, quickly yanking John into the next car, then hurrying him toward the next forward hatch, past rows of morose commuters sitting three abreast on cold vinyl contour benches, the air thick with tension, body odor, and clashing aftershaves. Again Jessie glanced over her shoulder and saw the detectives approaching the pass-through door. Time was running out. Jessie had hoped that the train would pull into the next station in time for them to make a quick exit unnoticed, but now it looked as though she would have to resort to Plan B, which was basically a desperation maneuver.

They reached the next forward hatch—which was adjacent to the small metal booth in which the engineer huddled, commandeering the train—and Jessie grabbed John by the shoulders. "Listen to me, John," she uttered. "Things are getting a little shaky now, so I'm gonna create a little bit of a diversion. All I want you to do is stick to me like glue. You understand?"

He told her that he understood.

"Okay, gimme the Beretta," she said, and reached into the satchel.

Behind them, the rear hatch was sliding open, the faces of the detectives appearing in the gap. Jessie grabbed the gun, then turned to the engineer's booth. She started knocking hard on the panel with the butt of her gun, and some of the passengers must have seen the weapon because a wave of hushed whispers rolled across the seats.

The booth door finally cracked opened, and the skinny little engineer peered out through his Coke-bottle glasses. "The hell's going on?"

"Stop the train!" Jessie pointed the nine-millimeter at the bridge of the engineer's nose.

"Wha—?" It took a moment to compute, as the engineer gazed cross-eyed down the barrel.

"Stop the goddamn train! Do it now, and do a hard stop!"

"Yes, ma'am." The engineer was already turning toward the console in front of him—a rack of gauges, indicator lights, valves, and a waist-high enclosure with two aluminum handgrips sticking out the top. One was the dead-man's stick, which controlled the speed, and the other was the brake.

The engineer yanked the brake.

And the results were much more dramatic than even Jessie had anticipated.

36

The Face of Death

ON AN EPOCHAL scale of disasters, it was *not* one of Chicago's most significant. The granddaddy of them all, of course, was the great fire of 1871. Then, in descending order of historic import, one might mention the Haymarket Square riots of 1886, the Eastland pleasure-boat disaster of 1915, the various and sundry gangland shootouts during Prohibition, the violence that erupted during the Democratic Convention in 1968, and maybe even the flood of 1992.

As far as the city's current subway system was concerned, it had certainly seen its fair share of disasters in its long and illustrious history. From the time the first underground lines were built in the late 1930s, there had been derailments, electrocutions, suicides, and all manner of foul-ups in the great subterranean caverns. The third rail alone—which continuously buzzed with enough juice to fry a small platoon—had taken its share of victims over the years. Needless to say, the momentary chaos that ensued after the emergency brake was thrown at Jessie Bales's request paled in comparison to most subway incidents.

But that didn't mean it was any easier for John and Jessie to get away.

"Go! Now!" Jessie's voice was nearly drowned by the tidal wave of noise following the sudden stop—the keening, screaming passengers, their newspapers, shopping bags, briefcases, and umbrellas clattering across the floor, the engine hissing like a great beast in its death throes. The two cops had careened along with everybody else, one of them landing in a heavyset woman's lap, the other landing on the floor, his skull cracking hard against a metal handrail. Now the train was swarming with pandemonium.

The doors automatically opened, revealing a scarred cement wall only inches away.

Jessie grabbed John's sleeve and hurled through the gap, and they tumbled outside, landing on ancient wet stone five feet below train level. Jessie nearly dropped the Beretta, then fumbled it back into the satchel around John's shoulder. The air was thick with the sharp tang of overheated metal, and a veil of smoke was rising from somewhere beneath the track. Inside the train, the chaos was still boiling over, which gave Jessie enough time to clutch at John's arm and worry him toward the front of the train, moving through the oily gray fumes.

They followed the battered rail apron, as prehistoric and desolate as a Pleistocene era boulder field, and John had some trouble moving, but Jessie kept him going, their shoulders brushing moist tunnel walls on one side, and the hot grimy metal of the train on the other. They heard the sound of the doors clacking shut behind them, echoing through the gloom. The smoke was thickening.

"Stay against the wall," Jessie whispered to John as they moved deeper into the shadows beyond the train's headlamp beam. The acrid smoke was heavy in the air now, obscuring almost everything in its thick, blue-gray fog. The ground was vibrating faintly beneath them as other trains approached in the distance, passing other junctions. Jessie blinked, the noxious fumes making her eyes water.

Out of the smoke, a triangle of forking tunnels materialized magically, one continuing to the left, another tributary cutting off to the right. "This way," Jessie said, pointing toward the tributary.

Jessie went first. The light dwindled immediately, and the smoke seemed to thicken—where the hell was it coming from?—and the path became exceedingly narrow, with a fossilized rib of iron embedded in its cinder floor—probably an old freight tunnel—and Jessie had to concentrate on her footing in order to lead the way. She was hoping they would come upon a ladder or a service hatch leading up to street level. A moment later, the path took a sharp turn to the left, then narrowed even further—barely eighteen inches across—and Jessie had to press her back against the filthy stone just to continue on.

After another minute of struggling, Jessie glanced over her shoulder.

John was gone.

"*John!*" Jessie hissed the word—half a whisper, half an urgent holler—spinning around, scanning the dense fog behind her. It was so dark now, and so smoky, the tunnel seemed to have no shape, no beginning, no end. How did it happen so quickly? Jessie felt dizzy, off balance.

"Jessie?"

The sound of John's hoarse reply was a galvanizing electric spark in the darkness, making Jessie's arms prickle with gooseflesh. He couldn't have drifted too far. "John, where are you?" she said. "Can you hear me? Try to follow the sound of my voice."

"Jessie?"

"I'm here, John, just follow—"

There was a sudden noise that made Jessie's spine straighten like a column of ice—a faint cracking sound, like wood collapsing—and all at once she remembered something she had neglected to tell John. *The tunnels, the bizarre catacombs under Chicago's subway system!* Originally built in the late nineteenth century, designed for telephone cables, they made up more than sixty miles' worth of hidden passageways, many of them barely wide enough for a human to negotiate. Legend had it that Capone used them in the twenties to transport contraband from one speakeasy to another. In 1992, when the Chicago River breached a hole in a restraining wall, there was rampant subterranean flooding, and several office buildings directly over the tunnels were filled with river water and errant fish. Nobody ever bothered to clean up the tunnels after that, and today they were a moldering, vermin-infested no-man's-land, the closest thing to hell the Windy City had to offer.

All of this ran through Jessie's mind in a microburst as she heard the sound of wood collapsing, creaking and groaning through the darkness.

Somebody had taken a wrong step, plunging through a rotten floorboard into the darkness below.

And for the first time since she had taken John's case, Jessie Bales had no idea what to do.

Death found himself huddling in a womb of shadows. He felt woozy from the unexpected incident, from the struggle to get off the train, from the smoke in his lungs, and he worked on controlling his breathing, gathering himself. The muffled clamor of voices echoed off the moist stone walls around him, voices from the smoke and shadows, from the darkness above him, from the shadows below, voices from inside his own head, moaning, pleading, begging for mercy. They were the kinds of voices with which he was very familiar—this man who fancied himself as Death—like the cries of a woman in ecstasy, or a group of commuters surprised by the sudden jarring stop of a subway train.

Or a subject awakening on an operating table.

Death crouched there in the steel blue fog for quite a few moments, taking long measured breaths, slowing his own heart rate down to between fifty and sixty beats per minute, clenching and unclenching his dexterous fists, and waiting. Watching. His legs were cramped from running through the alleys and streets, then sitting in the rear of a crowded subway train, but he ignored the pain. Physical pain can be short-circuited by a transcendent mind, and Death's mind was exceedingly enlightened. He concentrated on the task at hand, finding another sacrificial lamb, another sheep who had wandered too far from the flock, too far from the crowded train cars. Death would sweep one up, carry it away, and transform it into something beautiful, something resplendent.

This was how Death worked—always aware of the pain, the loneliness—and this was why he thought of himself as Death.

He unbuttoned his jacket—he wore a turtleneck underneath, covered by a tasteful charcoal-colored vest. He unsnapped a jeweler's pouch, which was strapped inside the vest like a holster, and began to sort through the delicate little stainless-steel instruments nestled inside. There were several syringes, most of them filled with formaldehyde, atropine, or a strong anesthetic to act as a hemostat in order to retard bleeding. He loathed making messes, and he always tried to avoid bleeders. Bleeders were difficult to handle, slippery. The hemostat allowed him to make incisions out in the real world without getting blood all over the specimen, not to mention himself and everything else within a twenty-foot radius. There were other instruments inside the pouch, things like graded forceps for sealing off arteries, Langeback retractors for manipulating skin and tissue, and at least a dozen curved dural blades and scalpels of various sizes for making incisions. The largest instrument—and by far the heaviest—was an Adson bone saw, a rubber-handled device that could snap a truck axle in two.

Death pulled a syringe of atropine from the pouch and started breathing low, steady breaths, fixing his gaze on the distant veil of smoke.

A specimen was emerging from the haze like some mythical specter. A large one, a very large one. Death had not yet taken a subject so enormous; this could be difficult.

The young man seemed to be searching for someone, perhaps a girlfriend lost in the chaos. Dressed in black leather jacket, black pants, and scuffed black jackboots, the boy was a sepulchral vision in the smoke-filled tunnel, his face full of surly misanthropy, eyes glinting with anger, cryptic tattoos across his knuckles, along his collar. He was fiddling with a small camera, his gaze darting about the shadows. Suddenly a small canister of film slipped from his hands and clattered to the floor, and the young behemoth knelt awkwardly, scooping up the film, glancing over his shoulder as though he were being naughty.

Death flexed his legs, then rose to his full height against the moldering stone wall.

He started edging toward the young man in black, a smile on Death's face, a reassuring smile. There were other voices echoing nearby, like ghosts in the smoke, but the big boy in black ignored them and just kept fiddling with his camera, staggering through the foggy shadows, moving farther and farther away from civilization.

"Excuse me—!" Death called out from the darkness, speaking in his most congenial voice.

The specimen froze like a big dog hearing a high-pitched whistle.

"Excuse me—sir—!"

Death took a few steps closer, the syringe of atropine cupped in his palm behind his back, and that irresistible warm smile on his face, that cookies-and-milk smile that seemed to say, *Hey, neighbor, don't worry, we're all in this crazy old world together,* and the young man wavered for a moment, turning toward the voice, squinting to see through the smoke. Recognition blossomed suddenly on the young man's face, and he was about to say something, when Death approached with the sweetest expression on his face.

"I'm sorry to do this to you, but I could really use some help," Death said in a cordial voice, sounding as though he might be collecting money for Catholic Charities. "My wife was hurt in the—"

The first blow came out of nowhere.

Billy Marsten's head snapped back with the force of the blow, the impact cracking delicate bones above the bridge of his nose, sending a blast of cold through his skull. It happened so quickly, so nimbly, that at first Billy thought he had bumped his head on something, a light fixture or a stalactite hanging down in the dark tunnel—as an overgrown kid, Billy had been accustomed to striking things with his head—but then he felt himself swooning, falling into the arms of the shadow-figure like a child collapsing into the bosom of a loving parent, and the fireworks went off in Billy's field of vision, and the ringing filled his head, and the massive pain stabbed him like a machete between his eyes. Spasming in the stranger's grip, Billy thought he was having some kind of a seizure now, or a stroke, and he dropped the camera.

Plastic pieces shattered on the hard-packed cinder floor.

The figure continued embracing Billy, holding him upright, whispering, "You've been chosen."

Billy looked into the eyes of the beast, a pair of cold steel buttons, and the realization washed through Billy—*Of course, my God, of course, it was him all along*—and then Billy was trying to speak, trying to straighten up and say a few final words to the man who would kill him, but Billy was nearly unconscious now, and he was having difficulty speaking, and the last thing he felt was a sudden pinprick in his arm, and he looked down and saw a needle injecting clear liquid into his bloodstream, and he started shivering, the pain swallowing him now, the cold unfurling in his joints. He started convulsing. He looked back at the monster, and saw that the monster had reached for something with his other hand, something metallic, something polished and gleaming in the dim light, and all of a sudden that sharp metallic thing had risen to Billy's eye, and now the metal glimmered brightly in Billy's eyes, blinding him, and the last thought Billy had before collapsing was pure sorrow—a grief that was absolute and all-consuming—not for his own imminent death but for something far more personal and intimate. In the remaining nanoseconds of his life, Billy Marsten was completely devastated by the fact that he had neglected to get a good photograph of the monster.

Then the scalpel pierced the upper part of Billy's eyelid and impaled his frontal lobe.

Ending Billy's Thing forever.

37

Fan Letter

He cradles the meat in his arms, watching the change coming over it again, and it's both fascinating and horrible. . . .

The light is going out of the man's eyes like a candle flame flickering out, the tiny sparks in the centers of the irises dwindling, contracting, shrinking down until there is nothing but a needle-prick of life. Then the fire finally goes out and it's incredible. Deeply moving. He looks down at the victim's hands, and they are closing, curling inward like the petals of a lovely flower at sunset. It is so sublime, watching this unraveling of life, this gradual shutting down.

He suddenly gazes up at the heavens, repulsed, horrified, and he screams, expecting to hear his own voice, but he doesn't hear his own voice, he hears something else: the voice of the Other. Throaty, whiskey-cured, the voice pours out of him like a liquid clarion call, pure poison, infecting the air with its singular message:

I AM A KILLER—

—no—

"No!"

Eyes blinking, opening suddenly, congealed with mucus, still in the dark, still asleep, but stirred by the after-echo of his own voice in his ears.

"Wha—?"

John McNally's brain was under siege for a moment, the darkness completely disorienting him, the fever-burst gripping his body, chills rolling up his spine, this throat clogged with sudden panic. It took him several frenzied moments to figure out he was lying prone on a hard, cold surface, soaking wet, his arms and legs weighing a ton, feeling too big for his clothing. Had he awakened in another hospital? Had he sustained another attack of amnesia? Was he doomed to live out an endless serial-loop of awakenings such as this, alone in the dark, completely helpless and oblivious? Or perhaps the entire ordeal from the moment he had left the Reinhardt Clinic had been a dream.

He tried to move.

It was futile, his body welded to the dark, wet floor, his spine wrenched, throbbing with pain. He tried to take a few deep, steadying breaths and think, think back to the events that had led him here. His eyes were adjusting to the dark now, and he saw that he was lying in a couple of inches of sulfurous, stagnant water. He could nominally make out the shapes around him, the walls of the narrow freight tunnel in which he had fallen, the leprous stone sweating filthy, viscous liquid, the stalactites of frayed cables overhead and broken rusty rails embedded in the floor and running off into the darkness. The stone was the color of moldy rye, and the air smelled of rotten earth, toxic and foul.

Jessie.

Yes, that was how he had gotten here. Images of the afternoon began flashing in his mind—the alley down the street from the precinct house, the tattoo parlor, the loading dock. The lady detective had led him on a foot-chase with the police, and they had ended up in the subway, *the subway,* yes, that was how it had happened. He had stepped on that foothold of rotting wood, and the wood had collapsed, and he had plummeted into the dark.

Something twitched on the ground to his right.

He sat up suddenly, jerking backward instinctively, rearing away from the object in his peripheral vision, partially obscured by the deeper shadows. The object was pale and rubbery, and John started thinking it was another killer possum or some other putrid little creature eking out a living in this hellhole. But the thing just lay there now, and John managed to rise up into a sitting position—despite his twisted spine and woozy head—so that he could take a closer look.

The human head was propped upright in the puddle of gore next to him.

John's body hardened suddenly into icy paralysis as he gaped at the head. It sat there almost as if it were staring at John, ruined nerves still twitching, the eyes still geeked open, the flesh still supple and shiny like an overripe melon, the blood still seeping from the jagged, torn neck in freshets, indicating a recent decapitation, perhaps only moments old, and the features frozen in that bizarre, yawning grimace, that adrenal death mask of terror—a young man with dark hair, dark eyes, and a smudge of partial tattoo below the left ear—and John couldn't move, couldn't breathe, he could only stare at the glistening thing as the involuntary collation of data streamed through his mind in a succession of herky-jerky thoughts: Was this meant for him? Was the perpetrator still lurking in the nearby shadows? *Watch out! Run! Run, you idiot!* But John's body weighed a million pounds now, and his ears were ringing, and his temples were tom-tom drums doing "Cherokee," and he could not tear his gaze from that damned severed head that was starting to look like an obscene joke, like a waxy mannequin's head. There was a deep gash above its left eye, and something poking out of its gaping mouth, something other than a bloated tongue, something that didn't belong there. At first, it looked like a delicate little feather. Curly little filaments, light brown and shiny. Then, all at once, John realized that it wasn't a feather. No. It wasn't a feather at all.

It was human hair.

Struggling to his feet, heart tumbling in his chest like a faulty bearing, John began to back away on weak knees, his gaze still riveted to that horrible apparition with the hair sticking out of it. He managed to reach up to his scalp, and he felt an itchy patch of skin behind his ear. He started repeating very softly under his breath, "No way, sorry, no way, no—" and his mind was shrieking, *Look at it, dummy, it's real,* and he tried to swallow but he couldn't. The worst part wasn't the gaping, contorted expression—

(sketches of weird, distorted heads)

—no, no, on the contrary, the worst part was the fact that John recognized the face.

Memories spurted through John's nervous system like fast poison, the name—BILLY MARSTEN—a neon sign igniting in John's brain, blinking harsh white light, images magically materializing in John's mind—gauzy and indistinct at first, but gradually sharpening, coming into focus. *Letters.* A drawer full of letters.

A fragment from one of the letter floating in John's imagination:

"Dear Doc,

You don't know me, but I've long admired your brilliant legacy—your cold, calculated reign of terror—and with all due respect, I just think you would be the ultimate subject for a doctoral thesis—"

John blinked suddenly, the memory shattering like a sheet of ice.

He kept backing away, backing from the carnage, away from the horror, his mind racing—*the kid had called me "Doc" in his letter?*—and now, in his peripheral vision, John saw his leather satchel lying on the ground a few feet off to his left. He leaned down and scooped it up. The satchel contained his lifeline at the moment, the hideous journal his only storehouse of information and hard evidence. He continued backing away, unable to tear his gaze from the severed head.

Something touched his back.

Whirling around instinctively, John yelped like an animal, and he put up his hands as though shielding his face, but there was nothing there, only a wall, and he realized he had struck the edge of two intersecting walls.

John hunched over and wailed vomit.

There was nothing in his stomach, of course, so the only matter that was expelled onto the cold concrete was a thin strand of bile. He heaved, and his shoulders hunched, and he heaved some more until all the nausea and disorientation poured out of him, and all that was left was a cold, scoured feeling. He straightened up and looked at the head lying across the tunnel. It lay there like a pasty white malignancy. John regarded it for another moment, the questions roiling in his mind. *Billy Marsten.* Who the hell was Billy Marsten? And how had he gotten here? And why had he sent John such a strange fan letter?

John wiped his face and shivered. It was time to get the hell out of this tunnel—away from this terrible thing on the ground—and try to find Jessie. Let somebody else deal with this murder.

John turned and started down a perpendicular tunnel.

And the darkness swallowed him.

He couldn't have traveled more than the length of a city block when he heard footsteps.

Fountains of chills poured up John's spine, down his arms and legs. He quickened his pace along the wall, his mind racing now, the dark closing in on him. The stone felt like crusty-dry modeling clay, and the air was acrid with rot, augering up John's nasal passages, but he kept moving along, moving toward the faint sounds. He reached into the satchel, fished around for a moment, and found the Beretta's grip. He pulled the weapon out and thumbed the hammer back. The gun felt awkward in his hand, heavy as a brick, and he was sure he had never fired one in his life, but he was prepared to fire if he had to.

A bruise of pale light materialized twenty yards ahead of him, and he moved toward it, his heart hammering in his chest. Beneath him, the ancient rails glimmered, rails that once hauled God-only-knew-what across town, trails that now gleamed like veins of petrified silver. The rotten-egg smell was choking him, but he ignored it and focused on the sound of those damned footsteps as the faint light rose ahead of him. A dull orange stain, intensifying with each painful yard he traversed. The air was charged with a hot chemical smell, and the unmistakable sound of someone else's footsteps under his own—dammit, there *was* somebody else down here with him—and he rushed toward the light, his entire body vibrating with animal-gut instinct, pure panic, the footsteps nearby, closing from somewhere beside him—over him?—and he saw the opening straight ahead, another intersection of passageways, flickering in bare-bulb yellow.

He reached the opening just as another figure loomed to his left.

John threw his arms up involuntarily, the gun slipping from his right hand, skittering across the floor, and the figure collided with him. It was like getting hit by a battering ram, the blind momentum slamming John hard against the stone wall, then sending him sprawling to the ground, stunned and gasping for breath, clawing at the gravel. The intruder had struck the adjacent wall, then had tumbled to the cinders as well, sending rock dust and debris down on both of them.

John managed to get a lungful of air finally, rising to his knees, backing away as though from a wild animal, panic sizzling in the air. *Where was the gun?*

The other figure was still ten feet away, breathing hard, gasping for air.

"Who are you?" John demanded, rising to his feet, scanning the floor for the gun or a weapon or anything he could use to fight this monster.

"Chrissake—who the hell do you think it is?"

The smoky, raw voice was familiar, and John froze as the intruder managed to rise up against the adjacent wall, her face coming into view in the dim light, her hair matted and dirty, her cheeks streaked with soot. Part of her blouse was soaking wet and clinging to her statuesque form—probably from schlepping through the filthy underground.

John gawked at her, then managed to utter, "Thank God."

"I'm glad to see you too," Jesse wheezed, bending over to catch her breath. She gathered up the front of her blouse and wrung it dry. Filthy, brackish water dripped between her fingers. "Lovely place down here, isn't it?"

John swallowed the metallic-sweet taste of panic. "You all right?"

"Just peachy." She nodded, catching her breath.

John shuddered, chills traveling up his spine, and he leaned against the cold stone, taking deep breaths. "There's something you should know, Jessie, something I just found."

"What are you talking about?"

John told her about waking up in the tunnel and finding the severed head.

Jessie listened closely, her expression tightening, and when John was finished, she whispered, *"Jesus God Almighty."*

John nodded. "I think somebody's following us—"

Jessie suddenly threw up her hand, cutting off his words. "Wait, John, hold on a second—!"

"What is it?"

Jessie was cocking her head toward the blackness of the tunnel behind them, listening, and now John could hear what she was hearing, and it sounded like more footsteps, delicate footsteps crunching through the cinders, and now John's whole body was crawling with goose bumps, and he nodded. "Yeah, maybe we better—"

"That way." Jessie pointed toward the narrow tunnel ahead of them. "Ought to be able take that tunnel all the way across town to Union Station."

"Union Station—how the hell do you know that?"

Jessie grabbed his sleeve, and started ushering him toward the tunnel. "I watch a lot of *Beauty and the Beast*—c'mon, stop asking stupid questions and let's get the hell outta here."

38

Falling

THE AMTRAK DEPOT was located at the corner of Canal and Jackson, across the street from the old Union Station. Rising up against the brutish Chicago skyline like a massive chockablock Erector set, the depot was a faux Art Deco monstrosity that served as a transportation hub for the upper Midwest. Signs were fashioned in the old railway style—harkening back to the days of Chattanooga choo-choos and Pullman porters—but upon closer inspection, the place had a tired, artificial quality, like an old shopping mall. Jessie found the place by pinpointing a strategic manhole cover just east of the South Branch River, then helped John climb up through shafts of filthy light into the cacophony of traffic noise and teeming sidewalks. Passersby barely noticed the twosome emerging from the sewer like deranged guerrilla warriors, soaked to their respective skins in filth.

This was Chicago, after all, where people minded their own frigging businesses.

Once inside the station—and momentarily safe—Jessie had gone directly to the ladies' room while John had purchased tickets. Jessie had used the hand dryer to dry her blouse, then splashed icy water on her face to clear her head. Her hair and makeup looked monstrous, so she primped at the mirror for a while, trying to salvage things with soap, water, and spit. She emptied her bladder, then sat there in the stall for another moment, breathing long, deep breaths, girding herself for whatever chaos was in store for her, thinking about Kit, trying *not* to think about the severed head in the underground. She couldn't stop wondering how she had gotten herself mixed up in this insane game. God help her, but she was starting to believe in John McNally's innocence. The man, or his helplessness—she was unsure which—had stirred something deep inside Jessie, something beyond words, and now she felt as though her entire life had been leading up to this moment.

By seven-thirty she had emerged from the rest room and had managed to locate a phone booth near the escalators, and now she was listening to the strident, high-pitched protests of her seven-year-old.

"But Mrs. Fitzgerald said you would be home by six o'clock at the latest, she said six o'clock, she said you promised her six o'clock."

"I know, Boodle, but some things came up."

"What things?"

"I can't go into it right now, but everything's fine. I'm just going to have to spend another night on the job."

"Mommy, please, I want to sleep in my own bed tonight. Tomorrow we got arts and crafts, and I gotta bring a leaf from the backyard."

Jessie sighed, squeezing the receiver a little tighter. "I understand, honey, but there's nothing I can do."

"You always say that," the voice replied.

"Watch that sassy mouth, young lady," Jessie said, wanting a cigarette badly.

"I'm sorry, Mommy, but you always said a promise is a promise."

"You're right, Boodle, I made you a promise and now I'm breaking it, and you're right to be upset. But you gotta understand my position. You're getting to be a big girl now, and I think you're old enough to handle this."

"I don't like it when you say that, Mommy."

"When I say what?"

"When you say I'm getting to be a big girl."

"Why?"

"Because it always means I gotta do something I don't want to do."

Jessie smiled in spite of her crackling nerves. "Yeah, well, maybe that's what being a grown-up is all about."

"Doing stuff you *don't* want to do?"

"That's right, honey."

"But Mommy, that's not the way it is when you're all grown up. When you're all grown up you get to do the stuff you *want* to do."

There was a pause then, and Jessie wondered how Kit might interpret her mother's latest endeavor. Was she helping John McNally because she wanted to? Jessie looked at her watch. It was getting late. Then, all at once, Jessie got an idea. A way to ameliorate her daughter's mood. "Maybe you're right, Boodle," Jessie said finally. "Maybe I'm doing something right now because I want to do it. But sometimes there's a lot of things you want to do at the same time, and you only have time to do *one* of those things, and you just hope the people you love will understand."

Jessie waited for a response. There was silence on the other end of the line for a moment, then Kit said, "I don't get it, Mommy."

"Do you know what I'm doing right now, Boodle?"

"No."

"I'm helping that man named John McNally."

More silence, then a rustling sound, then finally: "Is John McNally okay?"

"Yes, honey, he's fine, but he's in a lot of trouble, and he needs me; he needs both of us."

After another pause: "When do you think you'll be back?"

"Before you know it, honey—"

A shuffling noise outside the booth grabbed Jessie's attention for a moment, and she turned and glanced over her shoulder.

John was standing outside the booth, waiting restlessly. He had cleaned himself up as well, but he still looked shaken, drawn. It was unclear how long he had been standing there. Jessie wondered how much of the conversation he had heard. Jessie turned back to the phone and said, "Gotta run, Boodle—you be good, okay?"

"Will I see you tomorrow morning, Mommy?"

"Hopefully, yeah," Jessie said. "Now put the phone to your forehead and lemme give you a big smooch." Jessie loudly kissed the mouthpiece. "Love you, Boodle."

"Love you too, Mommy."

"Bye-bye, honey."

"Mommy—wait!"

"What is it, Boodle?"

"Be careful."

"I will, I promise."

Jessie hung up the phone and stepped out of the phone booth. "Sorry about that," she said to John. "Kit's getting to be such a little old lady."

"It's okay," John said. "Our train leaves in twenty-five minutes."

"Let's go," Jessie said, starting across the terminal toward a set of automatic doors.

John grabbed her, and gently pulled her back. "Jessie, wait, hold on a second." He was measuring his words now, his eyes burning with fear. Jessie could tell he had been agonizing over something. "I'm pulling you into this thing," he said. "This nightmare. You should bail out now, okay? Go back to your daughter."

"John, look—"

"No, listen to me. I know enough now to track down my own identity. I'll pay you whatever I owe you—"

"Stop." Jessie held up her hand, looking deeply into his eyes. "I'm in this thing now, okay? In for a penny, in for a pound."

"But—"

"Don't, John. Just don't. Don't take away the missing-person case of the century. All I got left are cheating husbands and lost German shepherds."

After a long moment, John managed a pained smile. "Okay, let's go."

The gate area resembled a modest little airport. Rows of styrene contour benches sat bathing in low inverted lighting, with scattered pockets of people waiting for their trains, softly chatting, reading newspapers, and checking schedules. Jessie and John were waiting outside Gate E, standing next to an elderly one-armed black man in a fedora hat and Hawaiian shirt. Three seats down the aisle, another old-timer, with a full white beard, sat playing a harmonica. A young couple sat near the ticket taker's podium speaking in some eastern European dialect.

Jessie and John were fidgeting now, their gazes shifting from door to door.

They had purchased one-way tickets on the 805 International, a superliner that circled around the Great Lakes, then looped up into Canada. East Lansing, Michigan, would be a midpoint stop, about six hours away. If their luck held out, they could make their exit from Chicago without being spotted and be in East Lansing by the wee hours. They could get a motel and start piecing together John's past by morning. But then what? Jessie couldn't help wondering how her involvement would shake down. She was already looking at major slammer time, aiding and abetting a fugitive, obstructing justice, tampering with evidence, God knew what else. But something told her that John McNally was no ordinary head case.

"Ladies and gentlemen," the ticket taker said, appearing at the podium, speaking into a microphone. A plump African-American woman with designer eyeglasses so huge they looked like triple-pane windows, she spoke in an officious monotone. "We'll begin boarding the International to Flint, Stratford, and Toronto in just a second, if you'll line up at Gate E, passengers to Toronto first . . ."

She called off the cities, one by one, the farthest destinations first, and eventually Jessie and John got in line. They had no luggage other than a damp leather satchel filled with notes, photographs, a madman's diary, and a nine-millimeter Beretta. Thank God Amtrak didn't have metal detectors; train hijackings had gone out of style right around the time the horseless carriage was coming into vogue.

Moments later, Jessie and John boarded the enormous superliner—these trains always seem bigger in real life, each car rising up nearly twenty feet off the ground—entering through an open doorway in back, passing through a luggage area on the first floor, climbing a set of metal stairs, and entering the massive seating area on the second floor. A generous aisle was flanked on either side by pairs of spacious recliners. The floor lights gave off an eerie luminance, accompanied by the soft rumble of the engines somewhere far off to the front. Jessie motioned John toward the farthest pair of recliners, which sat facing the front pass-through door. They settled into their seats—John by the window, Jessie on the aisle—and waited for the train to roll, gazing nervously over their shoulders, expecting to see a cop boarding the coach at any moment.

None appeared.

Five interminable minutes later, the train lurched into motion.

Jessie let out a long, pained sigh, then settled deeper into her seat as the coach began to pitch and sway softly, the crackle of the conductor's voice sizzling softly over the loudspeaker in a thick French-Canadian brogue— "Welcome aboard the International, ladies and gentlemen. Our destinations this evening are Hammond, Indiana; Michigan City; Niles; Kalamazoo; East Lansing; Flint; Port Huron; Stratford, Ontario; and Toronto. And for those of you who are so inclined, we'll be opening up our café car in the back of the train in a few minutes, where you'll be able to purchase beer, wine, and cocktails. I remind you, there is no smoking. Thank you for riding Amtrak, and have a pleasant journey." And then Jessie looked over at John and saw that he was not looking quite as relieved as she was feeling; in fact, he was looking positively spooked, his eyes still shifting around the dim interior of the coach car, darting from seat to seat.

Jessie looked over her shoulder. There was only a handful of other passengers lounging here and there as the train gently crept out of the station, the muffled clatter building beneath them, the light changing from a dim incandescence to the golden glow of magic-hour coming through the windows. Near the back, a young black woman in a Chicago Bulls T-shirt sat with a toddler clinging to her breast, dozing fitfully. A few seats forward, an elderly couple was breaking out a deck of cards. Three seats in front of them, an obese man in a well-worn business suit was staring out at the passing landscape, the weedy, overgrown railyards and featureless Orwellian buildings.

Turning back to John, Jessie laid her hand on his arm and squeezed reassuringly. "Gonna make it through this, Sport," she murmured. "Gonna get some food and some coffee, and we're gonna piece together some memories, and we're gonna get to the bottom of this thing."

Their gazes met.

It was an odd moment for Jessie, sitting there in that softly pitching coach car as it lit out toward the darkening horizon, the dying light shimmering in John McNally's eyes, all the doubt and fear and half-formed memories churning in his tortured expression. Jessie could tell he was on the threshold of a breakthrough—maybe even a breakdown—and *she* was his only lifeline. She felt a strange sort of twinge in the center of her chest, a jolt of emotion. May God strike her dumb, and may the elders of all great detectives strip her rank and send her to the Gulag of Eternal Goofballs, she didn't care anymore. The truth was, she was falling for this poor son of a bitch. She was *falling* for him. And the sooner she faced that fact, the sooner she would be able to deal with it.

John must have seen the revelation sparking behind her eyes because he swallowed hard all of a sudden, awkwardly looking away. "How am I ever going to repay you for all this?" he muttered softly at the shadows beneath the seats.

"We'll work the financing out," Jessie replied. "Don't you worry about that." Then she pointed at the satchel sitting on the armrest between them. "Now, why don't you get that notebook out and let's start retracing these memories you had down there in the subway."

John did as she suggested, and they started working just as the train began its eastward course toward the gathering darkness of northern Indiana. Behind them, half a dozen coach cars rolled along, full of weary travelers dozing and reading newspapers and gazing out the windows at the clear night sky darkening like a shroud.

Seventy-seven passengers in all, counting Jessie and John.

One of them completely oblivious to the fact that this would be her last journey.

Part Four

A Box Full of Snakes

I was not in safety, neither had I rest, neither was I quiet; yet trouble came.

—Job 3:26

39

Skeletons

"HE CALLED ME 'Doc' in his letter—Billy Marsten—so let's say I'm a doctor of some kind—"

"What's it say in the journal? Anything?"

"Does it matter?"

"Yeah, actually, I think it matters a lot," Jessie said, the muffled clacking of the rails beneath them punctuating the tension. "Even though we don't really believe this journal is you, it *is* your handwriting, and if nothing else, there might be more clues in it."

John thought about it for a second. He hadn't yet read the entire hundred-plus-page diary—he hadn't the stomach or the courage to go that far. He couldn't remember seeing any reference to being a doctor in the twenty-five or thirty pages he *had* suffered through up to now, but there *was* the reference to implantations and surgical techniques. Would that indicate that the narrator was a surgeon? John *did* recall glancing at a section in the journal that looked like recollections of past misadventures and indignities.

There was another clue, however—a part of the puzzle that John had been avoiding. It had to do with his own behavior over the past couple of days. From the moment he had fled the cop in the woods outside the Reinhardt Clinic right up until moments ago, he had been witnessing some fairly awful things—the photos at the Wagon Inn, the slain desk clerk at the transient hotel, Billy Marsten's remains in the subway. And while John had been horrified by these things, he had apparently accepted them on some deeper, almost *clinical* level, as though they were simply bits and pieces of data. Was this because he was a practitioner of some sort? Or was it due to something darker, more sociopathic, in his nature?

John remembered staring at himself in the mirror.

The eyes of the beast.

"Okay, wait a minute," he said suddenly, digging the tattered notebook out of the satchel. "There's a section here in the middle that might have something . . ."

He began thumbing through the pages.

Outside the window, the pitch-black night billowed and furled like a flag as the train sped through the desolate countryside, somewhere between Hammond and Michigan City, Indiana. Every few moments, a signal light would streak by, or the distant wink of a farmhouse, but mostly there were the shifting noises of the coach, and the muffled drumming of iron wheels on iron rails, and the occasional chorus of the air horn from the engine, curling around the train on the wind currents like an insane aria. Although they had been in transit for less than an hour, John felt as though he had entered another universe, a sort of timeless limbo where neither God nor the devil could get at them, and all they had to do was sort out the broken filaments of his memory until the light returned and everything made sense.

Fat chance.

"All right, here's something," John said finally, running his index finger down the tight, mechanical scrawl at the bottom of a page, his vision blurring slightly. Even though he had just consumed three cups of black coffee and a rubbery chicken sandwich, he was still exhausted. He hadn't slept since he had passed out the previous night at the Blue Island Hotel. But he *did* remember reading a little bit of this odd reminiscence before blacking out that night.

John began reading aloud to Jessie, speaking softly, so that he wouldn't be heard over the noise of the train:

" 'They know my history now, they've dug up the skeletons, gone all the way back to the dark ages when I was just entering my residency, assigned to shadow that old cocker Morrisey at that hideous little trauma clinic. I was a rookie in every way, full of naïve juice and grandiose ideas about revolutionizing the field, making a name for myself, getting rich, blah, blah, blah. Alas, plastic surgeons are a restless breed, unrestricted by anatomic region or system, prone to improvisation, innovation, grandstanding. I was no different. And I was not about to let a few minor substance abuse problems—methamphetamines and alcohol, mostly—get in the way of my dreams.' "

John stopped for a moment.

"So Marsten knew you were supposed to be a plastic surgeon," Jessie said after an awkward moment.

"Maybe, maybe not." John stared at the journal as the train passed another signal, the Doppler jangle echoing, the yellow light ghosting through the coach's interior. "The thing is, we don't really know if the 'Doc' in this journal is real."

Jessie regarded him for another moment. "What are you saying? The journal's imaginary?"

"I don't really know, Jessie."

"What do you make of the meat imagery? Or the *bacon* references in the file?"

John shook his head, completely mystified by it, and told her he had no idea.

Jessie made a few more notes in her notebook. "Gonna have to look up a Dr. Morrisey, maybe check out the trauma clinics around the region." Then she looked up at John. "Concentrate on it for a second."

"What do you mean?" He looked at her. He had a feeling he knew where she was going with this, and it made him feel very uncomfortable.

"I mean, concentrate on being a plastic surgeon, you know, the act. Think about it, see if it conjures anything. See if you can remember."

John shook his head. "I don't have to, Jessie, it doesn't resonate. Not at all."

"But you said you remembered graduate school and academics, and studying like crazy."

John tried to control his anger. "Look. All I said was, I remember vivid images of being in the graduate stacks at MSU night after night, but when I try to pull back and identify my field of study, it's like the lens goes soft-focus. You see what I'm saying?"

Jessie nodded, but before she could say anything else, John raged on.

"I can prove to you I'm not this guy, Jessie—I'm not some head case recording his sicko ideas for posterity. I don't talk like this guy, my speech patterns are different—I mean, I don't even *think* like this guy. These kinds of traits are not simply erased by amnesia."

"John, I never said—"

"Let me read you something else." He looked down at the journal, saw where he had left off, and continued: "'Morrisey and his little cadre of cretins knew I was becoming something special, a prodigy, a man with ideas, a man with vision, and it frightened them. They arranged to have that skinny bitch from the Gold Coast come to me during my first month of residency—what was her name?—Speakman. Yes, that was it—Gloria Speakman. A scrawny little piece of jet-trash, with her capri pants and rose tattoo and ratty little poodle dog. If I encountered her today, I'd take a white-hot speculum and dig out her ovaries, but alas, the cunt is gone with the wind. Amazing. All I do is make a subtle little remark about the quality of her inner thigh, and she drops a rape charge in my lap. Ruins the career of (potentially) the finest plastic surgeon who ever practiced.'"

John paused for effect, then added, "You see? This isn't my voice—I mean, this isn't even remotely like my voice, amnesia or not."

Jessie touched her lip. "But it's another little tidbit we can use."

"What is?"

"This guy was busted during his residency. That's assuming this is a real person."

John took a deep breath and sighed. "That's the real question, isn't it? I mean, if the bogeyman is real, then what's the connection to me?"

"At this point, we can't rule anything out."

John drilled his gaze into her. "I'm not a multiple personality, Jessie."

There was another pause as the train continued to pulse through the darkness.

Jessie looked down at her notes for a moment, then looked up at John. "Back in the subway, when you flashed back to your childhood."

"I remember, yeah."

"Seems like the further back you go, the more clearly you remember things."

"I don't know, I suppose that's true." John looked out at the night, the blur of vapor lights streaking by. All at once, he remembered something else about his childhood, an image. It was as though his sinuses had just opened, and he could smell the odors of his childhood, the pine needles and manure and grease, and he could see the flickering images of Fess Parker splitting rails. "I remember growing up in a little place right outside East Lansing," he said. "Haslett, it was called—a rural subdivision, really— farms, trailer parks; and I remember our place, this long, narrow trailer buried in the trees at the end of a dead-end cul-de-sac. My dad really made that thing a palace—you know, the imitation-bamboo wallpaper and the tiki furniture, and the TV in the corner—a little twenty-one inch Muntz. Used to watch a lot of TV in that trailer. Favorite shows were *Daniel Boone* and *Bonanza,* and later I watched *The Man from U.N.C.L.E.* religiously."

Jessie gave him a fleeting smile. "I loved *The Man from U.N.C.L.E.*" She gazed back at her notes. "You remember anything else about your parents? Mom stayed home, Dad was an insurance agent. They treat you well? Were they good parents?"

"Far as I can remember, they were fine. No tawdry tales of abuse."

"You were a bookish kid, though, right? Not a lot of friends?"

John shrugged. "That's what I remember."

"High school rolled around, and you were completely absorbed in the books, right? The classic geek? No dates?"

"You could say that, yeah."

"By the time you got to college, you were a total recluse, right? A full-blown bookworm?"

John nodded. He was starting to feel queasy again, as though his stomach were being peeled from the inside out. Something important was straining the envelope of his amnesia, and it was sending chills up and down the back of his legs.

"What did you do with it, John?" Jessie was clearly picking at the wound, trying to tweak something lose.

"What do you mean?"

"I mean, how did you deal with it? The isolation, the alienation. You know. People have coping mechanisms, ways of playing the cards they're dealt."

John thought about it for a moment, but it was futile. Even the most introspective nonamnesic with the world's greatest therapist would be hard-pressed to pinpoint a direct link to his childhood. And yet . . . something was worming through his subconscious, threatening to burst through the membrane, something significant. His heart was beginning to chug, and his mouth had gone dry. He wanted a drink badly. He wanted to go back to that café car and suck down a pint of Tanqueray and drown the worm and kill the witch and stop the noise in his head. Instead, he looked at Jessie and said, "I have no idea what shapes a person's destiny."

"There's something there, dammit, between the lines," she insisted, jabbing her finger at the notes. "Something unspoken, *something,* I'm sure of it."

"I can't help you, Jessie."

"What did you study in college?"

John kept shaking his head. "It just gets . . . vague."

"Think hard. Push it."

John was fidgeting now, the soles of his feet prickling as though the floor were electrified. How does a person *think hard* anyway? Is it a cartoonish exercise in brute cerebral force? Like Popeye madly pacing the length of his boat, clenching his fists, wincing until smoke starts pouring out of his ears? John felt like his skin was about to catch fire, like his skull was three sizes too small for his brain. Finally he rose to his feet. "I'm sorry, but I gotta get outta here—"

He squeezed past her, then entered the aisle.

"Where the hell you gonna go?" Jessie was taken by surprise, fumbling with her notes.

John was already halfway down the aisle, moving toward the far door, which led passengers into the next coach. Jessie followed him. John reached the threshold and paused, his heartbeat thumping in his ears, his throat full of dry sawdust, his sort joints creaking. He tried to move, but a wave of dizziness washed over him, tossing him against a chair back.

"John, what is it—?" Jessie was right behind him, reaching out for him.

He made another move toward the door and tried to slide it open, but the train jerked suddenly.

John fell against a window, the sound of the train's air horn trumpeting loudly outside the glass, a series of signal lights streaking past the car. The train was slowing, the conductor's voice crackling through a nearby speaker—"This stop is Michigan City, Michigan City, Indiana. For those of you disembarking, please check the seats around you for your belongings, and have a pleasant evening in Michigan City, Indiana"—the sound of the air brakes hissing, the train spasming, jerking, shoving John against the window.

Jessie reached out and grabbed his shoulders to steady him. "What's the matter, John?"

He tried to speak, but his brain was a piston now that had frozen midcycle. Somewhere outside, the sound of drumming was rising in the night air, the sound of sticks on metal, congas maybe. Some kind of Afro-Cuban percussion music drifting through the darkness. Silvery white light was flashing in the window.

The train stopped.

"John—?" Jessie's voice was a million miles away now, barely audible under the music.

John turned toward the window just as a beam of white light suddenly slashed across the train. John blinked. Outside, under a metal awning, figures were moving in a pool of sodium vapor light, their shadows dancing across the cobble-brick pavement of the train station. Half a dozen kids of various ethnicities, dressed in high-tops and baggies and gang colors, were dancing to hip-hop percussion music. One of them was wailing on an inverted garbage pail, and another one was sweeping the beam of a halogen camper's light across the dancers with theatrical flourish.

"John—?"

The camper's light swept across the train and flashed in John's face.

Something burst deep down in John's midbrain like a water main rupturing, and all at once memories started flooding him on great surges of brilliant-colored light and great waves of sound—*the echo of audiences applauding, the squeal of pulleys and cables and counterweights turning, the enormous curtains parting, the clang of stage lights flaming on, the brilliant magenta light illuminating ornate settings, the glare of spotlights in his face, the smell of hot makeup, the clamor of voices, the feel of burlap on his skin, the rush, the adrenaline rush—FLASH!—a woman crying, orchestras swelling—FLASH! FLASH! FLASH!—the sudden glare of impossibly bright WHITE LIGHT!!—*

The train lurched suddenly, and John stumbled backward against a seat.

"John, talk to me." Jessie was shaking him now. "What's going on?"

He looked at her, blinking, trying to focus on her face as the train pulled away from the dancing teenage boys and the sweeping halogen camper's light. The coach car was pitching and yawing gently now, the Michigan City station shrinking away into the blackness behind them. John swallowed the coppery taste in his mouth and said, "I remember what it means, Jessie. I remember it now."

She was baffled. "What it means? What *what* means?"

He looked at her, then said evenly, "The method."

40

Broken Toy

IT STARTED IN Russia a hundred years ago.

In 1898, a renowned stage actor named Konstantin Stanislavski, working out of the Moscow Art Theatre, invented a system of stage acting that quickly caught on among the post-czarist Bolshevik intelligentsia. The system was based on "feeling" the emotions inherent in a play's text. Stanislavski applied this ingenious system to the works of Chekhov and Gorki, and soon became the world's premiere acting teacher, interpreting such great plays as *Uncle Vanya* and *The Cherry Orchard.* Stanislavski wrote a famous book, *An Actor Prepares,* which became the seminal source of inspiration for followers of this system; and in the twenties he toured Europe and America, spreading his philosophies from Stratford-on-Avon to Broadway. Stanislavski became so successful that by the time of his death in 1938, his system had become the most prevalent theory of acting in the world.

Americans adapted his teachings throughout the forties and fifties, creating such influential acting troops as the Group Theater and the Actors Studio. Practitioners Elia Kazan and Lee Strasberg taught Stanislavski-based techniques, such as mentally recalling past experiences, reliving traumas, and dredging up long-forgotten sense memories in order to get inside the skin of a character, re-creating the truthful emotions required to convey the message of a play or a film. These techniques bred a new generation of actor. Marlon Brando, James Dean, Paul Newman. The world of acting was forever revolutionized by this intense, brooding new approach.

They called it The Method.

And this was precisely what John was explaining to Jessie in the club car of the Amtrak International train en route to East Lansing when she suddenly stopped him.

"Okay, wait-wait—wait—slow down, please." Jessie raised her hand, cutting off John's rambling dissertation. They were sitting at a small banquette in the rear of the narrow dining car. The little kitchen area behind them was as deserted as a Fotomat on New Year's Eve. The dining steward, a portly little gentleman in a white jacket, was perched on a stool next to the rear hatch, listening to a Cubs game on a transistor radio, paying no attention to them. A dozen other banquettes—six on each side—sat mostly empty, except for the last one on the right, the one near the front hatch. A lone woman sat there, nursing a Miller Lite, staring at a *National Enquirer* spread out neatly on her tabletop. Her bad dye job was piled up on top of her head like a scoop of butterscotch ice cream.

"Am I going too fast?" John asked.

"Not exactly," Jessie said. "I'm familiar with the Method-acting thing—although I never knew where the term came from—but what I really want to know is, what the hell does all this have to do with you?"

"Everything, everything. Look. Senior year in high school, I was miserable, utterly miserable. I remember my dad was dying a slow death from cancer, and Mom was scrambling to supplement the medical bills, working night shift out at Lansing Steel. I remember thinking, if I just drove off the edge of the world some night—you know, took a dip into the Red Cedar—everything would be easier for everybody."

Jessie nodded slowly, knowingly. "Sounds familiar."

"Yeah, well, you know teenagers. Very melodramatic. I remember I had terrible insomnia in those days, just relentless, and I would stay up nights either reading or staring at the TV. One night I saw an old rebroadcast of *On the Waterfront*."

"Brando."

"Precisely."

"And you identified with it?"

"No, not exactly, not at first. What I saw was this weird kind of freedom in that stevedore that Brando played, something I'd never seen before—in life *or* in the movies. I remember thinking, *This guy is totally pathetic and needy and a real loser—and Eva Marie Saint still wants him.*"

Jessie nodded. "The scene in the taxi—what was it?—'I coulda been a contender.'"

John closed his eyes, remembering the brilliant scene between Brando and Steiger: "'Charlie, aw, Charlie, you don't understand. I coulda had class. I coulda been a contender. Instead of a bum, which is what I am.'"

"That's the one."

John looked at her. "The very next day at school, I went and signed up for the senior play. Can't remember what it was that year, some banal farce, but I got a small part. I was galvanized by it."

"You wanted to be an actor."

"It was more than that—I mean, I *immersed* myself in it, I lost myself in the craft, and I—I—I read everything I could get my hands on, especially books by and about Stanislavski. I guess it was a way to turn all my short-comings into something like benefits—all the doubts and the loneliness—it was a way to turn the pain into something attractive."

"So you went on to study acting in college?"

John started to say, "Yeah, I was in these—" and then he stopped himself.

The overhead dome lights flickered for a moment, and the club car shimmied. The muffled drum roll rose up beneath them, the train rushing over a deserted switch platform in the middle of nowhere, sending chills up John's spine. What was it? Something was still blocked in the back of his mind, something to do with college, studying acting at MSU, something in his past. It was as though his memories were blooming like a poisonous flower, opening up from his childhood on, until they revealed a cancerous black spot right around college. At that point, everything went dark. What in God's name happened back then?

"What's wrong?" Jessie was staring at him.

"Uh, nothing, I'm fine, it's just . . . I'm remembering things in stages, and it's a little jarring."

He took a deep breath, then fished in his pocket and found his keys. He brought them up into the light and stared at them, studied them, wondered about them. There were a few cheap copies, silver-plated, with square shanks. There was a larger one with a plastic guard over the shank—probably his car key—and there was a smaller one, a tarnished-brass color, with a round shank. The smaller one had a delicate cut pattern, and John stared at it, wondering what it opened. He closed his hand over the key and squeezed it as though he were squeezing a talisman.

The light flickered again, and John looked over his shoulder. He saw the woman with the *National Enquirer* had vanished, leaving the tabloid and the empty beer bottle behind. Now it was only John and Jessie and the dozing steward in the club car. John turned back to Jessie. "Sorry," he murmured. "Still a little shaky."

"Tell me about college," Jessie said.

"I got accepted into Michigan State's theater school—not exactly a prestigious program, but it was close to home, and I could keep track of my father—and I became obsessed with acting. I acted in everything I could possibly find, from student productions to summer stock to local dinner theater, and I studied under the—"

Again he stopped.

"What is it, John?" Jessie was staring at him.

The noise in his head was back—the watery pulsing in his ears like a fetal heartbeat—the sparking white flares in his gaze, punctuating his panic. His temple was aching furiously now, and his mouth had gone bone dry, and he kept squeezing that delicate brass-colored key to the arrhythmic beat of his thoughts. It was as though the memories of his college days had triggered some chemical reaction deep in his brain, and now his vision was going all blurry—

—as he squeezed that key harder and harder.

"Judas Priest!" Jessie's voice snapped John out of his delirium.

He looked down at his hand.

It was sticky with blood, the deep crimson underneath it spreading in a blot across the white tablecloth. He jerked back. The keys dropped to the table, beads of blood clinging to their edges. Evidently John had inadvertently squeezed the key so hard it had cleaved his palm. He tried to stand, but his legs got tangled in the metal posts beneath the booth. "I'm okay," he uttered sheepishly.

"What the hell happened?" Jessie was helping him up, lights flickering.

"I'm okay, I'm . . . fine."

"John, what's going on?"

"Gotta . . . get to a bathroom," he muttered, grabbing the bloody keys, stuffing them back into his pocket and pushing himself away from the table. He staggered drunkenly down the aisle toward the far door, past slabs of windows billowing darkly, past the deserted banquette at which the blond bouffant had been sitting, reading her tabloid. Across the metal threshold, and then through the pass-through door. The hatch was automated, and it rattled open the moment John struck it with his shoulder.

Jessie was right behind him.

John staggered through the empty coach toward the metal balustrade, cradling his bloody palm in his free hand like a wounded bird. He reached the stairs and descended the steps two at a time, and when he reached the lower level, the train pitched suddenly and tossed him against the luggage rack. Jessie appeared at the bottom of the stairs. "John, wait a second, goddamnit, talk to me."

"I'm okay, really, I'll be right back," he croaked, then managed to slip inside the door marked GENTLEMEN.

The lavatory was surprisingly large, more of a lounge than a rest room, with a corrugated iron floor and a center cubicle featuring two stainless-steel sinks and toiletries lined up along steel shelves. There were three stall doors lined up along the left wall. The train pitched again, and John staggered for a foothold on the iron flooring. Then he moved over to the first stall door, and he swung the door open.

At first, the lifeless body slouching on the toilet looked soaking wet.

John reared backward instinctively, the sight of the woman with the butterscotch bouffant lying bloody and mutilated on the commode screaming silently up at him, her livid face canted upward, her expression furrowed as though crying out to God in her final moments. Her dress was dark and sodden with blood around the torso and armpits. Blood was puddled on the floor beneath her, tendrils spreading on the corrugated iron. Someone had amputated both her hands and both her feet, the stumps still glistening wetly. She looked like a sad, little, broken toy.

"Oh—no—Jesus—God—" John was gibbering now, touching his mouth with his trembling bloody paw, backing away from the abomination in the stall. He spun around toward the shadows behind him, looking for the culprit. Expecting Jack the Ripper to jump out at him at any moment.

The sound of muffled knocking behind him: "John—*John,* for Chrissake—!"

Somehow John managed to motivate his shock-flimsy legs, and he wobbled over to the door.

"John—!"

With one desperate movement he threw the door open, grabbed Jessie, and pulled her inside the lavatory. He slammed the door so hard it made his ears ring, but he barely noticed it now because the soles of his shoes were tacky with blood, and the fetal heartbeat was pulsing-pulsing-pulsing in his ears, and Jessie's frantic voice seemed out of sync with her lips as she grabbed him, shook him.

"What's the matter?" she demanded.

He grabbed her arm and spun her toward stall number one, and he watched her expression congeal, her eyes widening, her mouth going slack as she looked down at the dead woman with no hands or feet. Then Jessie whirled instinctively, gazing around the room, eyes shifting involuntarily.

"Jesus Christ, Jesus—whoever's doing this—he's on the *train*—he's watching us—he's here—he's—"

John suddenly clamped his hand over Jessie's mouth.

Sudden noises outside the rest room door.

"Sir—?" The gravelly voice of the dining-car steward. "Everything okay in there?"

John looked at Jessie, and he could see by the panicky fire burning hotly behind her eyes that she was fresh out of clever ideas.

41

One Way Out

"SIR—? CAN YOU hear me?"

The steward had one of those guttural, stentorian voices you hear coming out of drill instructors and traffic cops, a rich, cigar-cured baritone with just a hint of pent-up rage, which, even muffled by the latched door, was making John's flesh crawl. He drew his hand away from Jessie's mouth, and Jessie just stood there, frozen, wide-eyed, stunned silent. Somehow, amid all the shock and indecision, John managed to slide over to the door and make sure the lock bolt was engaged. He turned back to Jessie, momentarily losing his balance, his shoes sliding on the slime-slick iron.

He looked down and saw the blood.

It was seeping out of the stall—as dark as pine tar in the dim light—a narrow ripple inching toward the door. It was twelve inches away. John looked up at Jessie, and he saw her looking at the blood, and she was probably thinking exactly what he was thinking, and they both jumped when the muffled knocking returned.

"Sir—I heard a noise—you okay?"

John swallowed needles of panic, then spoke up: "Yes, yes, I'm fine, just a little motion sickness."

"Can I help you, sir?"

"No, no, thanks, I'm feeling better already," John was saying as he turned toward the sinks.

Jessie was already clawing at the towel dispenser, yanking out brown paper towels. She rushed over to the door, knelt down, and started sopping up the blood. But it was too late. A dribble of it had already seeped under the door. *"We gotta get outta here,"* she whispered.

John looked around the lavatory for a window and saw none.

"Sir—!" The voice was booming outside the door now, the lock jiggling. "Is that blood? Are you okay?"

"Almost done!"

Then things began to fall apart, because the steward was slamming into the door, the delicate little bolt straining with each impact, the hinges rattling, and Jessie was on her feet again, going for more paper towels, and John grabbed her and shoved her against the door, motioning to the bolt, motioning for her to brace the door, but the steward was ramming the door harder and harder now, again and again, straining the hinges, and John was going for more paper towels, when the sound of the bolt snapping filled his ears.

The door burst open.

The portly steward came stumbling into the lavatory, slipping on the blood-sodden paper towels and the slimy iron, arms pinwheeling, and all at once he went down with a massive thud. The entire rest room shivered, sending bottles of aftershave toppling out of their cradles. The steward looked up and saw the blood, and something snapped behind his eyes. The train shimmied suddenly, the overhead lights sputtering, the lavatory rocking, as John and Jessie tried to slip past the dumbstruck steward and get out the door.

The steward clutched John's pant leg, pulling him back inside the lavatory.

John managed to stay on his feet.

Jessie tried to intervene, attempting to kick the steward off John, but the steward was a scrapper—the stocky little son of a bitch—and he dodged her blow, rolling across the floor, twisting John's leg until John lost his balance and went down. John hit the iron hard, and his breath puffed out of his lungs. Now John was gasping for air, trying to see through watery, blurry eyes, as Jessie tried to grab the steward's shirt, but the steward was moving quickly now—very quickly for a portly little man—shoving her across the lavatory. Jessie slammed into the far stall, knocking open the door, landing on her posterior directly on the toilet seat, momentarily paralyzed, dazed and breathless.

The steward climbed to his feet and saw the carnage in the first stall. "Lord have mercy," he murmured under his breath, a gleam of mad heroism in his eyes as he turned toward John.

John was rising when the steward attacked.

The fat man engulfed John like a tidal wave, tight little fists battering at

John's soft places, and John was trying to fight back, but the steward was ablaze with anger and the hard-packed muscle that years of hauling tubs of dirty dishes had built. All John could do was shield his face and try to turn away, but the steward had John by the shirt now and was slamming him into the wall by the door.

The first impact rattled John's skull and sent fountains of sparks across his line of vision, and the second and third bolted down his spine, the pain shrieking between his shoulder blades. Then John was flailing at the portly steward, grabbing at the man's uniform, tearing at his face, kicking, clawing, yelling garbled, inarticulate pleas: "Stop—I didn't—*dammit!*—I didn't do this—she was here when I came—"

All at once the assault flagged, and the fat marauder abruptly paused, turning away.

Jessie was standing behind him, tapping him on the shoulder like she had some bad news.

What happened next transpired over the space of an instant, but in the lens of John's thunderstruck mind it seemed to occur in dreamy slow motion, like one of those stunning old Leni Riefenstahl documentaries—Olympic athletes in Nazi Germany diving off the high board in super–time-lapse—the gorgeous curve of Jessie's torso twisting backward, the line of her right arm winding back as though she were about to pitch a fast ball, the grimace on her lovely angular face, all teeth and flaring eyes, and, finally, her fist, like a shiny white-knuckled meteorite, coming hard at the steward's face.

The sound of Jessie's fist striking flesh and bone was like a pistol shot.

Cartilage popping, the fat man seemed to levitate out of his shoes, whiplashing backward hard, completely stunned by the force, the accuracy, the certainty—the sheer there-ness—of Jessie's haymaker. A sound like a rusty honk burst out of the steward's nasal passages as he slammed, back first, into the wall. Then he faded to the floor, his eyes glassy with pain. Jessie was staggering a few feet away, wincing, holding her hand. "Son of a *bitch!* That hurts!" she hissed through clenched teeth.

John managed to stumble over to Jessie and check her hand for any obvious damage. "You okay?"

"Yeah—*shit!*—I think so."

"Thank you once again," John muttered.

"It was nothing, really."

"I think we better—" John stopped suddenly when he saw that the rest room door was flapping open, banging against the jamb, and that there were figures in navy blue Amtrak uniforms coming down the stairs outside the door. John rushed over and slammed the door, but the lock had broken off in the scuffle, and now only a broken curl of metal hung from the groove. He spun toward Jessie and said, "We're trapped in here, Jessie."

"Maybe not," she said, then reached out and grabbed his shirt. She dragged him over to the third stall—the stall in which she had unceremoniously landed during the fight—and yanked him inside, slamming the door and locking it. Then she spun John toward the wall, and John looked up and saw the beautiful, glorious window, the lovely window, the picture-perfect window, with its three-foot-wide frame that was big enough for a linebacker to negotiate, and before John knew what was happening he saw Jessie fiddling with the metal flanges on either side of the frame, and the sounds of shuffling footsteps were pouring into the lavatory behind them, and now Jessie was grunting and groaning, and the window's ancient seal was cracking, and John's adrenal gland was about to explode—

"Somebody's in there! The other stall!" the voice clamored across the lavatory.

The window came off and clattered to the floor.

A torrent of noise and wind stormed through the stall, whipping John and Jessie back against the door, and the wind smelled of cinders and diesel and rain, and it stung with the acid-moisture tang of the wastelands, and John realized at once that the train was still barreling through the night, seventy, maybe eighty, miles an hour, and he knew what they had to do. No alternatives. No other choices. One way out.

"You go first," Jessie ordered him in a terse, steady voice. She had her game face on; her left eye was twitching. Out the window, the sound of metal keening. Were the brakes coming on? Was the train slowing?

"Call the depot security!" another voice was yammering outside the stall door.

John grabbed the window ledge with blood-slick hands, lifted himself up, and swung his leg out the gap until he was sitting there like an idiot on a mechanical pony, the wind buffeting him, curling around him, slapping him in the face. The roar of the metal monster was drowning everything else now, and John looked down at the rushing rapids, the gravel apron like whitecaps breaking in the Indiana night, and John winced at the painful pounding in his chest. The train was slowing. Up ahead, the track was curving around a dark patchwork of farm fields. John knew what he had to do— he knew exactly what he had to do—but he couldn't make his body work anymore. He was glued to that goddamned ledge like a rusted statue—

Jessie shoved him.

He had no time to scream, or react, or think, or even register the wind draft shearing the top of his skull, tossing him sideways—airborne, he was airborne—because the wind was a shrieking banshee.

Then he landed hard, his right buttock absorbing most of the impact on a muddy strip of earth beyond the apron, the g-forces immediately catapulting him forward. He tumbled head over heels down a wet, grassy embankment, the odors of manure and stone dust and rich black loam like an animal roaring in his face. He slammed against a weathered fence post.

His body vibrated for a moment from the sudden stop and the cold shock of the fall.

A moment later, he managed to lift his gaze to the train speeding off into the dark.

At first, in the blur of his pain and panic, he saw only the red taillights like candy cinders glowing garishly off the rear of the dining car, shrinking away into the black, moonless void, taunting him. He rose to kneeling position in the weeds, wiping tears and sweat from his face, heart slamming in his chest, trying to see the open window. Where was Jessie? John tried to stand, but his legs were still weak. It felt as though his lungs were filled with cement, his spine twinging hotly, his eyes burning, but he concentrated on the lower rear of that dining car, and that open window—now a quarter-mile away—and he saw nothing.

Jessie, for God's sake, what are you doing? His mind was racing hysterically now, all sorts of scenarios flashing across his consciousness. *Don't leave me now, Jessie, please—*

He froze.

About a hundred yards in the distance, the train's running lights were vanishing. Behind it, where the track curved, the smooth horizon line was broken by the crumpled silhouette of a figure lying prone in the weeds next to the rails. Arms and legs akimbo, body twisted sideways, she looked as though someone had carelessly dumped her from the train like a bundle of dirty laundry.

"OhmyGod," John was uttering now as he climbed to his feet, then started staggering frantically toward the figure.

The figure wasn't moving.

42

The Darkness to the East

APPROACHING THE SHADOWY form in the weeds, eyes stinging with panic, John tried to stay calm, focused. Jessie lay motionless, her face turned away from the tracks, her skin soiled with cinder dust.

John came closer and his scalp crawled with dread, his stomach turning icy cold. It looked as though Jessie were grimacing with her eyes closed, but it was hard to tell in the darkness. After all they had been through, John couldn't believe that Jessie would be the one to get injured. John swallowed back his terror as he knelt down by her face—afraid to touch her, afraid to utter a word—finally managing to croak a feeble "Jessie, can you hear me?"

Her eyes fluttered, then focused on him. Her breathing was shallow.

"Jessie!" John was paralyzed with emotion, trying to see through watery eyes.

She tried to speak, her breathless moaning barely audible above the buzz of crickets. "Goddamn racquetball . . ." she murmured finally.

"Excuse me?" John could hear his own blood rushing in his ears.

Jessie swallowed hard, wincing. "Phyllis Strickland and I played a couple of years back . . . like I'm some kind of jock . . . *Jesus* . . . what was I thinking?"

"I don't under—"

"My damn *back,* is what I'm saying." Jessie's eyes glimmered in the darkness. "I just *had* to be Miss Davis Cup and dive for that backhand."

John was trying to recover, trying to breathe normally again. He felt like embracing her. Instead, he stroked her forehead and said, "Can you move?"

"I suppose, I don't know." She tried to move and winced at the sudden twinge.

"Take it easy," John said, and gently urged her back to the ground.

"Two slipped disks for one lousy moment of glory." Jessie was staring at the sky, looking annoyed.

"Just take it easy," John said. "We'll get you some help."

"I'll be fine, just gimme a minute."

She took some deep breaths, her lungs rattling faintly, and John gazed down at her, down at her toasted-almond tresses and her Cover Girl lips and her incredible cheekbones—God, those cheekbones looked so exquisite in the darkness, like sculpted marble—and all at once the noise in his head began to fade, the siren-squall of fear, the aftermath of discovering that poor woman in the lavatory, it all began to ease slightly as John concentrated on this reluctant guardian angel. "What happened, Jessie?" John said finally, his mind settling enough to allow him to think.

"Conductor burst in on me just as I was about to jump," Jessie said. "Screwed up my timing, that's all." She managed to sit up, and John held on to her for a moment, steadying her. "I'll be fine," she said after another moment of deep breathing.

"Can you stand?"

"Gimme a second." Jessie swallowed hard then, and took one last deep breath.

Then she struggled to her feet.

John rose and stood next to her, his arm gently around her back. "You gave me quite a scare, lady."

Jessie looked at him smiling wearily. "I didn't know you cared."

At that moment, if he hadn't been so disoriented and terrified, John might have blushed.

He turned away and gazed across the field. They were standing on the edge of a big commercial soybean farm, the night sky a canopy of brooding black clouds, the land so dark and flat it looked almost like an ocean at dead calm. And that clean, rich, fecund odor drifting on the wind—John remembered that smell from his childhood. It was strange, though, how much the odors, more than anything else, were making him remember. The olfactory sense was the most evocative of all.

John turned to Jessie. "You feel like walking?"

Jessie shrugged. "Sure as hell not gonna stand around here all night."

They followed the train tracks at first, until they came to a crossing. Then they followed the access road. They walked for nearly twenty minutes, and the countryside was as still and quiet as a church, which was driving John mad—the silence seemed alive, palpable—and he filled the stillness with nervous conversation. They discussed that poor woman in the lavatory, and the fact that her murderer must have been lurking just out of sight, waiting, biding his time. But how had the monster managed to sneak on to the train? They discussed John's memories, his foray into Method acting, and the strange black hole in his mind around his senior year in college. Jessie bemoaned the unfortunate fact that they had left the satchel on the train—not to mention their fingerprints—but, thankfully, Jessie had grabbed the Beretta before chasing John down the aisle. It had been stuffed into the back of her khakis when she had fallen from the train, and she had landed on the damn thing, which had bruised her already tender back. But now at least they had a weapon. Other than that, all they had were the clothes on their bodies, a little cash, and John's headful of reconstituting memories.

By the time they reached Highway 20, they were so weary they couldn't talk anymore.

They decided to hitchhike.

It took a while for the right vehicle to come along, but, sure enough, just as they were about to give up and keep walking, a faint beam of light appeared behind them, piercing the low-lying spring fog like a beacon, accompanied by the rumbling vibrations of a big truck. Soon, the noise and light rose up, and an eighteen-wheeler appeared behind them like an iron carnival, running lights flashing, horn bellowing. The truck roared past them, taillights flaming on, air brakes hissing. John and Jessie limped after it, thanking their lucky stars.

When they reached the cab, John climbed up the metal steps and opened the passenger door, revealing a cluttered interior and a leprous little troll in a Caterpillar cap and greasy flannel shirt sitting behind the wheel. He was peering over a shotgun seat full of cardboard boxes. The yellow dash lights shone off his wizened face. "Happy to give y'all a ride," he drawled. "Only catch is, y'all gotta ride back in the trailer."

"In the trailer?" John glanced over his shoulder at the huge box trailer with the Bigelow tea logo on its side.

"Yessir," the trucker nodded, then pointed at the boxes next to him. "I'd like the company, but it's too damn cramped up here for passengers. The rear door's unlocked. Y'all just hop on in and make yourselves comfy."

"That'll be fine, sir, thank you," Jessie was saying, and was already turning toward the trailer.

"By the way—you folks heading to Detroit?" the trucker asked.

"Lansing," John said, backing down the steps, trying to mask his nerves.

"I'm heading right through there, buddy. I'll blow the air horn when we're gettin' close."

John thanked him, shut the door, and started toward the back, but then the driver's voice was calling after him. "Hey—buddy!"

John went back to the cab, climbed up, and peered in at the troll.

"Gonna have lotsa privacy back there . . ." The troll grinned, revealing a rotting gold tooth that gleamed in the dimness. "Plenty of time to enjoy that long-legged gal."

John nodded sheepishly. "Yeah, right, absolutely right, thanks."

John went around back to the trailer, shaking his head, thinking, *Yeah, sure, it's a wonderful night for romance.* The trailer doors were already open, and Jessie was waiting for him. She helped him up the step rail, then pulled the double doors closed behind them.

The truck rattled on its merry way.

The thirty-foot box trailer was loaded to the gills with cartons of Bigelow tea. Stacked on rows of pallets along either side of a narrow aisle, the tea rose to the ceiling, every flavor and cut imaginable, from loose pekoe to exotic flavors. The air smelled of humidors and cinnamon, tobacco rich and minty, and a single overhead bulb flickered dimly, illuminating the space. John had to brace himself against a box of Earl Grey as the trailer shivered over a series of bumps.

"Take a load off," Jessie said wearily from the end of the aisle.

John made his way over to the low-lying stack of shrink-wrapped chamomile on which Jessie was sitting. She had spread out a packing blanket over the tea boxes, and as John settled down, the boxed creaked and complained. The aroma of dried flowers wafted around them. "I can't get the image of that woman out of my head," John said finally.

"There's something about heads," Jessie said, fishing in her blouse pocket for her crumpled pack of Carltons. Only one broken cigarette left. She thought about smoking it, then tossed it away.

"What do you mean?"

"Heads—distorted heads in the file, a severed head in the sewer, your own head virtually erased, all this talk of some head case on the loose—I don't know."

"I don't remember reading anything in the—" John jerked suddenly toward the rear, toward the firecracker pop of a stone hitting the undercarriage.

"Easy does it, Captain," Jessie said, and put her hand on his shoulder.

John took a deep breath, settled. "Sorry—still a tad jumpy, I guess."

"I'd be worried if you weren't."

"Thanks," John said, and then noticed that Jessie had not yet pulled her hand away. She kept it on his shoulder, gently squeezing, comforting him, and all at once John felt an incredible rush of warmth radiating up through his bones, making his nerve endings tingle. He tried to come up with something clever to say, but he was completely tongue-tied.

"One good thing," Jessie said finally.

"What's that?"

"We know you didn't murder that woman on the train."

John nodded, then looked at her. "I want to thank you, Jessie."

"For what?"

"For sticking with me."

She shrugged, her hand patting his shoulder softly. "Just doing my job."

John managed to smile. "And to think I was starting to worry about you."

"What do you mean, worry about me?"

"I was worried sooner or later you were going to pull that Persuader business on *me*."

"Persuader?" She gave him an odd look. "What are you talking about?"

"That trick you pulled in the tattoo parlor, with the behemoth in the sweaty leather."

Jessie grinned. "Oh, *that*."

John nodded, then looked into Jessie's dusky-emerald eyes and saw the shadows falling across her face, accentuating her angles—*Thank you, dear Lord, for your infinite wisdom and skill in sculpting those otherworldly cheekbones*—and all of a sudden he felt a sudden jolt of heat surging through his tendons, images from his past flickering in his head, the lonely nights, the solitary hours in the graduate stacks, the longing, the longing for a friend, a companion—why had he been so lonely?—and now this magnificent woman, with her cheekbones and nails and right cross like Mike Tyson, accepting him, trusting him—*why?* "Jessie, I hope you don't think—"

She leaned over and kissed him on the cheek.

It came out of nowhere—just a simple peck, nothing too provocative—but it cut off John's words, and for an awkward moment they both sat in silence, staring at each other. John reached up and felt his cheek as though he had been stung. He groped for something to say, but he couldn't find any words. His heart was racing now. He wondered if Jessie was having the same thoughts, feeling the same sort of mawkish, adolescent affection.

"I'm sorry, John—" Jessie started apologizing. "I probably shouldn't have—"

This time it was John's turn to interrupt the flow of conversation. He reached out and pulled her into a gentle embrace. He was surprised to feel the dampness on her back—she must have been sweating profusely—and the slight trembling in her bones, and her smell, God, even under the stench of the sewer water, it was bewitching to John, the faint trace of perfume, and spearmint, and cream rinse, and heat—it felt as though he had just been injected with heroin. He found her lips and kissed her. She responded silently, pressing her mouth down on his, and then they were clinging to each other, clinging desperately in the noisy silence of the rocking semi-trailer, clinging and kissing and stroking, their heartbeats pulsing like bellows, the air a heavy mélange of tea leaves, rot, and scented oils —wonderful smells, wonderful—and they held each other like this for the rest of the trip—too unnerved to make love, too terrified to let go of each other.

And for the balance of the ride, John forgot about the cold night rushing outside the membrane of the trailer, and what lay ahead of them in the darkness to the east.

43

Ripples in a Black Hole

THE PREDAWN SKY over Lansing was like milky glass, the faint glow of light behind it like the dim wattage of an old Tiffany lamp. In fact, the entire community was somewhat worn and antique, like an anachronistic little gaslight on the corner of two busy streets. Founded in the mid-nineteenth century, Lansing was the capital of Michigan and a strange sort of relic from the mass-production age, a low-slung brick-and-mortar outpost of the automobile and manufacturing industries. But unlike Flint to the north, with its prehistoric husks of dead bodyworks, or Detroit to the east, with its mean streets and downriver foundries, Lansing was still a hermetically sealed little world unto itself, planted smack dab in the middle of rich farmland. A melding of cultures so disparate, they often seemed as though they might split the community apart at the seams.

The reason for this unlikely mélange was undoubtedly the university.

Michigan State University was founded in 1855. One of the first land-grant universities in America, it was situated on the east side of town and came to be known as "Moo U" to local bon vivants. Over the years, the campus spread like kudzu across the banks of the Red Cedar, down into the soybean fields south of Mount Hope and Forest Akers. By the late seventies, MSU had become the largest university (in square acreage) in the entire United States, covering more than two thousand acres of ivy-fringed red-brick classroom buildings, dormitories, labs, and experimental farm fields.

The northeast corner of the campus was the oldest, dotted by clusters of Victorian manses and groves of century-old hardwoods. Most of the old gothic dorms and study halls were whiskered with foliage, the copper trim and gutters moldering green, the ancient mansard roofs drooping like old swayback horses. The constant wear of transients had given the place a withered patina, a kind of Ivy-League-meets-the-Midwest slump to many of the buildings. And each morning, around dawn, the pale new sun would strike these enclaves first, giving them an eerie kind of phosphorescence. The air would smell of wet pine and asphalt, and the sky would turn the color of freshly cut granite.

It was at this precise moment in the new day that John and Jessie arrived on foot.

They came from the east, from across Hagadorn Road, after walking a couple of miles from the point at which the tea truck had dropped them near old Highway 69. They were exhausted, their clothing damp with perspiration and grit, their feet sore. John was especially weary. His injuries had flared up in the wee hours, riding in that unforgiving trailer, and now his joints had ground glass in them. But he could barely feel the pain, and he barely noticed the fatigue. He was positively vibrating with anticipation.

Ahead of them, the old dormitories rose against the morning sky like beacons, the sight of them sparking synapses in John's midbrain, flashes of raw memory, glimpses of his past. This was ground zero.

"Incredible, incredible—I remember that building—*Jesus,*" John was murmuring, pointing at the green-fringed bricks and vaulted windows of the dormitory fifty yards ahead of them. They crossed the parking circle and walked onto the lawn. As they approached the building, the chiseled frieze above the arched doorway came into view. The Romanesque letters said ABBOTT HALL, and above it, in the second-floor window, someone had positioned strips of masking tape across the pane that said HI!

"You remember living here?" Jessie asked, pausing near the front stone steps. She was speaking softly, careful not to awaken any sleeping coeds.

"I remember spending a lot of time here," John said. "Can't remember if I was a resident or not."

Jessie looked at him. "Girlfriend?"

"God, no, I never had time for that kind of thing. Too consumed with the acting—you know—angry young man, all that stuff."

"Sounds like a laugh riot."

John smiled. "All right, Inspector, you got me, I was a total bore, I admit it."

Jessie poked his shoulder. "You said it, Sport, I didn't."

There was an awkward stretch of silence.

"The administration building," John said at last. "That's where we should start. They have all the student records in their database."

Jessie pointed at the dormitory. "Don't you want to go in, try to rattle loose some more memories?"

John told her he would rather do the rattling at the administration building.

"Can we at least get some coffee first," Jessie pleaded.

"Come on," John said, ushering her toward the street. "We'll stop at the union on the way, and we'll get some of that delicious campus fare."

The trip across campus was like a walk through a ghost ship, the horticulture gardens a dead tableau of shaded lawns and dark buildings, the silence broken only by the occasional sprinkler system or excitable bird. Along the way, Jessie felt another tremor of uneasiness—something she'd been feeling at regular intervals every since they had embarked on the train the previous afternoon—making her certain that a dark presence was following them. It had occurred back on the Stevenson Expressway, a small Japanese sedan hovering three car lengths back, just beyond the fringes of her side mirror's reach. And then again in the alley outside the precinct house, and again in the subway, and again while hitchhiking along the highway last night. Even safe in the shadows of the semitruck's trailer, Jessie hadn't shaken the feeling. Was this the dark presence responsible for the gruesome murders in the subway and on the train? Jessie had not yet mentioned the feeling to John, and she was neglecting to mention it right now.

Five minutes later, they arrived at the student union building and went about the business of gathering their bearings. The cafeteria was not yet open, but Jessie convinced one of the fry cooks to make some coffee and scramble some eggs. Then they sat in the empty cafeteria for nearly an hour, discussing their next move, discussing John's past at the school, discussing the best-case scenarios and the worst-case scenarios. By nine A.M., their veins were full of caffeine and they were ready to mount their assault on the administration building.

It took them ten minutes to cross the quad.

By the time they arrived at the enormous steel-and-glass monolith known as the Hannah Administration Center, the morning's business was already in full swing. They made their way to the clerical center and found a sympathetic-looking woman in a powder blue pantsuit pecking at a CRT terminal. After giving her an elaborate song and dance about having a kid who wanted to enroll in the school of drama, the lady finally nodded and stiffly rose from her swivel chair.

"This way," she said, then turned and led Jessie and John over to a small carrel behind a stack of files. The carrel was equipped with a CRT and a keyboard, and the woman leaned down and booted up the proper information. The screen flickered suddenly, busy graphics appearing. "Just type in the key words," the pantsuit lady instructed.

Then she turned on her heels and walked away, leaving Jessie and John alone with MSU's history.

At first, the search seemed futile. Jessie sat on a desk chair in front of the screen, feverishly typing commands, scrolling through endless listings of student productions and course offerings, and John stood behind her, looking over her shoulder, uttering snippets of half-forgotten names and dates, the database full of strangers, anonymous class descriptions, and obscure plays, and then, out of nowhere, came *Rosencrantz & Guildenstern Are Dead,* the Tom Stoppard farce.

A moment later, the cast list was glowing in green diode letters across the screen.

"OhmyGod—yeah," John muttered, chewing what was left of his fingernails.

The name *Jonathon McNally* was glowing halfway down the list like a blast of amphetamines, a gut-rush straightening John's spine, the lines swirling through his mind—*"Death is not anything . . . it's the absence of presence"*—and memories of treading the boards, the dry silver light in his eyes, mnemonics in his head, remembering the lines, the little mental crutches—*the knight has a light when he enters stage right*—and then more roles flashing across the monitor—John as Layevsky in Chekhov's *The Duel,* John as Max in *Bent,* John as Eddie in *Hurly Burly,* John as Mick in *Plenty,* John as Gibbs in *The Hothouse,* and on and on—

—and then it ended.

John flinched suddenly as though a surge of electricity had just bolted through his forehead. The computer screen flickered with listing after listing of plays and cast members, but John had vanished from the ranks. And the disappearance had coincided with a sharp jolt in his brain, a sudden ripple in that black hole in his memory. Something significant had forced him out of the theater.

"Where'd you go?" Jessie said, staring at the screen.

"I'm not sure . . ."

"Maybe you graduated."

"No, no, that's not it," John said, a sharp, keening sensation in his head as he stared at the screen. "Wait—right there—what's that?"

He was pointing at a small blurb at the bottom of the screen, a memorial of sorts, dedicating the entire theatrical season to a drama professor named Stanley Brunner, and Jessie stopped scrolling for a moment and let the blurb rest center-screen, and John stared at the glowing block letters—DR. STANLEY BRUNNER—and reached down and touched his fingertip to the screen and felt a spark—

John jerked backward suddenly, again feeling as though he'd been shocked, banging into the desk behind him, knocking a stack of documents to the floor.

Jessie swiveled. "You okay? What happened?"

"I'm fine . . . I'm . . . sorry . . . I'm fine . . . really." John was gathering up the scattered fliers, trying to ignore the dozens of transistor radios tuned to different stations in his head—*Dr. Brunner?*—and all at once John flashed on a possibility that hadn't occurred to him at first. A reason why he had vanished off the cast lists. "Jessie, do something for me," he said. "Type in key words for other graduate departments."

"Like what?"

"Like psychology," John said. "Teaching-assistant lists, master's candidates—stuff like that."

Jessie tried a few key words, and it took a few attempts, but she finally struck pay dirt. Evidently, at about the same time that young Jonathon McNally had vanished from the theater scene, he reappeared in a different department as a *psychology* graduate student. "Looks like somebody changed his major."

The screen glowed with the heading COLLEGE OF SOCIAL SCIENCES, and John's name was near the bottom, on a list of past master's candidates.

John's mind was swimming with fractured memories now, voices buzzing. "I remember leaving the theater department—I do—I can't remember why—but I do remember leaving it all behind, going into psychology . . ."

Jessie was staring at the screen, thinking, as John continued agonizing.

"Why psychology, though? What the hell was it that turned me away from theater? Was it this Dr. Brunner dying? There's got to be something there, but it's . . . still vague . . . I don't know, like it's distorted by that black hole in my memory. I remember the coursework vividly, though—developmental psych, clinical psych. I had an old doctoral adviser—what was his name? Kane? No, not Kane . . . *Cohen!* That's it. Shelly Cohen. Sweet old man."

Jessie was typing something now.

"Jessie?" John was looking down at her, the screen flickering. "What are you doing?"

"Just got an idea. What was you psychology adviser's name again?"

"Cohen."

She typed in a few more key words and waited for the computer to cycle. "I don't know why I didn't think of this earlier, sitting in the middle of a university. Chrissake, I'm really slow sometimes."

A name and address winked onto the screen.

Jessie copied it down.

Then she rose out of her seat and started to lead John toward the exit, explaining to him just exactly what they were going to do.

44

Memory Lane

"YOU SURE I can't get either of you something to drink? Some juice? Wine?" The old man was sitting behind a cluttered desk in the middle of a cramped little office on the fourth floor of the psychology building. The room was brimming with books, memorabilia, and tchotchkes, and the old man was the lord of the manor. Bald as a wrinkled honeydew, with thick granny glasses and graying chest hair like steel wool poking out the top of his Hawaiian shirt. He fixed his milky brown eyes on Jessie. "Miss Bales?"

"No, thanks, Doc," she said and winked at him. "Somebody's gotta drive."

The old man turned to John. "Jonathon?"

"I'd love some," John said, and Jessie noticed that John's fists were clenched in his lap.

The old man turned to a side drawer, rooted out a bottle of tawny port, and filled a couple of demitasse cups with trembling, liver-spotted hands. He handed one of the cups to John, then lifted his own, taking a delicate sip, savoring the taste for a moment. John polished off the wine with one fierce gulp, then pushed the empty cup across the desk. "Mind if I have another?" he asked.

Jessie put her hand over the cup. "Maybe we oughta just take it nice and easy this afternoon—we only got a couple hours of sleep last night." Jessie shot a look at John and John nodded sheepishly, then Jessie turned back to the professor and winked. Feeling a tad claustrophobic in the ancient little office, Jessie was sitting on a ladderback wooden chair near the window, next to John. It was a classic intellectual cubbyhole, crowded with shelves of books and yellowed documents filmed in dust and memories. The air smelled of musty pages, stale coffee, and mentholated rub, and everywhere you looked there were photographs. Photographs of the professor with college VIPs and visiting dignitaries, countless shots of his late wife, his children, grandchildren, and extended family members. It was a room steeped in the past, and Jessie was hoping that Professor Emeritus Sheldon L. Cohen, Ph.D., would serve as a doorway into John's past as well.

She knew her idea was a long shot at best, but it was something that Jessie had been wondering about ever since she had met John McNally. And now that they had finally tracked down somebody who not only had the ability to do the deed but the willingness to pull it off, she just couldn't resist. Old Shelly Cohen was their ace in the hole.

"Wine's good for the circulation," the professor commented somewhat pedantically, belting down the last of his vino. Then he turned to John. "Have to admit, Jonathon, I never thought I'd see you again."

"I'll be honest with you," John said, "I have no idea what condition I was in—or, for that matter, what frame of mind I was in—when I left the school."

"You were in no condition to do anything."

"Can you tell us about it?" John asked nervously.

Jessie watched the old man as he took a deep breath before speaking.

"You were always the moody type," he began, measuring his words. "Always with the brooding and the moods. I worked with you for nearly two years, I never saw you smile, not one smile. What kind of person doesn't smile? I used to feel so sorry for you, but you were an impeccable student. Driven. 'Take a break sometimes,' I used to say, but no, not Jonathon. Had your nose in the diagnostic-and-statistical manual night and day."

The professor paused, swallowing dryly, and Jessie wondered if the old geezer was battling an illness. He had that washed-out, jaundiced look old men get sometimes after surgery. "You said John was in no condition to do anything," Jessie said. "What did you mean?"

The professor looked at Jessie. "It was toward the end of Jonathon's thesis—if I'm not mistaken, I think it was *The Effects of Posttraumatic Stress on the Multiple Personality Disorder*—and I was getting more and more worried about the boy. All the obsessing over the degree, spending night and day in the stacks, I was worried he was going overboard. Maybe taking drugs. His health started going, his moods got darker and darker, he was a mess." The professor shrugged, then looked at John. "You never even said good-bye, Jonathon. After the degree was conferred, you never even dropped by to say fare thee well. You were like ... an engine on overdrive . . . and I was afraid your gaskets were going to blow."

There was an awkward silence then, and Jessie seized the opportunity. "Listen, Professor Cohen," she said, "you understand why we're here, right?"

The professor shrugged again. "If what you say is true, then Jonathon has suffered something beyond my comprehension. Amnesia is the silent sickness. I can't imagine how disconcerting it must be."

"Then, you'll help us?" Jessie asked.

"I'll tell you everything I know."

Jessie shook her head. "No, you don't understand, we need you to do more than that."

"What could be more than that?"

Jessie looked into the old man's eyes. "We want to try hypnosis."

Professor Cohen's eyebrows arched like caterpillars undulating. *"Hypnosis."*

Jessie nodded. "Yeah, I really think it's the only way to break through to John's *recent* memories—which seem to be the most blocked."

There was the briefest of pauses then, and Jessie could feel John's gaze on her, scalding her with fear. Jessie watched the professor, and for a brief instant it almost looked as though the old codger's eyes were twinkling with pride. "You kids came to the right place," he said, then grunted as he rose out of his chair. "We'll just need to find a comfy spot."

John snapped his gaze back toward the professor and said, "You want to do it *now?"*

"No time like the present," the old man murmured, then started going through his drawers.

John seemed uneasy all of a sudden. "Don't you think I should . . . *prepare?"*

"No need," the professor said, pulling a shoe box from his bottom desk drawer. "You have the desire, the urgency. It shouldn't be too difficult."

Jessie put her hand on John's arm. "I'll be right next to you, Sport."

John looked into her eyes, and again Jessie felt the sheer terror in his gaze, the primal dread of opening that box full of snakes in his head and sticking his hand inside. She softly stroked his arm, nodding.

Finally John turned to the professor. "Okay, great, yeah, by all means, let's do it."

The old man had already opened the shoe box and pulled out a small wooden object about the size of a clock radio. "We'll use this little baby to help you along," he said, and held up the metronome. It was a walnut job with a long brass arm clamped at the top and a dial at the bottom. The old man motioned at the door. "The lounge should be empty this time of day, if you don't mind climbing a few stairs . . ."

John nodded tersely. "Let's go."

The psychology building was typical of the older departmental buildings on campus. Constructed in the innocuous style they used to call Georgian, it was a rickety five-story tower of ivy-rotted bricks and mortar, worn down by decades of Michigan wind and weather. The corridors were so narrow, the parquet floors so old, that the hallways made snapping noises as people traversed them. The stairwells smelled of mildew, the shadows deepening as one neared the uppermost floor. The lounge was the only room on the fifth floor, a meager little attic den bordered by ancient louvered windows that reeked of stale cigar smoke. When Jessie entered the room, she expected Quasimodo to jump out at any moment, the place was so withered and gothic. The north wall was an enormous wheel window with tarnished copper mullions and the hands of a great clock that probably hadn't kept time since World War II.

"What is this—the belfry?" Jessie was glancing around the airless room.

"Our little den of iniquity," the professor said, turning on a couple of overhead lights. There was a leather couch against one wall, and a hardwood coffee table strewn with books, dirty ashtrays, and scattered chess pieces. The professor pointed at the corner window. "Have a seat, Jonathon."

Jessie watched as John walked over and dutifully took a seat on a tattered settee near a large arched window. The glass panes were old—beveled and chipped at the corners—and the pale afternoon sun was filtering through them like light through antique Waterford crystal, throwing sharp refractions across the cracked plaster walls. In the distance, spires of aging dormitories stood in harsh relief against the treetops. Jessie found a folding chair, positioned it in front of John, and sat down.

"Now, Jonathon, before we begin"—the professor was rolling a swivel chair in front of John—"we're going to do a simple test to see how accommodating you're going to be to the trance state." The professor put the metronome on the window ledge, then turned and leaned down into John's face, close enough to kiss him on the lips. "Just close your eyes for a moment and clear your mind, and when you open your eyes, I want you to imagine a point in the distance beyond this room, and I want you to stare at it. Ready?" The professor cupped his hands over John's eyelids. "All right . . . open."

Jessie watched the professor pull his hand away as John's eyelids fluttered open.

"All right—that's good, Jonathon, that's very good," the professor gushed. "You can relax now, and we'll start our little trip down memory lane."

Then the professor began the process of putting John into a trance.

Jessie was surprised at how simple and straightforward it was. She had envisioned the old Bela Lugosi movies, with the watch-fob pendulum swinging back and forth—*"You're getting sleeeeepy, very sleeeeepy"*—but Dr. Cohen's method turned out to be quite mundane in comparison. He felt John's wrist for his pulse, then dialed the metronome to the exact same rate as John's heartbeat. The instrument began to click. The professor asked John to close his eyes again and think of an elevator—not just any elevator, mind you, but a magic elevator—and John's on this elevator, and it's the most peaceful feeling he has ever felt, and then the professor was taking John down, down, deeper and deeper, into a sort of sleepy ennui, and the professor asked John to feel his fingers beginning to tingle, and his forearm beginning to feel light, and eventually John's hand began to levitate off the chair's arm.

—click—click—click—click—

Jessie watched as the professor kept guiding John deeper and deeper into the trance, the elevator descending farther and farther, and all the while John's hand kept rising higher and higher, until it was shoulder height, and that's when the professor started suggesting that the elevator was descending down through time, and the deeper it went, the further back it was traveling, and then the professor started asking John questions—asking him if he was relaxed, and if he felt comfortable in the elevator, and if he was ready to get off the elevator and take a look around his past—and John murmured something about being ready.

—click—click—

At first, the professor took it nice and slow, opening the elevator floors during John's adolescence. John still had his eyes closed as he described the sensation of walking out through the elevator doors, emerging into the landscape of his childhood, his hand still elevated next to him as though he were testifying. He spoke in low, even tones about Dad and Mom and high school, and the poor man's voice was so full of pain and loneliness that

Jessie's heart was breaking all of a sudden, because she remembered her own childhood tribulations, and she rubbed the moistness out of her eyes and stared at John's floating hand.

—*click*—*click*—*click*—

The professor said softly, "John, listen closely. I'm going to bring you back to the elevator, okay?"

"Yes," John said flatly, his expression loose, completely catatonic.

"We're back inside the elevator now," the professor droned, "and we're going to a different floor, all right?"

"Yes."

"Up past ladies' lingerie, past housewares, past lawn and garden. We're approaching a recent year, okay? The elevator is stopping, and the doors are about to open, Jonathon, and you're gonna get to see your recent past. We're gonna get a taste of what you've been up to lately. Is that okay, Jonathon?"

"Yes."

"All right, here they go, the doors are opening—*now.*"

John jerked as though electrocuted, nearly tipping backward over the settee.

"It's okay, Jonathon, you're safe, you're simply observing, understand?"

"No—no—no—*God!*" John's eyes were suddenly pressed tightly shut, his face squinting as though pointed into the sun. Jessie's heart started beating faster. John was shuddering now, breathing faster, harder.

"What is it, John?" Jessie heard herself saying the words, though her voice sounded faint, distant.

"We're with you, Jonathon," the professor was saying, softly reassuring.

"No—*God*—please!" John looked like a child in a dark forest.

The professor's soothing voice: "What are you seeing, Jonathon?"

"I'm—I'm—I'm—I'm—no!" His voice yelped like a wounded animal. Jessie felt her blood running cold, cold as ice water in her veins. This wasn't supposed to happen like this, not like this.

"Jonathon?"

"I'm—I'm—I'm—*hunting!*" His face was contorting now, brow sharp, lips curling away from his teeth, a rage-rictus that in that horrible split second reminded Jessie of a wolf, a cornered wolf. Something terrible was unraveling behind those closed eyelids. "I'm hunting . . . I'm, I'm, I'm *hunting a human being.*"

The professor shot a glance over at Jessie, and Jessie returned it. The professor looked at John and said, "You're searching for a human being,

Jonathon? Who are you searching for?"

"Not searching! *Hunting—hunting—HUNTING!* I'm hunting him down like an animal, and I want him so bad I can taste it, I'm so close . . . I'm creeping low behind a building . . . it's an alley, the smell of disinfectant, a bare yellow bulb inside, and, and, and . . . I can see the shadows up ahead . . . I'm so close . . . I've been hunting him so long . . ."

Jessie was paralyzed, her throat constricted, but she managed to say, "Who, John? Who are you hunting?"

Eyes pressed closed, nostrils flaring, John said, "The killer, dammit!"

Jessie and the professor looked at each other, then Jessie looked back at John. "The killer? Who's the killer?"

John hissed the word: "Glass."

45

Arthur Glass

THE TRUTH BLOOMED like a flame the moment John laid eyes on the distorted reflection in the pane of broken glass behind the tenement building. Caught in the shimmer of moonlight, distorted by the cracked grimy window, his own face looked haunted, eyes deep-set and darkened by years of rumination, jaw grizzled with whiskers, sandy hair spiky and unkempt. How had he gotten here? Here in this godforsaken alley behind this ramshackle tenement in the middle of nowhere?

(*the method*)

It all came flooding back to him—the events that had led him here, creeping down this dark alley on the outskirts of Joliet, Illinois, closing in on a killer's lair, hunting down a monster no one else even believed was real. In that horrible instant, glimpsing his own face—his own haggard face in that broken window—John McNally realized exactly who he was. He saw the years of studying criminal behavior, absorbing bodies of literature, reviewing case studies, obsessing over modern mass murderers, learning how predators think . . .

John McNally: self-styled criminologist . . .

He tried to move, but his body had tightened like a rusty spring. He knew it was all a memory—a mere hypnotic vision—but he was trapped in the reality of this thing, terrified by the taste of metal on his tongue, the odors of garbage and pollution gusting in from nearby factories, and the realization that he was seeing his true self. He crouched down low and crept past the rear of the tenement house until he reached a chain-link fence, then he paused and gazed through the fence at the crumbling foundation of the building. There was a dim yellow light burning behind the basement window. A silhouette was moving down there in the cellar, doing horrible things to some poor unconscious woman stretched out on a metal table.

"Arthur Glass is the killer?"

The voice pierced the memory like an amplified public-address announcer. It was Jessie's voice, and the sound of it had a calming effect on John. He realized she was nearby, listening, observing alongside Professor Cohen like a Greek chorus, and it was John's duty to report back to them.

"Yes," he whispered, and the sound of his voice was modulated and hollow in his ears, as though he had an invisible helmet over his head.

Jessie's voice: *"And you've been hunting him all this time?"*

"Yes."

"This is what you do? You're a cop?"

"No."

"Then, what are you, John?"

Crouching on the hard, cold gravel by the Cyclone fence, his heart racing, his skin tingling, John tried to form a reply, but the answer was complicated: He wasn't a cop—that much was obvious—but he was more than a psychologist. He could remember being kicked out of the Association of the Study of Criminal Psychology because he had clashed with the steering committee on acknowledged profiling techniques. He could remember feverish correspondence with the FBI's Behavioral Science Unit and Investigative Support units throughout his early years as a criminologist and researcher for the American Psychiatric Institute. He remembered the day he lost his license, the shame and the resentment—all because he had been inebriated during a luncheon and had argued with the keynote speaker over scientific method. All because nobody wanted to acknowledge John's radical new techniques of getting inside the mind of a serial murderer.

After another tense moment of crouching behind that ghostly fence, John said, "I'm a psychologist, and I study serial killers; I try to track them down."

The disembodied voice said: *"This is what you do for a living?"*

"Yes."

There was another stretch of taut silence, then the sound of Professor Cohen's voice resonating like a pipe organ. *"And this is what you were doing when you had your accident?"*

John thought about this for a moment, and he was starting to reply, when a noise drew his attention to the cellar window ahead of him.

The yellow light still glowed behind the slice of dirty glass, but the silhouette was gone.

"John? Are you okay?"

John crept toward the corner gate, staying low, duck-walking, keeping his eye on that narrow basement window. He slipped through the gate, then waded through broken litter and discarded bottles strewn across the leprous little courtyard. Broken glass sparkled in the sodium vapor light. John approached the window, heart racing. He was too close now. The FBI had warned him, even the local cops had warned him—don't get in the way, don't get too close—but here he was, huddling in the chilled darkness outside this grimy basement window, smelling the sickening sweet stench of pollution, the hairs on the back of his arms stiffening. He took another step, and all of a sudden he saw the outline of the stainless-steel gurney in the shadows of the makeshift laboratory. There was a woman lying on it, her half-nude body draped in surgical blankets, the instruments gleaming on the tray in the half-light—

The woman sat up.

John jerked backward, his legs tangling, stumbling, falling on his rear in the dirt. The naked woman had sat up and was screaming now, turning toward John, clawing at the glass like a cornered animal, her eyes wild, her toothless mouth contorted, hair frazzled, flesh spackled with blood. Her silent scream was permeating the glass. John tried to gather his bearings and get back on his feet, but the woman's gaze was luminous with terror behind the grimy glass, and John's heart was pounding so hard it felt like a sledgehammer in his chest.

"Well done!" a voice cried out from the dream-darkness behind John.

"Wha—?" John spun around and saw the face of a killer reflecting the cold light of a streetlamp.

"You found me, Brother John," said the man named Arthur Glass—the same man who would one day come to a clinic to kill John—and he was smiling, his cold blue eyes gleaming. That Nordic face, that chiseled Willem Dafoe face. The face of a killing machine. Dressed in a white medical smock marbled with blood, he pulled something from his pocket that gleamed in the moonlight.

"No—!" John dodged the first strike at the very last moment, barely avoiding the blurry arc of the metal. Then John whirled and ran.

Time seemed to warp suddenly, and the memory began to take on the strange, jumpy continuity of a dream. John was running down the narrow cobblestone alley behind the tenement for a moment, and then he was sprinting across a vacant lot scarred by trash and tire tracks, and he could see the forest in the distance, and he could smell the predator on his tail, the sound of Glass's nimble footsteps like those of a jackal, and he could feel the whisper of a paper-thin razor on the back of his neck—

"John, you're breathing pretty hard, you better come back to us—"

Now John was running through the shadows of trees, swallowed up by the black void of the forest, running for his life, running, running, and the moon was a million light-years away, and now there was only John and the beast on his tail, and John was cursing himself with each painful stride—he should have listened to the disciplinary committee, and the FBI, and the rep from Behavioral Science, and the cops—he never should have gotten this close!

"John, what's the matter? What's going on?"

Then the faint strips of light dead ahead, looming larger and larger, then the shafts of silvery light cutting through the trees and then vanishing, and the distant rushing sounds of traffic, the whine of eighteen-wheelers, the scream of a truck horn, and John realized he was nearing the highway. Behind him, the killer's footsteps were looming. John glanced over his shoulder suddenly and saw Glass a few paces back, his pale face full of manic intensity, his eyes wild—it's a big party, a big game, *whoooopeeeee*—and then Glass was pouncing with the blade raised and—

John whirled and darted out onto the highway.

The sound of the oncoming truck was a hurricane full of fury and light.

"John—what's happening?" The professor's voice was a million miles away.

The truck tires shrieked, and the entire scene seemed to implode.

The image of the night highway curled inward like a great billowing blanket, whipping inside out to reveal the image of a cluttered little teacher's lounge on the top floor of an old Victorian building. John whiplashed back in his chair, his head snapping painfully, the sudden silence like a clanging cymbal, the air sparking hot with static electricity. John sat there for a moment, punch-drunk, paralyzed, as Jessie lurched across the room to his side, her hands like a salve on the coiled muscles of his neck.

"What happened? What did you see, John?"

"I—I saw—I—" John was having trouble speaking again, his vocal cords strained and raw, his mind spinning, the silence completely disorienting. He had just seen his entire existence summed up in a single scenario, the reason why the police were after him, the reason why the FBI suspected him, the reason why John was so confused by the diaries and the photos and the artifacts and the memories. *John had gotten too close.* His theories and speculations had been too specific. How could anyone know *that* much about a killer's method? How could it be anyone but the killer himself?

(*or a man obsessed with murder*)

"Okay, John, take a breath," Jessie was saying, stroking his shoulder.

"I'm . . . okay," John muttered, glancing across the silent room. It was getting dark outside, and the shadows in the corners were deepening. The air had a golden quality to it. The professor sat across the lounge, trembling gently, the dying light from the window making his grizzled face look like faded parchment.

"Can you tell us what you saw?" Jessie would not take her hand away from John's shoulder, bless her heart, she was completely rattled. Her eyes were wet, and her expression was a mixture of anxious panic and ebullience. It made her look like a child.

"I think I saw . . . my accident," John said. "The killer . . . *Glass* . . . I caught him . . . but he came at me with a knife, and he chased me out onto the highway."

Jessie managed a tepid grin. "You're a regular hero, McNally, you know that?"

John shivered. "I don't really think—"

Across the room: a creaking noise.

All heads turned toward the northeast corner of the lounge, where the dusky light slanted in through the clock spire, sending long, oblique shadows across a series of shelves, and just for an instant John thought he heard floorboards creaking, but then his ears adjusted to it and he realized it wasn't a creaking noise at all, it was human.

Two hands clapping.

The air seemed to tense suddenly as if it were a living organism, John standing up fast, knocking his chair backward to the floor, and Jessie standing, whirling instinctively toward the clapping sounds, and the professor rising and backing toward the door as if a wild animal had just slithered into the room through an open window, and John was frozen, gaping at the shadows from which the applauding noises were emanating, his mind vapor-locking, realizing two things almost simultaneously—one, the door across the room was half ajar; and two, whoever was standing in the shadows in the corner had probably sneaked in at some point during the hypnosis procedure.

In the northeast corner a figure was emerging from the shadows.

The moment was so surreal, so unexpected, so stunning, that the room seemed to turn crystalline for a moment, like a diorama filled with porcelain figurines. Then John took a step in front of Jessie, partially because of instinct, partially because of sheer, mind-numbing shock. He tried to say something, but his mouth was wired to his overloaded synapses, so all he could do was stare at the broad-shouldered intruder moving into the golden light as if performing some theatrical magic act.

John heard Jessie inhale suddenly.

Time seemed to stand still.

"Bravo," the tall man enthused, clapping heartily, strolling across the room toward his subjects.

He seemed bigger now than he had when he first appeared at the clinic, impersonating John's brother. Well over six feet tall, he wore expensive designer clothes and a designer hairstyle, and all at once his angular features were coming into full view, the magic-hour light shimmering in his icy-blue eyes. His skin looked burnished, perhaps even surgically enhanced. He was slightly out of breath.

"The pretty lady is right," he said finally. "Brother John is a true hero."

Nobody moved, nobody breathed.

The entire universe seemed to hang in icy, suspended animation, like a film that had jammed in the projector.

The intruder seemed to be enjoying it.

This was indeed a glorious moment, and it certainly hadn't been easy.

From the moment Glass had shown up at the Reinhardt Clinic—playing the role of brother, then vigilante cop—the relentless pursuit had taken its toll. Especially last night. Last night he had nearly lost the twosome after they had jumped off the train. Ten minutes later, after the train had come to an emergency stop at the next station—and the police had descended in a flurry of flashing blue lights—Glass had managed to slip off the last car and slither through the crowd. Then, almost out of desperation, he had crossed a neighboring farm field and flagged down a motorist. Killing the driver had been easy, but the final step had required more than a little luck. Driving the stolen car eastward along Interstate 94, he had suddenly come upon two hapless hitchhikers wandering the night—and *hallelujah,* it turned out to be McNally and the lady detective! The rest had been simple—passing them, hovering just out of sight while the trucker picked them up—it was almost as though Fate had been conspiring to bring Death and McNally together.

"I just adore heroes," Arthur Glass added as he took another step closer.

"Wait—wait a minute," John blurted, and they seemed to be the only words he could muster.

"Sorry, Brother John, but the waiting is over."

Glass reached behind his waist and pulled something sharp from his belt. The scalpel looked incandescent as it rose up into the yellow light.

The waiting was indeed over.

Part Five

The Endless Time of
Never Coming Back

*The dead keep their secrets, and in a while we shall be as wise as they—
and as taciturn.*

—Alexander Smith,
Dreamthorp

46

Sinkhole

JOHN WAS DIMLY aware—in the horrible instant following the appearance of the scalpel—that there was movement behind him, jittery movement, but he wasn't quick enough to catch it in his peripheral vision, and, God knew, he didn't want to turn his back on the beast, the beast with the sandy razor-cut hair and the chiseled face and frosty blue eyes, coming slowly yet inevitably toward him with the confidence and cavalier manner of a surgeon washing up for the day's final operation.

"Goddamnit, think it over, Glass." Jessie's voice was coming from behind John, sounding like a piano string tuned several octaves too high. "I'll shoot you fucking dead where you stand—"

—and now John knew that Jessie had the gun in her hand, and that she was probably going to shoot now and ask questions later, and John only got a chance to spin toward her—

—then things were happening too swiftly even to register in John's racing mind.

The scalpel was soaring across the five-foot gap, and John was spinning toward the east wall in the nick of time, the whisper of the blade on the back of his neck, his legs tangling then, sending him careening over the back of the settee. John hit the floor hard, and the gun went off behind him. The sound was a ball-peen hammer striking John's skull, and he slammed into the baseboard, ears ringing, cordite choking him, but he knew the bullet had missed Glass, he knew it, he knew it, because the porthole window had shattered behind him and Jessie was screaming, and John tried to rise up, twisting around to see better, squinting through the blue haze and the dying light, and he saw the old man clawing at the door, and the black blur swooping down on the professor like a bird of prey, and John was struggling to his feet then, hollering, voice sharp as though addressing a wild dog—*"Leave them out of it, Glass!"*—but the incessant ringing in John's ears and the dizziness made him trip again, and he tumbled to the floor, thinking—*Where's Jessie, dammit, where is she?*—and the black blur was somewhere else then because Jessie was screaming behind John, the gun going off again—*BAM! BAM! BAM! BAM!*—four times, popping high, puffing wild asbestos dimples in the ceiling, chewing through fixtures, fluorescent tubes shattering, spraying fine, sparkling dust—

—then John whirled around just in time to get clobbered in the face.

At first he thought it was a human fist that had struck him across the bridge of the nose, the impact so abrupt that it seemed to drown the noise in the room suddenly to a dull buzzing drone in his ears, and for one surreal instant John stood there on wobbly knees, staring at the three-foot length of hardwood in Glass's hands, a board that looked as though it had come off the antique doorjamb. Then John tried to say something, but his jaw was cast in cement, and he felt a warmth seeping down his pant leg, his bladder loosening.

Then he folded.

It felt as though the ancient floor had suddenly leaped up at him, slamming into his face, the entire lounge tilting on its axis. All around him, the shapes of hulking furniture and archaic wallpaper and geometric patterns on the parquet floor were getting all blurry, watery, curling around the edges, darkening like the edges of an old newspaper burning up. He tried to find Jessie in his clouding field of vision, but all he could see were enormous black tasseled loafers coming toward him at a crazy angle, the shoes of a giant, making thunderous booming noises with each monstrous stride—

—BOOM—BOOM—BOOM—

John was fading, the light dimming, the floor getting soft like quicksand.

—BOOM—BOOM—

The gargantuan loafers were only inches away from his face now, and John could smell the chalky odor of the floor, and he tried to stay afloat, tried to move, tried to speak, tried to howl, but the floor was a sinkhole now, and the light was almost completely gone, and he was sinking deeper, deeper, into the floor, into the warm dark nothing—

—his last conscious thought was *regret,* regret over getting a woman as wonderful as Jessie Bales mixed up in this thing.

Then he sank under the surface.

And then there was nothing.

—darkness . . .
. . . broken colored glass . . .
. . . a pale slab of meat . . .
. . . and eyes like candle flames flickering out, a pair of tiny sparks in the
centers of the irises dwindling, contracting, shrinking down until there is
nothing but a needle-prick of life, and a pair of hands, slowly closing, curl-
ing inward like the petals of a lovely flower at sunset, the flesh going from
pink to ashen gray . . .
. . . dead . . .

47

Penned in Blood

. . . a faint nimbus of light . . .

(meat)

. . . a sound like a train coming in the distance, the headlight shimmering through heat rays, the noise of the iron wheels rising . . .

(broken glass)

"No!"

John's eyelids were fluttering then, the dim light flickering in his mind. He was paralyzed, prostrate on the cold surface of a tile floor, eyes blinking frantically. How long had he been unconscious? How long? He had no idea where he was or why he had been knocked out. He managed to lift his head sideways off the floor—the pain like a rusty spike through the bridge of his nose—and he focused on the middle distance. All at once, he remembered everything. He could see the broken porthole window of the psychology building lounge, the night sky roiling with dark clouds outside, and across the room, the settee was overturned, pushed against the wall, and the door was standing ajar.

"Jessie—?"

There was a body on the floor near the doorway.

"Jessie!" His heart thrumming in his ears, the coppery taste of blood in his mouth, John forced his body to move. First his arms, singing with pain, then his legs, stiff and sore beneath him, he struggled to his feet with a great drunken effort, then staggered over to the door.

The professor lay in a Rorschach pattern of blood across the faded green tile.

John knelt down by the body, his own hands trembling convulsively, his brain still vibrating dissonant images and noises. At first glance, it looked as though Professor Cohen—whose grizzled face was cold and pale as limestone—was wearing a ruffled tuxedo shirt, the deep crimson florets running down the length of his thick belly, but then John realized the florets were glistening wet, and the filigree was part of the professor's own flesh, and the blood was still seeping in gouts down the sides of the old man's torso, and John realized the professor had been gutted.

John turned away from the monster's handiwork, gagging, stomach heaving. *"Jesus-God—not Shelly—Jesus—why—why-why-why—?"*

John swallowed his horror and looked back down at the old man. In death, the professor looked oddly tranquil, not unlike the way he had always appeared in life, very comfortable in his own portly skin, and all at once John was paralyzed with grief, because he was remembering the old man now, how the old codger had probably saved John's life on more than one occasion. Sheldon Cohen had given the young John McNally advice, direction, occasionally a place to get a home-cooked meal, a love of big band swing, an endless supply of magnificent potato pancakes, and maybe even *hope.* Most important, Shelly Cohen had been a friend.

And now look at him . . .

The room was spinning now, a carousel of cruel images burning into the retina of John's mind, a topsy-turvy nightmare funhouse distorted by the rising adrenaline rush, the air rancid-sweet with the smell of the slaughter, and John started backing away from the professor's body, whirling slowly, taking in the whole room, the obvious question suddenly bombarding his mind—why had the beast allowed *John* to live?—and now the sound of sirens outside, probably Department of Public Safety cops summoned by a neighboring teacher working late hours. What did they hear? What exactly happened, and how long ago had it happened?

John tried to take a few deep breaths, gather his bearings, make his mind work.

The realization struck him suddenly like a burst of static in his head.

Jessie.

The room was empty except for the professor's body and various signs of struggle. Jessie was gone, and there was no sign of her, no sign, no sign whatsoever. John rushed over to the window and gazed through shattered, jagged glass at the dark campus, the moonlight filtering down through the elms, and the deserted walkways, the silent, impassive nightscape staring back up at him. His blood was coursing through his veins now like quicksilver, and he felt as though he might vibrate out of his skin, he was so electrified with terror.

The sirens were getting closer.

John looked down at the floor then, and his terror boiled over into rage.

The writing snaked off the blood puddle beneath Professor Cohen like tiny scarlet tributaries, then swirled across the faded parquet in delicate brush strokes, the fingerpainting of a mad artist, and John had to stare at it for quite some time before registering any of the words in his fractured mind, but soon it became clear that the writing was a verse, a hideous, obscene poem—a clue—scrawled across the lounge floor specifically for John's eyes only.

John read the words.

Outside, the squall of sirens was looming, perhaps a mile away now, the roar of engines and the whoosh of tires on pavement rising beneath it, and John realized at once that he had better get out of there because he was close to madness himself, his mind was so full, so full of memories and pain and black rage, and now this terrible rhyme written in blood across the ancient wood of the lounge was buzzing in his head, and he could barely see straight as he stumbled across the room, past the lifeless corpse of Professor Cohen.

He was halfway out the door when the gleam of blue metal caught his eye.

It was lying on the floor behind one of the overturned chairs, wedged against the baseboard. John rushed over and scooped up the Beretta, wondering if it had any ammunition left in it. Jessie had fired it several times, but John was fairly certain that there were at least a couple of rounds left in its clip. He knew nothing about guns, but he was prepared to use one. Now that the beast was on the loose. Now that John knew who he was. Now that the final gauntlet had been flung to the ground. He stuffed the gun behind his belt—a flourish that would once have seemed ridiculous to him but now only served to bolster his seething resolve—and then he ran out.

He took the narrow stairs two at a time, his heart chugging, his brain white-hot with panic.

When he reached the first floor, he made his way down the rear corridor and out the north portico. The night air was a poultice on his damp skin and his superficial wounds, the wind bracing as it stung his face, the sirens piercing the air.

He sprinted across a deserted loading dock, over a low fence, and into the shadows of a maple grove. He could hear voices in his head now, voices from his past, but mostly Jessie's voice, and she was saying, *"Forget it, John, don't try to be some goddamn hero . . . it's not worth it . . . you should just get the police and get this guy,"* but John was on fire now, blazing with rage, and he was not about to abandon the only woman who ever really trusted him. He knew just exactly what he had to do. The beast had taken Jessie strictly as a challenge, as bait, as a way to draw John into the final round of play. John knew this for many reasons. He knew this because this was how the beast operated. He knew this because he had played the beast many times in his head. Most important, John knew this because of that obscene verse penned in blood on the floor of the psychology department lounge.

It was repeating over and over in John's mind as he headed north toward the outskirts of the campus . . .

> *My one faithful brother, My love for you still true,*
> *To share the taste, The original sin, In "H" your*
> *fair maiden waits for you.*
>
> *In "H" our final rendezvous.*

48

Macrosurgery

THE SPECIMEN MOANED behind him, her voice disabled by the duct tape across her mouth.

"Quiet, please," Glass said, speaking with the slightly distracted air of a specialist gazing at a chart at the foot of a patient's bed, not even bothering to glance over his shoulder at the shifting shadows of the backseat, where the specimen lay. No time for bedside manner. He was on a mission, a mission that might seem harsh at first, but was actually informed by love and tenderness. He kept his rubber-gloved hands on the steering wheel, and he kept the Camry wagon at a steady forty miles an hour as he explained, "We'll be arriving at our destination in a few minutes. You'll be more comfortable there, I assure you. So, for now, you'd be well advised not to wriggle or try to escape, because it will only make matters worse."

The subject was silent then, the hundred milligrams of Nembutal keeping her manageable. Conscious but manageable. Glass usually preferred his specimens unconscious, as least during the procedures. But this time, the subject would have to be conscious. *This* time, the operation would require a certain . . . dialectic. The patient would *have* to be fully awake. Lucid. Alive and kicking, as it were.

This is how Glass thought of his masterpiece—his Grand Experiment—as a surgical procedure. *Macro*surgery, perhaps, but surgery nonetheless. Everything he had accomplished up to now—every project, whether successful or unsuccessful, whether skillful or sloppy—was mere preamble to this magnificent operation. It mattered not one whit that the medical establishment would call his experiment an aberration and a fluke, or that no journal in the land would publish his findings, or that the greatness of his endeavor would be ignored. He wasn't doing this for any sanctioned authority.

The man who thought of himself as Death was doing this for love.

He gazed through the windshield at the white lines clocking past the beams of his headlights. Grand River Avenue was a graveyard this time of night, the silent, dark parking lots glistening with broken glass, the empty cars lined up like tombstones bathing in sodium light. He was heading east, heading toward ground zero, and his chest was burning from the inside out, as though all his rage and sorrow were being cauterized by a white-hot dagger twisting in his gut. It was terrible and sublime in equal parts, like a ritual suicide performed by some lone Buddhist monk. His world was about to change, it was about to be transformed by the Great Experiment, and the anticipation was almost too much to bear. Once and for all—if Fate was willing—he would finally put an end to the heartache and come face-to-face with his true—

Steel claws dug into Glass's shoulder.

"Ouch!" The car swerved and Glass twisted around, getting a glimpse of his attacker. The redheaded woman had somehow worked her bound hands under her legs, and now she was clutching dumbly at Glass's shoulder with both her hands, trying to throw the car out of control, her eyes watering, gleaming in flashing shadows. Glass wrenched himself free.

He pulled over to the curb, turned around, and regarded the specimen.

This one was a scrapper; no doubt about it. Even through the Nembutal daze, her clothes damp with panic-sweat, her hennaed hair matted against her moist face, she was still fighting back. Glass got the feeling that she was less interested in escaping than she was in simply hurting him.

Glass punched her in the face.

Jessie's head whiplashed backward against the rear seat, her body spasming.

"Miss, you've got to face the fact that it's going to be a little unpleasant until we disembark," Glass told her evenly, watching her bound arms flapping and flailing impotently in the air like a baby's arms, her eyelids fluttering. Her eyes seemed to focus again on Glass, and she tried to claw at him with her high-fashion nails, but her hands were uncoordinated from the Nembutal, and then Glass struck her again, hard, across the bridge of her nose. She bounced against the seat. The tape had come loose now and was hanging off one corner of her mouth. Glass smiled sadly and said, "It'll all be over soon, I assure you."

Jessie stared at him through wet eyes, her nostrils flaring with rage and rapid breathing. A tear glistened on her cheek. She tried to speak: "puh-hhh—thehhh—soh—"

"What was that?" Glass said, sounding genuinely interested now.

"—puhhh-thehhhtik—ahhhsssshhhhhoo—"

Glass frowned for a moment, then realized what she was trying to say. "You're saying I'm a *pathetic asshole?*" Glass nodded. "I'll accept that."

He struck her again, hard enough to make his knuckles tingle.

The woman convulsed against the seat, her legs and wrists still bound tightly, her eyes rolling back in her head, showing the whites. Then she deflated, and she was suddenly still, lying in a heap on the seat.

Then Death put the car back into gear and pulled away from the curb, continuing on his way.

49

Théâtre du Grand Guignol

AS IT TURNED OUT, John remembered the exact address of his office, although he had to spend five minutes fishing through the keys, shoving each one into the office dead bolt before finding the match. It was maddening how fragmented and incomplete John's recollections had become—remembering addresses but not specific keys—and it was highly ironic that it was one of the Ace Hardware copied keys that eventually worked on his office door, and not the magical brass key.

The door cracked open like a wax seal breaking on an old document.

A thin beam of light sliced through the darkness, illuminating the faded Oriental rug, the corner of an old pine desk, and the edge of a scuffed file cabinet. John's heart was pumping furiously as he slipped inside the dark studio apartment above the dry cleaner's and turned on the light.

Memories called out to him.

They spoke to him from the dusty framed certificates and photographs on the wall, from the overstuffed file-cabinet drawers and the plastic spinner crammed with jazz cassettes, the titles meticulously alphabetized from Albert Ammons to Lester Young. They whispered to him from the bulletin boards plastered with crime-scene diagrams, maps, photos of victims, intricate notes and doodles. They called out from inside desk drawers, from the articles he had published, from the countless letters he had written to law-enforcement agencies, from the obscure little artifacts he had kept over the years. They yelled at him from the little clown statue sculpted by John Wayne Gacy, from the threadbare silk panties that Richard Speck had sent him from prison, from the dusty audiovisual cart in the corner where the videotapes were stacked and cataloged, most of them rough, hard-core

S&M—women being tortured, beaten, and whipped—most with titles like *Forced Entry* and *Dominatrix Without Mercy,* most of them titles that John had forced himself to watch and digest, masturbating to some of them, getting as deep inside the mind-set as possible.

They howled at John from the battered-pine library hutch in the corner, where shoe boxes full of letters from Billy Marsten sat indexed and cataloged. Some of the early letters had seemed harmless enough to John: Gossip passed through the Internet, and some college kid latches on to the "outsider" aspect of John's working methods. Other than being slightly antisocial—not to mention severely morbid—Billy Marsten had seemed harmless enough. At least, initially. But the more Billy followed John's career, the more suspicious John had become. The letters would ramble on endlessly in their childish scrawl about John's ability to "disappear" into a sociopath's soul, and golly wasn't that cool, and gee whiz I'd sure like to meet you someday. And when the FBI had started harassing John as a suspect, the kid had become even more obsessed. After a while, the letters were coming at a rate of two or three a week, and John had started treating Billy as a suspect himself.

At least, up until recent events.

But mostly the memories shrieked at John from the east wall of the office, where the gallery hung. Most of the pictures were color plates torn out of art books, some of them framed lithographs, others crudely drawn copies of pencil sketches—screaming figures seated in stark cubicles, distorted heads, gaping mouths, and strange, voluptuous paintings of slaughtered cattle and sides of beef and people with grotesque head wounds. All of them rendered in the distinct style of a British artist named Francis Bacon.

Francis Bacon.

John walked over to the east wall and took a closer look at one of the paintings, a dark, velvety portrait of a terrified man seated on the throne—his blurry, open-mouthed face full of primal fear—with two enormous sides of beef hanging behind him. The legend below the frame read FIGURE WITH MEAT, 1954, and John stared at it, eyes burning, remembering how he had immersed himself in the aesthetics of Francis Bacon. John had believed that Arthur Glass was obsessed with Francis Bacon, and had even gone as far as posing several of his victims in Baconesque tableaus. John wanted to understand the appeal of Francis Bacon's art to a sociopath, so he had become obsessed himself.

This had been John's "method" as a criminologist, and this was why he had been shunned for so many years by both the clinical and the law-enforcement establishments, forced to eke out a living as an anonymous corporate consultant headquartered in this squalid little office above the Key Club Cleaners in Okemos, Michigan. Every few months John would publish an article in the *Journal of Applied Criminal Psychology* or offer assistance through the mail or the Internet to some out-of-town agency, but mostly he would concentrate on his own "projects," working the wee hours every night, inventing diaries, painting pictures, recording himself speaking in the voices of killers, speaking in tongues, *Method acting*. It was weird, it was macabre, it was disconcerting to everyone he came into contact with— even the professional profilers—but John didn't care. It was all for a good cause: stopping a killer.

One killer in particular. A man whose handiwork John had been studying for decades. John's obsession. *The Surgeon*. The Feds had always called him "Unknown Subject"—or "UNSUB Number 2033B"—but John had always believed him to be Arthur Trenton Glass, a name that John had seen on the return envelope of a personal letter. There had been so many reasons why John had been obsessed with the case. Glass was like a plague of locusts, his MO turning up every few years—two or three hideously mutilated bodies baffling the FBI unit—and then nothing. Complete dormancy. But John had always felt a strange connection to the case. He'd been hooked into some bizarre frequency from the start, and eventually he started receiving anonymous postcards with cryptic notes written on the back. "Cruel is the strife of brothers," said one, quoting Aristotle. "Brother brother, where do your cells go to play?" said another. John had been convinced these cards were from Glass.

John kept staring at that Francis Bacon painting and all of a sudden his entire body was crawling with chills.

The file.

He remembered sending a file folder brimming with evidence—postcards, Francis Bacon sketches, photographs, mock journal entries, and copious notes—to the FBI, and he remembered their reaction. They had treated John like a crackpot, like a suspect, and they had disregarded everything in the file. They had questioned John relentlessly, and put him under surveillance, and now John realized what had happened to that file. Jessie had stumbled upon it in the Homicide squad room back in Chicago. The same photographs of Glass, and the same Francis Bacon sketches, and the same journal entries. Jessie had stumbled upon John's file back in Chicago, and now the authorities knew that John and Jessie were working together.

If only John had been a little less zealous in his pursuit of The Surgeon.

If only John had gotten help once he had cracked Glass's method and discovered the location of Glass's little hideaway. Maybe Jessie Bales would be chasing down some lost dog right now or happily taking snapshots of some cheating husband, instead of . . . God only knew what.

If only, if only, if only . . .

John turned, walked across the room, and took a seat behind the cluttered desk.

"I just adore heroes," John announced to the empty room, speaking in a flat baritone, trying to get inside Glass's speech patterns, trying to get inside Glass's mind, trying to access some "Glass-like" part of himself. The sad fact was, John McNally was about to attempt something that could indeed be construed as heroic, and it was making him sick. He was trembling now, so uncontrollably he was having trouble simply thumbing through the old documents on his desk. It was bad enough that most of his memory had been restored in one great paroxysm of pain and terror, the final curtain of his amnesia peeling away like the last act of the Théâtre du Grand Guignol, but now his only ally in the world—big, gorgeous, tough Jessie Bales of high cheekbones fame—had been snatched by the very object of John's morbid obsession. It was as if the ghosts of his inner life had finally turned against him. He needed a drink. Badly. He pulled the Beretta from inside his belt and set it on the desktop. He vaguely remembered keeping something wet and fiery in one of the desk drawers. He tried a couple, his hands shaking convulsively now, and finally hit pay dirt inside the bottom right drawer.

The dark bottle of Tanqueray was half full, nestled in a hank of papers.

John took it out and set it on the desk blotter, staring at it for a moment, considering it. His mouth was so dry it was prickling, his lips cracked, his nostrils burning. The bridge of his nose was still throbbing where Glass had walloped him, but it was nothing compared to the fear, and the rage. Just a few jiggers, just to take the edge off, just to steel his nerves. *What are you waiting for?* He stared and stared at the bottle, and he realized there was something else bothering him, beneath all the bitter memories, beneath the sad truth of his pathetic existence, swimming like a shark. Something important. One last memory that he had yet to decode—

—flesh like a pale slab of meat, eyes like candle flames flickering out, a pair of tiny sparks in the centers of the irises dwindling, a pair of hands, slowly closing, curling inward like the petals of a lovely flower at sunset, the flesh going from pink to ashen gray—

"Good Lord, I just adore heroes!" John closed his eyes and tried to steady himself. He tried to understand this last shred of death in his mind, a memory that had been haunting him ever since he had started to recover: the death of another human being, experienced up close, intimately. it was not one of his "virtual memories" from some case study or some sympathetic memory he had manufactured in his mind to understand better the mind of the killer. It was raw experience, the product of a real-life event, and that was what was so terrifying about it. "I truly do love heroes," John growled. "I truly do . . ."

John reached out, unscrewed the bottle cap, and laid it next to the bottle.

He paused before picking up the bottle, mostly because he was starting to feel as Glass felt, and Glass would never go after an enemy stinking of gin, no sir, Glass would be as sober as a choir singer on one of his kidnapping sprees. But the bottle was gleaming now in the low light, and the magic liquid behind the dark-green glass was beckoning John, the promise of that numbing goodness in his belly, all the terror dampened so wonderfully. He turned away for a moment and saw past the file cabinet, toward the rear of the studio. Almost as an afterthought, a small living space had been arranged behind a rickety Chinese divider—a cot, a small kitchenette with a sink, a two-burner stove, and a secondhand minifridge. There was a bedside table laden with framed photographs, and the moment John saw the photos he felt a pang of recognition in his gut.

He went over to the cot, sat down, and took a closer look at the pictures.

There were no surprises: a couple of pictures of John and his ex-girlfriend, Gail, posed against the bulwark of a large sailboat docked off Lake Michigan. Gail was a mousy little woman with a quick wit and a vindictive streak, and her tiny agate eyes stared out from the photographs, reminding John of her razor-edged passive-aggressive tendencies. She used to call John "the Prince of Darkness," right up until the day she walked out on him. There were other photos of John—as a little boy, with his mom, in the little yard behind their trailer, building a lopsided snowman. Years later, John sitting at his dad's bedside in an anonymous hospital room. Another shot of John with a long dead pet—

"Wait a minute," John murmured at the empty silence, picking up one of the photographs. The one with the snowman was a faded black-and-white snapshot from the early sixties; John was probably seven or eight years old. There was a partial glimpse of his late mother along the right border, her figure bundled in a threadbare coat, her haggard face creased in a smile. Behind the snowman, out of focus, but still plain as day, was the ramshackle backside of the trailer home: a thirty-five-foot length of aqua-blue aluminum siding and narrow windows, with huge, rusty propane tanks along the bottom edge like ballasts. "Good God in heaven," John murmured, "I truly do admire these poor white-trash souls who fancy themselves heroes."

Of course!

He sprang to his feet, nearly overturning the tiny cot, then rushed back to the desk. He was still trembling convulsively as he picked up the Beretta and checked the clip, but now it was the palsy of adrenaline, because John knew, he knew, he knew, where the beast had taken Jessie, and he knew where the beast was waiting for him—*"In 'H' your fair maiden waits for you. In 'H' our final rendezvous"*—and John was amazed he hadn't realized that "H" had meant right off the bat, because "H" was an abbreviation for the little hamlet of Haslett, Michigan, and Haslett was where John was born and raised, and Haslett was where the trailer still sat in a forlorn little junk-yard off Marsh Road, a scrap-metal place owned and operated by one of John's relatives, a crusty old great-aunt named Joanne Prescott. John re-membered Aunt Jo, a real curmudgeon who had always harbored an inex-plicable soft spot in her heart for both little John-John and the trailer in which her niece had raised the boy.

The clip suddenly tumbled out of the Beretta's stock, clattering loudly on the desktop.

John jerked, started at the sudden sound, and the pinball clicking of nine-millimeter rounds rolling around the desk blotter, and he looked down at the remaining bullets, and he realized that *this* was the moment of truth. This was what his life had finally become. All the obsessive rumination and Method acting and psychic manhunting had boiled down to this: a few blunt-nosed bullets rolling around the edges of his repulsive diagrams, notes, and journals. He gathered up the bullets, inserted them back into the spring-loaded magazine—he had seen Jessie do this, and was now surprised at how easy it was—then stuffed the clip back into the Beretta's grip.

Then he picked up the bottle.

Before taking a sip, he paused one last time, thinking about his old trailer home. He hadn't seen the thing for nearly twenty years, yet it still lay in some protected blister in the back of his memory like a black pearl. He could still see its cinder-block porch steps, his mother's bedraggled petunias lining the walk, the white metal awning that always made that falsetto whining sound when the wind picked up. Of course, by now it was more than likely a mere heap of charred steel, but what it had lost in structural in-tegrity it had surely gained in resonance. It was the perfect place for a showdown. The beast knew this, and John knew this, because John was part beast himself, and now it was time to tear that part out of himself once and for all.

He flung the bottle against the far wall, and the wet, green fragments exploded.

Then he shoved the gun back into his belt and walked out of the office.

50

Broken Colored Glass

HOMESTEAD SCRAP AND Salvage was situated in a boggy clearing about a quarter-mile due east on Lake Lansing, just off Marsh Road. John had decided to utilize a cab (he had stumbled upon a taxi earlier that evening as he was fleeing the bloody scene at the psychology building, and he had paid the cabbie well to take him across town to his Okemos office and then wait outside for further instructions). He'd had the cabbie drop him along the shoulder of the dark two-lane about a mile from the junkyard. Then John walked the rest of the way, off road, huddling behind the trees. At one point, a couple of police cruisers roared past him, lights churning, sirens yowling, but luckily no one saw him. No one suspected a man would be walking through this muddy, stinky overgrown forest of white pines, his shoes sucking in the mire, his heart pounding furiously.

John wasn't sure what he was going to do when he encountered the beast. Arthur Glass was more than brilliant, he was smart. John expected Glass to have the upper hand. At first. But John was inside this thing now, he was drawing on some strange reserve of energy, some long-buried sense memory. Strange images were popping and sputtering in his mind, as though the gelid, clammy darkness around him were a faulty television signal—*colored glass shattering like diamonds, the sound of a skull cracking*—and soon John was "becoming" again. Transforming. Silent, focused, galvanized, he felt buoyant, flushed, the surface of his skin prickling in the night air.

He was going to beat Glass at his own game.

By the time John reached the junkyard, the sky was a funeral shroud.

The air was spun glass. It was the emptiest hour of the night, the deepest dark, when everything seems crystallized in aspic. The front gate to Homestead Scrap and Salvage was a whitewashed X of metal poles flanked by scarred concrete ramparts with enormous, sun-faded block letters— HOM TEAD SC AP—and the whole thing was illuminated by a pair of ground-level spotlights busy with insects. John walked around the light beams, staying discreetly in the shadows, and went over to the high chain-link that bordered the property. Through the fence he could see the caretaker's office across a dirt clearing about fifty yards away. The little shack was lined with hubcaps, the front window so greasy and dark it looked opaque. John assumed that his great-aunt must have surely relinquished the daily management to a younger man or woman. Old Aunt Jo was probably in her seventies by now.

John did a cursory scan of the front acreage, seeing nothing but junked cars and old kitchen appliances lined up in the shadows like prehistoric husks in some messy archeological dig. No trailers. He went around the east side and walked along the Cyclone fence, passing skeletal remains of old Buicks and Plymouths, their metal oxidized beyond recognition, their windshields so ravaged with cracks they looked like delicate lace. The place smelled of burned rubber and old tar, and it was making John's head throb. He reached around and felt the Beretta's grip stuffed inside the back of his belt. It felt like a living thing, a rough, scaly thing.

Stay inside the performance, stay centered, you're The Surgeon now, feel the sickness, feel it. The voice in his head was an old acting teacher— what's his name?—the words repeating like a mantra.

John reached the end of the fence line and realized there were no trailers at this end of the junkyard. He walked over to the Cyclone fence and pressed his face against the links, trying to see beyond the mountainous formations of wrecked automobiles and scrapped metal silhouetted against the moonless sky. In the darkness it was impossible to see too far beyond the middle of the yard, but there *was* a strange sound coming from somewhere inside the fence, somewhere nearby, a chugging sound, like a steam pipe or a pressure cooker, a sibilant hissing noise getting closer and closer and closer—

—until John turned to his right.

The barking noise exploded in his face, a frenzy of fangs and fur. The scabrous little pit bull was only inches away, roaring at him from behind the fence, sending John stumbling backward, sprawling to the ground. John looked up, momentarily dazed. The dog was an angry dervish, yellow eyes blazing, banging its leathery snout against the fence. John could feel the moist heat of its breath.

"Jesus—Jesus Christ—" John tried to shake off the buzz in his head, the adrenaline making him sick, making his ears ring. He rose to his feet, backing away from the animal, swallowing the sugary, metallic taste of blood in his mouth. He must have bit into his tongue.

He turned toward the darkness to the east and got his first glimpse of the trailer.

John froze, and the air around him froze, and the noises of crickets and night breezes seemed to halt suddenly like a stage cue in a play. The trailer sat in the distance, cloaked in shadows, planted in an overgrown vacant lot behind the junkyard, as pale as a huge alabaster coffin. Vegetation had rioted around its foundation, tangling it in wild juniper and prairie grass. Some of the narrow windows had been covered with ancient particleboard, and the siding had weathered to a dull, colorless gray. The cinder-block porch was gone, as were Mom's petunias, as were the propane tanks that young John-John had once imaged were rocket boosters designed to blast him out of his painful, lonely existence.

Pulling the gun from his belt, John started toward the trailer.

The barking sounds were fading under the thunder-rush of John's blood and the timpani beat of his heart as he crept toward the little rust-pocked aluminum home. He wondered if Glass was huddling inside the trailer at this very moment, watching, waiting, loving every moment, Jessie tied up on the bed next to him, groggy and bloody from the inevitable torture. John remembered seeing Jessie cock the Beretta by sliding the top mechanism back, so John did likewise, and the gun clanged with a satisfying *ping!* John approached the battered, cardboard-lined front door—the same front door that little John-John had banged so many times, coming in and going out, so full of childhood angst and unfocused energy—and raised the Beretta, gripping it tightly in his left hand, allowing his right hand freedom to open the door.

—you're the predator now—

He put his fingers around the rusty metal doorknob and turned it.

As he had suspected, the door was unlocked. It creaked open a few inches on loose, rusty hinges, and John paused, just for an instant, taking a quick breath, readying himself. Then he yanked the door all the way open with one violent movement, swinging the Beretta up and out, tendons twitching, arm trembling, eyes wide as searchlights, as he entered the pungent darkness of the trailer home.

Nothing jumped out at him.

All he could see were shadows, familiar shadows from his forgotten past. Shadows of the tiny kitchenette to the left, the miniature stove, the filthy exhaust hood, and the hallway leading into claustrophobic bedrooms. Shadows of the little living room to the right, the threadbare Hide-A-Bed sofa still pushed against the front windows, the TV cart canted against the heater, the TV long gone, the frayed cables sticking out of the wall like malignant whiskers. But no beast, no welcoming committee, no fiendish serial killers jumping out and going *boo!* Only the sad shadows of his childhood and the thick, rubbery aroma that always clung to the polyester curtains, conjuring waves of memories like an uninvited parade of ghosts.

At length, John relaxed his arm and let the Beretta fall to his side.

He had been wrong about Glass ambushing him here; and John McNally was rarely wrong about such matters.

He went over to the kitchenette and tried to turn on the dome light. Much to John's amazement, there was a tincture of juice left in the light's congealed batteries, and the dull yellow glow illuminated the trailer's walls. John turned slowly, surveying his boyhood home, a wave of sadness washing over him as palpable as tepid water. Aunt Jo had left the trailer pretty much intact. Most of the knickknacks were still on the walls, the bric-a-brac still on the cheap Kmart shelves, the faded family photos still dangling off yellowed tape hooks on the veneer paneling. John took it all in through eyes welling with tears, the meager little history of his world captured in broken Hummel figurines, fake crystal, chipped plastic molding, and decorative plastic flowers, and the pain almost took his breath away. He blinked suddenly, the tears tracking down his cheeks, burning his eyes, thinking that he had lost Jessie for sure now, and that he was destined to be alone with these forlorn memories for the rest of his miserable life, and that all he had ever wanted to do as a kid was the right thing—

—something sputtered hotly in the back of his mind, an unexpected image.

Broken colored glass.

He whirled toward the opposite wall across the kitchen. There was a small aluminum shelving unit mounted to the wall above the foldout table. Among the crumbling cookbooks and yellowed recipe folders—his mom's specialty had been bread pudding, made with stale bread and leftovers, always delicious to John, warm, filled with raisins, soaked in milk—a few old tattered photo albums and scrapbooks had been stuffed into the mix. John's hands were sweating now as he went over to the shelf, his mind racing, wondering if there would be something in the scrapbooks, another clue perhaps, *something*. From the moment he had come out of his comalike sleep more than a week ago, he had been plagued by that one recurring image of death buried in his head—so personal, so specific—

(*the flesh going from pink to ashen gray*)

—but now John had a feeling he was nearing the end of the journey.

He wrenched one of the photo albums from the shelf and started going through the yellowed plastic pages. Most of the photos were from the sixties—family picnics, Thanksgiving, Christmas 1962, John-John's first bicycle. He started thumbing through the book faster and faster, some of the photos slipping from their pages and fluttering like dead leaves to the floor. The droning, buzzing noise was back in John's ears, and he started to glance madly from photo to photo, frantically searching for some shred of evidence, some sign that he wasn't going stark, raving crazy. He grabbed one of the scrapbooks, tearing through the pages, newspaper clippings flashing by in a bittersweet blur—John's first Boy Scout merit badge, John's track team winning the state finals, John's high school graduation— and then he was grabbing another scrapbook, more yellowed clippings, more painful memories—high school, summer stock, reviews of plays that John was in, snapshots of John in costume, John as Puck in *A Midsummer Night's Dream,* John as Nathan Detroit in *Guys and Dolls,* John as—

Something yellow and brittle slipped from the scrapbook and flitted to the floor.

The silence crashed.

John picked up the faded newspaper article, taking a closer look, reading the headline, the words barely making sense, as though John had been stricken with some weird attack of dyslexia. Then, gradually, like a watermark coming into clearer focus on a canvas of white, the headline registered in his mind, the words jumping off the page and piercing his frontal lobe, making his flesh crawl.

The last doorway finally opening.

51

Tony Giddings

THE DATELINE WAS Haslett, Michigan. The item was written by Mike Hughes, special reporter for the *Lansing State Journal*. Probably circa 1974 (although it was impossible to tell for certain, since the top margin of the newsprint had been torn away). From the prominence of the headline type, and the number of the column inches, it appeared to be a first- or second-page article in the front section—

AREA DRAMA TEACHER DIES

Local drama teacher, Stanley Brunner (59), of 1226 Kensington Drive, Okemos, was found dead early Saturday morning at the Little Red Barn Theater in Haslett. Brunner, a full tenured professor at Michigan State University, was renowned for bringing serious theater to the community, as well as training some of the rising stars of the regional theater scene . . .

—and John was trembling now, holding the faded clipping under the dim light of the stove, his heart palpitating so loudly it sounded audible in the silent trailer. All at once the events of that night nearly twenty years ago were flooding back into his consciousness:

It's a rainy night in late April, and John is rehearsing an upcoming performance of Rosencrantz and Guildenstern Are Dead *with his best friend, Tony Giddings, for their drill sergeant of a director, Dr. Brunner. John and Tony are both sophomores, and they're working at the Little Red Barn for extra credit. John is Rosencrantz, and Tony is Guildenstern.*

The problem is Dr. Brunner. The man is a tyrant, a monster with a mercurial temper, infamous among both university and local community theater people as a sadistic taskmaster who physically assaults you if you do so much as drop a line. Only five feet seven inches tall, with a mane of wild silver hair, Brunner usually overcompensates for his diminutive stature through verbal humiliation and pure cruelty.

On this particular night, Brunner's coming down extra hard on Tony Giddings. A gangly boy with unruly jet-black hair and a nervous manner, Tony is one of John's few trusted friends, and he does not respond well to intimidation. The more Brunner leans on the boy, the more Tony flubs his lines. Finally, Brunner starts physically slapping the boy around, physically slapping him every time he drops a line, calling him a faggot and a sissy and a discredit to the art form. Finally, Tony snaps—just mentally snaps—and starts striking back—

—and now, in the dim light of the trailer, John blinked away the tears. He could barely see the newsprint:

Brunner's body was found shortly after 1:00 A.M. Saturday by a night watchman, Bernard Saulkin (67), of Haslett, and two theater students, Tony Giddings (18), of Grand Ledge, and Jonathon McNally (19), of Haslett. Police were summoned to the scene shortly thereafter. "We can't be sure until we get the coroner's report," Sergeant Edward Miller said at the scene Saturday. "But from eyewitness accounts, it looks like the victim was killed by a falling light truss."

—but that wasn't how it happened, no, that wasn't it at all, the sights and sounds of that horrible night echoing now in John's memory banks—

—when Tony starts hitting back, the teacher goes berserk. He grapples Tony to the floor and starts strangling the poor kid, and all John can do is stand there, screaming, begging them to stop. But Brunner is throttling the boy now, strangling the life out of Tony, and John finally acts on pure instinct. He rushes over, grabs Brunner, and tries to peel the maniacal teacher off Tony, but Brunner is out of control now. The teacher twists around and slugs John in the face, sending John reeling backward, careening to the floor. John shrieks a wounded battle cry, climbing back to his feet and shoving a lighting stanchion toward the teacher. The pole—laden with heavy stage lights and knots of cable—slams down on the back of Brunner's skull.

The resulting impact makes a horrendous noise—a sickly thudding

*sound, followed by an eruption of breaking glass—and Brunner gasps at
the unexpected pain, sliding off the boy and flailing at the air. Tony is gasping too, holding his throat, but all John can do is gaze down at the fallen
teacher and all the broken colored glass strewn about the stage like brilliant gemstones. Staring down at the kaleidoscope of shattered stage light,
John feels the years of pent-up anger and emotion and resentment erupting.*

Something inside John snaps.

(broken colored glass)

*John pounces on the silver-haired teacher, clawing at the older man's
throat. Brunner is groggy and tries to fight back, but John is strangling
Brunner now, and once John starts he can't stop. Brunner's face changes
color, his flesh turning ashen white, his wild eyes smoldering, silver hair flying in all directions, and John just keeps strangling him, slamming his skull
against the stage floor again and again, long past the point at which Brunner loses consciousness. John just keeps slamming that sadistic old fucker's
head against the hardwood, the sound of Tony's voice piercing the violent
haze.*

*"Do it—Johnny! Kill that motherfucker! Kill him! KILL HIM,
JOHNNY!! KILL HIM!!"*

*When John finally realizes that the teacher's eyes have gone all milky
and unfocused—and that just maybe the old fucker isn't breathing anymore—John stops, and he lets go, and he watches the silver-haired man's
head drop to the floor.*

*"You did it, Johnny—you did it—you're my man," Tony is mumbling
now, backing away toward the stage wings, rubbing his hands, trying to decide whether to run or scream or laugh.*

*John just sits there, transfixed, staring at the old fascist asshole's face
nestled in a carpet of shattered colored glass, staring, staring and thinking.*

*Sometime later, a voice speaks up: "Okay—I know what we're gonna
do—listen to me."*

*Only a few minutes have passed, maybe seconds—John isn't sure—but
he hears Tony speaking in measured tones. "We're gonna say it was an accident. Yeah. That's what we're gonna do. You stay here, Johnny, and I'll go
get some help, and we're gonna say it was an accident. Do you hear me,
Johnny?"*

"Sure, whatever," John mutters, staring at the dying man.

Tony runs out of the theater.

One of the eyewitnesses, Giddings, confirmed Sergeant Miller's suspicions. "That building is so old," a shaken Giddings said from the Lansing Police Department headquarters earlier today. "It was just a matter of time before something like this happened." Myron Korngold, the owner of the Little Red Barn Theater, could not be reached for comment.

John's alone with Brunner now, alone in the silent theater, with its broken colored glass and paint-thinner smell, waiting for the police to come. The strange thing is, John isn't frightened anymore, he isn't repulsed. He isn't even worried as he watches the life drain out of the teacher. The only way to describe what John is feeling now is a horrible sort of fascination.
Fascination.
John sees the light going out of Brunner's eyes like candle flames flickering out, a pair of tiny sparks in the centers of the man's irises dwindling, contracting, shrinking down until there's nothing but a needle-prick of life. Then the fire finally goes out and it's incredible. Incredible. John looks down at the man's hands, and they're closing, curling inward like the petals of a lovely flower at sunset, his flesh going from pink to white to an ashen gray.
John is watching a life come to an end, a life he has taken, and the worst part, the most hideous part, is the fact that John feels no remorse—
"No—!"

John was hunched over the trailer's sink now, mumbling to himself, "No, no, no, no, no—not true—" and the tears, the big, fat, salty tears, were dripping into the rusty steel sink where he had dropped the clipping, the tears pinging loudly, like raindrops on a tin roof.

Eyes closed, John began to cry silently.

The memory was shivering through him like a cold injection, the last click of a Chinese puzzle box, revealing the whole picture. And John stood in the pungent gloom of that trailer, sniffing back his tears, thinking about how the secret death of Stanley Brunner had changed the whole pathetic arc of John's life. From that fateful night on, John McNally had become obsessive, a haunted man. All his passion for the theater, his love of acting and his fascination with the method, all of it had gone sour, curdling inside him, transforming into a morbid obsession with death. For months after the incident, John had gone into seclusion. Clinically depressed. Lost. The nightmares robbing his sleep, his dark secret festering inside him.

But he still had his gift, thank God.

The gift had saved him, his acting gift, the ability to turn raw feeling into expression. He began to read about murderers, serial killers, and he found himself turning them into projects, characters, empathizing with them. Not *sympathizing* by any stretch—John hated this part of himself; but in some ways, he could now feel a killer's sickness, understand the need, the hunger, all because of a secret little apocalypse in a small, dilapidated theater—

A sudden noise across the trailer yanked John's attention to the front door.

Footsteps crunching in the gravel.

John spun toward the kitchen table on which he had set the Beretta, grabbed the gun, and cocked the hammer back without thinking. But it was too late because the door was already opening, and time had suddenly bogged down in John's mind—he wasn't ready for this, he wasn't prepared to fight the beast—and now the shadow slipping inside the trailer was hooded, dark, and carrying something large and metallic, and John tried to aim the gun—

"Drop it—scum-bunny!"

The twin barrels of a twelve-gauge shotgun materialized in John's face.

John froze, the pistol still gripped in his hand, raised at the intruder, who was still shrouded in shadows, the hood of a nylon Detroit Lions wind-breaker obscuring his face. John had no intention of firing, no intention whatsoever, because firing would surely mean death, but he couldn't move. The intruder gently pressed the barrels against the tip of John's nose and said in a gravelly voice, "I believe I told you to drop the hardware."

"I'm trying," John said somewhat sheepishly, wondering why his arm wouldn't move.

Eventually he managed to lower the pistol.

The intruder took a step closer, letting the shotgun drop to waist level. "That's better," she said, tugging off her hood. Her mischievous brown eyes were buried in wrinkles, the top of her thinning gray hair pulled back in a tight ponytail. Her weathered face was the color of brick. She looked to be somewhere between 60 and 112.

"Aunt Jo—?" John felt as though the clock had suddenly been turned back about thirty years.

The woman stared at him for a moment, then a spark of recognition flitted behind her eyes. She smiled, and the creases on her face deepened like old bark. "It ain't Julia Roberts . . ."

52

Original Sins

"DON'T TELL ME you gotta run, Johnny, because I can tell when some-body's in deep shit and needs my help, all right?" Joanne Prescott was sit-ting on a metal lawn chair outside the trailer, smoking a Winston 100, the shotgun lying across her lap, the ratty little pit bull curled up at her feet. The dog's name was Weiner and it was pretty much harmless, according to Jo. At the moment, though, it was snoring like an old Bowery bum.

"I know I sound like a lunatic, but I've really got to get going," John said, pacing across a patch of dirt next to the lawn chairs. He could see the faint orange glow of Lansing on the horizon just beyond the trees, and he felt his chest seizing up again, like an iron vise was squeezing it. It was edging to-ward four A.M. and there was no telling what Glass was up to. The thought of that psychopath torturing Jessie was making John's flesh crawl. Mostly because John was in the mind-set now, and he knew what a trophy Jessie was. What a prize! But John could not figure the location. Where would he take such a prize? Where would he go to be alone, undisturbed? John had to get out of there right now and figure out his next move, but the last thing he wanted to do was burden his aunt with all the gory details. Besides, John was worried that he was endangering her by merely talking to her.

What if Glass was nearby, lying in wait?

The old woman took a drag and blew smoke out through her nostrils. "You show up in the middle of the night like some kinda goddamn ghost—"

"I apologize for sneaking in," John said.

"—and now you can't even tell me what's wrong, what's happening in your life?"

"It's complicated."

The old woman rolled her eyes. "Oh. Well. By all means, don't weigh my brain down with all the facts and figures. A lady can get so confused."

John kept pacing, shaking his head. "All right, suffice to say, I'm in a little bit of a jam."

"Coppers after you?"

John looked at her. "How did you know that?"

Joanne jutted her chin proudly. " A woman knows certain things."

"What else does a woman know?"

Joanne Prescott looked down at her mongrel dog and scratched it behind the ears. "I always liked you the best, Johnny. You were my favorite."

John smiled, remembering how kind his aunt had always been to him. "The feeling's mutual," he said softly.

"You remember the time we went fishing up to Duck Lake?"

"Of course—how could I forget it?"

"You cut your hand on that old bullhead."

"Bled all over the boat."

"You hated every minute of it."

"Until I got home."

The old woman giggled. "You wanted to get right back in the car and go back."

"You got it."

A pause.

"What's happening, Johnny?"

John took a deep breath and stopped pacing. "I'm supposed to meet somebody."

"O.K. Corral?"

"Something like that."

Joanne shook her head slowly, as though commiserating over some sad, lost era. In the darkness, it looked as though her eyes were liquid. "You always were such a serious boy, your head so full of heavy thoughts."

"Yeah, well . . ."

"Even when you were appearing in all those shows out to the Little Red Barn—and boy, your uncle and I were sure proud of you back then—you still seemed kinda—what?—*moody*. I dunno. Maybe it was just—"

"Wait a minute!" John froze in his tracks, interrupting her, glancing out at the eastern horizon, the realization like a punch in the gut.

"What?"

"Give me a second here."

"What is it?"

Snapping his fingers, thinking, John said, "What did you just say—just a second ago?"

The old gal shrugged. "Uh, I said, you always seemed kinda moody when you were in them plays out at—"

"That's it!"

"What?"

"Nothing, nothing, um, I've got to go," John was murmuring now as he turned and went back to the trailer, his scalp crawling, his skin flushed. He knew where Glass was waiting for him now. *He knew.* But how in the world had he missed the clue? The poem: the words scrawled in blood on the floor of the psych building. It was all there. *"To share the taste, The original sin, In 'H' your fair maiden waits for you."* "H" did indeed refer to Haslett, but not the trailer. It was the right town, wrong locale. "H" referred to another part of Haslett, a part even closer to John's tortured soul. Glass had taken Jessie to ground zero. Of course. *The original sin.* Glass must have discovered John's dirty little secret. But how? How in the world had Glass uncovered something that was unknown even to the cops?

"Wait a minute—*Johnny*—where the hell you think you're going?" The old woman sprang to her feet, the pit bull stirring beneath her. She went over to the trailer and stood outside the door, the shotgun still propped under the crook of one arm, as John rummaged around inside the trailer for something. "Johnny, answer me!"

John emerged with the Beretta, awkwardly fumbling with its safety clasp. "I've got to go, Aunt Jo, I'm sorry. I can't tell you any more than that."

"That's it? Just gonna skedaddle without another word?"

He went over to the old woman, kissed her on the cheek. "I'll be back—hopefully tomorrow—and I'll tell you the whole story."

"You gotta be kidding me."

"You've got to just trust me on this," John said. "Please, just trust me."

Then he turned and started toward the east edge of the property.

He got halfway across the dirt yard when his aunt's gravelly voice suddenly called after him.

"Wait a minute, Johnny!"

John paused, gazed over his shoulder, and saw the woman rushing through a rear gate and into the shadows of the junkyard. She made her way between stacks of ruined cars, then into the little caretaker's shack. She was in there for only a moment, clicking on lights, banging metal drawers, then she returned with something wrapped in an oily rag. "Here," she said, approaching John with the bundle. "That Italian piece is shit for close quarters. You oughta be packing something sturdy and powerful."

She handed him the bundle and John pulled the rag away from a stainless-steel handgun with a four-inch barrel and a small scopelike device on the top.

"Ever since your uncle died," the old woman explained, pointing at the gun, "every redneck in Ingham County's been courting me. Fella down in Lansing Brewing Company—name of Shorty Simms—he's got this thing for guns, and he's giving me stuff all the time. He gave me that contraption last spring, said it was the best bet for home security. That's a Colt .357 Trooper—border-patrol model—with a laser sight. You ever shot one of them babies?"

John told her he didn't know the first thing about guns.

"All the more reason you should be packin' something powerful, easy to shoot—like the Colt. Here. Lemme show you."

The old woman took the Beretta away from him, then showed John how to turn on the Colt's laser targeting device, which sent a tiny, hair-thin beam of crimson light across the misty atmosphere of the junkyard. She explained that all you have to do is put that little red dot on the son of a bitch and squeeze the trigger. Then she gave John a box of Winchester silver-tip .357s and a couple of speed loaders, and she showed him how to load the gun quickly. John was hardly paying attention, he was so wired, so pumped with adrenaline.

He knew where the beast was waiting for him now; he knew for sure this time.

"I've got to go, Aunt Jo, really, thank you, thank you for everything," John said, and it was almost as though he were thanking the woman for a lifetime of watching after him, caring for him when his dad was too sick to stand and his mother was losing her mind.

"Don't mention it, kiddo," the old woman said and kissed John's forehead.

John started across the lot.

Just before slipping away into the shadows of Marsh Road, he heard his aunt's voice one last time. John paused and looked back at her.

She was standing on the edge of her property line about fifty feet away, shotgun in her hand, Weiner the pit bull standing next to her, wagging its tail. "Whatever the game is, Johnny," she said softly, *"make sure you end up winning it."*

John nodded at her, then turned and headed east into the dead, black darkness.

53

The Little Red Barn

It was astonishing how vividly John remembered the labyrinthine streets that wove through Haslett.

The lake road was called Detweiller Drive and it curled around Lake Lansing in tight turns and switchbacks, evoking memories around every corner, of toboggan runs in the winter, of bike rides in the summer, of midnight hikes and camping expeditions in the spring. At this time of night, the ancient asphalt was an endless ribbon of black, the thick corridor of oaks and white pines blocking out all ambient light and sound, the air smelling of humid rot, swamp gas, and imminent rain. John was hyperalert now, moving briskly through the darkness, his footsteps echoing flatly in the woods, the gun digging into the small of his back.

As he walked, he found himself preparing, recalling all the imaginary journals he had constructed, and the photos and the fantasies. It was second nature to him now, now that his memory had been fully restored, now that he had been pushed into this hideous corner. Just close your eyes and get inside a killer, go back and draw on that terrible sense memory. The feeling. The delicious feeling of letting all the rage come out into one beautiful explosion, of wrapping your fingers around that horrid little man's throat, then squeezing, squeezing, until the beast was gone. The most powerful sensation a man could feel, a primordial feeling, and John was going back to that place and absorbing every last rad of energy.

It was the only way John could destroy the beast: by *becoming* one.

It was sometime later—it was hard to keep the passage of time straight in his current state of mind—that the road widened slightly, and a wooden signpost materialized out of nowhere:

LITTLE RED BARN THEATER—NEXT LEFT.

John could feel every cell in his body buzzing, working, as he made the turn and entered the small, deserted parking lot. Memories swarmed in his head like angry bees, making his arms and legs rash with goose bumps. He could hear the ghost of Stanley Brunner out there somewhere in the soft drone of crickets: *"Stop mumbling, McNally, and get inside the man! Inhabit the character, for God's sake. Don't just read the lines!"* Thankfully, John McNally had learned his lessons well. He was indeed inhabiting the monster now. He was inside Glass's head, and it sent an inchoate charge through the air.

It was positively erotic.

Pausing, looking around, John felt the tiny hairs on the backs of his arms standing up. The trees and wild brush had encroached on the lot somewhat, the overgrown limbs dropping down across the parking spaces, the weeds sprouting up through the cracks in the cement, but the place was still as John remembered it. A tiny little oasis of culture in the hardscrabble woods of a blue-collar enclave. John remembered taking breaks out here with Tony, smoking cigarettes in the cool night air, talking theater, talking method.

Straight ahead, behind a thicket of elms that ran along a split-rail fence, lay the theater.

John pulled the .357 from his belt and flipped on the laser sight. His heart was racing so fast now, it felt as though it might just flutter up his esophagus and out through his throat, and he had to swallow a few times just to steady himself. His blood felt effervescent. But he no longer could tell whether it was fear or some kind of primal, homicidal ebullience. He was so far inside Glass now that he had come out the other side of his own identity. He had no name now, no personality. Only a pair of single white-hot purposes: to kill the killer, and to save the fair maiden.

He thumbed the hammer back on the .357, then started around the edge of the trees, staying low, letting the luminous thread of scarlet scan the darkness ahead of him, the red dot playing across the weeds. John wanted to be ready. He wanted to be mentally prepared to see the theater. He thought he was ready. He thought he was mentally prepared.

Then the theater materialized out of the shadows like a ghost ship.

The sight of it made John physically recoil, as though he had just stumbled into some kind of magnetic field. He paused, huddled behind a tree for a moment, and gazed up at it. The place moaned at him. It was a wounded place, the outer shell of weathered clapboard siding sunken like the flesh of an old face. Battered pine-shingled turrets rose up defiantly into the night sky, the original, cheery Cape Cod design long since worn away to bare rotted wood. The luscious rose trellises, the creeping Charlie and thick ivy that used to festoon the arched entrance, were now withered away to spindly webs of dry vines like moldy hay clinging to the walls, clogging the window wells and choking the gutters. To the left of the front entrance was an oblong arched window.

There was a dim yellow light burning in the lobby behind the window.

John tightened his grip on the gun and took a deep breath, girding himself, gathering his bearings. He had been right about Glass. This was the place, the final rendezvous, John was sure of it. If he could just stay in the mind-set, stay centered and ignore the ache, ignore the fear being stirred up by this little reunion, he might have a chance. The key was staying in character. John took one final breath and then crept out of the elms.

He remembered the side entrance, near the back loading dock, just off the backstage area. Keeping low, covered by shadows, he made his way across the front lawn—which was crisscrossed in shadows, the only outside illumination coming from a sodium streetlamp out beyond the parking lot—to the north portico, then around the side of the theater and along the crumbling cinder-block foundation. The side of the building was just as John remembered it, scarred siding and rows of cracked, boarded lancet windows, like an old church.

He reached the loading dock.

The backstage door was an iron hatch stained with graffiti and still padlocked. John started looking around the litter-strewn pavement for something with which to force the door open, and he was crouching down in the gravel, awkwardly gathering up a rusty old tire iron, when the sound of ancient squeaking hinges caught his attention. He straightened up in a flash, spun toward the door, and aimed the tiny red dot.

Then he exhaled.

The door had lazily come open on its own power, urged by the wind. He went cautiously over to the entrance and saw that the padlock was still secured to its broken lock plate, but the door had long ago broken free of its moorings. He swallowed the metallic taste in his mouth, then aimed the gun at the darkness behind the door.

The red dot vanished.

He stepped inside.

The first thing that struck him—more than the absolute pitch darkness, more than the familiar pasty-mildew smell—was the cold. It was as cool and damp as an old cellar in here. Close. *Fetid.* As though the sweaty old costumes and curtains had molded and ossified. He stood there for a moment, just inside the loading-dock door, filling his lungs with the dank air, letting his eyes adjust to the darkness. Muscles coiled, fingers tingling, he was holding the gun with both hands—emulating some ludicrous police show he had seen a million years ago—waiting for the bogeyman to jump out at him.

The silence stretched, the sound of his heart like a skin drum.

At length, his eyes adjusted to the dark, and he began to see familiar images. He was standing in the rear of the backstage area, a cavernous reach of painted concrete and unfinished walls filled with the shadows of over-turned scenery flats and wardrobe racks. The sour memories were beginning to seep into John's consciousness as he touched each silhouette with the poisonous red dot. He remembered many a sweaty night, huddling behind these flats, smoking nervously, trying to get to the core of some character, trying to draw on some painful experience long since repressed. He had a strange taste in his mouth now, sugary sweet, acrid. As his eyes adjusted further, he saw that the place had deteriorated more than he had expected. Pigeon dung and feathers covered the floor, and nests of leaves and twigs clogged the corners. Strange shapes hung from the ceiling, attached to frayed cables, broken counterweights, and rusty pulleys.

Across the room, a dim strip of light shone under the curtain leading into the wing.

John felt goose bumps crawl across the back of his neck, his stomach muscles clenching. It was the feeling an animal in the wild must get when the scent of a predator is on the wind, the fight-or-flight instinct kicking in. That thin thread of light under the curtain was beckoning him, taunting him. Glass was most certainly on the other side, probably waiting for John onstage, probably waiting to spring some elaborate trap, and, just for an instant, John felt the urge to make a big entrance. Raise the gun and burst onstage, blasting up a storm, shooting anything that moved. Brunner would have appreciated it. But instead, John crept silently over to the far wall and found an inner door.

He opened the door as quietly as possible and slipped into the darkness behind it.

John felt his way down a series of three wooden steps, each one creaking noisily under his weight—*great, great, just a great way to announce yourself to the beast*—then turned and crept down a narrow aisle and into the theater.

As he entered the auditorium, John stayed low behind the seats, scanning the darkness on all sides for the enemy. The auditorium was empty and silent, most of the seats tattered and torn, some of them gone, uprooted like rotted teeth in an ancient mouth. John could smell the odors of the sticky-sweet floor, the mélange of cologne and sweat that had mingled over the years, impregnating the upholstery. Glancing over his shoulder, he tried to see what was on stage, but all he could make out were huge wooden trees blocking most of the stage, their gnarled limbs jutting off the wing—probably remnants of some past summer stock production of *Peter and the Wolf* or *Little Red Riding Hood*—silhouetted in the dim flicker of a bare bulb hanging high above the lighting truss.

It was the same bare lightbulb that Stanley Brunner's acting company had once utilized for rehearsals.

John heard a noise then, a weak, muffled mewling sound coming from the stage.

There was a pop, like a flashbulb going off somewhere near the stage.

John ducked, realizing suddenly that it was the sound of an old parabolic stage lamp flaming on, throwing a pool of magenta light onstage.

What happened next occurred with the surreal speed of a dream, because John was moving on instinct now, forgetting about being vulnerable, for-getting about keeping the red laser dot poised, entering row B-B, center section, rushing toward the seats in the middle of the theater to get a glimpse of what in God's name was up there onstage amid the make-believe trees and flickering incandescent light, and as John approached the center seats, the object onstage came dimly into view.

John instinctively raised the .357.

But he didn't pull the trigger.

He just stared.

54

Into the Wooden Forest

THE RED DOT was in Jessie's face, blooming in her eyes, and she tried to speak but her mouth was a swollen, blood-encrusted knot of pain, and she tried to move but the Demerol had made her so groggy, so groggy, so groggy, she could hardly lean one way or the other. But *goddamn*, what a stupid way to die—what do they call it in the army?—friendly fire? The drugs must have been messing with Jessie's perception of time, because she felt as though she had been tied up on this stage for weeks now, months, alternating between scalding tears and smoldering rage. She couldn't stop thinking about Kit, and what a raw deal the poor kid was getting, losing her mother in such a stupid scenario. If only Jessie had played this thing smarter.

She tried to call out again, tried to call out to John, but her lips were puffy and useless on the side where Glass had repeatedly struck her, the blood dried in a crusty patch on her chin.

"Don't—!" she finally managed to utter. "John, don't shhhoot—!"

"Jessie?" John was coming down the outer aisle now, coming toward her, swinging the laser sight this way and that—and where the hell did he score a piece like that, anyway?—his eyes wide as saucers as he approached.

"Back—!"

"Take it easy, Jessie, I'm here." He was coming toward the stage steps, the luminous thread of laser sight stitching through the darkness. In the darkness, his eyes were watering, electric-hot. She had never seen him like this. He looked like a cornered animal. "Are you okay? Are you all right? *Jesus!* What did he do to you?"

"Gah-dammm-it, John! Stay back—!" Jessie was trying her best to form complete sentences, to articulate the simplest concepts of staying the fuck away, staying back, but her body was a bag of wet sand now. Glass had really done a number on her, the son of a bitch, beating her senseless, then filling her full of sedatives, then dragging her inside this godforsaken little theater and tying her to this makeshift operating table. Best Jessie could tell, the contraption was constructed out of cannibalized parts, pieces of actual surgical gurneys bolted together, complete with casters underneath and armrests on either side. Glass had used nylon straps to bind Jessie's ankles and wrists and torso to the cold laminate surfaces, then he had fixed the back of the thing to the ceiling cables, raising her upright as though she were on display, like a piece of brisket in a butcher's window. There was even a queasy sort of crucifix-like flavor to the thing that was making Jessie very uncomfortable. How long had she been tied up to the thing? Hours? Days? Forced to listen to Glass's endless psycho mumbo jumbo about life being a stage, and all of us being merely players, and Jessie being the core of some great experiment. Why the hell couldn't Jessie have been kidnapped by a normal psycho? Why the hell did she have to get snatched by Sir Lawrence-fucking-Olivier?

"I'm here, Jessie, I'm here," John was murmuring as he came across the stage, his .357 raised and ready. He reached her and put his arm around her, and the sensation of his touch made something shift inside Jessie. A dam cracking, fracturing, threatening to break.

"Jesus Chrissst, John—don't you know a trap when you see one?" Jessie uttered as best she could, staring up into his eyes.

"Can you tell me what happened?"

"Nice gun—where the hell did you get it?" She cocked her head at the .357.

"A friend gave it to me. Where's Glass? Where is he? I'm gonna get you out of here."

John began tugging at the nylon straps, and Jessie started shaking her head. "No—no—there's no time—"

"I'm getting you out of here—"

"No, John, listen to me, he drugged me, it's too late—"

"I'm not leaving you—!"

"John, goddamnit, didn't you hear what I said? It's a goddamn trap—" She felt the strap around her ankles coming loose, and then she felt John's hands working at her wrists.

"I got you into this," he said, then he paused and looked into her eyes.

"I'm not leaving you."

Then the dam burst, the emotion washing through Jessie like a tidal wave, and the room got all blurry as big, salty tears filled her eyes—and, goddamnit, she hated it when that happened—and the tears started rolling down her cheeks, and she looked up at him and said, "I'm scared, John."

"I know, kid, you and me both. Now tell me where Glass is."

"I don't know. I—I—I remember he left me here." Jessie was trying to remember what Glass had done, trying to recall what he had said before he vanished. Her mind was in free fall, the events of the past few hours like the wind rushing past her, and she couldn't latch on to anything. She vaguely remembered Glass ranting about his greatest achievement, injecting the Demerol into her shoulder and then backing away into the shadows behind the stage as though he had just planted a bomb. Maybe he *had* planted some kind of trap. Maybe he was preparing to press the button right this moment.

"Jessie! Stay with me," John said. He was still wrestling with the straps around her wrists, but he couldn't quite get them loose. "Think! Where did Glass go when he left you?—think hard!"

"I don't know. I, I can't remember."

"Was he armed?"

"Armed—?"

"Did he have a weapon?"

"He—was—"

A faint noise out in the empty seats.

John swung the .357 toward the darkness, the red beam slashing through the shadows.

Jessie tried to see through her tears, tried to focus on the darkness beyond the stage, but the magenta fire from the stage light was blazing in her face. She swallowed the urge to weep like a child, and she decided *not* to give this sick bastard the satisfaction. Instead, she focused on John, and she focused on her feelings for him, and she focused on how she was going to take him out for a goddamn steak dinner if they got out of this thing with their respective skins intact. John was holding the gun with both hands now, jerking it toward a creaking noise to the right, then to the left. He looked stiff and mechanical, trembling with emotion, like a broken toy soldier, and Jessie would have giggled at the incongruous image if she weren't so terrified. She started to say something when John's voice erupted.

"Glass!"

The word was a terrible mantra in the darkness, echoing in the dark auditorium, reaching down into Jessie's core and twisting her guts. She hadn't realized how much she hated this freak, how much she wanted to tear his throat out with her teeth. It was bad enough that he had beaten her, and dragged her halfway to hell, and tied her to this jury-rigged slab of laminated wood. The worst part was that he had frightened her, frightened her out of her wits, and no man frightens Jessie Bales and gets away with it.

"I'm here—isn't that what you wanted?"

John's voice was strained to the breaking point now, and Jessie suddenly started feeling bad, *very* bad, as a matter of fact, because for the first time since he had materialized out of the shadows, John McNally was sounding as frightened as Jessie felt. And deep down in some secret, private compartment in her brain, Jessie was sure that this was exactly what Glass wanted.

"Why me, Glass? Why the obsession with me?"

Another sound, closer, maybe behind the stage. Like a floorboard creaking. John spun toward it, the red beam cutting through the motes of filth. "It doesn't matter, Glass," John said softly now, addressing the darkness, his voice almost hollow-sounding, hoarse, like someone who had just undergone major surgery. Or someone who was *preparing* to. "You think you're ripping open an old wound, tearing me apart inside. I couldn't care less anymore."

That's when Jessie saw the shadow emerging from the wooden forest behind John.

Her scream was too late.

55

The Soul Thief

JOHN HEARD JESSIE shriek just as the dark presence leaped out of the scenery flats behind him.

He whirled at it, gun raised, and fired off a wild shot way too high in the air, the gun bucking in his hand—a violent spasm that John had not anticipated—the bullet gobbling the top of a plywood tree, a puff of wood dust exploding, the blast so loud it made John's ears ring. The figure engulfed him then, before he knew what was happening, and he was thrown backward, off balance. The gun went sprawling across the hardwood platform, and John careened to the floor. Arthur Glass landed on him like a battering ram, and John felt something sharp digging into his shoulder, a splinter of wood, a shard of broken glass.

"*John!*" Jessie's voice was a billion light-years away, swallowed by a black hole.

John was fighting for his life now because he saw the gleam of the shiny thing in Glass's hand, and John grabbed at Glass's wrist and tried to force the blade away—was it a scalpel?—and it was impossible to get a good glimpse at Glass's face, the man was wriggling too violently, revealing only flashes of feral blue eyes, perfect teeth, flared nostrils. Then something shifted, like heavy machinery retracting suddenly, and Glass rolled off John as abruptly as he had appeared out of the darkness—why had he retreated so quickly?—and all at once John saw an opportunity, a single white-hot instant of clarity: *the gun.* It lay just out of reach across the stage, the gleam of chrome-plated steel, less than ten feet away.

Glass was heading for the shadows upstage, and John had one chance, one tenuous chance, to get to the pistol.

He dove for the gun.

His shoulder took most of the impact, slamming hard as he landed, skidding wildly across scarred hardwood, and he managed to scoop up the .357 in one awkward swipe, and he tried to quickly aim it, quickly shoot it, but he couldn't, he couldn't, his finger was outside the trigger guard, and the gun was as impotent as a cold piece of lead. Across the stage, Glass was vanishing behind the scenery flats, and John struggled to his feet, aiming the pistol with both hands—the red dot falling on a dark shape—and squeezing off the five remaining rounds.

The air seemed to pop open like a pressure cooker as five successive blasts roared out of the .357, sparks and kickback spitting in John's face, the slugs chewing through the scenery thirty feet away, wood pulp splintering, shrapnel spraying, hellfire and damnation erupting in the magenta glare, and the sound of Jessie's desperate scream like a tea kettle boiling over. Then a wave of silence crashed, and John stood there for a moment, empty gun still aimed in sweaty hands. His ears were ringing. Glass was gone.

A frenzied moment passed.

"John—John, listen—John, it's a trick," Jessie was gibbering now across the stage, kicking her legs against the slanted table. Her eyes were blazing. One of her wounds had opened up, and her cheek was glistening in the glare of magenta stage light. "Are you listening to me? John!"

"I'm gonna get him," John said, fumbling with one of the speed loaders, trying to load it into the cylinder with trembling hands.

"John—wait—listen to me!"

"He can't get away this time, Jessie—"

"John—please—please—just—just—get the fuck outta here—!"

"I'm gonna get him," John murmured again, finally forcing six blunt noses into the cylinder. His hands were shaking convulsively now. He clicked the bullets home, pressed the release, snapped the cylinder back into the stock. It didn't matter that his legs were ablaze with pain, or that his eyes were burning, or that his shoulder was twinging where Glass had stabbed him. It was all fuel for the fire in John's brain.

"John, c'mon, please, John, whattya doing—?"

"Don't worry," John said as he started across the stage. "Just gonna finish what I started."

"John—wait! John!—"

John had already slipped into the darkness behind the fake trees.

He moved through the moldering upstage curtains, their dark, tattered fabrics hanging from pulleys high above the platform. The darkness and stale air engulfed him, and he quickly searched the shadows for any sign of the beast. Holding the gun tightly in both clammy hands, blinking away the sweat in his eyes, John swung the barrel to the left, then swung it to the right, then heard a noise up in the rafters and swung it up, the red dot landing on an iron catwalk.

Nothing.

He swept the laser thread back down at the darkness ahead of him and continued on. He was dimly aware of the sound of Jessie's voice behind him, pleading with him to get out of there. The voice was helpful. It provided a reference point.

Something moved to his right.

John swung the red dot toward a hulking shadow and fired—once!—twice!—three times!—and the sparks coughed up from the gun, a strobe light in the darkness, the bullets ripping through a pair of wardrobe mannequins, puncturing Styrofoam limbs, the arms and legs and heads hurling off in flash-frame glimpses. John stood there for a moment, heart racing, ears ringing, blinking away the retina burn, the images of mannequin body parts glowing in his field of vision.

He continued on, past the last curtain, into the dark landscape backstage.

Another sound, to his left, a creaking noise, and John spun toward it. The red dot touched a human face, and John squeezed the trigger. The blast bellowed, a blue flame leaping across the darkness, and the human face shattered. Shattered into a million hairline fractures.

A mirror.

It was a makeup mirror, reflecting John's own face, and John stared at it for a moment, feeling strange. Lightheaded. The image of his own distorted face floating in the darkness of the backstage wings was making him dizzy. He crept over to the mirror, keeping the gun raised and ready. He felt drunk, disoriented. Perhaps it was the shock, the inevitable exhaustion. He stared at his fragmented reflection, the image in the mirror swimming, warping. John turned away from the mirror and his legs got tangled.

He stumbled to the floor.

The entire room seemed to lurch on its axis, the g-forces pressing down on him, and he tried to lift himself back up but his head weighed a thousand pounds now. He knew this feeling well, this thick, inebriated haze. He had gotten to this point many times after a night drowning himself in the depths of a green bottle. But it didn't make much sense right now, with his heart chugging in his chest, his shoulder aching, throbbing. Why did his shoulder hurt so badly?

John dropped the gun and felt the place where Glass's scalpel had slashed him. It was tender to the touch. He looked down at his shirtsleeve and saw a tiny puncture mark above his bicep, the fabric spotted in blood. A puncture mark. *A puncture.* The realization flooded through John on the tide of hideous warmth radiating up his legs at the moment, spreading through his tendons, up his spine. It felt as though his body were being microwaved from the inside out, the feeling was so warm, and John realized that Glass had not stabbed him with a scalpel at all.

Glass had stuck him with something infinitely more troublesome.

"Jessie—!"

John's voice was weak all of a sudden, and he scooped up the pistol with tingling fingers, and he started crawling back toward Jessie, but now he was moving like a newborn, his movements tentative and shaky, his coordination all syrupy and weak. The warmth had penetrated his bones now, the tingling sensation shooting up his spine. It felt like a dream, a terrible dream where the world slows down, and the bogeyman comes at you from behind.

Almost on cue, the sound of footsteps creaking loudly behind him.

"Jesss—"

John tried to call out, tried to make it back through the curtains, but his jaw was cramping now, his body cast in cement, his joints seizing up like a rusty engine. The footsteps were looming behind him, and John tried one last frantic attempt at calling out.

"Jehh—"

It was futile. Something was working inside John's bloodstream. He could hear the footsteps looming behind him, only inches away. John clutched the .357 as tightly as possible, then turned around.

Glass was standing over him.

It took a few moments for John's watery eyes to register the costume into which Glass had squeezed his substantial form. At first, it looked as though Glass had put on a derelict's getup for Halloween, the garb a bit tattered, dyed in shades of dirty browns and grays and blacks. But the more John looked at it—and right now the seconds were stretching into an eternity—the more he recognized the wardrobe: the faded brown waistcoat and threadbare tunic shirt, the knee britches and dusty leather riding boots, the tattered cravat around his neck. The costume was seventeenth-century England—*Shakespearean England*—and the alkaline, mothball smell of it trumpeted in John's brain.

(*Rosencrantz and Guildenstern*)

"Nn-no—" John tried to speak, the chemicals flushing through his bloodstream, mixing with the adrenaline that was coursing through him now, the revelation like a razor through his sternum.

Glass was dressed as Guildenstern, the hapless highwayman from the Stoppard play.

"Yy-you're—"

"Yes, Johnny, I am he," Glass announced, slipping off his moth-eaten tricorn cap, giving a little bow. "Your humble servant, Guildenstern . . . or is it Rosencrantz? I can never be sure."

John blinked as though he were just splashed with acid, his face burning up. Glass was quoting the play, the Stoppard play, but how could he know it? How could he know that John and Tony had been rehearsing that very play the night of Brunner's death? How? *How?*

Unless . . .

"After all the intrigue was over," Glass said suddenly, his gaze burning into John, "you avoided me, Johnny, you avoided me like the plague."

"Y-yyou're not—"

"You still don't remember, do you?" Glass said. "You don't remember that hackneyed piece of shit I wrote our freshman year—what was the title?—*The Soul Thief*? You don't remember that saucy little roman à clef I banged out on my little Underwood? All the references to the starving young artist, Arthur T. Glass? Remember, Johnny?"

John felt as though he were stapled to the floor, his face blazing with fire.

Over the space of an instant, all the little squares on the Rubik's Cube in John's head were clicking into place, sending jolts of burning magnesium through his nervous system: the early months of his friendship with Tony Giddings, the endless hours in coffee shops listening to Gidding's self-indulgent Beat poetry and one-act plays that would never be finished; the strange phone calls in the wee hours, the strange behavior and even stranger obsessions; and the most glaring clue of them all—the initials *A* and *G* pulsing in John's mind like neon ghosts—Arthur *G*lass equals Anthony *G*iddings. *All* of this engulfing John in one great paroxysm that made his flesh crawl icy-hot.

Somewhere in the darkness behind him, the sound of Jessie's voice calling out: *"John!!"*

"You've done s-ss-something," John slurred his words at the monster. "Y-y-your face—"

Glass reached up and stroked his jaw. "It wasn't long after the little debacle I decided to forsake the theater, get into premed. My word was *indeed* plastics—plastic surgery, that is—and I could have been a great one, but I was on a more cosmic mission." He brushed his flaxen hair back, winking at John like an aging lothario winking at an old lover. "I did take advantage of professional courtesy, though—nothing extraordinary, mind you, just a little nip and tuck, a new hair color—so simple, yet so effective."

"I can't mmm—Can't mmmooh—"

"It's called succinylcholine," the surgeon said cheerfully, his icy-blue eyes twinkling in the dim light. "Large-animal vets use it to calm horses on the operating table. It creates interesting effects at certain dosage levels. You should be approaching complete paralysis right about now. Does that sound about right?"

John raised the gun and tried to squeeze the trigger, but the trigger weighed about six thousand pounds and John couldn't budge it.

"Enough of this horseplay," Glass quipped, and took the gun away from John. "We've work to do."

John's hand fell to the floor like a lead weight.

56

Chemistry

IT WAS AS though John has been shrunken inside his own body and now was a tiny frightened parasite riding along inside a big, fleshy dead carcass. Glass went about his business like a good highwayman. The gun was tossed into a trunk, and John was dragged like a huge sack of peat moss back through the tattered curtains toward the stage. John could still move his eyes, could still see fairly well, could still breathe, and he found he could speak nominally well if he took his time and formed simple sentences.

"Why? Why me?" John was trying to stall, trying to buy some time.

"Well . . . let's see . . . I could tell you it was because you ignored me after the Brunner incident." Glass was dragging John through the ruined wooden trees and unidentifiable scenery flats as he spoke. "Or I could tell you it was because of the delicious irony—you becoming a hunter, me the hunted—all because of the same original trauma."

"What-what are you talking about?"

"The social implications, Johnny. Think about it! Two relatively normal boys, traumatized by the same event, each choosing diametrically opposed paths. One's evil, one's good. It's downright mythic!"

"It's also absurd—"

Glass shrugged and kept dragging Johnny toward the magenta light. "You're right, Johnny, you're always right. It was none of those things. It was something more . . . *elemental*." Glass stopped for a moment, swallowing back the unexpected swell of emotion, his eyes shimmering now. "Years after we parted ways, I started missing you, Johnny. Something fierce. I'd lost my innocence by then, and had just started my little unauthorized *procedures,* when I ran into a brief article in the *Journal of the American Medical Association.* It was all about this cocky new profiler taking unsolved cases, annoying the Feds, writing speculative journals in the point of view of the killer, channeling the killer's thoughts. Fascinating stuff, John. Just brilliant. When I found out it was you, and you were working on one of my *own* little indiscretions, I had an epiphany—"

"You started sending me postcards," John said sourly.

"We're brothers, Johnny, in every sense of the word."

"It's over, Tony."

"The name's Arthur Glass, thank you very much," he said flatly, then continued dragging John into the cold, magenta firelight.

"I'll m-make you a deal," John said with a slur. "Please listen to what I have to say."

"Let me guess . . . you don't mind if I do whatever fiendish thing I have planned for *you,* but let the lady go. Does that about sum it up, Johnny?"

"Something like that," John said.

Glass smiled sadly. "You're not exactly negotiating from a point of strength."

Jessie's groggy, drugged voice suddenly rang out across the stage: "John! *John!* Are you all right!?—"

"The lady is a feisty one, Johnny," Glass said as they approached. "I'll grant you that."

"F-ffuck you!" Jessie slurred. "What the hell'd you do to John?"

Glass ignored her. "I gotta tell you, though, I would have pegged you for someone a little more genteel."

"Please," John said again, and felt himself being dragged across the stage. It was such a strange sensation, being moved yet feeling no movement. He could see his lifeless limbs hanging beneath him like sandbags, his numb arms flopping loosely in Glass's grasp, and he could sense himself being dragged over to an enormous crate in the corner, being propped against the crate like a rag doll. He could smell the chalky odors of the stage, the hot tungsten of the lights, and he could even feel the heat on his face.

But his body was a cold piece of meat.

(figure with meat)

John watched Glass wander off into the shadows beyond the opposite wings. Across the stage, Jessie was straining against the wrist straps, eyes closed, veins bulging in her neck, fighting some rising narcotic wave. John tried to move—just an inch, just a centimeter, just a twitch—but it was like trying to budge some enormous granite monument. He could feel the cold sweat that had broken out across his forehead, a pearl of moisture dripping into his eye, stinging him, making him blink. Which was a good sign. That meant *some* part of him was still able to feel. A rattling sound suddenly came from the darkness across the stage, a ratcheting noise, and a squeaking, as though Glass were assembling some diabolical child's toy.

A moment later, Glass reappeared, pushing a waist-high hospital cart with one hand, and carrying a metal stool with the other.

Jessie was starting to say something else but froze when she saw the cart.

"Hard to believe, Brother John, how far we've come," Glass mused as he pushed the cart—tiny wheels squeaking delicately—over to Jessie's gurney. He sat the stool down next to the cart. Jessie stiffened when she saw what was on the cart: a metal tray covered in white linen, the gleaming tips of surgical instruments sticking out the bottom. Scalpels, forceps, clamps, retractors. It seemed to take the wind out of Jessie's sails—what little there was left of it—and she fell silent.

"How did you . . . find me?" John said as calmly as possible, still trying to stall. He was staring at that horrible metal tray full of surgical steel. He knew the key to survival was keeping Glass engaged in conversation for as long as possible.

"It was laughably easy," Glass said, carefully folding back the linen, revealing the polished steel instruments. Jessie started straining against her bonds again, eyes wide, her chest rising and falling swiftly. "The first place I looked was Haslett," Glass explained. "I knew you wouldn't stray too far from the nest."

"But when I caught you . . . you tried to kill me," John said.

Glass stopped as though waiting for John to figure out the rest. "I never intended to kill you, Johnny," he said finally. "You thought I was coming after you with a knife, but it wasn't a knife at all."

Another pause.

"It was a needle," John said at last.

"Precisely! I realized you had tapped into my very thoughts, into my methods, and it was quite wonderful. I realized you and I were inextricably linked, and I had to do something about it. I lured you to that basement, Johnny. But then Providence stepped into the game."

"You're talking about the accident, getting amnesia," John said, trying to think of some strategy, some way out of this nightmare. His body felt like a straitjacket. His legs were cast in stone.

"Right again," Glass said, sorting through the instruments, choosing a fresh hypodermic. He started to prepare another dose of some unidentified drug. Jessie's eyes widened. Glass said, "I was busy while you were ensconced in that clinic, John, cooking up my Grand Experiment. I wanted you to *live* the life, not just imagine it. Stanislavski can only take you so far, Johnny. Pretty soon you have to dip your hands in the wound."

"I don't know what you're talking about," John lied. He had all kinds of ideas. But right now he could not take his eyes off that shiny hypodermic needle in Glass's hand.

"It's all about bringing us together," Glass said, turning to Jessie and injecting fluid into her arm.

"Oowwwww—!" she howled, wincing.

"LEAVE-HER-ALONE-YOU-PATHETIC-MONSTER-OR-I'LL-KILL-YOU-I-SWEAR-TO-CHRIST!!"

John's outburst was so sudden, so violent, so innate, his scream so primal, that his entire body shuddered involuntarily backward suddenly, slipping off the side of the crate and collapsing to the floor. At first John thought he was going to suffocate under the weight of his own bones—his chest seemed to weigh a thousand tons—and all he could see were the broken lighting trusses overhead, the starburst of magenta light pouring down out of the parabolic lamp.

Then Glass was kneeling over him, grasping handfuls of John's shirt, lifting him up. "Pay attention, dear brother," Glass was hissing now through clenched teeth, his eyes like glittering opals. "This will be the defining moment in your life—"

"I'm not your goddamn brother!"

"—a peak experience, Johnny."

John looked up into the eyes of the beast. "Why? That's all I want to know."

Glass tightened his grip on John's shirt. "Why does a cell divide? Any ideas? Why does any strand of DNA win the genetic lottery? Why does God snatch a seven-forty-seven out of the sky, killing every man, woman, and child onboard? Any theories?" Glass paused for a moment so that John could come up with something. The moment passed. Glass leaned in close, so close now that John could smell his breath again, the odor of hot tar masked with stale mint. "Blame it on the molecules, Brother John. We're the same stuff; it's just chemistry."

John closed his eyes. "Do whatever you want, just don't hurt the woman."

"You don't understand, Brother John," Glass said with a trace of ebullience in his voice. "It was never my attention of hurting your maiden fair. On the contrary. I want to transform the lady, I want to forge a new spirit. I want to use her essence to bring us closer together, Brother John, because ultimately it's *you* that I've been searching for all along—*you*—you're the one, John. You always were the one."

Glass gave John a bear hug then, as though greeting him after a long absence.

For a moment John thought Glass was going to kiss him, but then the surgeon hefted John's body off the floor and started dragging him over to Jessie's gurney. John watched his own limp legs dangling beneath him, his dead heels scraping the ancient hardwood. He tried to move, tried to writhe in Glass's grasp, tried with all his might to tear himself away, but his limbs were bags of crushed ice. Glass carried him over to the stool and propped him up on the metal seat like a favorite doll. John looked down at poor Jessie and saw that her eyelids were drooping, a spot of drool on her chin. She was only semiconscious, barely able to hold up her head.

"I've made a study of your career, Brother John," Glass was whispering in John's ear now, standing behind him. "You've got the compulsion. You've got it more than I. The need. It started with Brunner, but it's blossomed since then."

John felt his brain melting, his essence shrinking inside him. Glass had his arms snug around John's torso, supporting him on the chair, and now Glass was moving John's arms like a ventriloquist's dummy. "All the method acting—thinking like a killer, flirting with the pathology—it's deep inside you, John, I can smell it. I'm an actor myself. Remember? I know the craft. The urge. The compulsion. I've been waiting for this moment all my life. You're the one, Johnny."

"I don't—I—I don't know what—" John looked down at the tray of instruments glimmering in the stage light, and the sudden revelation sliced through him like a machete, rending his soul apart. He finally understood what Glass had in mind. "No . . . wait . . . wait," John was babbling now.

Glass reached around John with his free hand and ripped open Jessie's blouse, exposing her bra, sending half a dozen buttons flinging off into the darkness. The buttons made chittering noises as they bounced across the stage. Glass selected another hypodermic—this one made of metal, with a bigger plunger and a more substantial needle—and injected a local anesthetic into Jessie's abdomen just below her rib cage.

Then Glass turned his attention back to John.

"The drug that's in your bloodstream," Glass murmured softly in John's ear, maneuvering John's left hand over the tray of instruments like a child playing with a stuffed animal at a carnival game. "It not only causes temporary paralysis, it also causes intermittent spasms where your fingers will just simply seize up."

John watched in horror as Glass pinched John's fingers around a scalpel.

Jessie's eyes opened momentarily, widening, fixing themselves on John.

A tear began tracking down John's cheek, and then another, though John could barely feel them.

Then the sharing began.

57

Borne of Nightmares

"P-PLEASE . . ." John begged in a quavering, choked voice, his eyes welling up again. He could barely see through his tears now, but his bleary vision was still good enough to watch the horrors opening up before him. The pale curves of Jessie's tummy exposed to the glare of the stage light, the shimmer of the polished blade, and John's own hand making the first incision.

The edge of the scalpel touched the smooth flesh beneath Jessie's breast.

Dark arterial blood bubbled from the incision, gleamed in the magenta light.

"That's lovely, John, well done," the puppeteer encouraged from behind, after slicing six centimeters' worth of epidermis. Jessie's eyes were glassy now, dilated and fixed, shimmering with terror. She was buzzing with Demerol, but still conscious. "Now let's get that bleeding stopped before we make another incision," Glass said.

John watched the nightmare unfold, his lifeless arm being swept over to the instrument tray, the blood-beaded scalpel being dropped into a stainless-steel pan, then another instrument being plucked up with dead fingers like a set of fleshy tongs. The new instrument was a tiny clamp, no bigger than a pair of manicure scissors.

"The clamps are for pinching off blood vessels and arteries," Glass instructed, positioning John's dumb hand over the incision, which was now sodden with blood. "So the patient doesn't bleed to death."

The clamp was put into place along the flap of the incision, the sight of it making John ill, making his stomach muscles clench and twist, making his brain vibrate with a new emotion as pure as distilled alcohol. *Rage.* It was smoldering inside him now—pure, molten rage—for a life spent thinking monstrous thoughts, rage for living in the dark, rage for all the lonely days imagining what it would be like to kill, to hunt, to terrorize, to devour, rage, rage, rage and shame, shame for a life spent obsessing over this beast, and shame for getting a woman like Jessie trapped in a box full of snakes, and now the tears in John's eyes were no longer tears of pain and horror but the tears of raw anger, as though his pain had finally denatured itself, cauterized itself into its essential raw element, and that was good, that was very good, because it was helping John think, helping him clear his mind and think, and remember, remember something he had forgotten: a minor little detail that had gotten lost in the shuffle.

John glanced down at the bottom of the slanted gurney without moving his head.

The straps around Jessie's ankles were still unbuckled, lying loose across the floor. John had forgotten about those straps, those goddamned straps that *he* had unbuckled, and from the looks of things, Jessie had forgotten about them as well. John looked back up at Jessie, her partially nude body strapped to the stainless-steel rack, head lolling, eyelids at half-mast. Then John peered down at the stool, and he saw several things at once—the positioning of his own legs, flaccid with paralysis, angled off to the right; the position of Glass's legs to the left; and the position of Jessie's feet—she was still wearing her black leather boots, the high-fashion kind with the Italian buckles across the side—her right foot canted off to the right, dangling only inches from the floor, dangling near Glass's. The idea struck John like a sledgehammer blow to his frontal lobe.

Glass was swinging John's arm back over to the tray, urging his numb fingers around another scalpel.

"Jessie—I'm *sorry!*" John spoke loudly, sharply, trying to rouse her from her drugged stasis. "I tried to persuade him, Jessie, I tried."

Glass paused for a moment, turning to glance at his accomplice. "That's not necessary," he said, a trace of revulsion in his voice.

"I just want her to know how sorry I am, how I tried to persuade you," John said, his voice uneven. He was practicing the Method one last time, channeling the seething rage inside him into heartache, remorse, tremendous sorrow. The tears started building in his eyes, then tracking down his cheeks. He was accessing another sense memory—this time, sitting at his father's bedside at Landing General twenty-five years ago, watching the old man die, wishing that he had told his father how much he had always loved him—and John started weeping. "I tried, Jessie, you've got to believe. You've got to know how much I tried to *persuade him*—"

—and these last words were barked like a desperate command, with an emphasis on the word *persuade*—

—and Jessie's eyelids fluttered suddenly as though shocked by an electric current. Her eyes flickered with recognition. She peered over the side of the gurney and glanced down at her ankles as though she had forgotten to tie her shoes, and her eyes widened further, and all this happened in the space of an instant without Glass noticing a thing, but John was watching, John was watching it all. He stared into her eyes, and she looked up at him, then she looked at her belly, slick with blood, taut with a metal clamp, and John saw that same warrior glint in her eyes that he'd seen in the tattoo parlor and on the train—the glimmer of a wolf about to protect her cubs. Then John said it one last time—

"Persuade him—"

—and Jessie's foot leaped up suddenly, striking Glass hard in the groin.

Glass convulsed, the shock expelling from his lungs—

—as Jessie kicked him again, and then again a third time, as hard as she could—

—until Glass whiplashed backward, the tray of instruments flipping suddenly, end over end, sending dozens of sterilized instruments flying through space, as Glass continued to stagger, grasping at the air, gasping for breath, his eyes wide and wild, hot with surprise, tumbling to the floor. John felt himself slipping off the stool. He landed at the foot of the gurney, his legs tingling faintly, his arm twisted underneath his body. The drug was wearing off—he could tell that much even in the midst of all the tumult, the ache starting between his shoulder blades—but he still couldn't move very well. He saw the glimmer of a scalpel on the floor a few feet away.

It might as well have been in the next county.

"ENOUGH!"

Glass was screaming now, climbing back to his feet, his voice completely transformed all of a sudden, an angry, booming, patriarchal roar, and he stumbled toward Jessie, reaching out for her. John tried to will his arms and legs to move, but the best he could muster was to flop onto his belly, then start worming toward the gurney. Meanwhile, Glass was attacking Jessie, and Jessie tried to kick him off, but Glass was too strong for her and caught her foot, shoving the entire gurney to the ground.

The gurney crashed onto its side, the tubular steel frame snapping like dry kindling.

Jessie's left hand came free of its strap.

John watched, helpless, trying to make his legs work, trying to motivate his trembling fingers. Jessie was ten feet away, on the floor, cuffed to the overturned platform, clawing at a fallen scalpel only inches away from her. The clamp was still dangling from her incision, her torso black and glistening with blood. Glass was looming over her, breathing thickly, rubbing his groin. Jessie finally reached the scalpel, grabbed it, and spun toward Glass, and Glass jerked backward, then began to laugh, a half-maniacal, half-tortured chortle that sounded unlike anything John had ever heard—in fact, it sounded unlike anything John had ever imagined in his darkest thoughts—almost like a man in an electric chair laughing at his own death.

Jessie managed to sever the other strap that still bound her right wrist.

She rolled away from the fallen gurney, away from Glass—moving pretty well for someone with fifty milligrams of Demerol in her bloodstream—eventually striking a fallen scenery flat, her shoulder slamming hard against the jagged wooden pane, a spattering of her blood hitting the wood. The impact seemed to awaken her further from her drugged stupor. She struggled to her feet, wavering drunkenly, holding the delicate little scalpel out in front of her, holding her wound with her free hand, blinking, frantically trying to focus through the dizziness.

Glass stopped laughing.

He turned and walked across the stage to where most of the instruments had fallen, paused to scoop up a scalpel, then turned to face Jessie. He was still breathing fairly rapidly, and there was an expression on his face that was impossible to read. John saw it from where he was lying, and it put a shiver in his spine. It was the expression of a circus trainer about to discipline an errant animal.

"What are you ww-wwwaiting for, fffffreak?" Jessie slurred her words at him.

Glass nodded tersely, then lurched across the stage with scalpel poised.

Jessie got in one good strike, the edge of her scalpel nicking Glass in the arm, but Glass was much too fast and nimble, and he slashed out at Jessie's midriff when she was trying to spin away. The scalpel whispered through the shank of her oblique muscles, so cleanly it looked as though Glass had streaked her with a ballpoint pen. Then she yelped, jerking back and holding her side, blood glistening between her fingers. Ten feet away, John screamed a keening wail, the sound of it sharp enough to cut metal. Across the stage, Glass was slashing out at Jessie again, and this time Jessie dodged the blade, tripped over her own feet, and tumbled backward to the floor.

John tried to crawl toward them, his arms and legs tingling, brain swimming.

Glass was standing over Jessie, breathing hard, shoulders heaving with each gasping breath. Jessie tried to crawl away from him, but Glass reached out and grabbed her by the leg, and Jessie tried to wriggle but she was bleeding to death now. The clamp had come loose, and the incision had opened across her tummy, combining with the wound to her oblique, draining her. Blood as black as crude oil covered her belly. Glass knelt over her, eyes blazing madly, his body trembling with rage, raising the scalpel, preparing to bring it all to an end. Eight feet away, John saw the final blow coming, the terrible tableau frozen in time-lapse, the glimmering tip of the scalpel poised.

In that nightmare instant of clarity, like a glass figurine cast in a block of solid ice, John saw his entire universe crystallizing into one last act. An instantaneous blip of electrical energy deep in his brain, jumping from one synapse to another, firing a thought. A reaction born of dreams, of practicing parts in front of a mirror that no one has ever seen, of living the method—

—and John cried the words at the top of his lungs in the nick of time.

58

The Lizard Brain

"LET ME DO IT!"

On the edge of the stage, half buried in shadows, half bathed in purple light, the beast shivered above the woman, the tip of the scalpel stuttering in the air like the branch of a tree in the wind. The words had reached his ear at the last possible instant before the razor edge of the blade had come down, and the sound of the words—the inherent truth burning deep in their strangled wail—was just enough to trigger some deeply rooted switch in the killer's brain, which was in turn just enough to make him pause. Perhaps it was the sheer surprise at hearing such a declaration coming from John. Or perhaps it was the needy quality to Glass that John had always suspected, the loneliness, the desire to share something—anything—with another human being just like himself. Or maybe it was merely an involuntary twitch, curiosity perhaps.

"Please let me do it," John reiterated softly across the stage, his sincerity unimpeachable. "Let me put her out of her misery, Tony—*please*."

Glass seemed to be frozen with indecision, his arm still poised like a Renaissance statue of Lucifer over Jessie, the scalpel gleaming a weird rose color, reflecting the stage light. Glass was like a pitcher who had balked, stuck between pitching or turning toward the base runner, and the knife hung there like that for an eternally long moment—which probably seemed a lot longer to John, since Jessie was bleeding to death on the floor only inches away—the knife hanging in midair.

"Please let me do it, Tony."

For one frenzied instant, John imagined himself as a raging, hormonal twenty-year-old, and he thought of the greats—Brando, Kazan, Strasberg,

Steiger, Cassavetes—and he saw the Little Red Barn stage as it was twenty-five years ago, freshly varnished, festooned with the earth-tone façades and papier-mâché walls of Brunner's production of *Rosencrantz and Guildenstern,* and the rain was a tommy gun on the skylights overhead, and Brunner just lashed out at Tony Giddings for the last time, and John was dressed in his baggy highwayman's outfit, the greasepaint makeup oily and itchy on his face, creeping toward Brunner with anger tingling in his fingertips, pure unadulterated hate in his fingers, and now John wanted to kill another human being more than anything else in the world, he could feel it, he could feel the hate deep down in his marrow, deep down in the reptile part of his brain, but there was only one way, one way, one way to fool the beast—

"Help me, Tony," John whispered. "Help me put my friend out of her misery."

Across the stage, Glass was lowering the scalpel, and John could feel his legs again, well enough to begin crawling toward Jessie. There were tears on John's face now, real tears, real pain—the hallmark of a Method actor—but his fingers were dragging like limp simian digits on the floor. How much dexterity did he have in those fingers? How much had the feeling come back? Was there enough? Was there enough to do the deed? And if so, could John conceal his hidden strength? It would be the most important performance of John's life. Glass was turning slowly around to face him, and now John realized he would have to be the most convincing he had ever been, onstage or off. He would have to sell the Devil a barbecue grill.

Glass looked at him.

John said, "Please let me do it, Tony. Let me be the one to do it."

Glass pondered John, then glanced down at the woman on the floor. Jessie had passed out from the blood loss and exhaustion, but she was still breathing shallowly, her face the color of an eggshell, spattered with blood, her fingers twitching involuntarily. She certainly didn't have long to live. Glass looked back at John and something changed in the surgeon's gaze, something behind his eyes. A shimmer of emotion. A glint of joy that he had finally found the soul mate he was searching for. A long moment passed.

Glass smiled.

He knelt, reached over and pressed the scalpel into John's cold, numb fingers.

John sucked in a breath, lifting himself up—

—then drove the blade into Glass's chest.

The beast roared, stiffening as though electrified by some ungodly current, pulling John down on top of him. John had to lean on the knife with his entire limp body in order to keep from being thrown off, driving it deeper, deeper, deeper into the organs of the bucking bronco. Warmth spread between them, Glass's blood baptizing both men, and Glass was shrieking now—his voice high and shrill all of a sudden—wriggling under John, writhing, trying to tear himself away, but John was clinging to the beast, putting everything he had into planting that scalpel as deep as possible.

Glass finally rolled away, the scalpel slicing a groove through his aorta, various pulmonary arteries, and part of his left lung.

John dropped the blade.

Glass was twelve feet away now, partially covered in shadows, trying to stand up. His costume was soaked in blood, clinging to him, the clean diagonal tear seeping black in the gloom. He tried in vain to stand, then collapsed to his knees, then to his belly. He started crawling toward the darkness beyond the stage, and John watched in stunned, horrified fascination, the tears burning his eyes. It was like watching some jungle predator wounded in battle, limping off to die in private in the wooden forest, and a familiar feeling started rising inside John like a cold tide, the tingling sensation in the base of his spine, the buzzing in his ears, the heat in his belly as he watched the beast expire in the shadows—it was all so familiar—taking him back, taking him back to a rainy night twenty-five years ago, watching another beast die, feeling the lizard-brain rush back then as well, the primordial shiver of satisfaction—so sublime, so powerful—and now the currents deep inside John were colliding again, the primal soul taking over, spurts of adrenaline coursing through his veins, making him shudder again with that inexplicable, euphoric muscle-memory—

—as Glass finally collapsed in a bloody heap, and then was still.

And the silence was excruciating.

59

Permafrost

JOHN SWALLOWED THE sour, metallic taste in his mouth, took a few steadying breaths, and looked around the empty stage. He was still unable to stand, his arms and legs still relatively weak, but he had most of his feeling back, and his hands were working relatively well now, so he quickly crawled back over to Jessie. He looked down at her, and the shock of seeing her near death was like a sobering slap in the face.

Jessie was lying prostrate on the hardwood, her face as pale and smooth as ivory, her lips barely moving. John managed to cradle her head in his arms, the wetness spreading in his lap, the blood seeping out of her in gouts. He started to say something and then heard a muffled sound outside the theater, maybe an animal, maybe footsteps, he couldn't tell, but he didn't care. Jessie was dying. Working as quickly as his sluggish body would allow, John grabbed a roll of gauze that had tumbled to the floor next to them and started wrapping the incision. Maybe the initial cut had been superficial enough to give her a chance. Maybe the clamp had prevented her from bleeding to death. Maybe John would be able to get her out of here and to a hospital in time. Maybe, maybe, maybe—

The blood was pooling beneath Jessie like an aura, the deep red turning as dark as coffee in the magenta glare.

"Don't you *die* on me!" John's voice was garbled by tears and pain and terror now, real terror, because he was covered with Jessie's blood, and the sounds outside were getting closer, twigs snapping, something metallic clicking like a big clock. John tried to wrap his arms around Jessie in a half nelson, then drag her across the stage toward the exit doors.

John was halfway across the stage when he started wailing. "HELP!

SOMEBODY HELP US—PLEASE—HELLO—ANYBODY! PLEASE HELP US, PLEASE!"

He reached the edge of the stage and tried to stand, but his legs were still rubbery and weak, and he collapsed twice before giving up. He decided instead to drag Jessie downstage left, toward the ramp that had been constructed years ago for a handicapped professor to get onstage during rehearsals. He reached the ramp and was halfway down it—Jessie's blood leaving a glistening leech trail on the hardwood—when the sound of creaking wood echoed across the seats. John looked up—his legs getting tangled together suddenly—and Jessie slipped from his grasp.

Jessie folded to the floor of the ramp, and John tumbled off the edge.

He landed in the first row, banging his head on the edge of a chair, and the world seemed to flicker for a moment, his vision going all blurry and soft-focus, and he tried to climb back to his feet but could only rise to his knees, bracing himself on a chair, squinting at the darkness beyond the seats. Somebody was entering the theater, three dark figures, moving cautiously—John could barely see them through his tears and delirium—and one of the figures, the one in front, seemed to be carrying a large object that looked like a shotgun.

"Jesus-H-Christ, Johnny, what the hell kinda play you working on here?"

The familiar cranky voice was a slap in the face, awakening John from his daze, and he waved his hands in surrender suddenly because he could see the wiry old woman in the Detroit Lions windbreaker coming down the center aisle with her .306 raised like a divining rod. There were two men behind her in work clothes, one black and lanky, one white and bald, probably hired hands who worked at the junkyard. "Aunt Jo!" John tried to stand.

"Johnny—Chrissake! What the hell—?" The old woman was approaching John, lowering the shotgun. The two men were coming up cautiously behind her. She knelt down and said, "When I finally realized where you were headed, I decided to get the boys outta bed and come after you."

"I'm fine, Aunt Jo, listen—" John motioned toward the ramp, toward Jessie. "I need you to get my friend to a hospital right now."

"But—"

"*Please!—*"

The old woman whirled toward Jessie, went over, and checked her pulse. "Can't feel nothin'—can't tell if she's still kickin'. *Emit, Teddy!* Gimme a hand!" The old woman motioned to her boys, and the young men came over and scooped Jessie off the ramp. They started carrying Jessie toward the exit, and Joanne came back over to John, kneeling down next to him.

"I'll be fine, Aunt Jo, I'll be okay." John waved her off. "Just go get Jessie to an emergency room—fast—she's lost a lot of blood—*please!*"

"I ain't sure she's still alive, Johnny—"

"She's alive, dammit! And she's gonna make it!"

"But what about you?"

"I'm fine, goddamnit—"

Joanne glanced up at the stage, pursing her lips at the far shadows. "Is there somebody else up there?"

"Aunt Jo, please help my friend!"

The old woman handed him the shotgun and said, "I'll be back in a flash—don't you go nowhere."

"Don't worry," John murmured, taking the cold steel barrel in his hand, wincing at the pain in his joints.

The old woman followed the others up the side aisle, out the exit, and into the night.

John let himself collapse, flopping down on the tacky floor, all the tension leaking out of his body, the strange odor of his sweat permeated with the chemical smell of the drug. Outside, the sound of an engine swelling, gravel spraying under wheels. John tried to take a few deep breaths to steady himself, to clear his mind, but all he could think about was Jessie, and whether she would make it, and now the tears were gathering in his eyes again, and he began to weep softly, wondering whether it was all worth it.

The theater got very quiet.

There was a noise somewhere off in the shadows behind the stage.

John straightened suddenly, a cool wave of chills spreading over him, but then he relaxed, sighing, realizing it was just the ancient wood settling in the theater. There was no way in hell that Glass could still be moving around up there, not after having half his major thoracic organs sliced clean through. The wicked beast was dead. John could learn how to live in the sunlight now.

The bad dream was over.

The realization calmed John somewhat, and he exhaled and closed his eyes and tried to gather his bearings. His body felt almost normal again—still too weak to walk, but normal enough to stand up—so he slowly, painfully, struggled to his feet and turned toward the stage.

Arthur Glass was standing there.

John nearly jumped out of his skin, jerking back against the seats with a gasp. He instinctively threw up his hands and shielded his face. Glass didn't move, didn't speak, just stood there on the edge of the stage like Marley's ghost, his Guildenstern costume soaked through with blood, his face the color of fresh cement. His icy-blue eyes were milky with shock and pain, the stage light putting highlights on his sandy high-fashion hairdo. It looked as though he were about to deliver a soliloquy, his lips peeling away from his perfect teeth, but the words were jammed in his throat. John was paralyzed with a different drug now, a drug called sheer unadulterated terror. It looked as though Glass were trying to smile.

Then the surgeon's knees buckled and he tumbled off the edge of the stage.

Glass landed on one of the broken seats, ending up in a half-sitting, half-fetal position, as though he had timed and planned the fall like a veteran stuntman, his arms flopping lifelessly over the tattered armrest, a death rattle hissing out of his ruined lungs. Then he sagged in the chair, his jaw slack, head lolling to one side. John tried to back away, but he couldn't make his legs work or his eyes glance away from the beast. Something about the way Glass's face had come to rest, his eyes still open and fixed on John.

Something whispered out of Glass—a puff of air, hardly even a word.

John didn't want to hear any more dying words from this monster, didn't want to look into that icy stare, didn't want to see any more, but there was the little matter of John's legs being planted like tree trunks in the permafrost. There was no way in hell he was going anywhere. In fact, all he could do was stare at the dying man's face, the flesh metamorphosing from pink to white to ashen gray, the tiny pinpricks of light in the man's eyes dwindling, shrinking, like dots on a TV screen signing off for the day—

—and the faint sound of Glass's breathless whisper: "How did it feel?"

"SHUT UP!" John slammed his hands over his ears, pressed his eyes shut.

"How did it feel, John?"

John looked at the dying man, the ashen face and the gelid stare.

"Rosencrantz and Guildenstern are dead—" Glass uttered breathlessly, and then slipped away.

The smile lingered on the dead man's face.

Just as it would in John's imagination for the rest of his life.

60

Lime Green Cinder Block

THERE WAS A single dented pay phone mounted to the lime green cinder-block wall outside the processing unit at the Ingham County jail. John was forced to hold the receiver in both hands, his wrists shackled securely, as were his ankles, with heavy-duty steel chains. He was listening to the monotonous electronic buzzing on the other end as the hospital operator rang the ICU unit. Behind him, a beefy guard was breathing down his neck. John was trying to ignore him.

After more than an hour of questioning—first by a local Homicide cop, then by an FBI field agent from Chicago—John had been allowed his single precious phone call. Without hesitation he had dialed Lansing General Hospital to check up on Jessie. He probably should have called a lawyer, or somebody from the Behavioral Science Unit at Quantico who might vouch for him, or even little Kit Bales, but at the moment, John was beyond caring about anything but Jessie.

There was a click on the other end of the line, and then the brusque sound of a nurse's voice. "Intensive Care, this is Janice speaking."

"Janice, hello, my name is John McNally, and I'm calling about the status of a patient. She was brought in earlier tonight."

"Are you an immediate-family member?"

"Actually, no, but I—"

"I'm sorry, sir, but we're only allowed to give out information to immediate-family members."

"I understand that, ma'am, her name is Jessica Bales, and she was brought in earlier tonight, and I just wanted to know if she's out of surgery and if she's okay."

"Sir . . . I'm sorry . . . like I said, I'm not allowed to give out that information."

John bit the inside of his cheek hard enough to make it bleed. "Is she out of surgery? That's all I want to know."

"Sir, I'm really sorry. If there's something else I can help you with . . ."

John swallowed a mouthful of needles and tried to stay calm. According to his aunt, Jessie had been barely alive and was listed as serious upon arrival at Lansing General, but then was immediately rushed into surgery, her condition downgraded to grave. That was the last John had heard, and now he was panicking.

"All right, I'm her brother, okay, her stepbrother, from Philadelphia. *Please give me something.*"

There was a long, awkward pause on the other end of the line, and John heard the muffled crackle of an intercom, then a spurt of voices. Finally Nurse Janice replied in a measured, wooden tone: "Sir, you'll have to speak with the doctor, but I can tell you that the operation has been over for some time."

John blinked. "The operation is what? You said the operation is over? And that means . . . what? She's okay? Is Jessie okay?"

More muffled voices. "Sir, I'm sorry, but I have another emergency."

"Wait, wait, wait, wait a minute! Is she okay? Please just answer—"

There was a click in John's ear, and the other end of the line was disconnected—

—and John shuddered as though someone had punched him in the gut.

The operation has been over for some time.

John stood there for a moment, the receiver still clutched in his hand. It could have meant anything. It could have referred to the fact that Jessie was out of the woods, that she was going to make it just fine. It could have meant that the doctors had already treated her, had sewn her up and given her a transfusion—and it was not as bad as anyone thought—and she was now resting comfortably in postop. It could have meant any one of a million different things.

John hung up the phone.

"Let's go," the guard said evenly.

"Um . . . yeah, uh . . . can you give me a second?" John said, raising his hand, waving the guard back. "I just need to sit down here for a second and get my breath, okay? No big deal, I just need a second."

He sat down on the lime green bench in front of the lime green cinderblock wall and began to weep.

It took two guards to help him back into the interrogation room.

Epilogue

Closure

Time flies over us, but leaves its shadow behind.

—Nathaniel Hawthorne,
The Marble Faun

Soft, mournful organ music droned out of the back of St. Mary's Church, drifting across the parking lot until it was drowned by the gray mist coming down in sheets, unfurling off the chill breezes of Lake Michigan. The rain had started around noon, and now it was a blanket of misery over the tidy little suburb of Evanston, Illinois. No letup in sight. Which was precisely how John felt, standing under the church's long gallery roof, chewing his fingernails, wondering how he was ever going to get up the courage to go inside and face little Kit, not to mention the rest of Jessie's relatives. These were people who had shared intimacies with Jessie that John would never know.

He glanced out across the lot, beyond the trees to the east, beyond the rooftops of old Victorian painted ladies. Evanston was an old suburb, full of old homes, old money, old trees, and old El tracks that wound through the downtown area like an iron spinal column fossilized by cruel winters and endless wear. Jessie's mother was still a resident here. She hung her hat at the Oakwood Terrace nursing home over on Oak Street. Harriet Bales had helped choose the church, and John wasn't about to argue with the lady. After all, John had been acquainted with the Bales family for only a short time. The fact that he was even involved in this event was a miracle.

Come to think of it, the fact that he was standing here in one piece was pretty miraculous.

God knew, the past few weeks hadn't been easy. It seemed as though it had been *years* since that fateful evening at the Little Red Barn Theater. All the sleepless nights, the endless testimony at endless court proceedings, the interviews with one investigator after another, the interminable sessions with fellow clinicians, the roller-coaster ride of emotions, and the struggle to keep attending those AA meetings. Weeks of grim rumination had gone by before John had realized he was nursing one hell of a clinical depression. At first, his GP had prescribed an antianxiety drug called impramine. It had worked for a while, allowing John to sleep through the night at least, but his dreams were still as haunted and as desperate as ever, full of feral flesh and contorted faces, and toothy smiles plastered on the pale face of a dead man. Then he had tried a new antidepressant called Elavil—appropriately named for its tendency to elevate moods—but this drug had turned out to be a pharmaceutical Trojan horse. It merely opened up a channel to John's raw emotions, reducing him to gibbering idiocy at the mention of Arthur Glass's name. Finally, John was given eighty milligrams per day of good, old-fashioned Prozac. The Prozac seemed to work relatively well.

It had allowed John to start thinking about the future at least.

"John!" Behind him, the high-pitched squeal of a voice pierced the hiss of rain.

John whirled and saw a tiny gnome in eggshell lace trotting toward him, her delicate rinse-water curls bobbing in the wind, her freckled face bubbling with panic. Kit Bales clamored up to John and grabbed his leg. "Everybody says you're hiding out here!" she raved breathlessly. "I told them you'd never hide from something this important."

John scooped the child up into his arms and gave her a squeeze. "Who's hiding?"

"They think you're nervous," she said with a shrug.

"Who's they?"

"You know, Grandma, Aunt Treva."

"I'm not nervous," John said with a grin. "I'm just savoring my last moments as a free man."

Kit wrinkled her nose at him.

Right then, another figure appeared across the portico, hovering inside the rectory door. A thick-jowled bear of a man in a white liturgical gown and purple sash, Father Michael looked apoplectic with nervous tension. The priest was a hand wringer, a real nervous sort, and even now, as he squinted out at the storm, his face twitching softly, his hands were wringing busily, wringing the top of his silk armilla.

"About time to get things under way, Father?" John called to him.

The priest nodded. "Yes, John—we're all waiting."

John turned to Kit and kissed her cheek, smelling her baby-powder smell. "Come on, Boodle, let's go take the plunge."

John put the little girl down, and the two of them followed the priest into the church.

The sanctuary was luminous now with pastel light from myriad stained-glass louvers, and all the friendly faces out in the congregation were radiating encouragement, and all at once John felt whole. Maybe for the first time in his life. He could feel the tiny vise of Kit's hand around his, and he knelt down next to the little girl. "You ready for show time?" he whispered to her.

The little girl nodded.

John rose, nodded at Father Michael, and the ceremony began in earnest.

Organ music swelled, all heads turned toward the front of the room, and the priest slowly ushered John and Kit past the front pews, crowded with sniffling aunts and uncles, past the chancel rail, and finally up the wide steps—covered by a white runner—to the high altar. John took his place next to an old schoolmate with whom he had recently become reacquainted—a criminologist from Detroit named Dave Johnson—and turned to face the congregation. Kit stood on the other side, trying to look as grown up as ever, the world's smallest maid of honor.

A few moments later, the organist launched into the wedding march.

At the foot of the aisle, Jessie Bales materialized in a nimbus of white light.

She was accompanied by her elderly uncle Calvin on one arm, and her mother, Harriet Bales, on the other, and she came down the aisle with a slight limp, her posture bowed slightly from all the surgery. It had taken a couple of operations to get her insides repaired—her bowels had been perforated by that final slash of Glass's scalpel—but lately she'd been doing pretty well. She was singing along with her Reba McEntire albums again, and she was starting to scheme about a new investigative firm, with John as her partner. These were all good signs, very good signs. Nevertheless, it had been an uphill battle for Jessie.

Her therapist had come to refer to Jessie's problem as a form of posttraumatic stress disorder. Like John, Jessie had been flashing back to the horrors of the Little Red Barn Theater on a daily basis, but no amount of talk therapy or twelve-step programs or drugs had seemed to help. Fortunately, Jessie was tough. Not macho tough, like a lot of men. Or crazy tough, like some kids you see on the streets. Jessie had a kind of strange internal reserve. An indefatigable belief in herself. In Kit. In John. In the threesome's future together.

When she reached the altar, Harriet and Uncle Calvin each nodded in turn, grinning at John and winking at Kit, then returning to their seats.

Jessie grinned at her daughter, rolling her eyes comically, and then turned to John, *"Jesus, Johnny,"* she was whispering under her breath, keeping her bridely smile intact for the peanut gallery. "What's with the brooding out back?"

"Sorry, Jess." John grinned in spite of his nerves.

"I thought you were having second thoughts, for Chrissake."

"Second thoughts—what are you talking about? This was my idea in the first place."

"Your idea?"

"That's right—my idea—and, by the way, how the hell did you know I was out back? You were snooping on me, weren't you?"

"Of course I was snooping on you! I'm a snoop, for Chrissake! That's what I do."

The priest cleared his throat, shot an awkward glance at both of them.

Jessie fell silent, smiled tenderly at the priest, smiled tenderly at John, smiled tenderly at Kit, and then said very softly out of the side of her mouth, "I can't believe you're taking credit for this."

John took her hand as instructed, faced the priest, and whispered, "All right, maybe I'm trying to steal the credit for a good idea."

"It *was* a good idea, wasn't it?"

"Yeah, Jess, a very good idea."

"Thank you."

"Don't mention it," John whispered.

Then, as the priest began the long, convoluted ritual that is the Catholic wedding ceremony, John looked over at Kit and grinned and the child grinned back. Then John looked at Jessie's hand nestled in his. It was a large, sinewy hand for a woman, with garish nails painted bright fuchsia for the wedding. Then John noticed a thin scar along the outside of Jessie's thumb, and he realized that he had a similar scar along his own thumb. Very similar. He had gotten it at some point during the endless night in the Little Red Barn, either from a scalpel nicking him or from some other errant mishap. Jessie had probably gotten hers while struggling with Glass, and now John was gazing down at his own scar, then at Jessie's, then back at his own, and all at once John realized that neither scar would ever completely heal.

Neither would heal.

And maybe that was okay.

Maybe that was the way it was meant to be.

He gazed back up at the priest and started listening a little more closely to the words.